the CAT'S EYE

Fans Are Talking About
... *In the President's Service*

Ace has a rare gift to blend history and fictional characters, in a way that is both true to the facts and compelling to read. As a history teacher, it meant a lot to me that he structured this series to be both accurate and fun to read.

The *In The President's Service* books show Ace's writing at its most versatile—from wartime intrigue to personal crisis to murder mystery to political scheming, and then back again, all in the space of a small number of pages. And the story keeps the reader hooked from beginning to end.

If you are a fan of World War II fiction, of great detective stories, or of just plain old excellent writing, get into this series. Ace will not disappoint you!

—Mike Messner, Mountain View, CA

Ace Collins takes these short novellas to a new height. He researches and loves history so the details come out in his writings. All this series sheds new light on the people and places which played such a role in World War II. How some people tended to not be loyal to a flag but to the power they could gain by playing one side against the other. This made for some very tense moments as well as some very lethal enemies.

—Caliegh

These books remind me of the old serial movies on Saturdays back in the day! Can't wait for the next one. Helen Meeker started with *The Yellow Packard* and I have read them all. Keep them coming, Ace!!

—Helen

The reason I loved the story so much is because it has mysteries that weave together throughout the story to keep me glued to the book. I love the way the author piques the interest of readers by his brilliant storytelling. I am excited to read the next installment in this intriguing story. Thank you for writing with great details, having interesting characters, and a storyline that takes us back in history.

—Deanna

I read this on my computer and after realizing the book was complete, I had to look to be sure. Oh, my goodness, I need to find out what happened. Ace Collins, do you have Episode 9 finished because I want to read it!

This story takes place during World War II. Espionage, mystery, and kidnappings abound. It's fast paced and well written with researched historical facts. The scenes are in England, Europe, and the United States. The characters are well developed and continue to grow throughout. The author has an element of faith interwoven. If you want a clean, suspenseful story that moves quickly, *In the President's Service* is your series. *Shadows in the Moonlight* is Episode 8. Even though I have read only one other in the series, I could pick up what was happening.

—Sharon

Ace Collins makes this story build with intensity and suspense, introducing new twists and turns in the plot. Now in the third installment, Helen Meeker is severely wounded and not expected to live even if the doctors can find someone with her B- blood type. The Third Reich is using humans for guinea pigs to be able to build super soldiers who would heal completely at a remarkable rate when wounded. Helen needs a miracle as evil seems to be progressing on the war front. At the White House, the discovery of a mole infiltration sets everyone under a microscope until he or she is removed.

Not all the characters are working for the benefit or destruction of a nation as some are using the chaos war brings for selfish benefit. As I read the tale, I was kept guessing as to what was happening not only because of characters' actions or words, but sometimes because the author wasn't revealing what happened to certain players. The sacrifice called upon by the President in the story wasn't happening overseas or on the home front, but in ways many people didn't know of in this fictional plot.

I don't want to spoil the series for you, but one thing I will say is when a new major turn of events happens that puts the very foundation of American government at risk, I sure was surprised! I never anticipated or thought of that angle to the plot; it was not just amazing, but in my opinion raised the climax of the episodes up several notches.

All I can say is don't miss reading *In the President's Service A Date With Death #1, Dark Pool #2 or Blood Brother #3* and anticipate further episodes coming soon!

—**Lighthouse88**

Ace Collins is a master storyteller and historian. He has made me view war so much differently than my simplistic views before. Never had I considered there could be masterminds behind the major powers, minds not claiming loyalty to one nationality or another, but simply addicted to power.

—**Becky**

Ace Collins is a brilliant and masterful storyteller with great plots and characters. His research of history comes across in his books. This has been an amazing story of danger, espionage, suspense, twists and turns that keeps you on the edge of your seat.

—**Donna**

the CAT'S EYE

Library Cataloging Data
Names: Collins, Ace (Ace Collins)
The Cat's Eye—Book 14 In the President's Service/ Ace Collins
434 p. 21.6cm × 13.97cm (8.5in × 5.5in.)
Description: Elk Lake Publishing, Inc. digital eBook edition | Elk Lake Publishing, Inc. POD paperback edition | Elk Lake Publishing, Inc Trade paperback edition | Elk Lake Publishing, Inc. 2017.
Identifiers: ISBN-13: 978-1-946638-33-5 (e-bk) | 978-1-946638-34-2 (POD) | 978-1-946638-35-9 (Trade)
Key Words: Helen Meeker, Teresa Bryant, World War II, The Manhattan Project, Nazis, Suspense, Murder
LCCN 2017948778 Fiction

the CAT'S EYE

BOOK 13

IN THE PRESIDENT'S SERVICE

Ace Collins

 Elk Lake
Publishing, Inc.

Plymouth, Massachusetts

PART ONE

CHAPTER 1

Wednesday, November 18, 1935
9:45 a.m.
Farm just outside of Oslo, Norway

Though she deflected the compliments, Anna Olson knew her five-year-old daughter, Elga, was the most beautiful child in the area—perhaps in all of Norway. Her arctic-blue eyes were mesmerizing. Like magnets, they attracted and almost hypnotized everyone the child met. As the news spread of those clear and strikingly beautiful eyes, complete strangers traveled miles just to have a glimpse of them. Once visitors pulled their gaze away from Elga's eyes, they were just as struck by Elga's creamy, flawless complexion and her soft, wavy, straw-colored hair. She was literally the most beautiful girl most had ever seen—the embodiment of Nordic perfection. But in this rare case, beauty was far more than just skin deep. Beyond her obvious attractiveness, Elga radiated all the other qualities parents prayed for in their daughters.

She was reading by age three, playing piano at four, and now solving math problems that often stumped fifth graders. She was outgoing, friendly, talkative, and unassuming, as well as bright and curious, but she was neither spoiled nor conceited. All signs pointed to a great future, limited only by her dreams and her parents' meager resources. Yet, that Elga was seemingly unaffected by the adulation showered upon her was most remarkable. Every parent prays for a child like Elga, but in this rare case, the prayers were fully answered.

This Wednesday morning was much like all the others at the Olson home, beginning with a hearty meal provided by the farm's bounty, followed by daily chores. Elga followed her father through the fields, into the barn and down to the creek. With the work completed, the tall, lanky, and deceptively strong twenty-nine-year-old Sven hitched up a team of horses to a sixty-year-old wagon to make his weekly trip to town for supplies, leaving his wife and only child alone for a few hours.

As crime was unknown in this small, tight-knit community, he was unconcerned about his family's safety. As fate would decree, he should have been. He had no way of knowing people had been watching the house for weeks, their eyes drawn strongly to Elga. These were not the eyes of harmless admirers, but rather the eyes of those with intentions too evil to imagine.

Fifteen minutes after Sven left, Anna had cleaned up the kitchen, finished the breakfast dishes and started the laundry. The petite, blue-eyed woman was scrubbing her husband's soil-stained shirt on a washboard when she heard a knock on the door. After setting her laundry to one side and drying her hands, she made her way from the back of the tiny four-room home to the front door, where she smoothed her apron before opening the wooden entry. On the other side, she found two strangers.

"May I help you?" Anna asked, her tone showing both innocence and trust.

The taller of the two men, dressed in a long, dark leather coat, looked beyond the woman to where Elga played with her doll in the corner of the small living room. His expression stern, he studied the child for a few moments before nodding. A second later, his short, stout companion pulled a handgun from under his blue coat and without saying a word, fired three shots. In rapid order, the bullets entered Anna's chest, piercing her heart before exiting her back and digging into the wood-covered walls. As soon as the mother, her welcoming smile still on her face, slumped to the floor, the taller man stepped over Anna's now limp and bleeding body and roughly grabbed the stunned child. Before Elga could move, the stranger retrieved a syringe from his pocket, seized the girl's left arm and pushed the needle under her skin. Within ten seconds, she went limp. Sweeping the child up and stepping over Anna, her eyes open but unseeing, he stormed out of the house toward the road where his car was parked. Within five hours, the child with the startling blue eyes was on her way to Germany, leaving those who lived around the Olsons to ponder a horrific mystery that would likely never be solved.

CHAPTER 2

Monday, July 10, 1942
2:16 p.m.
The Wallace Estate, Wilmette, Illinois

In his twenty-seven years of police work, Roger Richards had seen death more times than he could count. Still, some crime scenes had crawled under his skin and into the deep recesses of his mind to resurface as haunting memories on long, sleepless nights. Most involved the murder of children; almost all the others were suicides. As he stood in the study of millionaire industrialist Michael E. Wallace's Chicago mansion, he leaned over to study a small woman—Asian, dressed in a kimono, appearing to be about forty. She rested on her stomach, her legs gracefully extended toward the desk. Her features were fragile, and her skin was pale. Her face, turned to the right, revealed a small bruise and scratch on her left cheek, likely caused when she struck the hardwood floor. Dried blood no longer seeped from a single bullet wound to her head. Yet, even viewed in a most horrid death, she was beautiful. Her tiny frame and delicate yet distinctive features gave the appearance of a porcelain, oriental doll, the kind popular before the war but relegated to attic storage or trash heaps after Pearl Harbor. And in 1942, all things Asian, perhaps even this small woman, now seemed tarnished.

About two feet from the woman's body was a snub-nosed thirty-eight. The black barrel shone in the afternoon sunlight now cascading through French doors. If things were as they appeared, Richards doubted there would be fingerprints on the weapon as the woman was wearing white lace gloves.

After unbuttoning the jacket of his blue, pinstriped suit, the cop crouched beside the body but touched nothing. Rocking back and forth on his size eleven, scuffed brown wingtips, his gray eyes took in the scene and imprinted on his brain the geometry that played into every case involving a gun. To fully comprehend a crime, to clearly picture the scene in his mind, there were angles to be figured and distances to be ascertained. They had to be combined with physics, including the strength needed to pull the gun's trigger and the force of the exploding projectile as the bullet left the barrel and entered the victim. In this case, the math and science didn't seem to add up.

What the cop observed showed the woman should have initially been sitting in the chair behind the desk. She then would have placed the gun to her temple and pulled the trigger. If that had been the case, she would have fallen forward onto the floor. But why was the weapon out of her hand? Shouldn't the gun have dropped under her as her hands had? Shouldn't it still be in her grip?

The cop leaned closer. The woman had evidently not

moved after she fell; nothing indicated anything but a dead drop, so she had to have died the instant the bullet entered her brain. If that were the case, why was the gun so far from the body, and why was there no blood on the barrel? And where were the powder burns on her skin?

Richards turned his eyes to the desk chair, a high-backed swivel model, upholstered in maroon leather. Surprisingly, there was no blood apparent on the cushion, arms, or back. In fact, the only blood obvious at the scene was the pool around the woman's head.

Standing behind Richards, observing his every move, was the home's owner. Michael Wallace—"M.E.," as he was known around the city—was a large man with graying hair, a stern face, soft jaw, and deep wrinkles likely caused by too much frowning or maybe a habit of sucking on cigarettes. As Wallace lit a Camel, the fourth in the past ten minutes, Richards could easily see he was agitated and impatient. But what Richards didn't observe interested him most. The man seemed neither stunned nor shocked and as years investigating homicides and suicides had proven, stunned and shocked are two distinctly different emotions.

Rising to face his host, the cop frowned and shook his head. Something smelled. In fact, everything about this business stank. With science and math, as well as human instincts not producing the right answers, he needed to shift his investigation in a new direction.

"What's the woman's name?" the cop not too gently demanded.

"Mayu," the man answered. His voice was strong, almost stoic. If he'd never seen death before—and how many businessmen had been around a gunshot victim—this was a bizarre reaction.

"And who was she to you?" Richards prodded.

"My wife."

"Your wife?" The answer came as a complete surprise. Richards expected the dead woman to have been employed as a servant, but never in his wildest dreams did he consider her to be married to the millionaire. As soon as the words were uttered, the cop wished he could have couched his response differently. They sounded too judgmental and harsh. But with no way to pull them back, there was now only time to wait for a reaction. He didn't have to wait long.

"Yes," Wallace barked, evidently offended. "Do you have a problem with my having been married to a woman from Japan?"

"No," Richards quickly assured him, "I'm not going to condemn you for that. In my way of thinking, everyone has a right to marry whom they please. But when a wife dies, the death is personal and takes the case in whole new direction, so I do need for you to tell me about her."

Wallace frowned. "Not sure what that has to do with anything. She was a woman I met on a business trip two decades ago. We fell in love, married, and I brought her back here. That's the whole story."

Richards shrugged. Emotions mixed in with math and science made him uncomfortable, yet even in times when anger and grief collided, he had to dig for answers. If he held back, he was not serving the victim.

"Mr. Wallace, what you've told me is only the outline and a short one at that. I need much more. In cases like this, I have to know possible motives, even for suicides.

No," he corrected himself, "especially for suicides." Though he doubted the woman had killed herself, for the moment, he thought it best to allow that explanation to stand, so he added a reinforcing phrase, hoping to bring out some vital information. "Mr. Wallace, I'm a couple of years too old to be drafted. The military doesn't want a man of my age. I've been in this business since 1928, working homicide for a decade. In that time, I've learned this. The act of taking one's own life is not something to be treated lightly. So why don't you explain to me why Mrs. Wallace decided to stop her own clock?"

Nodding, Wallace nodded, moved over to a chair placed next to a window and eased down onto the deep cushion. As the sun highlighted his graying hair, as he took a long drawn from a cigarette and allowed his eyes to roll toward the ceiling, with as his free hand, he drummed on the chair's arm. For a few seconds, he remained mute; and then, in a voice still devoid of emotion, spilled out the story of a marriage that sounded perfect until international events came into play.

"We were born in much different worlds," he began. "She was a descendant of Samurai warriors and very proud of her heritage. I was about as far from nobility as you can get. My father worked in sanitation, and I often wore clothing he dug out the trash. Somehow Mayu and I complemented each other perfectly. Our happiness only started with the two of us, but went well beyond us."

Wallace paused and looked at Richards. His expression suddenly became emotional, and his tone was sincere as he continued the story of a union that was both normal and exotic. "Sure, they doubted us at first, but in time my old friends enjoyed my wife's company almost as much as

I did. In fact, because of her intelligence, wit, and charm, she pretty much became the star of our social circle. While never the leader—she was too reserved for that—Mayu was the one person women turned to when they needed ideas on decorating. She even helped them with their children's weddings and coming up with new ideas for parties. She also arranged the flower displays for almost every social event in their homes and clubs. Over time, she became their go-to friend, the one they could always depend on. If they were sick, she brought them soup. If they lost a loved one, she was first to visit them. I thought they used her, but she never saw things that way. She just wanted to be accepted and needed. I believe she was."

"She sounds like an extraordinary woman," the cop suggested.

"She was that and more. Despite the fact she wasn't white, our friends even invited her into their clubs. She played golf and learned the latest dance moves. She was as much or more American than Carole Lombard or Bette Davis."

He paused, his brooding eyes pushing into slits. "And then Pearl Harbor changed everything. Suddenly, Mayu was shunned. People even went so far as to completely ignore her when we were out together. They'd greet me, but they wouldn't even say hello to her. Many suggested my wealth and influence was what was keeping her from being shipped to an internment camp. They were too stupid or blinded by prejudice to know that internment camps were only for Japanese living on the West Coast. So, our lives went from sunshine to dark in the blink of an eye." After smashing his spent cigarette in an ashtray, he added, "Needless to say, the party invites stopped, as did the drop by visits and phone calls. All of this was made even worse by the demands of war. As production increased at my plants, my business kept me away from home much more than before the war.

"If only we'd had kids. That might have helped fill her days. But we couldn't have children, and suddenly, she was alone. In a real sense, she was a prisoner in this big old house." He paused, then added, "I guess you could call her a prisoner of war."

Wallace pulled out and lit another cigarette. "She couldn't go home. Her childhood friends would have seen her as a traitor. They'd never approved of her marrying outside her kind. And yet, what could she do here? She couldn't go shopping, out to eat or even to church without being accosted or treated like a leper. Imagine her loneliness!"

Wallace's eyes went back the ceiling. For several moments, he watched the cigarette smoke hovering above his head. Then, with no prompting, he continued.

"You have to understand the Japanese mind to grasp what happened to her. She was consumed by guilt. She believed that, because she was my wife and she was from Japan, she was costing me all I held dear. I heard her once refer to herself as a cancer. And certainly, when my company began getting war contracts, I was investigated a lot more deeply than most are, simply because of her. And I'll admit to you, and everyone else, being shunned did bother me. I carried a lot of bottled-up rage over the way Mayu was treated. I can't deny that. I felt like I was being cheated and abused by my friends and even my own country."

The cop nodded. Without knowing, Wallace had given

him a motive for murdering his wife. But his words had also convinced Richards the man loved Mayu. So, did love trump the motive? Too soon to tell. More questions had to be asked.

"Mr. Wallace, how did your wife feel about the war?"

"She hated the war. Despite what she chose to wear when she ..." He paused as if trying to control his emotions before once more finding his voice. "Despite what you see her in now, she always dressed in modern western style. She loved classy suits, pumps, and hats. She closely followed the dress styles of that movie actress ..." He snapped his fingers, trying to recall a name before continuing. "She was in that big film about a decade ago, *It Happened One Night.*"

"Claudette Colbert," the cop offered.

"Yeah, that's the one. She bought movie magazines and watched all her films to see what Colbert was sporting." He pointed across the room with his cigarette. "The outfit she died in was the one she was wearing when I first met her in 1920. Today was our anniversary. She told me this morning that when she finished volunteering at the local kitchen that serves bums and outcasts—which she did every Monday and Thursday for a decade—she was going to make me a very special dinner." He paused and shook his head as he focused on his wife's dead body. "Maybe someone said something this morning that set her off and robbed her of her will to live. Perhaps putting those clothes back on was symbolic. Maybe she was ending our life together as we began. I don't know. None of this makes any sense to me except it's all the fault of this stupid war."

Wallace stood and walked over to the French doors, looking out on his grounds. "I can tell you this, she was an

American citizen, and she loved this country. She found her voice here." His tone softened as he turned to look once more at the limp body on the floor. "But a part of her was still Japanese. Perhaps the shame of what her people did weighed her down to the point where she couldn't live with it anymore. Maybe her death was actually a product of guilt—for something she had nothing to do with."

"Was there a note?" Richards asked.

"Not that I've found."

"And I don't think you'll find one," Richards spoke solemnly as he turned back to the body. He had as much information as he was likely to get, so now was the time to reveal what the math and science told him and then gauge his host's reaction. He sighed deeply before speaking. "I'm betting when we test her gloves, we'll discover she didn't shoot herself."

Wallace gasped, genuinely shocked. "What are you saying?"

The cop raised his eyebrows. "I'm not staking my reputation on my conclusion, but I think she might have been murdered."

Wallace looked from the body to Richards. "Then why did you ask me about motives for suicide?"

"Based on your call to the station, I assumed her death was suicide," Richards explained. "You told me a woman had killed herself in your study. Weren't those your exact words?"

"I was sure that was the way it had to be."

"Okay, then let me ask you this. Whose gun is that?"

"Mine," he replied. "I keep it in the side drawer of the desk."

"Did she know the gun was there?"

"Of course, she did. She'd watched me pull it out when I went on business trips and put it back when I returned. My friends knew my weapon was there too. Heck, everyone who knows me knows where I keep that gun."

"Did you move the gun when you found her body?"

"No!" he quickly and vehemently exclaimed. "I didn't touch anything."

"You just left her as she was?"

"Yes. I'd been at my office downtown. I came home, walked into this room and discovered her. I immediately called you."

"You didn't hear the shot?"

"No. As I just explained, it happened while I was gone."

"What about the servants?"

"We don't have any. Mayu insisted on taking care of the household chores and doing the cooking. She wouldn't have things any other way."

"So, she died alone?"

"I guess so. I mean … that's the only thing that makes sense."

Richard moved closer to the widower, set his jaw and fired off a completely unexpected question. "Mr. Wallace, did you love your wife?"

"What kind of question is that?"

"Did you love your wife?" the cop repeated, staring directly into the millionaire's face.

"Yes."

Richards grimly smiled. "My years of experience prove, more often than not, when a loved one finds the body of someone who has taken their own life, they rush over and pick up the victim in their arms as if trying to will them back to life. Most even admit to asking the dead person questions about why they did what they did. It takes a few minutes for a person's head to clear enough to call us, and when they do, their voice is either filled with emotion, or it's almost zombie-like. Also, they're almost always confused and lost. You displayed none of that when you talked to me on the phone. You sounded as if you were telling me about something no more important than discovering your mailbox had been knocked over."

"Are you suggesting I killed my wife?"

"I'm suggesting someone might have, and your reaction makes you the most likely suspect."

"I didn't," Wallace protested. He tossed the cigarette into the ashtray. "There is no way."

"Then you have nothing to worry about," the cop replied.

"I would never hurt her," the millionaire whispered. "Never once did I slap Mayu."

"Mr. Wallace, I hope you're telling me the truth. If you are, and if we find she didn't kill herself, then, in this war climate, you can likely give us the names of many people who had come to dislike or mistrust your wife since December 7th of last year. Maybe some of those are even in your social circle." Richards glanced back to the body. "There are people who see any person of Japanese origin as the enemy. They have come to the unsettling conclusion that by killing them, they are showing patriotism. I'm not suggesting you are the only one with a motive, but you did admit your wife's race was now affecting and limiting your life. You even pointed out just a few minutes ago how lonely you were and how angry you sometimes became."

Wallace didn't respond but instead reached for another cigarette. His hand was shaking as he lit up.

The cop shrugged as he once again turned his attention to the body. He took a few moments to reaffirm his earlier observations, then added, "Or maybe the medical examiner will prove my hunch wrong and the poor woman did kill herself. But even then, if she did find a way to fire the gun at the angle needed, and it somehow dropped where it dropped—which doesn't make mathematical or scientific sense to me—what likely drove her to suicide were the attitudes of those narrow-minded people in your social group who suddenly stopped calling her a friend. In a way, it is still murder!"

"I didn't kill her," Wallace forcefully spat, "but if someone did, I'll track them down and make them pay."

Richards looked at him and frowned. "That's my job!" Then he glanced around the room, doing a quick inventory, "Have you searched to see if anything's missing?"

"Of course not. I just assumed …"

"Do you keep large amounts of cash or perhaps jewelry in your home?"

"Not really. Mayu only wanted to wear simple things. I offered to buy her fancy bracelets and rings, but she'd have none of them. The only thing I own that has any real value is a piece of jewelry I bought some years ago on a European trip."

"Describe it."

"It's called 'The Cat's Eye'—an antique necklace supposedly owned by Marie Antoinette. As you would guess, in the middle of the setting is a large piece of blue sapphire that looks like the eye of a cat. Mesmerizing. I've grown so fond of the piece I named my yacht after the jewel. According to legend, the necklace is supposed to supply the owner with great luck."

Richards considered this new information as he walked over and looked at the French doors leading to the patio. At one time, the landscape of the estate was likely considered among the finest in the city but now had gone to seed. Bushes needed to be trimmed, furniture to be painted and a water fountain to be repaired.

"I need a gardener," Wallace noted from his chair. "I let ours go last year and just haven't had time to find another one."

"That small painted brick wall at the edge of the patio looks nice," Richards observed.

"I did that myself last month. I should have worked on other stuff at the same time, but I got wrapped up in plant work again."

Richards turned back to his host. "About *The Cat's Eye* ..."

"What about it?"

"Where is it?" the cop asked.

"It's in my wall safe, behind the desk."

"Would you do me the favor of opening the safe and showing the necklace to me?"

"But ..."

"Humor me. I just want to make sure the piece is still there."

Wallace moved slowly behind the desk, past his wife's body, to the back wall. He pulled a hinged photo away from the wood paneling, revealing a gray wall safe with a small circular red label just above the combination dial. He spun the dial using a four-digit code and opened the door. Reaching in, he retrieved several envelopes, along with what appeared to be stock certificates and a pocket watch. His jaw dropped as he examined the booty. Seemingly panicked, he pushed his face almost into the safe before exclaiming, "It's not here!"

"The necklace is gone?" Richards asked?

"Yeah."

"When was the last time you saw it?"

Obviously stunned, Wallace turned to face the cop. "Last week. That's when I had my father's pocket watch fixed. I remember looking at *The Cat's Eye* before replacing it and locking the safe."

"Who else knows the combination?"

"Just me and ..." His eyes dropped to his wife.

"No one else?"

Wallace shook his head.

The fact the jewelry was gone might not be tied to the woman's death. A professional thief could have stolen the piece earlier. The safe would not be that hard for a professional thief to open. Still, the cop's hunch that Mayu Wallace did not commit suicide became a bit more plausible. Until he heard from the medical examiner, Richards was going to treat this as a murder investigation.

"Mr. Wallace." The cop's words shook the industrialist from his mental fog. "When the crime scene boys get here, I'd like you to submit to a paraffin test to determine if you have fired a gun recently. Will you do that?"

Wallace, caught between rage and grief, nodded.

"Good. Now, for the time being, put the stuff back into the safe, but leave it open. Then, let's move to another room and wait."

Wallace replaced the watch and papers, then shuffled through the study door. Richards turned back to the body. Perhaps Mayu Wallace really had killed herself. Even though her death stretched the bounds of math and science, there were ways for the wound to be self-inflicted and the gun to fall and bounce or slide to where it ended up. But if Richards' hunch was correct, and she didn't kill herself, despite the missing piece of jewelry, he figured the husband was the logical one to have pulled the trigger. If that were the case, would a jury convict Wallace of murder when the victim was Japanese?

CHAPTER 3

Monday, September 28, 1942
3:40 p.m.
13th Floor, Lincoln Hotel, Chicago, Illinois

As she placed the phone receiver back into the cradle, Helen Meeker felt like a high school girl who was chairman of the prom committee but didn't have a date. She'd once called the shots, but now others were calling to inform her what tasks needed to be done. So many of the investigations and operations she'd started while working for the President in Washington were now being handled by others. Even her latest assignment, one that would again put her into the thick of the action, would not become a reality until she completed a job better suited for low-level FBI operatives.

Then, there was the state of her team. There were no original members left. Henry Reese was with the underground in Germany, Becca Bobbs and Clay Barnes were heading up their own units, and she never even got to talk to them for fear of blowing their covers. Yes, the three who worked with her now were solid, but each of them had been thrust upon her, not picked by her. She felt as if someone else were pulling the strings, and she was just a puppet.

With Napoleon Lancelot and Dizzy Vance out trying to find the local Nazi contact who had been working with Bauer, her one-time nemesis now buried in a Wisconsin pasture, she and the extraordinary but mysterious Teresa Bryant were literally cooling their heels in their secret, thirteenth-floor headquarters at the Lincoln Hotel. At this moment, Bryant, outfitted in dark slacks and black sweater, had her feet propped up on her desk as she filed her nails. The operative word for today was *bored*.

"Teresa, did you have a date to your high school prom?" Meeker asked.

The American Indian's dark eyes lit up as she answered the question with a question. "What does that have to do with anything?"

"It doesn't," Meeker replied. "It's just that I'm uninterested in and not at all enthused by our ongoing assignment."

"Which is?" Bryant asked, continuing to put her file to work.

"In a way, we're already working on it. But back to my question, did you have a date to your high school prom?"

"I didn't have a high school prom." Bryant was obviously uninterested.

"I had a date with Robert Wilson. Everybody called him Bobby."

"That's nice, Helen. I'm happy for you."

"Don't be," Meeker said. "I wanted to go with John Akins. I guess all the girls did."

"Don't take this the wrong way, but I don't care. Why don't you just tell me about the assignment?"

"I'm getting there," Meeker assured her. "Just give me a second to tie this all together."

"Tie what together?"

"Just hold on. Teresa, Bobby and I had a … what would my sister call it … yeah, a vanilla time. Going after Bauer was never vanilla, but with him dead, the folks we're assigned to track down are like spending an evening with Bobby while watching John kissing Betsy."

"Helen, please. I can't take any more."

Meeker shrugged. "Fine, let me put it this way. For our next *date,* we're not going after Public Enemy Number One or tracking down a lost gold shipment. We have to find out what low-life was feeding Bauer his information."

Bryant nodded. "Lancelot and Vance are on that right now. The person has to be working for or have contacts at Central State Bank. It's just a matter of researching the employees and tracing down the leads. I doubt if the task will take more than a week. So, considering all we've been through, I don't deem that much of a problem."

Meeker frowned as she moved from her desk to a wooden chair by the far wall. After smoothing her jade-green, pleated wool skirt, she sat down and gazed at the ceiling. From her desk, Bryan studied her partner for a full minute before breaking the silence.

"It's so dull. Whoever we find is not going to be the menace Bauer was."

"Oh, you're wrong there. Just because he was the worst and smartest you've dealt with doesn't mean there aren't scores who are even more devious, desperate and dare I say it, evil."

"Okay, fine. I'll give you that. But we have a shot at doing something really special, and we can't until we find the mole. Until we find and take that person into custody, we're stuck in Chicago. And if we take too much time, they might find someone else for the other mission, and we could be stuck in Chicago forever."

"There are worse places to be stuck. London, Berlin, and Paris are three examples. Bombs fall in those cities on a regular basis. Pretty much all we have to deal with is the smell coming from the stockyards." Bryant put her nail file down and leaned back in her desk chair. "Besides, where else do we have to go? After the blow up in DC, we seem to have been exiled here. Or at least you have. I guess I'm still free to go anywhere I want. The heat's not on me like it is you. But then again, the President did assign me to be your babysitter."

"Hey!"

"You know what I mean. You know I respect you. I usually trust your judgments and your abilities, but FDR did place me with you for a reason. You have a bad habit of attempting to do too much on your own. You need to quit trying to prove yourself."

"Or what? Do I just fade into a world where I'm just like every other woman ... a bit of eye candy who can whip up a great apple pie?"

"You know that's not what I mean. The President and I don't want to see you take needless chances. You need to learn to take a deep breath and depend on others for a change."

"We've been through this. I want to play alone because that way ..."

Bryant finished the sentence. "That way you don't have to feel guilty when someone on your team dies. Right?"

"Yeah," she admitted. "You never knew Dr. Spencer Ryan. He was a surgeon who joined my team. He was killed in a shootout. He wasn't trained for that and had no business being there. But who placed him in that position? I did! And he was the first of how many?"

"I don't know, but you never took on anyone who didn't believe in you or didn't want to be with you. And none of them died needlessly. They all gave their lives for something they believed in. Now stop griping about bland prom dates and our current assignment and go back to something you hinted at a few minutes ago. You indicated when we catch the mole, there's something important waiting for us. Unwrap that package and give me something to look forward to."

Meeker explained the news casually as if she was talking about taking in a Chicago Bears football game. "Okay, here it is. We have a chance to go behind enemy lines in Germany. The OSS would love to have us join the underground in taking out a Nazi research center."

Suddenly much more interested, Bryant leaned forward. "The atomic lab mentioned in The White Rose diary? The one Sophie Scholl wrote about?"

"Yeah. After all, we were the ones who told the President and the OSS about the lab. We deserve to be there as they go in for the kill. But we can't join that mission until we find the stinking mole who was Bauer's stool pigeon."

Bryant laughed. "I think you're mixing metaphors or something. You can't be both a mole and pigeon. Now, back to going on a mission behind German lines. Why us? Let's be honest, we don't have any more skills than a few million others, so why are we needed? I mean I'd love to go, but why not just drop in a unit of elite, specially trained members of the Army or the Marines?"

"Apparently," Meeker explained, "the powers that be in the intelligence department don't want anyone else to know the Germans are attempting to develop atomic weapons. Thus, because we already know, we got chosen." She shook her head and added, "I'm not even sure how much those on the underground's team will be told about the atomic research."

"So, behind the lines and keeping our team in the dark," Bryant said.

Meeker, her expression steely, said, "I want this job, Teresa. I worked with Holsclaw when I was on an earlier mission in Germany. He will be the leader. Henry will likely be on the team as well."

"I see." Bryant raised her eyebrows in irony. "How sweet, a lover's reunion. Now remembering your prom date suddenly makes sense."

"It's not that. I just trust those guys and feel we could add something special to the team."

"So, some folks do believe women have intrinsic value!"

"I wouldn't go that far. They seem to want women in the group because we will have a far easier time blending in."

"There are lots of females in the OSS. Why you and me?"

"How many have our experience and our training? How many can shoot and fight like we can?"

"Why not just bomb the place? Why put a ground team at risk?"

"According to Intelligence, it's too deep under the

mountain for bombers to do any damage. The mission has to go into the facility and set off explosions on the inside."

"That's likely suicide," Bryant cracked as she eased up onto a table and crossed her legs. "I have lots of courage, but I also have lots to live for."

"Dying's not an option. We're supposed to bring all the documents on the research back to Washington."

"So, we're really joining the underground just to be the human carrier pigeons that bring the information. We're not going along to do any of the dirty work?"

"That's the way it's supposed to play out," Meeker said. "But nothing happens until we unveil the mole. They want to know his contacts and what he's shared with Germany. They're especially interested in learning if he knows anything about our atomic research."

"Wait. We're developing atomic weapons as well? I've heard nothing about this."

"It's all hush-hush, but millions of dollars and thousands of our top minds are working on the project right now."

"Where?" Bryant asked.

"I don't even know," Meeker admitted, before adding a caveat. "You'll find this interesting. The German atomic research lab is not that far from Hitler's Bavarian retreat. Maybe we can stop by for supper while we're there."

"Yeah. I look so Aryan. He'd love me."

A warning buzzer caused both women to tense and turn their gaze toward the entrance to their secret headquarters. Silently they moved to their desks, retrieved their guns and stood ready to fire. After a series of preassigned taps on the door, a large black man entered.

"Mr. Lancelot," Meeker greeted him as she placed her Colt back on the desktop. "Do you have news?"

"I think I've got the name of the mole," the man replied.

"Do tell!"

"Dollars to donuts he's the vice president of the bank. His name is William Elliot."

Bryant eased into a chair, then asked, "And why do you think he's our guy?"

"Poker and the ponies," Lancelot explained. "He's up to his ears in debt, and it seems his one way to pay off the mob is by working for the only force in the world worse than organized crime."

"How was he recruited?" Meeker asked.

"My guess is Esther O'Toole knew about his debts," Lancelot continued, "and sucked him in. She likely introduced him to that guy who tried to kill you. What was his name?"

"Bauer."

"Yeah, the guy Big Jim called 'Darkness.' Anyway, based on what Vance and I've been able to uncover, Elliot's been working on smuggling secrets to Germany for at least a year."

"Even before the war?" Bryant asked.

"Oh, yeah," Lancelot replied. "We found some microfilm at his home that deals with something called the Manhattan Project. Wonder what that is?"

"Something we shouldn't know about," Meeker suggested.

Lancelot reached into his pants pocket and, after juggling it as if it were red hot, quickly tossed the small silver capsule toward his boss. "Then I sure don't want this."

Meeker caught the peanut-size container and studied it

for a moment before dropping it onto her desk. "Did you find anything else?"

"Some envelopes and small boxes with the same Buffalo, New York, address written on each … John's Antique Shop, 1012 Front Street. That capsule was in the first one I opened. At least we got there before that information could be passed on to the next contact as it works its way back to Germany."

"I'll see that Alison gets that address to the FBI," Meeker noted. "I'd guess there will be a going-out-of-business sale at 1012 Front Street very soon. Now, what about Elliot?"

"He never came back from lunch," Lancelot explained. "Vance is trying to track him down right now."

"Think he was tipped off?" Bryant asked, looking at Meeker.

"Maybe he has good instincts," Meeker suggested. "After all, the newspapers ran a story this morning on O'Toole's arrest. Perhaps he read the report at lunch and realized the mob queen might be talking." She turned back to Lancelot. "What can you tell me about Elliot?"

"He's thirty-five, athletic, well-educated, not married, and his parents are dead. Since I found boxes of ammunition at his apartment, I'd guess he owns a thirty-eight and likely carries the piece with him. And based on racing forms and notes we discovered during our search, he's still playing the ponies. I found a telephone number on a pad by his phone. I called and was connected to a bookie."

"Interesting," Meeker noted. "A normal guy gets a bad habit and suddenly finds himself in bed with Hitler. So, where is Vance now?"

"He's likely on the move. He has a list of Elliot's friends and is working his way through them."

"Helen," Bryant chimed in, "I'm guessing you're thinking what I'm thinking: It's all about numbers and odds."

"Yeah, we need to visit a bookie," Meeker admitted. She turned back toward Lancelot. "You still have that phone number?"

"I have a thing about numbers. If I read them once, I can remember them forever."

"Good," Meeker said with a smile. "Give me the number, and I'll get us an address. I want to close this thing out and get to Germany before the snows come."

"What's this about Germany?" Lancelot asked.

"It's a girls-only trip," Meeker replied. "We're going to ski in Bavaria and go to Octoberfest."

CHAPTER 4

Monday, September 28, 1942
7:19 p.m.
Mock's Diner, one block south of the Stockyards, Chicago, Illinois

Since her 1936 Packard was still being repaired, Meeker used a leased 1935 Hupmobile for the drive to the address linked to the bookie's phone number. Arriving at the destination, she parked the gray sedan on an almost deserted street directly across from the greasy spoon known as Mock's. The red, blinking neon sign in the dingy window promised the freshest meat in town. As the stockyards were just a stone's throw away—and the odor carried by the north wind proved that—there was likely some truth in the advertising, but the place was all but empty during the normally busy dinner hour, causing Meeker to question the quality of the diner's fresh beef.

"So," Bryant wisecracked, "I guess we should have worn formal dresses."

"It's the kind of dive that draws rats," Meeker quipped. "Both the human and rodent varieties."

"Our glamorous lives," Bryant returned. She eyed the

building a second time, then asked, "You think the bookie is on the second floor?"

Meeker nodded. Lights were showing through the five upstairs windows and from time to time, silhouetted the men walking behind the shades.

"Got to be. Too many folks pacing back and forth up there to be a residence. And note the phone lines from the pole to the building." Meeker took a deep breath and frowned. "I'd have to guess most of the bookie's patrons work in the meat-packing business."

"I don't think this joint would attract the white-collar crowd," Bryant agreed. "I'm betting Hoover was in office the last time those windows were cleaned."

"Guess I should have sent Dizzy on this outing," Meeker added. She grew serious as she looked over at Bryant. "You didn't know him when he wasn't sober. Before he cleaned up his act, this would have been Dizzy's kind of place. I'm glad it's not now."

"Helen, why do you think Elliot drove clear over here to bet? There are probably a dozen places much closer to the bank."

"Most likely, he was afraid of being caught. Bank officers aren't supposed to gamble. Frightens the stockholders and the customers."

Bryant raised her eyebrows. "How do you suggest we get up there?"

"Well, in the past three minutes, four guys have gone into the diner. Three have already come out. That's not enough time to eat, and they haven't been carrying any to-go orders. Let's assume they're being paid off for bets they won or making good on those they lost."

"Do you want to just go in, grab a booth and order?"

Bryant's tone reflected her distaste for what she was suggesting. "Then we can watch to see where the bettors go? I mean, that would be my plan, but I'm sure hoping you have a better one."

"Good idea," Meeker agreed. "It's simple, straightforward, and I hope we won't have to use our guns. Do you have the photo of Elliot Napoleon found at his apartment?"

"It's in my pocket. I'm not really hungry, so why don't I just wait out here."

Meeker laughed. "You have diffused bombs and faced down cold-blooded killers, but you don't have the stomach for a diner?"

"Stomach is an accurate description."

"What are you afraid of, Teresa?"

"Food poisoning. It's the worst thing in the world. It's like swallowing a rabid rat that has to eat its way out of your gut to get free. I speak from experience."

Meeker shook her head. "You'll live. Besides, suffering is good for the soul. Now let's go!"

As she opened her car door, Bryant shot Meeker a dirty look. Meeker saw and smiled. Maybe Bryant was starting to relax a bit.

"This is not a good idea," Bryant said for a final time as the women crossed the street and stepped up on the sidewalk.

When they pushed open the diner's front door, Bryant's concerns were suddenly in twenty-twenty focus. The dirty windows had only given a slight hint as to the condition of the floors and walls.

"I'd guess the health inspector doesn't know about this place," Meeker whispered.

"He might be afraid of it," Bryant cracked. "I'm speculating rats see this place and walk on by. Remind me not to go the restroom." Glancing at the floor, she frowned and asked, "Do we walk to the booth or just slide?"

Meeker ignored the observation as she stood in the entry and inventoried the building. The main room was forty-by-twenty, booths were placed along the street windows, and across the aisle, a long counter had stools for fifteen. The floor was too stained to determine its color, but the walls were dark green, the shade due more to accumulated grime than paint. While there was not a single customer in the joint, the same couldn't be said of the roaches. They appeared to be massing for a convention.

"This might well be the most dangerous mission I've ever been on," Bryant grumbled.

"Yeah," Meeker agreed, "let's take the booth back by the jukebox. That'll give us a good view of the door."

"I wonder how long I can hold my breath," Bryant muttered. "What is that smell?"

Meeker wouldn't even hazard a guess.

Behind the counter, a heavyset man—balding, fiftyish, wearing a stained apron over a white shirt—eyed the woman as they made their way to a booth. Only after they'd slid in, one on each side of the table, did he grab a couple of menus and amble in their direction.

"We serve tomatoes," he cracked, showing an all-but-toothless smile, "but rarely do they come as fresh as you two."

Bryant frowned, "How long did you take to work up that line?"

Raising his eyebrows and pushing the menus their way,

he countered, "Just my way of saying you babes are a lot better looking than our normal crowd. The last time a woman in a suit and heels came in here was before the Depression."

"Not surprised," Bryant sniped, "and I'd guess we're a lot cleaner than your normal crowd too."

"And you smell good," he said, laughing. "Welcome to Mocks. Now, what do you fine ladies need?"

"I take it you're Mock?" Meeker asked.

"No, I bought this place off Mock. My name's Bub."

Bryant forced a smile before asking, "Is Bub short for something?"

"What?" The man looked confused.

"Is it a nickname?"

"No, I was named after my dad."

Bryant cocked an eyebrow. "Your father's name was Bub?"

"Yep."

Bryant shrugged. "That may explain a lot."

"What's your grub choice?" Bub asked, apparently missing the meaning behind Bryant's barb.

"Bring me a burger," Meeker ordered. At the same time, she noted two men dressed in suits enter the front door. The pair waved at Bub, then strolled toward the back wall of the building. They rapped three times on a door, and a buzzer sounded. The men then disappeared through the door.

After the pair had exited the room, Meeker added, "Hold the onions and give me a Coke to drink."

Glancing toward Bryant, Bub asked, "What about you?"

"The same, and I want it done all the way through!"

"I'm the cook too," Bub proudly announced, "I'll get

back to the kitchen and put the patties on the grill. You want me to bring the drinks with the meal or do you need them now?"

"Keep them cold until you finish cooking," Meeker suggested.

"Whatever you desire, I will comply."

Meeker watched Bub mosey behind the counter and through a door she assumed led to the kitchen. Then she turned her attention back to the far wall. A minute later, the two men who had just entered reappeared. Smiling, they walked back to the front entry and exited.

"I know where we need to go," Meeker said to Bryant. "I also think I know the code to get in."

"You ready to make our move? I'm not real crazy about actually sampling what we just ordered."

"Hold off, Teresa. Let's wait for our food and see if anyone else comes and goes."

"You must have an iron-clad stomach."

A dozen men and two women passed in and out of the diner before Bub brought their burgers. None of the patrons ordered anything. They simply sauntered to the back wall, knocked three times and waited for the buzzer.

"You need anything else?" Bub asked as he set the food on the table

"No, thanks," Meeker replied, "this will do for now."

The bun looked relatively fresh though getting limper by the second due to the grease still oozing from the meat. On the bright side, the lettuce was almost green and the slice of tomato, close to red.

"Are you really going to eat this?" Bryant whispered.

"When you're undercover, you have to go with the flow."

"Remind me to never go undercover with you at a

mortuary," Bryant cracked. She waited for her partner to pick up the lubricious burger and take a few bites. "So, what do you think?"

"I don't think it'll kill you," Meeker announced.

"That's good to know. By the way, I'm picking the next place we eat."

As the women slowly consumed their burgers, four more men came into Mock's, strolled to the back wall, knocked three times and disappeared. Again, none of them ordered food.

"Isn't it amazing," Bryant noted, "we're watching folks who have no problem betting their hard-earned cash on ponies and numbers, but none of them feel confident enough to bet on the food in this place. That speaks volumes!" She paused to glare at Meeker. "If I get sick, you're holding my hand!"

"Just finish up the sandwich and quit grumbling. It could be worse."

"Fill me in on how?"

After Bryant forced down the last few bites and drained her Coke, Bub reappeared from the kitchen. Sporting a smile and a few more spots on his apron, he lumbered over to their table, his belly jiggling like Jell-O with each step.

"You need anything else?"

"No." Bryant jumped in before Meeker could reply. "What do we owe you?"

"Beef's hard to get," Bub explained.

"Don't even tell me what this was," Bryant protested in horror.

"No," he assured her, "it was beef. I even met the cow

before it was turned into burgers. I just meant with the restrictions and rationing, it's not easy to find or buy."

"So, you dabble in the black market?" Meeker suggested.

"I didn't say that. I'm just warning you things aren't as cheap as they were before the war."

"What's it going to run?" Meeker demanded.

Bub shrugged, "For the burgers and the Cokes, it's sixty cents."

Meeker reached into her purse, retrieved three quarters and tossed them on the table. "Keep the change. Let's go, Teresa. We have work to do."

While Bub turned his back to pick up the coins, Meeker, with Bryant hot on her heels, slid out of the booth and moved to the back of the diner. She pulled out her Colt and eased the gun to her right side, out of Bub's view, then knocked three times. A second later, the buzzer sounded. She turned the now unlocked knob and smiled.

"This is too easy," Bryant whispered.

The open door revealed a worn, dusty staircase leading to the second floor. Knowing Bryant had her back, Meeker fixed her eyes on the objective and began the climb the wooden steps, bowed from years of use. The twelve stairs led to a large open room. Sitting at six oak desks were half a dozen men, drinking coffee and smoking cigarettes. Each was talking on a phone and scribbling notes. None of them bothered to look up as the women appeared. So far, so good.

Meeker, with Bryant peering over her shoulder, observed the operation for a few seconds before a small, gruff-looking man dressed in a gray suit barked, "I don't recognize you." As he puffed on a cigar, his frown turned into a smile. "But I'll never turn away new customers who have your kind of curves. What can I do for you ladies?"

Keeping her gun out of sight, Meeker closed the distance to the man she assumed was behind the illegal operation. As she approached, he unbuttoned his suit coat, revealing a pronounced bay window lapping over his belt. His eyes took a complete inventory of her anatomy.

Meeker ignored his stare. "Are you in charge here?" she asked.

"I am," he replied, running a hand over his bald head, his eyes now somewhere between her waist and neck.

"Well, I need some information."

"On a horse?" he asked, his gaze still fixed on the same appealing spot.

"No, a man."

His demeanor markedly changed as he looked at her face and held up his hands. "If your husband's been losing money, that's not my business. You might as well turn around and head back to your kitchen. Folks who work with me trust I won't talk about my clients. Trust is what makes this business work."

"I think you'll want to talk to me," Meeker continued. She produced her gun and aimed at the man's suddenly concerned face.

A few seconds before, the room had been filled with voices asking for horses' names, racing venues, and numbers, but when Meeker showed her weapon, the joint became as silent as the grave. All six men manning the phones put the receivers down and became as still as statues. While Meeker continued to hold her gun on the manager, Bryant aimed hers in the direction of the hired help.

The manager finally worked up the courage to break the silence. "You a cop?"

"No, but I know some. And to ease your mind, I assure you that you won't have to break your pledge to your clients as you call them. I don't have a husband who plays the ponies. In fact, I don't have a husband at all."

The bookie whistled, "Somebody's missing out. I'll bet you're a tiger …"

"Don't go there," Meeker suggested. "Once again, and let me emphasize this, we came here for information, not action. Now, what's your name?"

"William."

"Just William?"

"My last name is Williams. My folks weren't too imaginative."

"Well, it's better than Bub," she assured him. "Okay, William. I just need to know about one of your clients who's in big trouble with the law. If you give me that information, we'll leave here and never tell Chicago's finest about your little operation. If you don't come clean, then you might find yourself using the showers at the local jail for a very long time. Do you understand me?"

"Yeah," he answered, his eyes once more trailing down her body.

"William," she warned, "Keep your focus on my face. My father told me a long time ago there's no using looking at things you can't afford. You got that?"

"Yes, ma'am."

With her free hand, Bryant pulled the photo from her jacket pocket and showed the man. "Have you ever seen this guy? And don't lie. I have no problem reading men, and I don't react well when I don't like the story."

"She means what she says," Meeker assured him. "And by the way, she's a Caddo Indian, and I don't think she has ever recognized any peace treaty between her tribe and us. On top of that, she has a surgeon's skills with a knife."

"You're some kind of dames," Williams noted as he nervously grabbed the photo. He studied the picture for only a moment before shoving the paper back at Bryant. "That guy's not coming back, so I've got no reason to lie."

"Spill the information," Meeker demanded.

"Okay, fine. He calls himself Dan. He's not real good at picking winners, but today he got lucky on some horses that ran in California. His long shots made him almost a grand."

"What do you know about him?" Bryant quizzed.

"Only what I told you. Look around, this ain't no social club. We don't ask who your parents are or where you live. He told me his name was Dan, and he paid his debts. That's all I needed to know. Still, hate to see him go. I made a lot of money off that guy."

"What did you mean by his not coming back?" Bryant asked as she kept an eye on the other employees.

"He told me he was getting out town," the man explained, "and it had to be a one-way trip."

"Where was he headed?" Meeker asked.

"He just said he had to disappear. There was another guy here who overheard and jumped into our conversation. When Dan told the guy he was hot, Spoons explained for a couple of hundred, he could get him on a boat to Canada. As they left together, I'm guessing, if he was lucky, that's where he was headed."

"Who is Spoons?" Meeker asked.

"He's a low-life. You could call him a cockroach in a suit."

"His family lives downstairs," Bryant cracked. "What's he do to make his dough?" Before Williams could reply, she belched. "That burger's going to haunt me all night."

"Did you actually eat downstairs?" Williams asked.

"Yeah."

"You two are real gamblers. Now, what did you ask?"

"What does Spoons do to earn a buck?"

"You want the truth?"

"Yes!" the women answered in unison.

"First, I need to know who you guys are. There is stuff I can't just spill without making sure you're on the level." He glanced at Bryant and added, "Believe me or not, there are things worse than Bub's cooking."

Glancing at Bryant, Meeker shrugged before turning back to their host. "We're private investigators."

He snapped his fingers, "Yeah, I knew I'd seen your face somewhere. Your picture was in the newspaper a few days ago. You're the one who used to work for the President. Helen, Helen, Helen …."

"Meeker."

"Yeah, that's it." For the first time since they'd drawn their guns, the smile returned to the man's face. "So, this is really government business then."

"You could say that."

"And you're not going to rat me out to the cops?"

"Not if you help us," Meeker assured him.

"Well, you've got the firepower, so I guess I'll have to trust you." The ringing of three different phones stopped the conversation. "Can my guys go back to work?"

"Sure," Meeker replied.

"Okay, boys," Williams announced. "Everything's under control. Get back to making us some money." As the men picked up their pencils and answered the phones, Williams leaned closer to the women and spoke in a hushed tone. "Spoons is a hired gun. The mob uses him when they want to take someone out. He's strictly local, but that doesn't mean he's not lethal."

"You sure about this?" Bryant asked.

"Yeah, real sure. And he's good. He doesn't leave clues, and he's not going to rat out those he works for. Because of what he does, I try to make sure he wins enough to keep him happy. In other words, all my inside tips are shared with him."

Meeker, her Colt still directed at the bookie, concluded, "So, Spoons hangs out here a lot."

"No, he just places bets or picks up money and leaves. But he hung around today. I didn't question him, just let him drink our coffee and sit on the corner of my desk. He didn't say anything worth noting until the guy you're looking for came in. Then he became strangely talkative. And that's not like him at all."

Meeker glanced toward Bryant, noting her solemn expression. She figured they were both on the same page. The hit man had likely been assigned to take out a possible leaker. Who was Spoons working for? She was sure the bookie wouldn't know that, so there was no reason to ask.

"Okay, William. What does Spoons look like?"

"Skinny, redheaded, about five-six, and he's as pale as a ghost. Today, he was wearing a brown suit, gray shirt, and no tie. Every time I've ever seen him, his shoes shine like new silver dollars, and he always drives a dirty gray, dented Chevy sedan. He lives about a block from Indiana

Harbor. I was there once to deliver some winnings. The place looks like a shack until you go inside, then it's real nice. When I was there, he showed me his collection of jazz records. He's real proud of those."

"I guess we need to go put a fork in Spoons," Bryant suggested.

Williams shook his head. "I'd rethink that if I were you. Remember, he kills people for a living. He's been doing the work since he was fifteen, so he's had lots of practice and is really good at his job. On top of that, he's as mean as a rabid wolf and has no conscience. I'll bet he makes gutter scum feel clean and streetwalkers think they're novice nuns. If I were going after him, I'd head over to the Great Lakes Naval Base and bring about a hundred of those boys with me. This isn't a job for girls."

"Thanks for the advice," Meeker noted. "And I think your roving eyes proved we're women, not girls. Now, you just go back to work. And if you'll forget we were here, we'll forget what you do for a living." She grinned. "Mr. Williams, do we have a deal?"

"You got one. But if you run into Spoons, don't tell him I was the one who gave you the dope."

"If we run into Spoons," Meeker replied, "we'll escort him to a new address where he'll have lots of roommates."

The women backed from the room, guns ready, then quickly turned and hurried down the stairs, through the diner, and out the front door. Once they were on the street, Bryant voiced what Meeker was thinking.

"Odds are Elliot's not going to make Canada."

"Let's hope we get to the dock before Spoons has a chance to make him disappear."

CHAPTER 5

Monday, September 28, 1942
8:41 p.m.
Indiana Dock, Waterfront, Lake Michigan, Chicago, Illinois

"Come on in," Eric "Spoons" Gaston called out. William Elliot nervously followed his host through the waterfront shack's door. "It's not much on the outside, but I've done a lot to make up for that inside these walls." Spoons glanced toward his guest and smiled. Elliot looked as though the hounds of hell were after him. While the hounds might well be on their way, the wolf would get to claim this prize long before they arrived.

Spoons pointed to a chair and made a seemingly innocent offer. "I'd guess you could use a drink."

"I just need to get out of the country," Elliot insisted, his tone elevated by fear.

"Why's that?" Spoons asked as he opened a cabinet and pulled out two glasses and a bottle of rye.

"Nothing you need to know about. When can I leave? I've got the money. I can pay you now. I just want to get on the road. In fact, I have to get on the road!"

"First have a drink; it'll calm your nerves, and then, I need to make a call. I've got a friend who runs a boat up to Canada a few times each week, and you'll be on it tonight. In fact, you'll be as snug as a bug in a rug. I guarantee it."

Elliot drained the liquor in one gulp. "Are you sure you can trust this guy?"

Spoons set his still full glass on the table and grinned. "I can trust him. He's a smuggler. He can't afford to go to the cops, and for a couple of hundred, he'll be more than happy to pick you up and drop you off. Now, I'm going to put on a record. Do you like music?"

"I guess so," Elliot muttered as he paced from one end of the room to the other. The drink had obviously done nothing to calm his nerves or lower his blood pressure.

"Why don't you sit down?" Spoons suggested. "Wearing out my carpet is not going to do either of us any good."

The guest shook his head. "I'm too keyed up. It's like there are eyes everywhere. I can feel people looking at me and sense them following my every move. I feel like I'm living in a nightmare. I thought I had my tracks covered. I thought I'd figured everything out, but I got in over my head."

"Most folks do," Spoons agreed, "but tonight your problems will be over." He picked up a record and grinned. "I love jazz. Maybe this will help you calm down a bit."

"I thought you were going to call the guy with the boat."

"He won't be at the dock until about nine. So just find a place to light and let the riffs and strains of really good music fill your head."

Smiling, Spoons put Coleman Hawkins's cut of "Body and Soul" on the turntable and set the needle in place. As the grooves in the ten-inch wax platter began to make a melodic sound, he looked back to his guest. Elliot had finally found a chair and eased into it.

"You're a godsend," Elliot announced. "I had no idea how to get out of town without being spotted. And then you popped up at Williams's, and everything fell into place."

"Timing is everything," Spoons quipped.

"Still, I appreciate it. When I read that …"

"When you read what?"

"Nothing," Elliot answered. "Just a story in the newspaper that kind of warned me the game was up."

"Well, at least you had a warning. I've known a lot of folks who don't get any advance notice. One moment they're on top of the world, and the next moment they are under the ground."

Elliot nodded. "I guess I am pretty lucky at that. After all, I had a great run on the ponies today. That must have been a sign." Seemingly a bit more relaxed, he glanced around the room and observed, "You must have a good job."

"Why do you think that?"

"This is really nice furniture, and the carpet is like a mile deep. That record player is top of the line, and the console radio must have set you back a lot of change. They don't give this stuff away."

"I do okay," Spoons assured him.

"If you don't mind me saying, I'm surprised you don't drive a nicer car or live in a better part of town."

"I drive what I drive and live where I live simply because I don't like to call attention to myself. In my line of work, it's not healthy."

"So, what do you do?" Elliot inquired. He was now feeling much more tranquil.

"Contract work. I'm a specialist. I get a call when someone wants me to help them make a business problem go away."

"You mean like cooking the books?"

"No," Spoons replied with a grin, "my line is not numbers, it's people. When someone has an issue with someone, they call me."

"What do you do with the people?" Elliot asked, confused. "Do they call you in to fire them, or do you just retrain them, so they fit in with the other workers or the job requirements? I always hated to can folks. Wish we'd called in an outsider to do it."

"Actually, I don't retrain them or fire them. I kill them." Spoons waited for the shock to register on his guest's face and then smiled. "In fact, I got a call on you today. Seems you've become a problem that can only go away when you stop breathing."

Elliot's face went ashen as his hands grabbed the arms of the oversized chair. With his unconcerned host looking on, he pushed himself upright, but rather than run for the door, he wavered, as if trying to gain his balance.

"You're dizzy," Spoons said as the music stopped. After reaching over and clicking off the record player and replacing the arm, he added, "Your drink was laced with enough poison to kill a herd of cows."

"But …" Elliot whispered.

"Your gut will start burning in a minute or so. My experience suggests you'll soon be in a lot of pain … intense agony … but it won't last long."

"You …" Elliot groaned as he reached for his stomach.

"I took care of a problem," Spoons explained as he casually walked into a bedroom. He returned a minute later with an eight-by-eight-foot piece of carpet. After dropping and unrolling the rug on the floor, he looked back at his guest and explained, "I replaced this last week. I got some bloodstains on this one, so I bought a new one for the area in front of the fireplace. It's imported. What do you think? Did I make a good choice?"

Elliot was still standing in front of the chair. Spoons casually strolled over and grabbed his guest under his right arm. "I'll bet you are having problems seeing, and you no longer have feeling in your hands and feet. Don't worry, that's normal. Still, I think you can manage a couple of steps. I'm going to lead you over to that carpet."

Elliot offered no resistance as he was dragged across the room. When he was in the right spot, Spoons let him go. With no one to lean on, Elliot staggered for a moment before falling to his knees and once more grabbing his stomach. In a few seconds, his strength gone, he collapsed on his side. He was still breathing, but for all practical purposes, he was gone.

Kneeling beside his victim, Spoons quickly went through Elliot's pockets, pulling out cash, identification, and a few sealed letter-sized envelopes. He pocketed the money and after moving back across the room tossed the other items onto the table. Easing into a reading chair, he turned on the light, grabbed the phone and dialed seven numbers.

"It's me. The job's done," Spoons announced.

"Have you gotten rid of the body?"

"No, but I will be in a while. My trusted friend is going

to take our guest out on his boat tonight and dump him in the lake."

"Did he have any stuff on him? By the time we got to his place, someone else had already cleaned it out."

Spoons glanced at the table, "A few envelopes. I'll let you decide if they're important."

"Anything written on them?"

"Just a second."

Setting the phone aside, Spoons reached over to retrieve the letters. After glancing through them, he once again grabbed the receiver.

"They are light. They couldn't have much of anything in them."

"Everything's on microfilm," the voice on the other end explained. "Now what's written on them?"

"Well, the first one has Bauer scribbled on the flap. The next one says B.S." Spoons laughed. "Now that pretty much sums things up."

"It means bombsight," the voice explained. "What about the other two?"

"DC is on the third one, and the last one says Manhattan."

"That's good, really good. You have what I gave him. I need the envelopes back so I can route them another way. They have to get to Germany along with another piece I have. They all need to be there in a week or so."

"Why the hurry?"

"I've already been paid," the voice explained.

"I'll give them to you when you pay me," Spoons cracked. "And, if what I found is that important, perhaps I deserve a bonus." He paused to check on Elliot before adding, "Oh, make sure I'm paid in dollars, not marks. I'll see you later this week."

Spoons hung up the phone and glanced back to the floor. His guest had expired, so the time had come to package him for shipping.

CHAPTER 6

Monday, September 28, 1942
9:33 p.m.
Indiana Dock, Waterfront, Lake Michigan, Chicago, Illinois

The air was cool, hinting of fall, and was bitter and brisk coming off the lake. Meeker and Bryant were ready for action but not dressed for the cold. After parking the rented Hupmobile sedan under a street lamp by a warehouse, they stepped out onto a brick street and cautiously made their way toward a pier. They had no reason to talk. They knew what and who they were looking for, though finding either was a long shot. How often did that happen?

As Meeker studied the deserted streets, a sobering realization set in, as chilling as the breeze. If Spoons had been assigned to knock off Elliot, the job had likely already been completed and whatever the man carried in his pockets long gone.

"Dead ends and dark alleys," she whispered.

"What?" Bryant asked.

"I don't like our chances," Meeker explained.

"I think they are better here than surviving the meal at Mocks," Bryant cracked.

Ignoring her partner's comment, Meeker continued, "We've got two choices in directions to search. I'll take one, and you take the other. We'll meet back here unless we hear fireworks. Then we race to the noise."

Meeker pointed to the street to their right. Bryant understood the directive and with gun drawn, slowly headed in that direction. Meanwhile, Meeker, sticking close to the old clapboard buildings, made her way down the nearer avenue. Except for the clicking of her steps on the bricks and an occasional moan of a foghorn, there was no sound. In the first half block, the only living things she saw were two cats under a street lamp and a possum perched on an alley garbage can. He was likely in for a much better meal than Meeker and Bryant had paid for two hours earlier. For the moment, along the Indiana Dock, Meeker and Bryant appeared to be the only people around. That realization was hardly comforting. They needed information to shut down the organization Bauer had served. They had to find out whom the group was working for and whether the mob or the Nazis were in control. They needed Elliot alive, and the clock was ticking.

As she stopped to assess the environment and inventory her eerie surroundings, Meeker shook her head and smiled. A grand joke had been played on her. She'd gone through college and law school and landed a job working for the most powerful man in the free world, but now, here she was walking down streets that even ladies of the evening avoided. The irony was as thick as the fog she'd once seen in London and seemed to be taunting her. She'd passed up marriage, motherhood, and a normal life to eat at cheap diners and dress down bookies and cons. Now she was trying to keep a lousy gambler who had sold out his country from being killed by a cockroach in a suit. What a life.

After watching a calico cat chase and catch a rat, then play with the hapless and terrified creature for a full minute before inflicting a lethal bite, Meeker once again moved forward. She walked past three warehouses, a small storefront that hadn't been open in a decade, and two shanties before noting a well-used and badly dented gray Chevy parked beside a junky, rambling shack. Lights shone through the paned glass. Bingo! The table was set. She'd found Spoons.

Meeker's instincts told her to wait for Bryant. The other woman would surely complete her search in five minutes, but her gut demanded action. After all, if there was a contract on Elliot, his time for breathing was limited. And, if Spoons was not going to kill him but help him escape, time was still not on her side. Every second counted. She stood in the shadows in front of a deserted house and studied the scene. Knocking on the front door was out, but waiting and watching was an invitation for Spoons to punch Elliot's final ticket. She had to get a look inside that house.

With her Colt drawn and ready for action, Meeker stepped out of the shadows and moved quickly across the street to the car. Crouching beside the sedan, she popped open the rear passenger door and glanced into the shadows of light framing the scene. On the back seat was a rolled-up carpet. Pulling a small flashlight from her purse, she shined it toward the end of the rug. The beam caught two brown shoes that just happened to be attached to legs.

Climbing into the vehicle, she crawled across the floor and shined her light at the far end of the roll. This time the beam illuminated a face, frozen in agony.

"Darn," she whispered. She was too late.

With Elliot dead, there wasn't much else to do. Even if he were captured, Spoons providing the name of the person who assigned the hit was highly doubtful. After all, a stretch in prison was better than walking the streets after ratting out either the Nazis or the mob. Still, Elliot might have had something on him he was going to pass along, something dealing with national security. So perhaps this wasn't a complete waste. Unrolling enough carpet to get to the man's front pockets was like wrestling a bear in a closet. Worse, the search was fruitless; the pockets she could reach were empty. Thus, to find out what had been there, she was going to have to take on a man with no morals and few fears. If only this could have been easy.

Putting away the flashlight, she crawled backward out of the car and set her Colt on the Chevy's running board. She then grabbed the end of the carpet, set her feet on the pavement and pulled the body and rug out of the sedan and onto the ground. After retrieving her gun, she went through each of the dead man's pockets a second time. She found one stick of Beechnut gum.

Elliot was past saving. Meeker tossed the gum aside, eased back onto the running board and safe from being seen from the house, tried to formulate a plan. Charging into the home would be suicide, and the city would frown upon her setting the shack on fire. The only smart option was to wait for Bryant. While killing time, she eased around to the front of the car and popped the hood. Spotting the coil that led to the stovepipe six-cylinder engine's distributor, she yanked the top wire out and tossed it under the car. She then eased the hood closed and moved back to the running board. At least if Spoons made it to the Chevy, he wasn't going anywhere.

Meeker focused her eyes on the far end of the street where she expected Bryant to appear. Suddenly, she heard a door open. She frowned; nothing was working in her favor. Glancing around the car's nose, she noted the gunman locking his front door. Like it or not, now was the time for action. Positioning herself behind the sedan's fender, she aimed her weapon and waited.

As Spoons turned toward the street, she barked out an order. "Raise your hands or face the consequences!"

As her words echoed along the empty street, the hit man dropped and rolled behind a tree. The odds now seemed to be back in his favor. He knew the turf, and she only had the Chevy for cover.

"What do you want?" he called out.

"You," she answered. "We need to talk."

"I've got nothing to talk about."

"The body in the back of your car says otherwise. Who put the mark on Elliot?"

"I don't know what you're talking about. Who's Elliot?"

"The dead guy I just pulled out of your back seat."

This time there was no immediate answer. The man hiding behind the oak remained mute, likely contemplating his next move. One second became ten, and an eternity later, the clock had counted off another minute.

"You shouldn't try to make a break," Meeker warned.

She glanced back down the street, looking for Bryant. Seeing she was still alone, she added, "I'm a really good shot."

"It's hard to hit a moving target in the dark," came Spoons' calm reply. "I know."

"I'll bet you do," Meeker agreed. "But I've managed more times than you can count to bring folks down in both day and night. In fact, my hauling in O'Toole is likely the reason you knocked off Elliot. Now here's the score. You can come out of this alive, wounded, or dead. The choice is pretty much yours. I'd rather not have to shoot my Colt, but I will."

"You're Helen Meeker!"

"In the flesh!"

"I've read about you," Spoons assured her. "In fact, there's a price on your head. I could retire on what I'd get for your scalp. So, you coming my way might be the biggest break I've had in a long time."

"Always happy to accommodate," she sniped. "Now, if you try to make it back to your front door, I'll nail you before you can get it unlocked. You obviously can't use your car. So that means your only exit that includes continuing to breathe involves trying to outrun the lead from my Colt. How lucky do you feel?"

Spoons' answer was both rapid and potentially lethal. From behind the tree, he squeezed off three rounds, two bouncing off the Chevy's bumper and the other piercing the radiator. As coolant began to drain onto the pavement, the man hustled across the shadowy yard and down the street. As she stood in place and followed him with her eyes, Meeker realized he was headed for an alley just thirty paces ahead.

"Stop, or I'll shoot!" she shouted, rising to her feet.

He answered by firing two wild shots over his shoulder as he sprinted toward what he was sure would be freedom. He was ten feet from his goal when Meeker frowned, then set her jaw. Leaning against the Chevy, she aimed and squeezed the trigger twice. Spoons stumbled forward and dropped. Why did everyone seem to think getting shot was better than giving up?

Her gun still ready, Meeker stepped around Elliot's car and, from thirty feet away, studied the scene. Spoons lay face down on the edge of the dirty, deserted waterfront street, his breath labored. Blood dripped from two gunshots wounds, staining the pavement. His life expectancy appeared to be measured in seconds. As always, Meeker felt regret. She hated killing, but this time she didn't feel any sadness. Spoons' final exit was appropriate. He'd spent most of his thirty-odd years wading through gutters, and now he was dying in one.

After waiting a full minute to be assured the killer was completely out of commission, she covered the twenty feet from the sidewalk to where the hood was fighting to breathe. His right hand still held the Smith and Wesson. Leaning over the body, she observed the places where the bullets had pierced his back, making two neat holes in his brown jacket.

After kicking the revolver to the middle of the street, she grabbed his shoulders and turned him over. His eyes were open, but unseeing. There was no time for last rites, much less any questions.

As she watched his chest rise and fall a final time, she thought of something her father had told her when she was a child. Those who carry a gun as a calling card almost always end up in the gutter, a prison, or a grave. There was rarely another option. This punk had paved that final route for who knows how many other men, including Elliot. She felt no pity, but there was no glory in killing, even a human cockroach. How she wished she'd had a chance to talk to him, to get the information he was taking to his grave.

Meeker glanced up as she heard footsteps rounding the corner. Bryant jogged over to Spoons, picking up his gun in her gloved hand. She approached her partner, shaking her head.

"I saw what happened and called the cops from the booth down the street. They're on their way." She then grimly added, "I told them with your pinpoint shooting, they'd need the wagon and not an ambulance."

"I preferred to have him alive," Meeker noted.

"He'd have still ended up in the ground. The state would have executed him before the snow melted." She shook her head. "Men with small brains should never play with guns."

"No one should," Meeker observed before shifting to what was now the most pressing issue. "We probably have five minutes before the cops get here. I'll go through his pockets; you take his keys and search his house."

"What am I looking for?"

"Anything that might have been in Elliot's possession. I don't want any government information to slip into the local police department's hands. If he knew about the atom, then someone likely fed him more information as well. Let's hope that hasn't slipped out."

"Helen, do think the Nazis have that good of a spy network in the States?"

"No," she replied, "but I'm convinced someone near the top of our chain of command has sold us out. They fed information to Bauer, and now they are feeding the line to others to take back to Germany. We have to find and stop that person before any more damage can be done. Millions of lives depend upon it."

Just before Bryant headed toward the house, she observed, "The bookie was right."

"About what?"

"Spoons made sure he had the shiniest shoes in town."

CHAPTER 7

Tuesday, September 29, 1942
6:41 p.m.
Mountain Top Estate, twenty miles north of Berchtesgaden,
Bavaria, Germany

Henry Reese stood in a grove of trees and studied the postcard-worthy surroundings. The team's new mission took them into a part of Germany so tranquil he could almost forget the world was at war. The scenery was breathtaking with fall colors, picturesque villages, mountaintop castles, locals wearing unique native dress, and clear streams running through deep valleys. Best of all, for two days he had not heard a single gunshot. Now, as darkness enveloped the landscape, the moon lit up a large German estate where an impressive and massive brick house rested on a plateau.

A half-dozen outbuildings, including an arena-sized barn, surrounded the mansion. Several acres of grass were so neatly trimmed they could have served as greens on a golf course. Reese noted a flat spot where a soccer field had been lined off and another place between the house and the barn with an elaborate array of playground equipment. Closer to the house was a swimming pool, and not far from the barn, an area was set aside for archery.

"They must have some amazing views from that third-story balcony," Gail Worel remarked as she eased up next to Reese.

"No doubt," he whispered, forgetting the huge estate as his senses filled with the woman he'd grown to love more than anything on the planet. After gently sweeping her into his arms and drawing her close, he observed, "It's a crazy world."

"It always has been."

"But more so now. People are killing each other for sport, or at least that's the way it seems."

"I don't think the war will last forever," Worel noted wistfully.

"It seems like it will last until there is no one left to kill. When you think of all the blood, suffering, and rage we've seen, there's no way we should be in love. There's simply no room for that now. Life is far too fragile, and this war is much too important to take the risk of giving away a heart." He shook his head. "That line was so bad it would have been ripped out of a movie script. Perhaps, before acting and sounding like a teenager with a bad crush, I should have stopped with 'there is no way we should be in love.'"

"Maybe there should be a way," Gail suggested. She laid her head against his shoulder and looked up at his face. "And I don't care if it is corny. I love all those things you said. You see, I think love might be our only real hope to drown out all the hate we've seen."

He nodded and looked back at the estate. "I do love

you. Someday we'll have a real wedding, not just a quick trip to the local constable's office."

"It was a nice trip," she assured him. "But I'll take you up on the other offer someday. I'd love to march down a church aisle in a white gown with my friends and family there to celebrate with me. I'd like to hear the organ play the wedding march and dance with my father. I think I'd even enjoy rice in my hair."

He filed those wishes into the recesses of his mind and vowed to make them come true. Pointing to the estate, he said, "Maybe we can live in a place like that. We can play lord and lady and raise a dozen children."

"I think two is enough," she replied. "When this war is over, I'm not going to have the energy to chase a dozen."

"Those people up there on that hill," Reese mused, "what do you suppose they do?"

"They breed." Underground leader Hans Holsclaw joined the two lovers, still locked in an embrace. "I'm sorry if I interrupted anything, and I didn't mean to eavesdrop. I noticed you weren't at the camp and decided to see where you'd gone."

"I'll forgive you," Reese said with a laugh. "At least we didn't share any embarrassing fantasies."

"You said they breed?" Worel asked as she slipped from Reese's arms. "You mean like cattle? I haven't heard any sounds of livestock. Are German cows quieter than those we have in England? Besides, there are no fences or pens."

The Dutchman mournfully shook his head and looked toward the home. "Have either of you ever heard of Lebensborn?"

Reece replied, "If my German's any good—and it has to be for this mission—it means 'fountain of life.'"

"That's exactly the meaning," Holsclaw agreed, "and this is one of the several places across Germany where the children, products of that special breeding program, are being raised."

"I don't follow," Worel said, sweeping a strand of hair off her face. "What kind of children live there?"

"In 1935, the Nazis developed Lebensborn in an effort to create a generation of perfect Aryan youth. They went about this in a couple of ways." He held up two fingers as he explained. "The first involved literally mating blond-haired, blue-eyed SS officers with females who possessed the same characteristics."

"You mean the government arranged marriages?" Worel asked innocently.

"Hardly," Holsclaw replied. "In many cases, the women and SS officers were already married to other people. In other cases, teenagers were taken from their parents and housed in special places for officers to use."

Stunned, Reese cut in, "So these girls were provided for the men's pleasure?"

"No," the Dutchman answered, "this was about creating a master race, not giving the SS recreational rewards. The women were told this was their duty, and the SS officers were simply there to fulfill a job."

"That's mind-boggling," Worel noted in disdain. "In fact, it's perhaps the most disgusting thing I've ever heard."

"In the world of the Nazis," Holsclaw assured her, "this likely is one of the milder crimes against humanity. I would argue it pales in comparison to other ways the children of Lebensborn were obtained."

"How's that?" Worel looked back toward the estate.

"They couldn't breed enough children, so they

kidnapped kids who displayed what were deemed the ideal Aryan traits. Those that were stolen from their parents were taught the Nazi way. The propaganda never stops. Their schoolbooks and even their bedtime stories reflect the ideals of the Reich. The skills they are taught are meant to shape them into warriors. If Germany is not defeated, many of the children living in that home on the hill will become the next generation of Nazi leaders."

"That's ghastly," Worel whispered in horror. "You mean to say these children are being raised by the state for the purpose of becoming the human show stock of a nation?"

"It's actually more than that," Holsclaw continued. "The values they're taught, the ideology that's poured into their minds each day, and the way they're treated create an impression they are superior to everyone else. In a very real sense, they are made to see themselves as vastly superior to all those who don't possess their traits and characteristics."

Reese took a few steps toward a meadow and looked out at the estate. Just like his new bride, this news was beyond his ability to fully grasp. He struggled with the thought of breeding a master race. "Just when you think there's nothing that hasn't been tried, you get a big surprise," he muttered.

"My friend, what you're having problems grasping is really nothing new. Some American slave owners did the same thing in trying to create a bigger and stronger generation of workers. The Romans had breeding programs for their gladiators. History is littered with other examples. This is simply an outcropping of that kind of thought."

"But this perfect Aryan look makes no sense," Reese

protested. "It goes against fact. Look at the Nazi leaders—Hitler, Himmler, Speer, Goring, and Goebbels—none of them fit that mold. Almost all of them have dark hair, they possess all kinds of body shapes, few of them are athletic, and show me one of them who any woman would consider handsome.

"It's ironic," the Dutchman agreed. "Those who decide what the perfect man looks like look nothing like the perfect man. If you think about the logic, that was also true of the American slave owners and those in charge of the Roman games. But you have to understand when Hitler sees himself in a mirror, he doesn't actually see his true reflection. He sees a person who is superior in every way. In his mind, he is a mental giant, a man with inexhaustible energy. The face he sees in the glass might not look like the children in this home, but in his mind, he is their father. Henry, I've found that extreme ego blinds even those with twenty-twenty vision." He let his words hang in the air before adding, "And that works in our favor."

"I get being blind to the truth," Reese replied, "but explain how that helps us."

"My American friend, those who are blinded by ego believe themselves to be godlike. They no longer look at things logically because they think with a wave of their hand or a pronouncement from their lips, they can wipe away everything that stands in their way. In their minds, they are always right, and nothing can stop them."

Holsclaw leaned against a tree and pulled a pipe from his pocket. He tapped in a bit of tobacco from a tin and lit up. After a few long draws, he blew the smoke into the air before continuing. "With America now in the war, the only real chance Germany has is to find a way to broker peace. When the Nazis were facing the Brits, they really had the upper hand. The English had no oil reserves and limited natural resources. They could only hold off Germany for so long before they would be fighting the war on grit and fumes. Yet the British were stubborn, and that frustrated Hitler, so he chose an easy target to pump his ego and attacked the Reds. But Russian winters were something he hadn't planned on. And, as you know, when supply lines broke down due to weather, that not only delayed victory, but losses began to mount. The Nazis were literally stuck in the snow. And then came December 7th. I think up until that day, the Germans still had an opportunity to control all of Europe. They still had the chance to take England and turn things around in Russia."

"A sleeping giant was awakened," Reese added, "and the America First movement, led by the likes of Charles Lindberg, was finally silenced."

Worel cut in. "On our side of the pond, we recognized the America First movement was driven by fear and prejudice as much as not wanting to be a part of the war. Many in your country blamed the Jews for every world problem. I remember how much that organization ridiculed Hollywood and Wall Street."

"That's in the past now," Holsclaw noted. "Having the United States in the war means the Allied machine has almost unlimited resources. The Yanks will just keep building and building in factories all over your huge nation while Germany slowly runs out of raw materials and fuel to keep up the fight. And all of this happened because one man was blinded by his own ego, and another fool decided to attack a giant that really didn't have the stomach or will to fight."

"Still, winning won't be easy," Worel countered.

"Winning will indeed take resolve and many years," the Dutchman agreed, "but in the end, the little god in Berlin will be taken down as long as we can stop them from building a super weapon."

Pointing to the estate, Worel asked, "When we win, what happens to those kids?"

"My guess is they will be reviled," Holsclaw said. "I think that's the only possible outcome. When the war ends, the SS and Hitler will be viewed as the devil's backbone. So those children in that house will be hated due to their association with the cruelest elements of Nazi Germany."

Worel's face went white. "Then we need to kidnap them and take them back to Britain." She pointed to the hill. "Look, there's practically no security. We could call for a plane, drop it in, and remove these poor kids from their horrible fate. We could succeed!"

"We have the men," the Dutchman admitted. "We might even be able to get them to a place where they could be picked up. But many of these children have been brainwashed for seven years. How do you erase that mental garbage from their minds?"

"It could be done," Worel argued. "We have to try."

"Could it be done?" the Dutchman asked. "What if one of them is the next Hitler? Would you want to unleash that on the world? There are likely some heading up the Allied movement who think it best to just bomb that home and wipe all those kids out rather than deal with the poison that has been thrust into their minds."

"You can't be serious!" Worel shot back."

Holsclaw glanced back to the house on the hill and took a few more puffs on his pipe. "I don't want to see them dead. If fact, I'd love to be noble and save them. But we're not here to save lives; we're here to take down a research center that might be creating weapons that could turn the tide in Germany's favor. The lives of those twenty or so kids pale in comparison to our mission."

"But ..." Worel began.

"He's right," Reese agreed. "I'm sorry those children are in that environment. I wish we could get them into a place where they might escape the cloud of Nazism. But, the fate of the world is at stake. We have to get to the mountain, do our scouting, come up with a plan, call in our orders for the needed materials, and be ready when the rest of the team is dropped to our position."

Worel was crushed. "It's not right."

"Right or not, it's time to move," Holsclaw said. "The safe house where we'll be staying is still several miles down the road, and we need to be there before dawn."

Worel looked longingly back at the estate, a tear running down her cheek. Reese wiped the tear away before resting his chin on her head. As he embraced the woman he loved, he noticed a blonde girl who looked about ten, standing in front of a window.

"I wonder who she is?" Worel asked.

"Likely a child who was kidnapped," Reese suggested. "She's too old to be a part of the breeding program."

Worel quietly wept. "That means somewhere, right now, her parents are missing her and wondering if she's alive."

Reese thought back to a case he worked with Helen Meeker and the toll two separate kidnappings had taken on their families. Guilt swept over him with the suddenness of a spring storm—a crying shame they couldn't bring a few children home, but regretfully, there were other things much more important that demanded their attention.

"Let's go," he whispered as he grabbed Worel's hand and headed back toward the bottom of the hill.

"Promise me something," she demanded.

"What?"

"When all of this over, when there's no more war, we'll save one of those kids and bring him or her home to our house." She looked up into Reese's eyes. "You see, I still think love can fix any problem."

"If it's possible," Reese assured her. "Now let's get going."

CHAPTER 8

As she raised her eyebrows, Helen Meeker's face displayed a mixture of disbelief and amusement as Napoleon Lancelot tried to steer three Scottish terriers into the group's secret headquarters. The energetic canines were pulling the muscular man forward, backward, and sideways. He might be able to handle almost any size man—he'd proved that several times since joining the team—but the canines were completely overwhelming him. One terrier had managed to wind his leash around Lancelot's right leg while another was all but yanking his left arm from its socket. The third terrier was showing far too much interest in his shoe.

Meeker leaned back in her chair and grinned. "What in the world are you doing?"

"It's a long story," the ebony-skinned man announced. He dropped the leashes and collapsed into a chair, allowing the dogs to explore the main room. The largest of the short-legged, black bundles of energy raced between two desks and down the hall. The smallest strolled directly into the wall, his blunt snout leaving a wet circle, before regaining his bearings and moving under a desk. The last of the trio ran into a coat rack, knocking it sideways, but he didn't react when it fell to the floor with a loud clang. If this kept up, the office would likely be in shambles by the end of the day. What started out as cute was quickly becoming ugly!

Meeker became concerned. "Napoleon, what in the world were you thinking? These pups are going to ruin this place in a matter of minutes!"

"Fala hasn't ruined the White House," he argued, "and he's the same breed of dog."

"Unlike the President, I don't have the Secret Service and a large staff to look after a trio of living fur balls. If these pups get into the lab, we'll be in real trouble. Equipment worth thousands of dollars is in there. And, if someone calls while they're barking, the consequences won't bode well for them or me."

While Meeker waited for an explanation, the most energetic of the group came racing back down the hall. He barked three times, then knocked over a wastebasket, spreading trash everywhere. Meeker crossed her arms and tapped her foot before setting her jaw and hissing, "Napoleon!"

The big man sighed. "It's not really my fault."

"Not your fault?" She pointed to the growing chaos. "This isn't your fault? Then whose fault is it? When you give me a name, I'm personally going to haunt them!"

"I didn't ask for the dogs. They were thrust upon me."

"You should have thrust them right back."

Napoleon shrugged. "That would have required more digging than thrusting."

"What are you talking about?"

"My uncle died and left me the pups in his will. I don't know what he was thinking. I mean, he left my sister three thousand dollars and a five-year-old Hudson. My cousin Joan got his house, and another cousin, Johnny, was given the furniture. I got the dogs. So far, I can't find anyone to take care of them. The way my luck's going, I might just get stuck with them forever. So, you see, it wasn't my fault."

Meeker got up from her desk and walked over to the pooch hiding under the desk. She kneeled in front of him and extended her hand, but he didn't respond. At least being ignored was better than being bitten.

"He's blind," Lancelot explained.

"Blind?" Suddenly, Meeker was concerned.

"Yeah, he was born that way. You have to talk directly to him, and you also have to help him get used to new places." Lancelot glanced around the large room, filled with a desk, tables, and file cabinets. "It would likely take him a few days to map this place out, so he won't run into anything. His blindness is likely the reason he's shy. But on a positive note, his hearing is amazing. In fact, my uncle trained him to find sounds."

Confused, Meeker looked back at the dog, "Find sounds?"

"Yeah, let me show you." Lancelot walked over to the door, "Come here, Samson." On cue, the dog walked to where he stood. "Now listen to this." Lancelot took off his watch and placed it near the dog's head. After tossing the timepiece to Meeker, he ordered, "Find that sound."

The dog barked once, then stood perfectly still. After

a few seconds of apparent deep concentration, Samson closed the five feet separating him from Meeker, now sitting on the floor, and gently put his nose against the hand holding the wristwatch.

"I'm impressed," Meeker admitted as she scratched Samson's head. "Now, I'm not sure what good that skill would do, but it's a great stunt. Do the other dogs know any tricks?"

"Yeah, Zeppo, the one over by the far wall that knocked over your trash can, is a great scent dog. He can trail almost anything. And Keller is deaf. She can't hear anything, but her vision is amazing. She seems able to see even in the dark, so she serves as Samson's guide."

"They make a good team," Meeker admiringly agreed as she pushed off the floor and returned to her desk. "Maybe someday our team will function as smoothly, but with a lot less noise and destruction."

"I can't break up that team," Lancelot insisted. "That was in the will. If I give them away, all of them have to go to the same home. I guess I'm going to keep them together with me. My new apartment allows pets, but I just didn't feel like I could leave them alone today."

"I understand," Meeker replied. "I'll give you a pass today, but let's not make this a habit. We don't need to be *terrierized*—pardon the pun—on a regular basis. Why don't you put them in the room where you stayed while we checked out your story? That would be safer than letting them roam free." The ringing telephone pulled her attention from the three dogs.

"While you get that," Lancelot said, "I'll round up the mutts and get them situated."

By the third ring, the dogs were on the way down the hall. Meeker answered with a chipper, "Helen here."

"It's Alison."

"Good to hear your voice, sis."

"Rising at your pipes as well," came the expected slang-filled reply. "You want the heads up on what the G-men dug up at the frog's pad?"

Meeker frowned. "I'm guessing you're asking me do I want to know if the FBI found anything in Elliot's apartment. But what does a frog have to do with it?"

"Elliot croaked."

"That's too bad. But yes, I do want to know if they found anything we missed."

"You're still the teacher," Alison assured Meeker.

Meeker guessed that being the teacher meant the others still had things to learn. "So, nothing new?"

"No, the go-to guy or gal in this caper is still very much like Claude Rains."

"I'm lost again," Meeker admitted.

"Helen …" Impatience was evident in Alison's tone as she was forced to explain what should have been obvious. "Rains starred in *The Invisible Man*."

"Okay, I'm following now. Anything else I need to know? And please translate as you tell me."

"Fine. There's a businessman in Chicago who has been involved in making bombsights for the Army Air Corps. He's been in a blue funk since his wife died."

Before answering, Meeker recalled finding an envelope in Spoons' home with a set of microfilm plans for a new bomb sight hidden under a stamp. Although seemingly not as significant as the information they'd discovered on the Manhattan Project, the plans that had been hidden on microfilm of the Pentagon or the docks of New York Harbor, perhaps this would put that tidbit in a more significant light. But what did this have to do with a dead wife?

"Alison, what does a grieving widower have to do with me?"

"That's the problem, Helen. His depression is affecting the way he does his job. The cops ruled his wife committed suicide last July. One of those investigating, a guy by the handle of Roger Richards, argued there was probable cause for murder, but when the clothes came out of the washer ..."

"Clothes? Washer?"

"Okay, when they sifted through all the evidence, the DA didn't find enough grounds to justify overruling the ME. By the way, don't you find getting information in black and white kind of boring? I mean, it's so vanilla pudding, no flavor, no beat, doesn't soar. If it were a book, no one would buy, much less read it."

"No, plain vanilla is fine. I like when we speak the same language. Now, where do I fit into this picture of a mourning man?"

"That's good," Alison suggested.

"What is?"

"The line about a 'picture of a mourning man.' It tells a story."

"Back to the facts, sis."

"Okay, once again in your native tongue, the rich guy whose wife cashed it in is Michael Wallace."

"Ah, he's known as the 'Big M.E.' in social circles," Meeker cut in, "a man with both power and money."

"Like Astaire and Rogers, they usually go together," Alison cracked.

"I guess you're right. Now spill with the rest of the report."

"I like the way you're yapping, Helen. Here's what else you need to know. Wallace has set up a cruise tonight on Lake Michigan. He's invited all those people he thinks might have murdered his wife, along with the investigating cop. So, the guest list is filled with suspected suspects. Don't you dig that?"

"Not really. Get to the part where I'm involved."

"Okay, sis. Wallace and the cop want you and Teresa there to help determine if Mayu Wallace did commit suicide or if she was murdered. Both men value your opinion so much, they'll let things ride with your assessment of the case."

"Mayu, interesting name."

"She was Japanese."

As she considered this unexpected bit of new information, Meeker's dark blue eyes were drawn to Lancelot, who had reentered the room. Thankfully, no dogs were with him.

"Alison, why is my decision about what happened in this matter so important?"

"Because the government needs Wallace to have his head in the game. As long as he suspects his friends and business associates of murdering his wife, he's not going to be fully focused."

Meeker shook her head. "Teresa and I are supposed to leave for DC tomorrow and then travel to London the following day. We can't afford to put the trip off."

"The Big Cheese ..." Alison paused before correcting

herself. "The President knows that, but this is only going to be a three-hour cruise."

"A three-hour cruise?"

"Yes, a three-hour cruise! I mean, what could possibly go wrong?"

"Okay, fine." Meeker was obviously put out. "But how is Wallace managing to get all of those he suspects to attend this floating party?"

"They think he's organized a pleasure jaunt to get away from the bad news of the war. A big meal has been planned, and the dress is formal. And in case you need some muscle, Napoleon will go along as your butler."

"I have a butler?"

"Just for tonight."

"The yacht's leaving at 6:00, so be at the Windy City Marina in plenty of time to board. By the way, the boat's name is *The Cat's Eye*. Wallace keeps the vessel in slip 213."

Resigned, Meeker replied, "Okay. I'll let the team know, and we'll get the garb necessary for the junket. Can you have Wallace get us a list of everyone who will be there?"

"I already have a list. I like boat rides and dressing up. Wish I was going."

"I wish you were taking my place. I'll do some research on Wallace and let Teresa or Napoleon study the guests. As soon as we finish, I'll hand him the phone, and you can give him the names."

"Anything else?" Alison asked.

"No. Bye, sis, love you."

"Smiling exit and sunshine to you, Helen," Alison replied.

"Hang on, here's Napoleon." As the big man got up to take the phone, Meeker explained, "She has a list of names. Jot them down. We only have a few hours to get a full work up on each."

"Got it."

Frustrated, Meeker got up and moved toward the door. She was being asked to play a game to cheer up a man when she should be preparing for a mission to take out a potential game-changing facet of the Nazi's war machine. The last thing she wanted was to slip into a gown and mix with Chicago's elite, but plenty of things she didn't care to do were required as long as she was in the President's service. Once again, she was reminded of going to the prom with the wrong date!

CHAPTER 9

Wednesday, September 30, 1942
5:55 p.m.
Windy City Marina, Slip 213, Chicago, Illinois

The lake wind was almost bitter cold, hinting at a winter that might arrive sooner than normal and with much more bite than usual. After parking, Helen Meeker, Teresa Bryant, and Napoleon Lancelot walked a hundred yards down the pier to the spot where *The Cat's Eye* was tied to the dock. Sea-going cargo ships would have felt minor league compared to the yacht. *The Cat's Eye* was long and sleek, with polished mahogany decks and enough chrome to outline a twenty-story art-deco building. As Meeker knew firsthand, M.E. Wallace's rig made the President's pleasure boat, *The Potomac,* look like an antiquated, stripped-down tug.

"So, this is how the wealthy live," Bryant cracked as she adjusted the hem on her jade-green evening dress.

"Would someone remind me what I'm doing here?" Lancelot asked, carrying one Scotty. "And why didn't someone tell me the party was on a cruise ship?"

Meeker, dressed in an emerald-blue gown, explained, "You're my butler."

"Yes, that's right. All butlers have college degrees," Lancelot replied, displaying a touch of the bitterness. He struggled over having to act the role of a second-class citizen.

"It's not my idea," Meeker assured him. "I need you here for both your brains and your protection. The fact that you're seen as a servant means folks really won't notice you. That gives you the opportunity to go places Teresa and I won't be able to visit and do things we can't do."

"Pardon me if I don't revel in being considered invisible," he announced.

"It works to our advantage," Meeker assured him. "If Mayu Wallace was murdered by one of those on board, I suspect you'll figure out who they were well before we do." She frowned as she looked at the bundle in the man's arms. "And why did you bring the dog?"

"I couldn't leave Samson at home," he explained. "He hasn't mapped out my place yet, so he keeps running into things. I mean he's blind, you know?"

"Yeah, I remember," Meeker assured him. "It might be good to have him around. I'll explain that he's mine, and I don't go anywhere with him."

"So now the dog is yours! As if a butler would be allowed a dog of his own."

Meeker smiled and cooed, "No, he's yours, all yours, but for tonight, both you and Sammy are undercover. Besides, if Wallace hates dogs, then perhaps this trip can end almost as soon as it begins." Turning to Bryant, she asked, "Did your homework reveal anything about this boat?"

"Yes, the yacht is a tribute to excess," Bryant began. "There are six bedrooms—each with its own bath, a full kitchen, a dining room, and a gathering room that includes gaming tables. There are two levels, three if you count the observation deck, and there is a four-man crew: a captain, a first mate, and two stewards who will likely serve the meal tonight. *The Cat's Eye* is powered by twin Packard twelve-cylinder engines. Wallace is a compulsive man and pays great attention to details. My research uncovered each bedroom is outfitted exactly the same way, and he inspects every room before guests arrive to make sure even the clocks are all wound and set to the same time. He also puts on gloves and checks for dust. Each gaming table sports new, sealed decks of cards. With his wife dead, he has even taken over determining the dinner menu and has specified a precise number of ice cubes in each glass."

"Not the kind of person I enjoy being around," Meeker noted. "What was the cop's name?"

"Richards," Bryant answered, "Roger Richards."

"Why does that name make me want to sing?" Lancelot asked.

"Don't," Bryant ordered. "It might cause the dog to howl."

Ignoring the warning, Lancelot began humming "Fly with Me." Samson whimpered along.

Ignoring the bizarre duet, Meeker asked, "What do we know about Richards?"

Bryant didn't have to check her notes. "He's single, bright, has a good record, and is the kind of person you'd want on your team if you were dealing with a complex case. By that, I mean he has a reputation of having an eye for details. As per Wallace's orders, Richards is supposed to have his case files with him, including notes, photos, the gun used in the crime, and even the clothes the victim was wearing the day she died."

Meeker's gaze returned to the yacht. A gray-headed man, wearing a white dinner jacket, stood on the deck, waiting for the trio to make their way on board. She knew from photographs this was M.E. Wallace. A few feet to the millionaire's right was a tall, good-looking man in an ill-fitting, thus likely rented, tux. He looked like a fish out of water or a cop off his beat, so she pegged him as Matthews.

"Keep Samson on a leash," she suggested as she led her team toward the gangplank. She then whispered what almost sounded like a prayer, "Perhaps we can quickly move through the evidence and determine if her death was murder or suicide. Then maybe we can turn this three-hour cruise into a sail around the harbor and back home."

"You are far more optimistic than I am," Bryant replied.

CHAPTER 10

Wednesday, September 30, 1942
6:10 p.m.
Windy City Marina, Slip 213, Chicago, Illinois

"Miss Meeker," Wallace greeted, extending his right hand, "I'm so glad you can join us. I'm anxious for you to meet those in attendance and talk to Mr. Richards about the evidence."

Meeker forced a smile. Wallace appeared to possess the strength and energy of a man two decades his junior. After pulling her hand back and making sure nothing was broken, she offered a greeting of her own, hoping her words didn't sound forced.

"Miss Bryant and I will be happy to look at your evidence and give our views. But I hope you won't be upset if the conclusion is not the one you want."

"I will accept what you say," he assured her. "Have you, during your well-chronicled adventures, ever met Mr. Richards?"

"No," Meeker quickly replied, her eyes moving from the industrialist to the gray-eyed cop. "But first, allow me to present my partner, Teresa Bryant, and our aide, Napoleon Lancelot." She figured Lancelot would be pleased to be called anything other than a butler. "Oh, and my dog, Samson. It will become obvious later why we couldn't leave him behind."

After shaking hands with both of his guests, Wallace directed a comment to Bryant that caused Meeker to cringe.

"I've been told you're as good as any male detective in the city."

Bryant raised her eyebrows. "You must have been misinformed."

"Really?" Wallace replied, surprised.

"Yes, the men might not measure up to Helen's and my standards," she quipped, tossing a biting grin toward Richards.

Obviously not sure how to respond, Wallace turned his attention to the dog Lancelot held. "He looks sweet."

"He's my secret weapon," Meeker told him. "Samson often discovers things we miss. By the way, Mr. Wallace, I understand you were in the service the first time we fought the Germans."

"I was in the Navy," he answered with a hint of pride.

"I've read your file," Meeker noted. "Munitions, I believe." She then turned to the cop and extended her hand. "I'm Helen Meeker."

"Roger Richards," he replied. "It will be a pleasure to have your and Miss Bryant's insights. By the way, the medical examiner on this case is also here. I thought you might want to interview him."

"The more facts we have, the better off we are."

Suddenly, Meeker felt the yacht moving. By instinct, she grabbed the rail and looked back toward the dock.

"All my other guests are already on board," Wallace explained. "Unless you want to stay on the deck and watch as we head out, we can join them."

"Normally," Meeker said, "I might just stay and enjoy the view, but as cool as it is tonight, I think it would be best to go inside."

Wallace led the way into the large dining room. Thirteen people were gathered in the room, eight men and five women, all dressed in formal wear. Most appeared to be in their thirties or forties except for a younger woman wearing a tight, red dress, and a stout, gray-headed gentleman in a wheelchair whose glasses partially covered his dark, beady eyes. His face was deeply lined, but he had a full head of hair that would be the envy of most men in their thirties. He was also surprisingly solid for a man who was either injured or handicapped. Wallace must have noted the object of Meeker's gaze because he leaned closer and gave her a full profile.

"That's one of my main competitors. His name is William Decker. Bill is likely the wealthiest man on board today. He has a number of different manufacturing interests and over the years has consistently beaten me on most bids."

"I take it he doesn't make devices like the bombsight you are currently producing," Meeker said.

"How did you know about that?" Wallace asked, obviously stunned. "That's supposed to be top secret."

"Don't worry," Meeker assured him. "It is. Now, why didn't Decker get the bid on the sight?"

"He wanted that one," Wallace assured her, still taken

aback by Meeker's knowing so much about his business, "but he was a few dollars too high. Yet, with the delays my plant has been experiencing, unless I can get things back on track, he might well have that contract soon. He has all kinds of other interests to keep him busy as he circles over my head like a hungry buzzard. His companies make safes of all sizes, burglar alarms, forklifts, mechanical doors, and even tractors. He's also into lumber, ball bearings, and sporting equipment. He's spent a small fortune over the past few years in expansion. In other words, he's made all of us borrow up to our necks just to keep up. In fact, he's bought out three of the companies that used to challenge me."

"Why's he in the chair?" Meeker asked.

"He was in an automobile accident a decade back. The accident killed his wife and left him crippled. It hasn't kept him from his work. He has a specially equipped car, and his office is set up for him to roll wherever he needs to go."

Meeker faced her host and spoke bluntly. "You sound like a man who doesn't care much for Mr. Decker. How's your relationship with him?"

"It's more one of mutual respect than friendship. We both recognize who the other is and know that keeping close is the best way to stop the other from getting too far ahead. We were once good friends, but that changed after his wife died."

Meeker looked to her left to make sure Bryant and Lancelot heard everything that was said. Bryant nodded slightly, acknowledging she was in step.

Meeker leaned close to Bryant and whispered, "I think it's time to begin unwrapping some packages. What do you say we start with the guy in the chair?"

"One pigeon is as good as the next," Bryant cracked.

Not waiting for her host to make the introduction, Meeker led her trio across the room to Decker. She smiled as she gently held out her hand.

"Mr. Decker, I'm Helen Meeker. This is Teresa Bryant and our associate, Napoleon Lancelot."

"I've heard a great deal about you, Miss Meeker," he replied, taking her hand in his. Like Wallace, Decker's grip was solid and strong. After admiring Meeker's dress, he turned to his right and charmingly noted, "And Miss Bryant is becoming a familiar figure in Chicago, as well. In fact, with so many of the best Cubs White Sox, Cardinal, and Bears players going into the service, you two might be the heaviest hitters in town." He paused and looked toward Lancelot. "What does your man do?"

"He's not actually our man," Meeker explained. "I'll let him speak for himself."

"About anything," Lancelot announced. "I have a college degree, I'm good with languages, and I serve the agency in whatever way it needs." He added with a grin, "The dog here is our resident bloodhound."

Bryant, who had been mute until this moment, chimed in, "We know a great deal about you and your many businesses. Decker Industries has been a part of this country for decades."

"More than eighty years," Decker responded with pride. "My grandfather began everything. He was a machinist. He was producing gasoline motors for farm equipment when most folks were still using mules. My father built the business from there."

Bryant nodded. "I see you're a fan of the color red. I know your company trademark has your name printed over a bright red background, and you're the only man in the room with a red tie and red socks."

"My wife was the reason the company changed its colors from dark blue to red. She convinced me that red stood out more. Since she died, I've always worn something red as both tribute and remembrance. I also find, as I am confined to a rolling chair, the bright red gives me a chance to be noticed."

"Your shoes are unique," Bryant added. She bent closer before asking, "Is that eel?"

"You have a fine eye," he replied. "I love the way eel shines. I have them made by a shop on the west side. The eel skin is brought in from the Gulf of Mexico."

"How long have you owned this pair?" Bryant quizzed.

Decker glanced down at the almost reflective shoes and shrugged. "I guess about two months."

"Look at those shoes, Helen," Bryant urged. "I don't think you'll ever see another pair like them."

Meeker smiled, but wondered why in the world was Bryant blabbering about footwear when tomorrow they were going on a mission to head off Germany's work on a super weapon? Nevertheless, Meeker quickly glanced down and nodded. "They're nice. Now if you'll excuse us, Mr. Decker, we need to meet the rest of the guests."

"What did you think of Decker?" Wallace asked as he guided the two women toward more guests.

"He's far more than he seems," Bryant offered, not bothering to explain what she meant.

"Molly and Jim Castle," Decker announced as he approached the four guests. "You no doubt have heard of Helen Meeker and Teresa Bryant. The Negro with the dog is one of their employees."

Meeker swallowed her words and reset the fuse in her brain rather than defending Lancelot. She had to remind herself this worked to her advantage. She wanted those present to underestimate the man with the dog, but she still found not saying something difficult.

"Very nice to meet you," Meeker said, speaking for everyone in her trio. She then casually scoped out the couple.

The Castles reeked of money. Jim's tux was tailored, his nails polished, and his dark hair far too perfect. He was much too pretty to be a man. Molly was a bit over five feet tall, outfitted in a black dress and at least three grand in jewelry … that is if the gems were actually real. Her eyes were clear and her makeup a touch overstated. Meeker pegged Molly as a former cheerleader and sorority officer.

Evidently sensing a need to bring the detectives up to speed, Wallace pointed out, "Jim's in stocks and bonds. Those who follow his advice almost always find the pot of gold at the end of the rainbow—and Molly is into spending everything Jim makes."

If the diminutive woman took offense, it didn't show. She just kept smiling like a beauty queen. Meanwhile, her husband sported a barely discernable grin as if he had already been assured the title.

Wallace began a second round of introductions. "And here we have Greg and Melody Steinforth. Not that long ago, Melody, using her maiden name, White, was a star on Broadway. Greg is a theatrical agent who also dabbles in diamond sales. You can't have a Windy City gathering without including these two."

As greetings were exchanged, and the couple made small talk, Meeker sized them up.

Greg, looking uncomfortable in his tux, puffed on a cigar. His hair was receding and what was left appeared to be dyed black. He was about thirty pounds overweight. Melody, about five inches shorter than her husband's six feet, had deep-green eyes and fair skin. She wore thick makeup and was a bottle blonde. Her gown would have looked good on her twenty years earlier, but tonight the outfit revealed way too much skin.

"I imagine the diamond industry is somewhat fluid right now," Bryant commented, attempting to peek into the couple's minds. "As I recall, most of the work used to be done in Holland, but with the war, I guess some of the cutting has moved to the States."

"We have seen an uptick," Steinforth agreed, "but getting the rare diamonds from South Africa is not easy. The U-boats have sent some shipments to the ocean floor."

Meeker nodded, "I see that Mrs. Steinforth has managed to corral a few for this evening. They are very beautiful."

"Thank you," the woman replied. Then she offered a glimpse into the family history. "Gregory used to buy me a new bracelet every time I had a starring role on Broadway. He did keep Tiffany's very busy."

"I'm sure," Bryant said. "As I recall, you did manage at least two starring roles."

As expected, the conversation immediately died.

Looking at Melody's glowing eyes and flushed cheeks, Wallace suggested, "You can visit more later. I want Helen and Teresa to meet the rest of our guests."

As their host stepped into the middle of the room, he pulled the trio close to him. "In the far corner are two more couples. The tall, graying man with the short, plump wife is Roscoe Taylor. He's a distributor of automobile parts. With no new cars being sold and old ones wearing out, he should be in gravy, but I hear he's still paying off debts from the Depression. Tolly's sweet, but her mind and a blimp have a lot in common—they're both filled with hot air."

Wallace cast his eyes slightly to the right before continuing his discourse. "The other pair is a bit more interesting. Andrew Bellford is a retired banker. The young thing by his side is not his wife. Bella Bellford is out of town, so Andrew opted to bring his daughter-in-law, Janet. His son, the woman's husband, in on a destroyer somewhere in the Pacific."

"What are you implying?" Meeker asked.

"Only that Andrew hits on everything that moves. And with his movie-star looks and grace, he often scores. There is talk that Janet is his latest."

"Class act," Bryant noted, her voice dripping with sarcasm.

Wallace continued, "Off to the port side, sitting at the table, are our final four guests. The Wickmans are on the right. Joshua is a broker who drinks too much. His wife, Kathleen, is the real brains of the family. She has a master's degree in art, and before the war, she made some important sales with paintings obtained from Europe. He is as crass and vulgar as he appears. She is elegant but has a sting like an angry wasp when provoked. The other couple is from New York."

Meeker eyed the pair. The man was small, slightly built, with curly hair and dark eyes. He resembled a weasel. His wife, with her closely cropped bob, appeared more rabbit-like. She was tall, plump, and nervous.

"Don't let their looks fool you," Wallace warned. "The Van Elffands are opinionated and loud. Scott would knife you in the back if it could make him a dollar. By the way, his business centers on importing furniture. Ellie's business is spending Scott's money, and she loves to discuss her family's supposed royal roots. She only has friends to use them. She is as loyal as an alley cat."

"Lovely crowd," Lancelot chimed in. "I think I prefer the folks in my neighborhood."

"I will say this for all of them," Wallace explained. "They're all patriots. They love America and wrap themselves in the flag every time they get the chance— for whatever that's worth. Hence, they now all hate the Japanese. And each of them turned on Mayu after December 7th. So, if she didn't take her own life, then each of them is a suspect. And because they all have money, they likely had no fear of being caught. If the cops get too close, there are people they can bribe."

"You don't have much regard for the local police," Meeker suggested.

"I feel about the same as I did back in the Capone era." He eyed his guests before continuing. "Money talks and that's the best reason to always have it. Being broke is worse than being dead."

"There are some," Meeker offered, "who wouldn't agree with you."

"That's because they've never had enough to really know the power money brings," he retorted.

"How about the man in the brown suit?" Bryant asked, wanting to move the subject beyond the value of wealth.

For the first time since they had entered the room, Roger Richards spoke. "The man leaning against the bar is the city's top medical examiner. His name is Stanley Renshaw. Renny, as we call him, can answer any questions you might have about the autopsy. I still think he's wrong in his assessment of Mrs. Wallace's ability to pull the trigger at the angle needed to inflict the wound."

Renshaw was likely in his late thirties. Nothing about him stood out other than his dramatically pale complexion. Bela Lugosi looked sun-kissed compared to this guy.

"I'd guess he never gets outside his morgue," Meeker quipped.

"Not often," Richards verified. "In this city, a lot of work comes his way, and he's understaffed."

"We'll have time to visit with him later," Wallace suggested. "Dinner is about to be served. After we eat, we can move to the gaming area, and the questions can begin."

"No," Meeker interjected, "we eat and then my team examines the case files and evidence. Then we'll go to work." She paused and glanced around the room before asking, "Do these people know the real reason they're here?"

"No," Wallace assured her. "They think it's just another of my outings. I've been having them for years."

Meeker smiled and said, "Good. When setting a trap, it's best to have ignorant prey."

CHAPTER 11

Wednesday, September 30, 1942
6:50 p.m.
Lake Michigan

As Wallace signaled that dinner was about to be served, Teresa Bryant pulled Helen Meeker and Napoleon Lancelot to the side. Once assured no one would overhear, she made her pitch.

"I think Napoleon needs to take Samson for a walk."

"So, I just skip supper? That doesn't seem like a very good idea."

"You'll be going hungry for a good cause," Bryant assured him. She glanced around the room before adding, "It would be wise if you were to look in every room on this yacht. Get a feel for the layout. If Helen agrees, I'd like you to find the case files and evidence Richards brought with him so you can study them even before he shows the materials to us." She stopped as the boat pitched a bit to the stern side and then observed, "The wind's coming up. That likely means a storm's brewing. Wallace isn't going to take us home until Helen gives him a verdict, and I'd like to get back to the dock before a real nasty bit of weather hits. After all, there have been about as many shipwrecks on the Great Lakes as in the Atlantic. In a storm, these are dangerous waters."

"Great," Meeker grumbled, "a three-hour cruise becomes a recipe for seasickness."

"I sensed the storm even as we boarded," Bryant explained.

"How?" Meeker asked, before waving off the answer. "You have to have some kind of gift from your ancestors, so I'll just accept the fact and move on."

"Should I do what she said?" Lancelot asked.

"Her plan sounds good to me," Meeker agreed. The yacht rolled a bit. "So, Napoleon, walk the dog and make sure you take a very long walk. Over dinner, Teresa and I will get an even deeper feel for the guests. Knowing their temperature and views might enable us to limit our suspect list. That is if the evidence really does indicate Mayu Wallace didn't kill herself."

"Fine," Lancelot grumbled, "but I'm taking some grub from the galley for the hound and me."

As the man and dog unenthusiastically exited the room, Bryant turned back to Meeker. "We're all going to be at the same large table. You take one end, and I'll grab the other. As you're the celebrity, I think you need to direct the conversation, and I'll try to read the body language."

"You suddenly seem very interested in this case," Meeker observed. "Care to tell me why?"

"Just a hunch and I'm not ready to share yet."

"You also seem to be suddenly in charge?"

"I didn't think you wanted this case anyway. But, I'm now finding this very interesting. I'm going to enjoy watching skeletons jump out of the rich folks' closets. And I'll bet there are going to be a lot of them. Not only is a storm brewing outside, but I also sense one building in here."

Meeker frowned. "Still seems like a redo of my high school prom to me."

As promised, Bryant remained mute during the meal, her eyes and ears fixed on those seated around the table. After the salad, one of the stewards set plates filled with vegetables, and another brought in a platter piled high with sirloin steak. The cuts had been prepared so a guest could request anything from rare to well done. Decker chose a steak that was almost raw, while beside him, Kathleen Wickman requested a cut that was nearly burned. As Kathleen watched the man in the wheelchair cut into his bloody piece of steak, her skin turned ashen. While Decker eagerly devoured the raw sirloin, she set her fork to the side, evidently having lost her appetite. She didn't look like she had the stomach for blood, but a quick look around the table indicated everyone else did.

As the guests filled their stomachs and drank imported wine, the conversation became a bit livelier. Having spent four hours that afternoon in a newspaper morgue, digging up everything she could on the guests around the table, Bryant had an advantage in reading those around her. She was aware of how many children they had and where they went to school. When the talk was directed toward business, she was also a step ahead of the game. During dessert, when Meeker steered the conversation to news of the war, new territory was finally covered.

"Are we going to win?" Meeker asked.

"You're the one who knows FDR," Scott Van Elffands pointed out. "What do you think?"

Meeker smiled as she dabbed her mouth with a cloth napkin. "We'll win, but the length of time it takes will depend upon the support we get on the home front. Our industry has to outproduce the Nazis and Japan, and our workforce, which now includes women, has to realize that each line worker's contributions are vital. We can't have plants that aren't efficient."

Decker grumbled, "You mean like those breakdowns that Wallace has been experiencing? What a sorry excuse for a factory! He's giving the war to the Japs and Huns."

"Just a minute," Wallace shot back, "I seem to remember some delays in your plants as well. Very few of us are used to working twenty-four hours a day and seven days a week. All of us have many people on our lines with no experience. If I were you, I wouldn't be pointing fingers."

"I'll point mine where they need to be pointed," Decker assured him.

Bryant looked from one rival to the other. Decker was smug though not agitated, but their host was beet-red and angry. If the table hadn't separated the pair, Wallace might have even slugged the wheelchair-bound man. Secretly, Bryant wished he had. The cad deserved a good lashing. After stretching his neck, Wallace glanced at his watch and cut a bite from the chocolate pie that had just been served. For the moment, an uneasy truce appeared.

Breaking the awkward silence, Meeker turned to Joshua Wickman and asked, "Who do you fear the most … Japan or Germany?"

"The Japs."

"Why?"

"They're not even really human," the broker barked as he took a gulp of coffee. "They don't think like we do. They don't have the same values. They're monsters who want to see us wiped off the face of the planet."

Meeker paused and took a sip of water, before calmly inquiring, "So I guess you looked upon Mayu Wallace as being a monster too?"

Wickman's eyes lit up. "I thought M.E. was crazy to marry her. She had no business being in this country. Kathleen and I only put up with her because of good manners. We should have spoken up much sooner. We all should have."

Meeker turned to Wickman's wife. "I'd guess he speaks for you as well?"

Kathleen looked uneasy as she glanced from her husband to Wallace. After ten seconds of awkward silence, she phrased her thoughts in carefully measured words. "It would have been better if she'd never left Japan."

Once more agitated, Wallace interrupted, "When you needed help with your insipid art shows, who was the only one who'd help you? Who was there when your kids both got sick at the same time, and you were buying art in Europe?"

Kathleen Wickman shrugged but didn't answer. She was ill at ease and growing more uncomfortable by the second. Soon others would likely share that feeling. This was now like a family reunion gone bad, and Meeker was about to open the door for even more ill feelings. Too bad they hadn't brought a ship's doctor. They might need one very soon.

"What about you, Mr. Bellford?" Meeker asked, looking to her left. "How did you feel about Mayu?"

The retired banker smiled, then spoke. "I had no contempt for the woman, but M.E. could have done better. And none of us appreciated having her forced upon us. He used his money to ensure we allowed the foreigner into our circle. If he hadn't been rich, it wouldn't have happened."

"Andrew's right," Roscoe Taylor added, as his wife nodded in agreement. "At various times, Wallace, because of his standing in the community, all but owned us and he, therefore, had the power to push us into doing things we didn't want to do. And associating with that Jap woman was one of them."

Greg Steinforth added, "But after December 7th, we were finally able to exclude her from our lives. In a way, the country's worst day was also our best."

Bryant observed the others quietly nodding in agreement. Only Molly Castle remained stone still. Taking a deep breath, the woman quietly offered a different point of view.

"Mayu tried hard to be one of us, but in the long run that was impossible." She glanced around nervously before adding, "I grew up on the West Coast around Japanese people, and I found them to be just like us in most ways."

"You what?" Wickman shouted. "You think they're as good as us?"

"Yes," Castle quietly but firmly replied. "Just like the Germans are as good as us too. The fact the world's at war doesn't mean that people aren't good. Some are just following the wrong leaders."

"That's unpatriotic!" Decker chimed in. "You should be ashamed!"

Jim Castle stood, tossed his cloth napkin down on the

table and yelled, "You can't call my wife that. She's as good as this country has."

Decker shook his head, "Then we're all doomed."

Meeker stood and waved her hands. Once she had everyone's attention, she asked, "Mr. Steinforth, your last name interests me. Where are your people from?"

"My grandfather come over from Germany in 1903."

"Whose side was he rooting for in the First World War?" Meeker asked.

"The US."

Meeker shook her head. "Despite his being born in Germany, he was still an American patriot then?"

"Of course."

"Then why should it have been any different for Mayu? Why do you judge her by a different standard?"

"Because she didn't look like us," Melody Steinforth admitted."

"So, the mere fact she didn't look like us means she was not one of us?"

"Yeah," Jim Castle added, "and you know that is true because the man you worked for, the President of the United States, has placed Japanese Americans in internment camps. That pretty much proves you can't trust any of them. But why are we wasting time talking about this?"

Meeker glanced at Bryant before sitting back down to drop the bombshell. In a calm and assertive tone, she announced, "We are here tonight because the lead investigator in the death of Mayu Wallace does not believe she killed herself. He thinks it was murder, and it seems that those around this table are the best suspects. Now, before Miss Bryant and I excuse ourselves to study the evidence, would any of you like to take back the words you just said?"

CHAPTER 12

Wednesday, September 30, 1942
7:01 p.m.
Lake Michigan

Napoleon Lancelot watched Samson curl up in a corner and close his unseeing eyes before turning his attention to finishing the last half of a steak sandwich. Beside him, Roger Richards spread out his notes on the suicide of Mayu Wallace, placing them on a table in Wallace's shipboard study.

"So, you're not a butler?" the cop asked as he stepped back to look at the evidence.

"Why do you ask?"

"I don't think Meeker and Bryant would have confidence in a butler reviewing this case file."

"What about you?" Lancelot demanded. "How do you feel about that?"

"I work with lots of good Negro cops. I trust their judgment just like I do the whites. Being smart has nothing to do with skin color."

"Okay, I'm not a butler," Lancelot admitted. "You must

not have heard when I explained earlier, but I'm a college grad, an expert in codes, and I am an agent in Helen's agency. She trusts me completely, or I wouldn't be here with you right now. So, turning to the evidence at hand, what makes you so sure this wasn't a suicide?"

"I never claimed to be sure," Richards corrected. "I just have a hunch."

"Why?"

"Why what?"

"Why do you have a hunch?" Lancelot repeated.

Richards rubbed his chin and shrugged. "Things just don't really add up."

"Add up?"

"Suicide is about emotions, but it's also about math and science. The angles have to be right, and there needs to be a formula that can be proven by scientific means."

"Okay," Lancelot conceded, "you have me interested now. Preach on!"

"May I ask you a question first?"

"Sure."

"If you're so bright, why aren't you in intelligence or something?"

"The FBI and OSS wanted me until they found out my skin was darker than yours. And even you'll have to admit that Negro cops don't work on white crimes. In Chicago, the black police are limited to their own areas of town. And we know they don't make the same money as whites do."

"Sorry," Richards said. "I've ignored the obvious for so long that I'm now blind to it."

"I'm not blaming you," Lancelot assured him, "though it wouldn't hurt for folks like you to speak up to your superiors and spell out the unvarnished truth and how unfair it is. Now show me why things don't add up."

Still uncomfortable, Richards nodded. "First of all, the angle of the wound. I don't see how a woman with arms as short as Mayu Wallace's could shoot herself in the temple in this fashion and not leave powder burns and bruising."

As Lancelot leaned closer to study the crime scene photos, a strong wind rocked the boat. The storm was picking up.

"It's really raining now," Richards noted as he glanced out a porthole. "Hope the crew knows what they're doing."

"Well, if they don't know how to get us home, your medical examiner likely does," Lancelot added as he studied a second photo.

"What kind of crack was that?"

"Renshaw spent four years as a pilot in the Coast Guard," Lancelot explained.

"How do you know that? He never told me."

"Today, Bryant dug up information on our guests, and I studied up on you and Renshaw, as well as all the newspaper coverage of the case. Renshaw had a spotless record while in uniform. So, you see, we've done our homework."

His earlier apprehension in sharing a stage with a Negro gone, Richards strolled back to the table, "So what's your verdict?"

As he picked up another photo of the dead woman's wound, Lancelot pushed Richards to explain more of his murder-not-suicide theory. "You said there were other things beyond the lack of powder burns and bruising that concern you in this case."

"Yeah, when we examined the gun, two bullets were missing."

"Did you ask Wallace about that?" Lancelot picked up the revolver as he waited for the reply.

"I didn't in our initial interview at the scene, but I did ask him when I took his statement downtown. He had no explanation. He claimed the gun was fully loaded the last time he checked it."

"Maybe she fired once before using it to take her own life."

"If that were the case, I couldn't find where that first shot went."

Lancelot put the gun down and turned his attention to the clothes Mrs. Wallace was wearing the day she died. As he examined the oriental dress, he urged Richards to continue. "What else makes you think this was murder?"

"There are two other things. First, there was no blood on the chair where she must have been sitting when she shot herself. Her head would have been well below the top of the cushion, but it was clean."

"Did you find blood anywhere else?"

"Only underneath the head where it had seeped out and on the wall behind the chair."

"Maybe she wasn't in the chair."

"That's what the ME thinks, but if she were lying down when she killed herself, the spray from the exit wound would have been much lower."

"And what was Renshaw's reply to that?"

"That she was kneeling, close to the floor, and the angle she fired was the reason for the blood flying as it did. The bullet ending up on an upper shelf, buried, ironically enough, in the Sherlock Holmes novel *A Study in Scarlet*."

Lancelot noted the book in the evidence box but didn't pick it up. "Do you have anything else?"

"If you look at the photos, you'll see her hands are under her body, but the gun is above her head on the floor. I know there are ways that could have happened, but the floor is wood and has no scratches. I think the odds against the gun bouncing or sliding to that spot are long."

"I'm curious about something else," Lancelot added, "but I'll hold off on that until Helen joins us." He then picked up the ME's notes and final conclusions. After reading through them, he looked back at the cop.

"The notes say here that tests on her right glove proved she fired the gun, so all the long odds you're talking about seem to have been trumped by this fact alone."

"Yes," Richards admitted, "and that was why Renshaw overruled every inconsistency I pointed out and closed the books on my hunches."

Lancelot reached into the box, retrieved a paper bag and pulled out the two gloves. The right one had a circle of bloodstains on the palm, while the left remained clean. Though the stitching on the bloody glove was slightly stretched, both appeared to be almost new. After placing the gloves back into the bag, the big man sat at the table, pulled out a pad and pencil and jotted down a half page of notes.

"What are you doing?" Richards asked.

"Just providing Helen and Teresa my thoughts on what you and I talked about and what I've learned. That will give them a chance to ask fewer questions and go right to the most important elements of this case. It is a time saver!"

"And what do you think?" the cop asked.

"Let me stew on it for a while. Now, have you had a chance to fully explore this boat?"

"Wallace showed me around when we first came on board."

"And your impressions?"

"Huge, well-appointed, comfortable, and very powerful."

"I agree." Lancelot placed his notes on the table. "But did you find the uniformity a bit unsettling?"

"What do you mean?"

"Follow me."

They exited Wallace's study and moved along a hall to a bedroom. After they entered and turned on the light, he asked the cop, "What do you see?"

"It's large, the furniture is high dollar, and it beats what most folks have in luxury mansions."

"Did you know there are five more just like it. They're all the same size, and they are all arranged the very same way. The curtains, the bedspreads, the paintings on the walls, and even the wind-up alarm clocks on the nightstands are exactly alike. Every painting on this yacht is precisely eighteen inches from the ceiling. Mr. Wallace seems to be a man who is compulsive about uniformity."

"They are all just like this room?" Richards asked.

"Before I met you in the study, I walked the dog to every corner of this boat and looked carefully at each room. It is almost eerie." As a sharp wind rocked the yacht again, Lancelot glanced back at the cop. "The storm is getting more intense. I hope we can wrap this up and get home before we find ourselves clinging to lifeboats."

"They're likely close to finishing dinner. As you didn't

find anything that can confirm my theory, we should be heading back to the dock soon."

Lancelot nodded. He could see the disappointment in the cop's expression, but for the moment, there was nothing he could do to change that.

CHAPTER 13

Wednesday, September 30, 1942
7:30 p.m.
Lake Michigan

M.E. Wallace led Meeker and Bryant, along with Cook County Medical Examiner Renshaw through a maze of passages to his study. With each step, Meeker sensed the man was becoming more tense and angry. Even when they began sifting through the evidence and studying Lancelot's notes, their nervous host kept shifting his weight from one foot to the other. The way his lips sometimes moved, he seemed to be silently talking to himself.

"Are you all right?" Meeker, distracted by his behavior, finally asked.

"What do you mean?" he snapped back.

"You can't stand still. You keep wringing your hands and playing with your shirt collar. And the color in your face indicates your blood pressure's obviously elevated."

"Those people were supposed to be my friends! I could live with them feeling uncomfortable after Pearl Harbor. I understood that, but to say what they felt about Mayu before the war—that really eats at me. Every one of those jerks needs to die."

Ignoring their host's threat, Bryant noted, "War and pressure tend to bring out insecurities and suspicions. There are two of us in this room who are well aware of that. We have faced them many times."

Meeker raised her eyebrows, and Lancelot smiled and nodded. Seemingly everyone, including her team, was ready to tear down all sense of decorum and reveal their innermost thoughts, fears, anxieties, and even prejudices. She wondered how long before this blunt honesty erupted into a volcanic rage.

Wallace checked his watch before adding, "I guess my nerves are on edge because of this unexpected storm. The weather report in this morning's paper didn't mention it. Tonight was supposed to be cloudy but calm. Where are all our competent meteorologists?"

"Probably in uniform," Bryant suggested as she studied a photograph taken at the crime scene.

"If the storm's getting worse," Meeker said, "I guess we'd better get moving."

That was far from her only reason for wanting to wrap this mess up quickly. Beyond having a plane to catch for DC, she had no desire to stay with any of these refugees from high society any longer than necessary. At this point, except for Molly Castle, all of them made her skin crawl. Did these people represent the America she and millions of others were fighting to preserve? Surely that wasn't the case. Most of those in Chicago and around the nation had to see things much differently. Shaking off her distaste, she turned back to Napoleon's written observations. Her intuition had been right about him. His instincts were dynamite.

Directing her gaze toward Wallace, Meeker demanded more than inquired, "Give me more information about your wife."

"I've got that in my case notes," Richards eagerly cut in.

"You have the basics," Meeker replied, "but I'm looking for things I don't see. Perhaps I'm even searching for things a man wouldn't think to ask about." She eased up on the corner of the sturdy oak table and crossed her right leg over her left before continuing. "A woman has to have a lot of courage to marry a man she barely knows, even if they live in the same town and have the same friends. How many of us would go halfway around the world to live in a culture we've never experienced? I know enough about the Japanese to realize that a native marrying outside her race and religion is simply not accepted nor done. What Mayu did would seem to be an act of either panic or rebellion. So here are my questions. Was she running from something at home? Did she marry you to escape something? Were you the love of a lifetime who caused her to toss out everything she'd been taught? Or were you, perhaps, a lifeboat, offering her a last chance to escape someone who was after her?"

Wallace pointed to a long shadow box on the far well. "Do you see that sword? That was a part of her family for generations and was carried by her ancestors five centuries ago. She was from a family of Samurais, and she was very proud of that fact. She knew the family history better than most of us know American history. Her wisdom sprang from what that history taught. Her people were a proud group who clung to old traditions while also having the vision to see a new world. She wasn't afraid nor was she running from anything. In fact, her courage as much as her beauty caused me to fall in love with her."

"Still, it would seem tradition would require her to marry someone within the Japanese culture. If she so embraced her heritage, how could she toss that away?" Meeker asked.

Wallace shook his head and frowned. "In another time, that answer would be yes, but Mayu's family had fallen under great suspicion because they had the courage to question the decisions of royalty. Accidents began to happen, and her brothers began to die. When I made that trip to Japan, she was the last of her generation still alive."

"So, you brought her to the United States to save her life?" Bryant observed.

"No," Wallace argued, "I fell in love with her because she was not afraid to stand up for ideas and concepts she believed in. I assure you, she wasn't using me. She was running from nothing. If I had not come along, she would have spoken out until they tossed her in jail. It was her love for me that caused her to leave. Nothing else. I could also see she needed to be set loose from a tradition that barred her from fully becoming the person she was meant to be. She deserved to live in a place where people are free to state what they believe."

Meeker prodded further. "She was a woman of courage, who was also running for her life?"

"Courage, yes, but she wasn't running. She never ran from anything. If only I had her convictions." He shook his head and set his jaw. He seemed to want to say more, but for the moment, he remained mute.

Meeker observed Wallace for a few moments before

turning to Richards. "Your notes indicate you initially suspected Wallace might have killed his wife. Is that correct, or am I reading too much into it?"

"No, Miss Meeker, you're spot on. When I conjectured it might not have been suicide, and it could have been staged, I began to assess who could have done it. Later, Wallace gave me the list of suspects, each of whom is here tonight, but I discounted those because of one reason."

"Which was?" Meeker demanded.

"The doors and windows were all locked," Richards explained. "And the doors have to be locked with a key. You can't just pull them shut and have them lock. He claimed he came home, unlocked the front door and went immediately to the study. There he found the body and called the police. In my viewpoint, he had to have killed her, or it was suicide."

Bryant chimed in, "I remember watching a Philo Vance movie where there was a locked-room murder case. I've read books with the same premise. Each proved there are ways for a locked-room murder if the murderer is clever enough."

"True," Meeker replied, "but it would take a lot of planning and preparation. The folks on this cruise might have had what they viewed as patriotic reasons to dislike Mayu Wallace, but I can't see any of them having the desire to plan the perfect crime just to act on that misguided sense of patriotism and hatred of the Japanese. And, while our files prove that Wallace ..." she glanced at their host "is a greedy and unprincipled businessman who puts power and money ahead of everything else, I honestly believe he loved his wife."

Meeker walked over to the desk and picked up the

gun. After making sure it was empty, she turned toward Renshaw. "Prove to me that Mayu killed herself! Show me how it was done."

"You have to be very flexible," the medical examiner explained as he took the weapon. He got into a fetal position, lifted his head about six inches off the floor, then extended his arm to a point where the barrel was about six inches from his temple.

"Now," Meeker ordered, "drop the weapon and fall." After observing Renshaw, she shook her head. "The hand you held the gun in didn't fall under your body."

The ME stood, then explained. "I know, but she was a small woman. The gun's kick would have caused her to drop the gun, and that reaction might have also caused her arm to land under her body before her head dropped. After all, her head would have been driven upward by the blast before it fell back down."

"Did she die instantly?" Meeker asked, taking the gun and placing it back onto the table.

"No doubt," Renshaw acknowledged.

Meeker picked up the bloodstained glove, studied it for a moment, then pitched it to Bryant. She observed her associate for a few seconds before turning back to Richards.

"Your only real suspect is Wallace?"

"Yes."

"I tell you," Wallace screamed, "I didn't do it."

"Not only is there no way in the world to prove you did," Meeker responded, "but your motives for wanting Mayu alive are much stronger than the motive for wanting her dead."

The cop sadly shook his head, "So I'm wrong. All of this was for nothing!"

Meeker took the glove from Bryant and returned it to the table. After picking up Renshaw's final report and glancing through it a last time, she frowned and looked over at Lancelot. He nodded. She then glanced at Bryant. Her dark eyes told Meeker all she needed to know.

"Mr. Renshaw," Meeker announced, "your final conclusions, based on the way you read the evidence, are logical."

"Is there anything else you need from me?" Wallace asked, disappointed and still angry.

"No," Meeker assured him. "You have given me all I need."

"Then, if you will excuse me, I'm going to go check with my crew and make sure they're prepared for the weather."

After their host had departed, Meeker made what seemed to be, considering what she'd just said, an unusual suggestion. "Mr. Richards, assemble everyone in the game room, including Mr. Wallace. Before we close this case for good, there are a few things I would like to clear up."

CHAPTER 14

Lying flat on his stomach, Henry Reese peered over the top of a rise at the research facility's entrance several hundred feet below. He had figured on seeing more activity. Yes, Nazi troops were guarding the underground facility, but they showed no more interest in their duties than sentries outside military bases in the United States.

The road leading to the facility had been paved recently and was wide enough for large trucks to meet and pass in each direction. The sentry hut had electricity and phone service. About a hundred yards to the north were a large, almost vacant parking lot and a garbage dump. Otherwise, there was nothing to give away what was under that mountain. The site looked like nothing more than a small mining operation.

"They're obviously not expecting company," Gail Worel commented from her position just to her husband's left.

"They believe no one knows about it," Reese whispered.

He scanned the area again, noting a barracks-style structure a quarter mile north. "I see where the German troops are housed. The building they've constructed would appear to hold about a hundred, but I really doubt if there are that many assigned to the mountain. My question is where do the scientists stay? For that matter, where do they keep the slave labor?"

Hans Holsclaw, also on his belly to Reese's right, solemnly provided the answer. "Our area contacts report the slaves never come out of the hole. At least not as long as they're breathing." He pointed to some railroad cars and a line of track just west of the entrance carved into the mountain. "The supplies come in via rail. They are unloaded there and taken into the mountain. The workers come in boxcars, brought here from concentration camps. They choose only the strongest men in those camps for this project. Within a matter of months, they are dead. The Germans either work them until they drop, or they become poisoned by radiation and die in pain and agony beyond what we can imagine. Both the work and what they are working with causes healthy men to literally waste away in days or weeks."

The Dutchman's ominous words were sinking in when they heard a motor. Reese grabbed his field glasses and looked down the road. "Looks like they've got company."

A minute later, a Mercedes sedan rumbled down the road and pulled up to the sentry post. After checking the driver's papers, the guard waved the vehicle forward. Once parked, two men, dressed in what looked like something out of a Buck Rogers movie, emerged from the back seat. Each held a helmet covered with matching material. They spoke briefly to the sentries before strolling through the entrance.

"Those men are either scientists or engineers assigned to create the ultimate weapon," Holsclaw explained. "They spend very little time in the facility with the workers. They have a separate lab where they do their experiments on splitting the atom. We're guessing they just come to inspect the work."

"How close are they to creating the ultimate bomb?" Reese asked.

"They're not there yet," Holsclaw assured him, "but I think they're further advanced than either the Americans or the Brits. Of course, all we know about this project, as well as those of the Allies, are rumors. No one who actually knows anything is talking about it."

Worel nervously shook her head before asking, "What else takes place in there?"

"The Germans are tired of having their labs and development facilities bombed by the Allies," Holsclaw explained. "The most important ones are now in that mountain. One reason slave labor is needed is to construct new rooms. You can see the mounds of dirt and rock they have removed, now waiting to be hauled off by rail. The lumber stacked beside the road is used to reinforce their work. One of our contacts, a barmaid in a local town where the men go on leave, has learned the rooms are fully ventilated and have walls and ceilings. In other words, they look very much like rooms you would see in an above-ground facility. This isn't just some dirt hole. This has a large series of sterile labs and offices for support staff."

"They're working on things beyond just the atom?" Reese asked.

"Our sources have revealed that the experiments in that mountain include new propulsion systems, work on firearms development, and even radar."

"So, most of the area is not poisoned?" Worel asked.

"Not as far as we can tell. The work with the atom is isolated to certain areas. The men we saw in the suits were obviously going into that area, or they would have dressed normally."

"Then why are there issues with radiation sickness for the labor force?" Reese asked.

"Because they handle the radioactive materials without any protective gear. We believe they are also subject to tests involving how a human body responds to exposure," the Dutchman explained.

"They are both mules and lab rats," Worel noted.

As that bit of news sank in, Reese returned his attention to the security around the mountain. "This doesn't look like it will be a tough job. It appears much easier than I expected."

"Never judge a book by its cover," Holsclaw warned. "Inside that mountain are scores of highly trained troops, many of them SS. And, with the type of construction you will find in the facility, we will have to plant explosives throughout the mountain to fully destroy it."

"Then how can we possibly bring it down?" Reese asked.

"We'll have to dress like scientists. We will have papers proving we've been sent by Berlin to inspect the facility and upgrade its defenses. We will also have our supplies with us. Therefore, our cover is viable, and because of that cover, we will be able to carry in the explosives. The problem will be distributing them."

"Have you got a plan for that?" Reese asked.

"Radiation detectors."

"What?"

"The bombs will be packed in boxes marked as radiation detectors. We will assume the role of inspectors dispatched to make sure no radiation is getting into the labs or other areas where the SS and the scientists work. Then we will distribute detectors throughout the facility to accomplish that task."

"Will they be on a timer?" Worel asked.

"No. We don't know how long getting them all in place will take. They will have to be wired in series. We can explain that precaution as a way of powering each detector. When we are ready to leave, someone has to push the buttons to begin the explosions. That person will have to be inside that mountain and then race for the exit."

"I'm the explosive expert," Reese dryly noted, "so that will be me."

"We will talk about that later," the Dutchman said.

"What about everyone who is inside?" Worel asked. "You've told us there are hundreds of innocent workers in that facility. They live, work, and sleep there."

"And," Holsclaw sadly noted, "they will die there."

She gasped. "You can't just kill them! That's murder!"

"We can't get them out and accomplish our mission," the Dutchman answered. "Yes, they will die, but that will enable many more to live. In fact, our work might just save the entire world."

"But …" she whispered.

"It's war," Reese noted. "Just like we can't help those kids back in the home, we can't save the conscripted labor in the facility. But better to have the mountain crush them than to be worked to death or die of radiation exposure." He allowed that bit of truth to sink in before turning back to Holsclaw. "Making bombs that look like these radiation detectors is going to take some time and a lot of material. I would guess it would be weeks or even months before we're ready to pull this job."

"We aren't making them," Holsclaw assured him. "They are being assembled in England. The rest of our team will bring them when they join us. Until then, we go back to our safe house and wait."

CHAPTER 15

Wednesday, September 30, 1942
8:10 p.m.
Lake Michigan

According to Meeker's instructions, Wallace's guests were assembled in the gaming room. When she walked in, she found them seated in chairs that had been arranged like a college classroom. They had been chatting nervously until the door opened and Meeker, Bryant, and Lancelot entered. The appearance of the three was an immediate conversation killer.

With all eyes watching their steps, Meeker and Bryant strolled to the front of the room, then turned and studied the formally dressed group. All but unnoticed, Lancelot stayed at the rear, taking a place between Richards and Renshaw. For the next five minutes, as Meeker and Bryant silently examined the uncomfortable guests, the only sound was the storm blowing outside, obviously getting worse. The yacht was now pitching much like grandma's rocking chair.

"Enough of this!" Perspiring heavily, Jim Castle barked

as he rose from his front-row seat. "I'm getting out of here."

"Unless you can walk on water, you're staying right here," Meeker warned. "Take a seat. And when your fanny hits the cushion, tell me where you were on July 10th, the day Mayu Wallace died."

He didn't hesitate to supply an alibi—the words flew out even before he was back in his chair. "I was with Molly in New York City at a convention."

"You both attended the convention?" Meeker asked.

"No, Molly spent her days shopping, but she was with me. We stayed in the Waldorf. I hosted a small cocktail party the night before Mayu died, so we both have a dozen or more folks who can prove we were in New York on the tenth."

Meeker looked to the couple sitting to the Castle's right. "What about you, Mr. Steinforth? Do you and your wife have a confirmable alibi for that day?"

"We weren't together," the man admitted. "I was also in New York, visiting with several different agents about bringing touring versions of current Broadway plays to Chicago. That's easy to prove." He glanced over to his wife. "I'm sure Melody can tell you where she was."

The woman nodded. "I was at home that day. I heard about Mayu's death on the radio."

"Can anyone confirm where you were during the time of the killing?" Meeker asked. "Do you have any witnesses?"

"I didn't leave home," Melody explained. "I was nursing a cold and didn't even put on my makeup that day. Anyone who knows me knows that I never go out without my face fully fixed."

"No doubt about that," Kathleen Van Elffands chirped. "It takes her more than two hours to prop up and paint that face."

Ignoring Van Elffands' dig, Meeker pressed forward. "So, Mrs. Steinforth, you have no alibi?"

"I don't guess so."

Meeker turned her gaze to the second row. "What about you, Mr. Taylor?"

The tall man shrugged. "My alibi is sound. I was in my office all day interviewing more than a dozen men for a position as distribution manager to replace a person who'd just been drafted."

"And you, Mrs. Taylor?"

Tolly nervously played with the cuff on her sleeve before finally responding. "I was shopping that day. I charged everything I bought, and the clerks always write down the time of purchases …" She shot an evil glance toward her husband before adding, "As per Rosco's instructions."

Meeker nodded and shot a look at Wallace. As he had been most of the evening, he was agitated and nervous. At this moment, he was checking his watch.

"Mr. Bellford," Meeker said, returning to her questions, "I believe you are retired."

"Yes, I am."

"Does that mean you were alone at home, or do you have someone who can vouch for you?"

"My wife can."

"That's convenient as she's not here and can't speak for you."

The redheaded man glanced toward the ceiling as if trying to gather his wits. Then he smiled and answered, "I do have a witness. A work crew was at my house, remodeling the kitchen. In fact, they were there all week. I stayed home every day to make sure nothing was stolen."

"Interesting," Bryant chimed in, "but I find that hard to believe."

"Are you saying I'm a liar?" Bellford demanded.

"Yes," Bryant bluntly answered.

"Prove it."

"I'll toss doubt on your statement," Bryant explained, "when Helen finishes her interviews."

Meeker looked at her partner and smiled. She wasn't sure what Bryant had, but she did look forward to giving her the floor. For the moment, there were five others whose whereabouts on the day of Mayu's death needed to be confirmed.

"Mr. Decker, where were you that day?"

"At work. I require all my employees to clock in when they arrive and out when they leave. Also, the attendant at the garage logs the arrival and departure of every car. In fact, as a matter of wartime security, the cars are searched before they enter or exit the garage. I believe Detective Richards, in his initial investigation, actually checked on my alibi."

"Is that true?" Meeker asked the cop.

"It is. I even checked on his phone calls that day as they all had to go through the main switchboard."

"Why did you check so closely on Mr. Decker?" Bryant asked.

Richards shrugged, "When I thought it was murder, Mr. Wallace placed Decker's name at the top of the suspect list."

"Why was that?" Meeker asked. "What motive could he have had?"

"I'll tell you the motive," Decker volunteered. "The car that spun out of control, killed my wife and left me in this chair belonged to Wallace. We'd been at his home that night, and my motor wouldn't start. He gave me one of his cars to get home. The brakes failed. I'm still convinced he set us up. He knew I'd see how fast that Cord would go and that I'd only slow down when I approached the sharp curve along the lake shore."

"That's ridiculous," Wallace yelled.

Decker demanded, "Then why, when my mechanic went over to pick up my car the next day, was he able to start it right up?"

"You likely flooded the darn thing that night," Wallace snapped. "I should have made you walk."

Meeker glanced from one man to the other. This was a bit ancient history that had not appeared in Richards' files or Bryant's research.

Wallace, again glancing at his watch, grumbled, "Can't we move this along? After all, we know what the outcome is going to be."

"Mr. Van Elffands," Meeker continued, after once again seizing control of the proceedings, "where were you that day?"

"At a warehouse, examining a recent shipment of antique furniture. Ellie was with me. She always gets first pick of what I buy for my shops."

"Is that true?" Meeker asked the woman.

"Yes, it is," Ellie confirmed, squeezing her husband's arm.

Meeker turned to Bryant. "Teresa, you had something you wanted to share earlier. Now might be a good time."

Bryant moved to the middle of the room and smiled.

"I will no longer be using Mr. or Mrs. before your names as that indicates respect, and I have none for any of you. In one way or the other, each of you is both a liar and a bigot." She glanced toward the retired banker. "Bellford, you told us you couldn't have killed Mrs. Wallace because you were home overseeing a kitchen remodel."

"That's right."

"You need to come up with a better alibi," Bryant suggested.

"Why?"

"Because you're broke and have been for a year. My research shows you've been selling off investments and property for the past ten months just to pay off your debts. And your wife is not where you said she was. In fact, I had Napoleon make some calls today because she has not been seen in several weeks. During that time, you have sold off all her jewelry. I figure the police will soon be digging in your garden."

Gasps filled the room. The eye candy, who had been sitting so close to Bellford, got up and moved to the back of the room. He took a deep breath as he tugged at his shirt collar. Finally gathering his composure, he looked back at Bryant.

"Are you implying I killed my wife?"

"Right now, that's not my concern," Bryant admitted. "I just want you to explain to us how you could be remodeling a kitchen when you are up to your ears in debt?"

Speaking just above a whisper, he said, "I didn't kill Mayu. I may have done a lot of things and deceived a lot of people, but I didn't kill that woman."

Bryant shook her head before dropping another

shocking revelation. "Everyone in this room is close to financial ruin."

"That's a lie!" Scott Van Elffands protested.

"Hardly," Bryant responded. "You couldn't have been looking at furniture that day. Your antiques come from Europe and your supply was cut off long ago." Turning her gaze to Wickman, she asked, "Does your wife know you're not only addicted to booze but to gambling? And Kathleen, you can't get the paintings from Europe to sell now either. The war has killed your business, and there is talk you're trying to purchase stolen art from the black market. The last thing you sold, six months ago, was smuggled into this country." She paused and looked at the guests before adding, "I can fully outline the financial issues of each of you and explain what caused them ... if you want me to."

"That won't be necessary," Roscoe Taylor quietly announced. "I don't know anyone who is in as bad a shape as I am. I'll never get out of the hole I'm in."

"Fine," Melody Steinforth admitted, "we're frauds, but what does that have to do with the death of Mayu? How could any of us benefit from it?"

Roger Richards stepped forward to speak. "The newspapers were never told that a valuable necklace was stolen from Wallace's home safe. The fact you each needed money makes all of you suspects."

"Correct," Meeker seconded, "so that leads us to who could have actually stolen The Cat's Eye and murdered Mayu Wallace. Except for the Castles, Decker, and Roscoe Jones, the rest of you had both motive and opportunity."

"You can't be serious!" Tolly Taylor shouted.

"My," Meeker smiled, "you do have some lung power.

But we have a large problem. Mayu Wallace died in a home where every door and window was locked. And on top of that, no one could leave and lock a door without a key. Mr. Richards' investigation proves there were no keys missing. Thus, it seems the only person who could have killed Mrs. Wallace was her husband."

"Wait," Wallace cried out.

Meeker cut Wallace off before he could add to his denial. "No, you didn't do it. Mayu died while you were still at the office. Richards confirmed that."

"Then, I was right," Renshaw said from the back of the room. "It was suicide."

"Well, I ..." Meeker began as the guests in front of her breathed a collective sigh of relief.

Wallace cut her off before she could finish. "So, she did kill herself. But each of you drove her to it. Your hate and exclusion gave her no reason to live. You dug her grave and pushed her into it. You filled her with shame, and she ended up killing herself to allow me to have a life without her dragging me down. You see, when you cut her off, you cut me off as well." He laughed a bitter laugh, dripping with acid, before adding, "But you won't get off. Now, each of you is going to pay."

"How?" Decker demanded.

Wallace pulled out a gun. "There's a bomb on this boat, and it goes off at ten. Each of you will be executed for what you did to my wife."

As the shocked group of guests looked on, Wallace quickly opened the door and slipped out into the storm. Before anyone could move, they heard the entry lock.

"You mean he's going to kill himself too?" Renshaw asked.

The question didn't need to be answered. Over the noise of the storm, they heard a boat engine start.

"He has a powerful launch that serves as a lifeboat and pleasure craft," Roscoe Jones explained. "It will handle this storm, so he'll be fine. This isn't a suicide; it's a mass execution."

Meeker glanced at Bryant before looking at her watch. They had fifty-five minutes to find and defuse the bomb. Before they could do that, they had to get through the strong metal door. This was certainly a new twist on a locked-room murder.

CHAPTER 16

Wednesday, September 30, 1942
9:22 p.m.
Lake Michigan

Meeker watched as the panicked guests observed Richards and Renshaw tear into the door. Using a steak knife and a table leg, they drove the hinge pegs out, and the entry sprang open. Just because they were out of the room didn't mean they were out of hot water. The grim reality was unless they found and defused the bomb, they had just over half an hour to live.

"I don't think we have a crew," Renshaw observed, as *The Cat's Eye* pitched back and forth in the high waves.

"Then," Meeker hollered over the wind, "I guess you'd better become the crew. You're the one with the Coast Guard training. Can you keep us afloat?"

"Well, at least until the bomb goes off."

"Get going," Meeker ordered. She then looked over to her team and Richards. "Okay, we have about half an hour to find a bomb. Teresa, you're the closest thing we have to an expert on board. Not that long ago I watched you defuse a bomb at a power plant. What do we need to look for and where?"

"Close to the fuel tanks makes the most sense." Bryant turned to Richards. "You arrived with him. Did he bring anything onboard?"

"No. But earlier today, he mentioned he served in World War I as a munitions expert. He could have set things up hours ago."

Meeker recalled, "At one point this evening, he started checking his watch on a regular basis."

"That started right after our meeting in the study," Bryant added. "That's when he likely set the timer."

"But why would he do this? Why kill everyone?" Richards asked.

"Because, in his mind, everyone was guilty," Meeker explained. "When he heard me emphasize the locked-room concept, he became judge, jury, and executioner. We can deal with his motives later. For the moment, let's focus on the problem at hand. On a yacht like this, where are the fuel tanks?"

"A bit earlier, I walked all over this vessel," Lancelot said. "The fuel tanks are directly under the back two bedrooms. That's also where the engine and the storage areas are, so it might take hours to find that bomb."

Bryant turned to the frightened passengers. "All of you are going with me, and we are going to search every corner around the tanks, looking for anything that has a timer hooked up to it. If you find it, let me know. Then I'll go to work."

"I can't go," Decker announced as he pointed to his wheelchair.

"Then on the off chance it might be in here or in the

galley, you cover those areas. Napoleon, you and Helen go through the bedrooms and look everywhere. Now let's get moving."

The parties split up as instructed and hurried down the hall leading to the bedroom corridor or to the stairs leading to the engine room. Meeker took the bedrooms to the left, and Lancelot, the ones to the right. She was on her hands and knees, searching under a bed when Lancelot rushed in.

"I've got something," he yelled.

"You found the bomb?" she asked, bolting upright. If he had, they might have been granted a stay of execution.

"No," he answered, "but the first bedroom I entered is missing a clock. I then checked the other bedrooms, and all the clocks are there. I'll bet that clock is Wallace's timer. It is nearest the engine room and the fuel tanks."

"Where's Samson?" she demanded.

"In the study."

"Bring him in here. He's going to listen to this clock and then find the missing one for us. If he does, he'll get fresh meat for the rest of the year."

As Lancelot hurried to retrieve the Scottish terrier, Meeker rushed to each bedroom, retrieved the four remaining clocks, then raced to the rain-swept deck and tossed them into the lake. Before they hit the water, she was on her way back to the upper hall. As she passed the door of the study, she saw Lancelot holding the clock up to the blind dog's ears.

"Where have you been?" he asked.

"I got rid of the other clocks. We don't have time for him to find five. We only need him to lead us to one." She glanced at her watch and then the door. "Come on, we've only got about fifteen minutes."

"You ready to go down?" Lancelot asked.

"Let's go."

The man scooped the Scotty into his arms and made his way to the engine room. After getting everyone's attention, he explained what was going to happen. Meanwhile, Meeker raced up to the bridge and had Renshaw kill the engines. With everything quiet and each person silent, Lancelot set the dog down. The anxious guests watched as the canine slowly moved around the room. One minute became two; two drifted into five. Time was running out as Samson methodically made his way from one stop to another, finding nothing.

"We're dead ducks," Melody Steinforth declared.

"It's what we all deserve," her husband whispered as his anxious eyes followed Samson. "How much time do we have now?"

"Maybe eight minutes," Bryant answered. "Samson has been everywhere and found nothing. Take him upstairs and search the bedrooms. We'll continue to look here."

Lancelot picked up Samson and carried him back up the stairs to the main hallway. Sweat poured from his brow as he tried to figure where to begin.

"Start where the clock was missing," Meeker suggested.

Lancelot nodded and pushed the dog into the room. Without hesitation, Samson moved across the floor to a large dresser, only stopping when his nose ran into the furniture.

"Pick him up and hold him," Meeker quietly ordered as she reached down and pulled open the drawer, which appeared to be filled with towels. She carefully removed the top layer and found the missing clock. It was attached to a fuse and two-dozen sticks of TNT.

"Get Teresa!" she calmly ordered.

Lancelot dashed from the room, while Meeker checked the clock. They had three minutes. By the time Bryant rushed in, the time was down to two.

"Can you defuse it?" Meeker demanded.

Bryant bent forward and nodded. "Yeah, but I'm not sure I have enough time."

"What are you going to do? Do you just guess and hope to cut the right wire?"

Bryant didn't answer. Instead, she pulled the drawer from the dresser, marched down the hall, up the stairs, and onto the deck. There, she tossed the drawer and its contents into the lake. She then turned back to her partner and announced, "I think that will take care of it."

"Will it go off?" Meeker asked, peering through the rain into the night.

"Maybe, but the wind and waves will have it well away from us if it does. And perhaps the water will make it too wet to explode. Wallace didn't make it waterproof."

"You know, I could have tossed it into the water," Meeker cracked, realizing the solution well after the fact.

"Then, why didn't you?" Bryant asked.

"I wanted you to have the glory. Now, why don't you tell Renshaw to restart the engines and get this tub home? Then meet me back in the gaming room. I'll gather the guests. We still have something to finish."

"Helen," Bryant asked, "I can understand why Wallace would want most of those who were invited on this cruise to die. I also get why the medical examiner and Richards would be on that list. But why us?"

"I have a theory, but we'll save that for another time. Let's get this barge headed home, and then let's finish what we started."

CHAPTER 17

Wednesday, September 30, 1942
10:14 p.m.
Lake Michigan

The passengers, feeling greatly relieved, gathered again in the gaming room. Meeker asked them to take the same seats they had before Wallace announced the presence of the bomb. Once the guests were properly situated, Meeker took the stage.

"As you can probably tell, the storm has diminished, and we're on our way back to Chicago."

"Thank the Lord!" Melody Steinforth exclaimed. "We may be broke, but at least we're alive!"

"Wallace will pay for this," Decker spat. "I'll make sure of that."

"You won't have to," Meeker cut in, "I will. But for the moment, with the bomb scare over and the weather calming, we still have a murder to solve."

"But," Roscoe Jones announced, "You said it was a suicide."

"No," Meeker corrected him, "it was Renshaw who

jumped in and announced he was right. I actually said that because of the locked home, the murder appeared to be a suicide."

"You mean it wasn't?" Jim Castle asked.

Before Meeker could speak, Bryant jumped in to explain an element that even her associates had missed.

"Mayu Wallace would not have killed herself with a gun. She was from a family of Samurais."

"You mean warriors?" Decker asked.

"Yes," Bryant continued, "and the women from those families take their lives in a ritual known as Jigai. They only do it when they've brought dishonor to their family."

"Well, the actions of December seventh could be seen as bringing dishonor to Wallace," Decker noted.

"She was not responsible for the attack," Bryant replied. "In fact, she was at odds with the Japanese royal family and evidently had been for years. But if she had taken her own life, she would have used a special knife and in one stroke, slashed the arteries in her neck. If you have ever studied Japanese history, you would know that."

"Maybe she didn't know how," Greg Steinforth suggested. "After all, she'd been away from Japan for more than two decades."

Bryant tried to be patient. "She would have known how because she would have been taught as a child. She would have tied her knees together, so when she fell, she would have been discovered in a dignified pose. Then, she would have slashed her neck. She would never have shot herself."

Meeker added, "Plus, when Renshaw recreated the crime to find a position in which she could have inflicted the fatal wound without leaving powder burns, he failed to consider something: Mayu's arms were about ten inches shorter than his."

"But testing proved the gun was in her hand when it was fired," Richards interjected, now arguing against his own theory,

"No," Meeker repeated. "The testing only proved the glove was on a hand when the gun was fired."

"Isn't that the same thing?" the cop argued.

"Not if you listened closely to what I just said." Meeker picked up the bloodstained glove and held it in the air. "This glove has rarely been worn. My guess is the only other time it was worn before the day Mayu died was the day she and Wallace met. Still, that was a long time ago. Even though the glove looks brand new, age can have a dramatic effect on stitching. The threads sewing this bloody glove together are stretched while the stitching on the other glove is not. That means someone else wore this glove, shot Mayu and then placed the glove on her hand. If you look closely at the top of the glove, you'll see tiny bits of blood splatter from the wound. If she'd shot herself, there would have been much more blood, and her hand would not have fallen under the body."

"So, I was right." Richards smugly announced.

Meeker looked back the cop and nodded. She then asked a question that had confounded even her. "Why were some of the crime-scene photos shot in color? I've never seen that before."

"Boy," Richards admitted, "that was a big mistake! One of the guys loaded the wrong roll of film in the camera. He'd bought that roll to shoot his kid's birthday party. Our lab couldn't handle it, and we had to send it out to be developed. The captain was not happy."

"I'm glad he made a mistake," Meeker noted. "There's something in those shots I would have missed if they'd been in black and white."

"Then who killed her?" Jim Castle impatiently demanded.

Meeker ignored the man as she dug deeper into motives and suspects. "All of you could have used the money you'd have received from selling *The Cat's Eye* necklace. All of you knew that Wallace owned the gem, and I have no doubt you knew where he kept it."

Greg Steinforth laughed.

"What's so funny?" Meeker demanded.

"That necklace wouldn't have done any of us much good," he explained.

Decker cut in, "Wallace told me it was worth a million."

"Everything he said was a lie," Steinforth noted. "It was never Marie Antoinette's, and he didn't buy it, he stole it."

"What?" Joshua Wickman asked. "You mean he conned us? I need a drink."

"Stay put," Meeker ordered, "and let him continue."

Steinforth stood, cleared his throat and pressed forward by clearing up the past. "Wallace was in Europe during the First World War. He got to know Mata Hari in the months before she was executed for spying. The necklace was hers. He lifted it from her apartment and then spirited it back to the States. Supposedly *The Cat's Eye* brought its owner good luck. As far as value goes, it had very little. The jewels were of common grade, and there was nothing special about the chain or settings."

"How do you know?" Decker demanded.

Steinforth smiled. "Because I examined the necklace

for the company that insured it. I even fudged a bit when I suggested a value of five thousand."

Decker, his rage showing in his face, bitterly and loudly disagreed. "M.E. told me it was worth a million to him. Not more than a month before Mayu died, he bragged he could sell it for a million or more."

"He was lying," Steinforth replied, then smugly sat down.

"Valuable or not," Meeker continued, "the bobble is missing. The investigation has revealed that. And five grand is still a pretty good motive for murder."

"But none of them could have opened the safe," Richards argued.

"That's not true. The color photos show the safe has a small red logo just above the dial. That means it was manufactured by ..." Meeker paused and turned to face the man in the wheelchair. "... Mr. Decker's company."

"I couldn't have done it!" he quickly shot back. "I was at my office all day. The records prove that. My car never left the garage, and it's the only car in this town adapted to fit my special needs. I can't drive anything else. Besides, I'm in a wheelchair, and I couldn't even reach that safe."

"But your company has the combination," Meeker noted.

"We have the combination to all the safes we make," he agreed, "but look at me! What you're suggesting is impossible."

Meeker glanced at Bryant and smiled. She then stared down at the man in the chair. "Do you remember when we met, Mr. Decker, that Teresa admired your shoes?"

"Yes, I explained they were eel and custom-made."

"Teresa, do you want to take over?"

Bryant nodded and moved toward Decker. "You also told me they were two months old, is that correct?"

"Yes, but what does that have to do with anything?"

"Decker, a man in a wheelchair does not create any wear on the soles or heels of his shoes." Everyone in the room looked down at the man's feet.

"You did your homework," Meeker commented as she also moved toward Decker. "You knew Mayu would be gone that morning doing volunteer work. You had no idea a fire prevented the charity's kitchen from opening that day. Rather than give her time to feed the poor, she stayed home, preparing for her anniversary. You left your office without anyone noticing and drove another car to the house."

"You're guessing," Decker snapped.

"Then, I'll continue to guess," Meeker smiled. "You had no problem gaining entrance to the home as your company's locks were also on every door. You likely went right to the study and opened the safe. That's when Mayu must have caught you and reached for her husband's gun. You took the weapon from her and hit her with it, knocking her out. That would account for the bruising the medical examiner believed was caused by her fall to the floor.

"But why would I need the necklace?" Decker argued.

Bryant cut in. "Your business is not as shaky as the others, so it likely wasn't the need for money. I think you grabbed the gem as a way of punishing Wallace. You blamed him for your wife's death. I'd guess it's true you were unable to walk for a while, and that made you bitter as well. Having something Wallace prized as much as he did *The Cat's Eye*, something he bragged he could sell for a million dollars, would have given you great satisfaction. He would never know what happened to the necklace and that would have brought you joy for years to come."

"Rubbish! What reason would I have had to stay in this chair if I could walk?"

Meeker smiled. "I'll take this one. Because you were well-served by the handicap. People felt sorry for you, and you took advantage of that to get business deals."

"My research," Bryant added, "shows you were 'Businessman of the Year' two years ago. Newspaper stories marveled at the way you overcame your loss. You were known as the man nothing could stop."

"But ..."

Meeker waved her hand. "Your business is in good shape. We found that out, but Wallace's was not. At some point, he must have either come to you for help or told you he was selling the necklace to raise funds to cover his mismanagement. What better way to really make him suffer for his sins than to take the one thing that could save his company ... and then use your power and finances to buy him out?"

"You're grasping at straws," Decker argued.

The guests looked on, fascinated, as Meeker pushed even harder.

"Decker, you didn't go to the Wallace home to kill Mayu, but after she had discovered you in the study, having opened the safe, you couldn't leave her alive to share with her husband what you'd done."

"You actually think I'd kill a woman over a necklace? Even if the fiction you're weaving were true, Wallace would never have called the cops on me. He would have just demanded I give the necklace back."

"Maybe," Meeker agreed. "But, he would have exposed you as a fraud. He would have told everyone that you could walk or he might have blackmailed you in order to shore up his company. You couldn't let that happen. As you were trying to figure out what you were going to do, Mayu began to come to. At that point, you panicked and shot her. Now you had a real problem, but you solved that by removing her right glove, putting it on and firing another shot, likely out into the garden. I noticed in the color photos a bit of the paint had been knocked off a new brick wall. That's probably where the bullet hit and bounced off. Then you took the glove off, slipped it onto her hand and laid her hand under her body. You dropped the weapon above her head, closed the safe, locked the garden door and made your way out of the house, even remembering to lock the front door too. You drove back to your office, parked the car somewhere on the street and entered through a back entrance. That was almost perfect enough for you to skate through with no one suspecting anything, but then Teresa noticed your shoes. By the way, based on the way your heels are worn, you're pigeon-toed."

Decker yanked a gun from his coat.

"Does everyone on this tub have a weapon?" Lancelot asked, incredulous.

Meeker remained calm. "You can't shoot us all, and you've got no place to run."

"The necklace wasn't even real," Decker grimly explained. "I took it to an appraiser, and he told me the thing was nothing more than paste. Wallace just kept ruining my life!"

Jumping from the chair, Decker, surprisingly quick, raced out the door onto the wet deck. The surface was not meant for custom shoes with leather soles. Before he could take a dozen steps, he fell, dropping his gun, which slid across the deck, under the rails, and into the lake.

Shaking her head, Meeker watched Decker struggle to regain his footing. She turned to Richards, who had his gun ready for action. "I'm through with this guy. Why don't I just let Chicago's finest take care of him."

As the cop pushed by, Meeker looked back at her other team members and announced, "One more thing to take care of before we can start our mission."

"Yeah," Bryant agreed, "I'd like to find out why Wallace wanted us at the bottom of Lake Michigan as much as you."

"I'm tired of this three-hour cruise." Meeker paused and smiled. "And I've got to buy a steak for a dog too."

CHAPTER 18

Thursday, October 1, 1942
3:40 p.m.
The Wallace Estate, Wilmette, Illinois

On the drive to the Wallace home, Meeker, Bryant, and Richards attempted to put the bizarre yacht trip into perspective. What began as a three-hour cruise had evolved into one of the weirdest evenings of any of their lives. As the trio silently contemplated how revenge had driven a man to such extremes, Bryant switched on the radio. She was surprised to hear a unique take on their adventure blasting from the speaker.

"This is Walt Gibson of WGN News. This morning, I had the chance to interview a haggard and worn M.E. Wallace. In the midst of a storm, this businessman heroically fought the waves in a small boat in an unsuccessful attempt to save some of our city's most prominent citizens. Let me share with you Mr. Wallace's own story of what happened on Lake Michigan

last night. You are about to hear M.E. Wallace in an exclusive interview ..."

It was horrible. I invited my friends to join me on a trip to get away from the war news. Then the weather caught us. My yacht had engine trouble, and we needed help. The radio wasn't working either, so my captain, two crewmen and I jumped into the launch. We were only a few hundred yards away from "The Cat's Eye" when an explosion ripped through the boat. Though the waves were tossing us in a myriad of directions, we spent an hour looking for survivors, but there were none. Sadly, we returned home and reported the news to the authorities.

"This is Walt Gibson again. Among those who are still missing and likely dead are local businessmen, Roscoe Taylor and William Decker, and Helen Meeker, a woman who once was at the President's side and had his trust. No doubt, our city and this nation will take years to recover from this loss."

Meeker smiled as she turned the radio off. She looked back at Richards, who was grinning in the back seat, and then over to Bryant, on her right. The news of their deaths was a bit premature.

Richards was the first to find his voice. "I'm not even sure what you would call that report."

"Alternative history?" Bryant suggested.

"Well, Wallace is about to get a visit from three ghosts,"

Meeker cracked. "I've been a ghost before, so this is nothing new to me, but you two might want to get into the spirit of things. Anybody bring any white sheets?"

Richards chuckled. "I'll try to figure out the zombie thing, but seriously, we should have alerted the authorities to the real story."

Meeker shook her head as she turned the car off the road and drove through the gates leading to Wallace's estate. "This needs to be a complete surprise. The fact he invented a story of his heroism just makes it that much better." As she parked the rented Hudson, she turned around to the cop. "You need to stay here until we signal for you."

"I don't get why," Richards argued.

"Because Wallace had a reason for killing everyone on that yacht except for Helen, Napoleon, and me," Bryant chimed in. "So why did he want us there? We have a theory, but we have to find out if it holds water. And you don't have to worry about Helen and me taking care of ourselves. We can do that just fine."

"No doubt," Richards answered. "I don't think Joe Lewis would stand a chance against you."

As the cop watched, Meeker and Bryant, both dressed in suits and heels, exited the car and strode to the front door. Bryant rang the doorbell. A few minutes later, a servant appeared.

"We need to see Mr. Wallace," Meeker announced.

The short, balding butler shook his head. "He is very tired and emotionally spent. He lost friends who were very dear to him last night. You'll have to come back later."

"I thought," Meeker said, "Wallace didn't maintain a domestic staff."

"I was hired after Mrs. Wallace passed away."

"And your name?" Bryant asked.

"Ferndale."

"Well, Ferndale, I think you might want to update your résumé."

"Excuse me?"

"We're about to visit your boss," Meeker explained, "and after our meeting, he will no doubt be living in a place where his needs will be met by people dressed far less formally."

Bryant pushed the door open and looked down at the well-meaning employee. "In other words, he will see us. Now, where is he?"

"But ..."

Meeker reached forward and gently took the man's chin into her right hand. After moving his head to meet her gaze, she spoke. "My name is Helen Meeker."

"But you're supposed to be dead," the man whispered, as the color drained from his face.

"I'm part cat," she explained. "Ferndale, take us to Mr. Wallace or my friend here will turn you over her knee and give you a spanking. And she can do it too."

Ferndale looked at Bryant, seeming to size her up, then whispered, "He's in the study. Follow me."

The trio marched from the foyer, down a hall to a back room. Before Ferndale could open the entry, Bryant suggested, "Why don't you go polish some silver or something. We'll announce ourselves."

"Yes, ma'am." He turned and hurried down the hall.

Taking the brass knob in her hands, Meeker opened the well-oiled door and led the way into the room where Mayu Wallace had been murdered. Without a word, she marched to the desk where Wallace's head was buried in a newspaper, ripped the *Tribune* from his hands and tossed the paper to the floor. Then she smiled.

"What in the world? You should be ..." The word never made it past his lips.

"Is dead the word you're looking for?" Meeker asked. "Richards is waiting out in the drive to haul you down to headquarters and book you on a list of charges so long the judge will take an hour to read them." Wallace moved his hand toward a desk drawer. "Don't try it! Teresa will blow you away before you even touch your weapon."

"The bomb?" he asked. His tone and body language clearly proved he couldn't believe what he was seeing.

"It's in Lake Michigan," Bryant explained. "We found it. Your handiwork is sleeping with the fishes, but we aren't!"

"But how?"

Bryant leaned closer. "Even a blind dog finds a bomb every now and then."

Meeker walked around the desk, pulled Wallace's thirty-eight from the drawer, and tossed it to her partner. "Now, I can understand why you wanted everyone on that boat dead, except us. What did we do to you?"

Wallace shook his head and remained mute. Perhaps he was in shock, or maybe he didn't have a real explanation for his actions. Meeker guessed the former.

"Wallace, there's only one thing that makes sense. Teresa, why don't you share what your research has revealed."

The Caddo woman smiled. "I'll be happy to." Her stern, dark eyes caught Wallace like headlights on high beam, burning through his face and into his brain. "You bank at Central State."

"A lot of folks do," he answered.

"And when you go to the bank, you always ask for the same person to handle your business ... William Elliot."

Wallace nodded. "He's a good man. I like dealing with the same person. It's one of my quirks."

"You need to find a new go-to guy," Bryant snapped.

"Why?"

"Because Elliot was recently taken out by a hitman. Helen and I got there a little too late to save him."

"I didn't have anything to do with that. I didn't even know he was dead."

"Maybe you did, or maybe you didn't. But your connection to Elliot was what actually provided us with the reason we were included on your little party list."

"I don't know what you're talking about," Wallace argued, seeming to regain a bit of his composure. "I thought having two of the nation's most famous investigators there would scare my friends. And if you had proven Mayu's death was suicide, I would have stopped the bomb. I was crazy for revenge." He snapped his fingers before adding, "I was literally insane."

"You were crazy for revenge," Meeker agreed, "and I have no doubt you loved your wife, but you really didn't need us to punish your friends. You're far too smart to have us there for no reason at all."

"So, if no one was hurt, then I'll plead temporary insanity. I have lawyers who can make that stick. I was so crazed by grief my mind wasn't working correctly."

"Don't plan your exit yet," Bryant suggested. "Elliot's gambling habits opened the door for him to work for the Nazis. You were the only one who demanded that Elliot handle your business. The FBI investigated where he was sending his microfilm plans for things like bombsights. The mob claimed they passed the stuff on but didn't know what was in it. And they also told the Feds they didn't pay Elliot."

Meeker leaned closer as she took over the interrogation, "So we theorize that when you made your deposits, you gave him extra money to cover the work he was doing for Germany. You also passed off plans for things you were building in your plants and other bits of information Bauer got to you. That's likely how he got the plans for the bombsight, which he didn't get to pass on because we intercepted it."

"You can't prove any of that," he argued.

Meeker sat on the corner of the desk, "You know, you might just be right. Just like we can't prove the problems at your plant were caused by deliberate actions. But while you're sitting in jail, contemplating the long list of charges you're facing, we can release to the newspapers that we have identified you as a German agent and you're cutting a deal to share all you know."

"You're grasping at straws," Wallace asserted.

"I'm not saying you would cut a deal," Meeker assured him, "but let me explain this way. We put the word out you're talking to us to reduce your charges. Then we also provide you with bail and let you stay in this house. How long do you think you'd last once the Nazis or the mob—whoever is calling the shots right now—put out a hit on you like they did Elliot?"

Meeker allowed the scenario to fester for a few moments before adding, "We have a trip to make, so we'll let Richards come in and take over now. The story of you being an agent and talking to us will be in the morning papers. You might want to know that the DA has agreed to charge you tomorrow morning and let you walk out of jail tomorrow afternoon. That likely means in about three days, your obituary will run in those same newspapers. Teresa, would you get Mr. Richards?"

"Sure thing," the other woman announced as she headed toward the door.

"By the way," Meeker added, "you should have stuck around last night. Decker was the one who killed your wife. She caught him stealing the necklace."

"What? But you said that with the doors and windows locked, it had to be …"

Meeker corrected him. "No, I suggested her death was suicide. After you had left, I explained how Decker, who can walk, panicked and shot your wife. So, if you had been a bit more patient, I never would have figured out you were on Hitler's payroll."

"My Lord," he whispered. "Decker killed Mayu?"

"Wallace, just like your friends, you got into financial straits. They had no way out, but you found one. Now the question is, did you approach Elliot or did he make the pitch to you?"

Wallace shook his head. Discovering his wife hadn't committed suicide seemed to cause him to rethink his position.

"What happens to me?"

"If you share all you know, I can fix your sentence, so you won't be shot or hanged. I'm not sure how we're executing spies now. Anyway, if I arrange for you to dodge whichever method we're currently using, you're going to spend time in a Federal prison. There's no way out of that."

He nodded. "But will they protect me to make sure no one kills me in prison?"

"You'll be protected … not because you deserve it, but because you have information we need."

As Wallace considered his options, Bryant returned with Richards. Meeker glanced over, signaling for them to remain silent. For the next five minutes, no one said anything. Finally, Wallace broke.

"Elliot approached me. He knew my company was on the ropes. I wanted to get the bombsight contract badly, and I bid too low. With the government watching, I couldn't cut corners as I had in the past when I was in over my head. I started taking money to share a few plans and slow down production. That kept me afloat and helped me beat Decker. That meant even more to me than staying in business. I wanted to beat him more than anything in the world."

Her voice cold, Meeker added, "You sold out your country for a few bucks and hatred for a rival?"

"Not really," Wallace replied. "I just kind of slowed things down a bit at the factory. And the plans I shared were actually older models that had gone out of production."

"Don't try to rationalize things," Meeker snapped. "Every time you slowed down production, you cost people their lives. So, there are men who died because of you."

"I didn't think," he admitted. He looked up, his eyes meeting Meeker's. "I was going to get out of the mess about the time Mayu was killed. She found out what I was doing and shamed me into changing my ways. I told you she was a loyal American."

"Too bad you weren't," Bryant countered.

"Who were your contacts?" Meeker demanded.

"The only one I ever met face to face called himself 'Darkness.' He was a tall, thin man."

"He's dead now. I know because I killed him as he was trying to kill me."

"That explains the calls from Washington," Wallace said. "The caller was a woman this time. She was taking over for Darkness."

"Who was she?"

"I don't know, but she called herself Sis. That was her code name."

Meeker leaned closer, "Do you have her number or address?"

"No, I don't. She contacted me, and every call she made was from a pay phone. But, she was the one who ordered the hit on Elliot. She was also the one who told me I had to get rid of you and Bryant."

Meeker stood and turned to Richards. "He's all yours for the moment, but I want you to hand him over to the FBI. I'll make sure they learn what I know."

Richards stepped forward, pulled Wallace out of the chair and cuffed him. Now humbled, Wallace stood before them, and Meeker took another verbal shot.

"*The Cat's Eye* Decker stole from you was a fake. Even if it had been real, Steinforth informed us the value was only a few thousand and that you'd stolen the necklace during the First World War. Yet, you told Decker it was worth millions. If you hadn't lied to him, your wife would still be alive." She paused, letting that thought sink in, before demanding, "What happened to the real *Cat's Eye*?"

"You're right," he admitted. "I was in over my head, and I sold it. I was doing anything I could to raise money. I had the fake made to keep my cover in case anyone asked to see the necklace."

"An illusion to maintain an illusion," Bryant cryptically suggested.

"I guess so," Wallace mournfully agreed.

"Before you take this whipped pup out," Meeker said as she looked at Richards, "you need to be aware of a few things. Teresa and I are going out of town. Before we leave, I'll write a couple of news releases and give them to Napoleon. Richards, you make sure those stories run in all the newspapers and are picked up by the radio stations." Meeker looked back at Wallace. I'm protecting you, so you'd better tell the FBI everything you know. If you don't, I'll set things up for Sis to finish you off like she did Elliot. Do you understand that?"

Wallace nodded. "Miss Meeker, I need for you to know something before you leave."

"Shoot."

"The reason I changed my mind on the deal with Elliot and Bauer was that Mayu was going to divorce me if I didn't. She told me she'd rather live in an internment camp than live with a traitor."

Meeker considered the irony. Of all the people she'd been with over the past twenty-four hours—the supposed cream of the city's social set—none of them had the character, substance, or patriotism of a woman born in Japan who had spent the last few months of her life being shunned because of her race.

PART TWO

CHAPTER 1

Thursday, October 1, 1942
8:29 a.m. (2:29 a.m. Chicago time)
Thirty-four miles northeast of Berchtesgaden, Bavaria, Germany

Henry Reese stared at a fried egg that seemed to stare back at him. His actual thoughts were miles away. He and Hans Holsclaw were sitting in the kitchen of a small, rural German cottage, but the American's mind was still on the hill where he'd studied their target just a few hours earlier. He took a sip of bitter coffee, then glanced toward the Dutchman. They shared a growing concern.

"Gail is having issues with the number of innocent lives that will be taken when we blow up that mountain."

"My men are no different," Holsclaw assured him. "We all feel it. But those lives are doomed anyway. They will either be worked to death, starved to death, or die horribly from the radiation. What we're doing is mercifully bringing that end a bit sooner." He paused and shook his head. "You and I both know that hundreds of thousands, if not millions, are being murdered by the Nazis in concentration camps. It's being whispered about everywhere. The best thing we can do for them is to end this war sooner rather than later. Perhaps our mission will help do just that, even if it does cost a few hundred innocent lives."

"I'm not ignorant or weak," Reese replied. "I fully grasp the scope of this war. Or maybe I should say, I grasp it as much as anyone can. But I don't enjoy killing."

"When you do," the Dutchman observed, "you will have lost the humanity that sets us apart from those we are fighting."

Reese nodded and thought back to what he'd observed earlier. The mission appeared simple on the surface, but when the unknowns were factored in, became overwhelming. They were going up against at least a hundred soldiers and who knew how many scientists. The men defending the Alamo might have had better odds.

"Can we really pull this off?" Reese asked. His voice showed no fear, but neither did he mask his obvious doubts.

"If you're asking whether we can get into the mountain, then the answer is yes. The Germans will view our paperwork and see it as valid since scientists come and go from Berlin on a regular basis. I honestly believe we can distribute and wire our explosives in one night. But, if you're asking if we will all get out alive, I believe the odds are against that."

Reese smiled grimly. The Dutchman's assessment was the same as his own, but there was one part of this job he failed to understand. Why did they have to bide their time in this safe house? Waiting only seemed to enhance their chances of being discovered. Why not just get it over with?

"Hans, why don't we just have the Brits drop in the explosives and go ahead and do it? I've got to believe they have them ready."

"They do."

"So why not just push on?"

"Life is about being patient." Holsclaw was stoic. After finishing his coffee and putting the cup in the sink, he turned and stared through a window. "I was raised on flat land. I could walk to the sea anytime I wanted. The mountains are foreign to me, and yet, I love them. There is majesty and serenity here I've never known anywhere else. Before breakfast, I walked through the trees and up to a ridge. As far as I could see was a tribute to God's creativity. There were no sounds of war, no screams of the dying and no babies crying for a father who would never come home. Then the illusion was shattered."

"By what?" Reese asked.

"By a German supply convoy most likely heading to the place we are going to blow up. The swastikas painted on the vehicles have a way of crushing peace and serenity like nothing on earth. As long as that symbol is there, peace will remain an illusion. Even when the sounds and smells of war are not with me, I still can't escape them."

Reese responded, "Which leads me back once more to the question of why we have to wait for the team they are sending in from America?"

The Dutchman turned from the window to face his friend and comrade. "From what I have been told, there are files that must be retrieved."

Reese shook his head, "Why couldn't we do that?"

"Because the information contained in those files is classified. We are not allowed to see it."

The American shook his head in disgust. "So, putting our lives on the line in what might be a suicide mission is not enough to allow us to view secret information. What a screwy war this is. I feel like I'm still working for J. Edgar Hoover."

"I don't think it's that," Holsclaw argued. "The folks who are meeting us will return to England and then to America. We will stay here. The odds of our being captured are much greater. If we are taken prisoner, we don't need to have any knowledge in our heads that might compromise our cause."

"We wouldn't talk," Reese snapped.

Holsclaw's brow wrinkled, and his eyes grew strangely sad. "I've known many who have made that claim, and almost all of them did talk. Both their side and ours have ways, my friend, of working you over until you will say anything to relieve the pain. None of us can fully appreciate our resolve until we are tested. Therefore, knowing nothing really is the safest way to fight this war."

As always, the thoughtful Dutchman was right. That was why he'd been such a successful leader in the underground. He fully grasped his purpose and didn't try to move beyond it. He also saw the big picture, such as at the house where the Germans were corrupting the minds of children in the Lebensborn program. Holsclaw knew helping those little ones would compromise their mission. He wasn't heartless; he understood his job was to do his job.

"You two have everything figured out?"

Startled, Reese looked up. How had the love of his life managed to sneak into the room without his hearing her footsteps? As he turned to greet her, he was awed that even in peasant-woman garb, she was still breathtakingly beautiful.

After several long moments of counting his blessings, he found his voice. "We're in wait mode."

Placing her arm around his neck, she bent to kiss his cheek.

"So, my bride, I guess we have a few days for a belated honeymoon."

"Not a bad idea," Holsclaw added. "On that note, I think I'll join my men in the barn."

CHAPTER 2

Friday, October 2, 1942
5:50 p.m.
The White House, Washington, DC

Meeker and Bryant waited in a small sitting room just one hundred steps from the Oval Office. Dressed in business suits, they sat in uncomfortable wooden chairs, waiting to receive their final orders before boarding a plane for England. In the background, a radio played news so unexpected it seemed like a joke.

"Did you hear that?" Meeker asked.

"Yeah, the Queen Mary took down a German cruiser."

"How in the world does a passenger liner sink a warship?"

The question was still hovering in the air when Alison Meeker walked in and closed the door behind her. After handing a file to her sister, she explained the oceanic mystery.

"It rammed it."

"What rammed what?" Meeker asked

"The Queen Mary rammed the Nazi ship," Alison repeated.

"Just ran into it?" Bryant didn't believe her.

"Yep, sliced that boat into two pieces."

"Wow, that has to be a first," Meeker noted. "Maybe it's a sign the war is starting to turn our way."

"Hang onto your paper greenery," Alison said. "There are still plenty of rounds to go in this fight. Now, it's time for me to deal your next hand."

So far Meeker was following her sister's words. The "hand" had to be their orders, and "greenery" was money. The question was, could she continue to keep up with Alison's unique way of communicating?

"Keep your blinkers open," Alison explained, "and make sure there's no wax between me and your gray matter. Smile while the indigo's still wet on the exam. It's an open book test because you're still the teacher's pet. Before you make with the big swim, you'll have to leap into a loony bin and chat up a wandering German hound."

"Okay," Meeker translated, "the first part was about staying awake, and the next was the material in the file concerning our mission behind enemy lines, but you've got me on the dog."

"Then let me give it your way." Alison was frustrated. "There's a Nazi in London in prison, and they want you to talk to him before you go behind lines."

"Who's the guy?"

"Rudolf Hess."

Bryant frowned. "The crazy German who flew to England last year on a supposed peace mission?"

"Yeah, the wacky bird was winging in an invitation for the Brits and Germans to kiss and make up. It seemed the queen's dance card was already full, so she counted to eight and gave him a big nein."

Meeker asked, "Why do we need to visit with the former Deputy Fuhrer?"

"Because he might know something about the mountain where you and Teresa have booked your skiing vacation. A cruise across Lake Michigan on a luxury yacht one night and a few days later, a junket touring the scenic Bavarian Mountains—what a life you have!"

"I'll be happy to trade with you," Bryant cracked.

"By the way," Alison added, "top shelf job on Wallace and that bit of icing came from the nation's big dog, not me or Fala."

"Assure the President it was our pleasure. Now, is there anything else? And please give it to me in English."

"Okay, there's a flight of Liberator bombers leaving Bolling Air Base tonight at midnight. You've got tickets on one of those planes. Be packed and at the base no later than dime ... I mean ten. They'll have flight suits for you to wear on the ride. You can study the file on the way."

"Good, that gives us time to grab something to eat," Meeker said.

"And," Alison added, "sew up your flappers and keep the ivory out of sight when it comes to the atom caper. Don't even yep out to the flyboys."

"We'll keep our mouths shut," Bryant acknowledged.

After Alison had escorted the women out a side exit, Meeker glanced over at her partner and posed the question neither of them could answer: "What would Hess know that is vital to the mission?"

Bryant watched a young woman, likely a White House staff member, flirt with two men in uniform. They seemed to be arguing over which guy was taking the gal out. Meeker's gaze followed to the spot where the mating ritual was playing out. She smiled and commented, "Teresa, I think we're in the wrong business."

"No doubt."

Alison laughed, "You all might always be flying solo, but I'm flying in pairs tonight. Tunes are always best on the flip side. Make like a bank and keep it safe, sis!"

CHAPTER 3

Meeker tossed the file she'd been studying by flashlight for the past two hours into her bag. She looked over at Bryant, bundled up in an Army-green heavy coat, gloves, and boots. Pushing herself off the plane's floor, she walked over and dropped down beside her partner. Leaning close, she spoke for the first time since they'd taken off from Bolling. The roar of the four engines forced her to almost yell.

"What do think?"

"About the mission?"

"Yeah."

"We've got it easy. The underground takes all the risks and blows the place up. We go in once, make contact, find the files and exit."

"It's not we," Meeker corrected, "it's me. Your skin's a little dark to pass as a member of the master race."

"Fine," Bryant replied. "I stay on top of the hill with a rifle and play look out."

"And if something goes wrong, you lead the cavalry."

"How about I'll lead a band of my people instead?" Bryant joked. She paused, waiting for Meeker's grin. "Those files must be really important for the President to make us the carrier pigeons."

Meeker agreed, "Yeah, not letting anyone else view them speaks volumes. I understand this is all about seeing whether Hitler is a step or two ahead of us on this one. I guess this is the world's version of keeping up with the Joneses."

"When the underground blows the place up, Hitler won't be ahead anymore."

Meeker looked across the plane before dryly commenting, "The Bible talks about weapons that can bring about incredible destruction, signaling the end of time. I've been thinking a lot about that recently. Perhaps we're there."

Bryant shrugged but said nothing.

Suddenly curious, Meeker turned to face her partner. "I'd never considered that you might not put much stock in the Bible."

"Why's that?"

"You're an Indian."

"Well, while your people were stealing our land and killing our men, women, and children, they were also distributing Bibles. We all had the chance to read the pages. In fact, it was your people who pretty much made us learn to read."

"And you have?" Meeker asked, before clarifying, "I mean read the Bible?"

Bryant frowned as if insulted. "Yes, Helen, I have. Now I have a question for you. You just talked about passages in the Bible predicting the end of the world. Do you believe everything that's in the Bible?"

Meeker nodded, "I guess so."

"So, you believe in Adam and Eve, the flood, Moses parting the Red Sea and Jesus was born of a virgin and came back to life after being crucified?"

"Yes, I think I do."

Bryant smiled and went mute. After a while, the awkward silence unnerved Meeker. She had to know what the other woman was thinking.

"Teresa, do you believe the Bible?"

Bryant shook her head, pushed off the floor and walked over to look at the ocean below. She remained there, holding onto a support beam as she observed the world beneath them, but said nothing. The silence was driving Meeker crazy. She was so tired of playing these games. Ever since they'd been thrown together, she'd ask a question, and Bryant would either spit out a cryptic response or follow with a question of her own. She'd reveal glimpses of her life and tidbits about what she believed, but never enough to get a firm grip on who she really was. Tired of mystery, Meeker pushed off the deck and joined her partner.

Over the engine's roar, she demanded, "Do you believe in the Bible? And don't answer that with a question!"

"If you're asking if I believe in God," Bryant answered, continuing to look down at the ocean, "I can tell you I do. The story of Jesus makes sense to me as well. But to be honest, I think my people have done a far better job of living like Christ than your people have. We have traditionally cared for widows and orphans and sought ways to live in harmony with nature. We have treated the earth and those who walk on it with respect. Which is far more than I can say about those who took our lands from us. The Spaniards, the French, and the English literally robbed us of all we had and stained the ground with our blood. How did that reflect Jesus?"

Bryant turned her eyes from the placid scene below the plane and studied Meeker. As she continued to open her heart and mind, her face remained emotionless. "So, Helen, it seems that long before my people read a Bible, we were living more like Christ than your people were then or now."

Meeker had no comeback. Bryant was right. Since the day the first whites came to American shores, native lives had been diminished. There was nothing Christian about the actions of those who'd robbed and slaughtered them.

"You see," Bryant continued, "I understand fully how Mayu Wallace must of have felt. I, too, have been distrusted, devalued, and shunned. I, too, am considered a second-rate citizen despite the fact my people were and remain the only real Americans, though I might add that name is completely wrong."

"Then why fight for us?" Meeker asked. "I'm not sure I would."

"Because as bad as your people have been and continue to be to mine, they are far better than Hitler and the Nazis." She shook her head, then added, "What can you tell me about Matthew 25:35-40?"

Meeker thought back to her days in Sunday school as a child and mentally turned the pages of a Bible given to her by her mother. In the deep recesses of her memory, she recalled bits and pieces of the verses Bryant had cited.

"I think," Meeker replied, "if recollection serves me right, that's where Christ talked about being like Him and reaching out to the least of these."

"And now that we've heard what Hitler is doing to the Jews, I choose to live out those verses."

"So, Teresa, you do take the Bible literally?"

"Possibly even more literally than you do," Bryant returned. She leaned back against the inside wall of the plane, feeling the engine's vibrations and closed her eyes. She remained that way until they landed in England. Only after they'd deplaned and placed their gear in an Army jeep for the trip to London did Meeker break the silence.

"I've been thinking a lot about what you said. You're right. The Indians got the short end of the stick."

"Actually, we didn't even get a stick."

Meeker climbed into the jeep, and Bryant joined her in the back seat. A sergeant approached, grinning as he eyed the two women.

"Your driver will be here in about ten minutes. You arrived a bit sooner than we expected. Do you need anything? Can I get you coffee, a Coke, or something to eat?"

"No," Meeker assured him, "just sitting in something that's not moving will be good for a while." After the young man had walked off, she turned back to Bryant. "You're a complex woman. You have so many different layers."

"And so many different names," Bryant cracked. "I still can't believe I shared one of them with you."

"Ah, Morning Star," Meeker replied with a smile. "I like it." She looked up at the sky. A British Spitfire was flying about three hundred feet above their heads. Her eyes followed the small fighter until it was several miles away. Then, without facing her partner, she said, "Mr. Roosevelt said you'd worked for several presidents."

"You find that hard to believe?"

Meeker faced the other woman, "Yeah, if that were the case, you must have been on duty when you were in diapers and worked right through grade school. So how old are you?"

Bryant chuckled, "I've been told that whites can never really tell the age of Indians."

"You didn't answer my question."

"No, I didn't, but I think it's time I pose another one for you."

"I'm tired of you answering my questions with questions of your own!"

"Then we'll end the discussion." Bryant dropped her chin to her chest and closed her eyes, driving Helen over the edge.

"What question were you going to ask?"

Bryant smiled. "You sure?"

"Yes!"

"Okay, I want you to really consider what I'm asking before you answer. Do you believe the Bible can be taken literally?"

Meeker wanted to jump right back with her reply, but instead, she held her tongue and glanced down at her wrist. Remembering they were now five hours ahead of Washington time, she took a moment to reset and wind her watch before answering, "Yes, I guess I do."

"Then," Bryant continued, "you believe Adam lived nine hundred and thirty years, Seth was nine hundred and twelve when he died, and Noah made it to nine hundred and fifty. And let's not forget Lamech, who only lasted to seven hundred and seventy-seven years and old Methuselah, who died at nine hundred and sixty-nine."

Meeker realized that she'd been trapped. Bryant had played her not by questioning the resurrection, but by digging into ancient Old Testament material.

"Okay, Teresa, maybe I don't take everything literally," she finally admitted.

"So, you don't really think a person can live for centuries?" Bryant asked.

"No, but what does this have to do with anything?"

"Helen, I was testing your faith. I was getting a handle on what you could really believe and what logic forces you to dismiss."

"What's my grade?"

Bryant shrugged. "No worse than a C. I just find it unusual that you can believe in the virgin birth and the resurrection, but can't let your faith grow to the point of accepting that folks in the Old Testament lasted for centuries."

"You do?" Meeker asked.

"It's far easier for me to accept that Methuselah lived almost a thousand years than to grasp the concept of Jesus being the Son of God, dying for man's sins and then rising from the dead. But if I accept one, then I have a much easier time accepting the other."

"But how can a person live that long?" Meeker asked. She then laughed and said, "And I'm asking as if you would know the answer."

Bryant smiled, "Let me toss this out. What happens when a watch or a clock runs down?"

"It dies," Meeker suggested.

"Even before my people had ever seen a mechanical timepiece, they understood that principle." Bryant pointed to Meeker's wrist. "I watched you just reset and rewind your watch, and it will live for another day. What if Methuselah, Noah, and Adam understood how to rewind their body clocks? And what if that skill was lost over time, and folks just lived until their body clock wound down, never realizing they could reset and rewind it?"

"You actually believe that?" Meeker asked.

Bryant grinned. "I think our driver's coming."

Meeker glanced toward a lanky GI heading their way before turning back to her partner. "This time you didn't answer my question, and I need an answer. Do you believe there's a way to rewind body clocks and somehow, in days long gone, man forgot how?"

Bryant nodded. "I not only believe it, but I also believe that some never lost that skill."

Meeker was dumbfounded. How could a woman of Bryant's intelligence buy into that?

"Good day, ladies," their driver's greeting pulled Meeker's gaze away from Bryant. "My name's Evans, and I understand I'm supposed to drive you. But why in the world do you want to go to Mytchett Place in Surrey? What could be in Surrey?"

"We're off to see a man about the war," Meeker cryptically replied.

"Hang on," Evans announced as he climbed in and started the vehicle.

A few moments later, the four-cylinder "Go-Devil"-powered jeep was exiting the base and heading toward England's capitol, but Meeker's thoughts were still stuck on the tarmac. She urgently wanted to revisit the conversation about rewinding a body's clock. Was Bryant hinting she was someone who still understood that skill? No, that couldn't be it. Meeker was being played. Her Caddo partner had set a trap just to confuse her. After all, surely the Bible didn't mean that Methuselah lived all that time? And even if he did, no one in today's world could live that long.

She glanced over at Bryant. She appeared to be in her early thirties, certainly not a day over thirty-five. Or was she?

CHAPTER 4

Sunday, October 4, 1942
12:15 a.m.
Mytchett Place in Surrey, England

Meeker and Bryant were briefed about the prisoner's mental issues before being escorted through heavily fortified gates and into an ancient home that now served as a prison for Rudolf Hess. The rambling, two-story, white stone structure in Surrey, just outside of London, was so completely off the radar that hardly anyone outside of MI6 was aware of its use as an interrogation center and prison for the most elite Nazis and spies held by the Allies. Nor did most know that after spending time in the Tower of London, Deputy Fuhrer Rudolph Hess had been secretly relocated to Mytchett.

Hess was a thin, balding man of fifty-five. When he'd flown to Scotland more than a year before to seek a way for Germany to forge peace with England, he was one of the most highly respected leaders in the Nazi government. What motivated him to hop into a Messerschmitt BF110 on May 10, 1941, and make his way to England remained a mystery. What had been confirmed was Hess had planned the trip for a year. The supposition was Hitler likely knew nothing about it. Apparently, no one in Germany or Britain had been enlightened either. After crashing his plane and being captured in Scotland, Hess claimed he was an ambassador for peace. But to the intelligence officers who visited with him, Hess's peace flight was really a case of a man simply flying off his rocker. He was evidently crazy, but that didn't mean the Allies just locked him up and moved onto other things. After all, this man had spent two decades as a vital part of Hitler's inner circle. He knew things.

Hess met Hitler in 1920 and helped him launch the Nazi movement. He quickly moved through the party ranks and was included in almost all the planning sessions. When Hitler came to power, Hess was looked upon as the Fuhrer's second in command. He held great sway with Hitler and therefore, was privy to information few others knew. British Intelligence tried daily to unlock his mind to gain access to potential keys to destroying the Nazi political machine even as the Allies fought the German war machine. Now, two American women were to try their hand at digging up something the interrogators might have missed.

MI6 opened the door and held nothing back. They could take the interview any direction they wanted. As a part of their strategy, Meeker and Bryant dressed in slacks and sweaters. Their hair was styled, and they had also added makeup, hoping to charm Hess in ways others could not during his months of debriefings. But, would sex appeal work on a man who strongly believed in the teachings of Hitler?

After being ushered into what was once the home's dining room, the pair waited at a long table for British troops to escort the German in for their interview. As time dragged by, Meeker leaned back in her chair and absentmindedly observed the room's now stark walls. At one time, securing an invitation to this home would have made guests feel on top of the world. She wondered who had dined in this room over the past few hundred years. Could a member of the royal family have been honored with a dinner fit for a king? Perhaps a few knights had played cards or discussed the fine arts right where she was sitting. My, how the war had changed things! Now a common American woman and a Caddo Indian were sitting at a table, waiting on the most notorious prisoner in the world to join them.

"Wonder what it would have been like to grow up in a place like this?"

Bryant cocked an eyebrow in reaction to Meeker's question. "It's nothing like where I spent my childhood."

"Which was when?" Meeker prodded.

"Don't you mean where?"

"No, Teresa, in your case, I think the when would be far more interesting."

Meeker was waiting for her reply when a door on the far end of the room opened, and a man dressed in an ill-fitting suit was escorted to the table. His face was drawn, his small eyes were barely open, and his thin lips seemed to be glued shut.

"You don't want me to stay?" a British Army officer asked.

"No," Meeker assured him, "that won't be necessary."

"He's not going to hurt you," the officer said. "He's pretty harmless."

As the British soldier left the room, Meeker turned her attention to the prisoner who had once been a very powerful man. In the 1920s, Hess had likely recruited more people to the Nazi cause than anyone. For years, he had Hitler's ear and his trust. Then, for reasons no one understood, he'd taken that flight. The reason for the flight didn't concern her right now, but there was another area where she hoped Hess could supply some information. With that goal in mind, she opened what would become a very informative interview.

"Mr. Hess," Meeker began in a tone more charming than confrontational, "do you grasp enough English to understand me."

"Yes."

"Thank you for meeting with us," she continued. "My associate's name is Teresa Bryant. We are obviously American. We are grateful to have this chance to share a room with the Deputy Fuhrer. We have obviously tracked your career for years. In fact, I would go so far as to suggest that without you, Hitler would have never risen to power."

"Thank you," Hess replied in a thick German accent, "but I can assure you the Fuhrer would have risen to power if I had never met him. He is an amazing man. God chose him you know!"

Meeker considered Hess's tone and expression. He was relaxed and seemingly believed what he was saying. As an American, she felt a desire to tear those beliefs apart, but in this case, that would likely do more harm than good. She opted to continue to heap praise.

"Deputy Fuhrer," she began.

He waved his hand, "When men and women speak out of the public eye, titles are not necessary. You may call me Rudolf."

"And you may call us Helen and Teresa."

Hess smiled, then noted, "They are both historical and strong names. You should be proud of them. Imagine the world of Helen of Troy and consider that one of Austria's great queens was named Teresa. We, well those still in power in Germany, will restore the world to the glory it has known in past ages. For too long, the world has been corrupted by commoners who have stolen the mantle of God's grace."

Meeker's face remained placid, but she questioned how Hess could believe what he was saying. Had those concepts been so drilled into him by his years spent with Hitler they were now a part of his very fiber? She would have loved to explore that point, but she needed to push the man in a different direction. To accomplish her goal, Meeker tossed out another pat line.

"I understand you're still very loyal to the Nazi cause."

With a nod, he announced, "The Fuhrer is the greatest man to ever walk this earth."

"So, you're proud of your service to Germany?"

"I have much to be proud of. I was a part of something wonderful. We took a nation that was in ruins and helped transform it into the greatest country in the history of the world!"

"Then I hope you can clarify this for me. Why did you fly to Scotland? Why did you desert your country?"

She'd struck a nerve. For the first time, his expression changed.

"I made the flight to ensure peace between two great

nations. There was no reason for us to be at war with those whose blood is the same as ours. I thought when Churchill heard me, he would join with us against the Jews and the Russians, as well as all the other human subspecies. So, this was not some rash move; it was completely logical. I was trying to expand our concepts, to fully explain them, if you will, to include more people into the Reich. I was offering a gift."

Hess was definitely unrepentant. While other interrogators likely viewed that attitude as a hindrance to gaining information, Meeker saw his recalcitrance as something she could prey upon and use.

"You must be proud of the German war machine," she noted.

"We have the best equipment and the best men," he bragged.

She smiled, "I think technological development will win this war, don't you agree?"

"No doubt," he assured her.

"I fear," she added, "that my country, the United States, is far behind yours in developing new weapons."

"Of course," he proudly bragged, "we have identified the best minds, and they are working on developments no one else can even imagine. Did you know we are even finding a way to bring back the aurochs?"

"What are the aurochs?" Meeker asked. She had absolutely no interest in going in the direction, but if it kept Hess in her court, she'd follow that trail for a bit.

Bryant cut in before Hess could answer. "The aurochs were huge European cattle. Much like our bison, they were wild and strong. They have been extinct since the 1600s."

"Very good," Hess complimented Bryant. "You are very well read for a woman of dark skin."

"You'd be surprised," Bryant said as she shook off the backhanded compliment.

Hess smiled as he waxed on about the cows. "The aurochs were a symbol of the majesty of Germany. They were bigger, stronger, and smarter than all other cattle. They couldn't be tamed. They are an important representation of our people, and after this war, they will once again roam our lands."

"Interesting, and impressive if you manage to do it, but that likely pales when compared to your work in other areas of technological research."

He excitedly nodded and continued, "Our planes improve on a weekly basis, but in time they won't be necessary. We're working on flying bombs that will rain terror without the aid of human pilots. When I left, there was talk of a bomb that would be like no other. I was told just one or two of them could wipe out a major city like London. Imagine one bomb that could kill millions … perhaps even tens of millions!"

Bryant asked, "Don't you believe the Allies are working on those weapons as well."

"Unless you have made great strides in the past year, you are well behind us," he stated. "Besides, you have a weakness that will prevent you from ever dominating the world."

"What's that?" Bryant queried.

"You see your enemies as human, while we see them as not being on the same level as us. Therefore, we can test our weapons on people rather than static targets. It is far more effective to know what a poison does and how it works if you are feeding it to a subhuman rather than a rat. The same holds true for a gun or a bomb. So even if you develop a super weapon, you will likely hold back from using it. Oh, you'll threaten the world with it, but you'll hesitate. And it has long been known, he who hesitates is lost. When we have that bomb, we won't warn anyone. We'll just drop it on London or Moscow and watch as the world kneels before us. Power comes not from knowing you can kill, but rather in proving you enjoy it."

The words, delivered in such an unemotional, matter of fact style, were chilling. Still, Hess might well have the two sides pegged correctly. There did seem to be limits— based on a basic sense of humanity and compassion—that handcuffed the Allies.

"Don't underestimate the Americans' passion for killing," Bryant warned. "My people found the United States relished the use of force to wipe out entire populations."

"And who are your people?" Hess asked.

"The American Indians."

"Ah," he noted with a smile. "But like the Jews, the Negros, and Gypsies, your people are lesser humans. You are not the chosen ones."

Bryant smiled. "Time will tell."

"Listen!" Hess pointed a finger at Bryant. "Our scientists have developed drugs that fuel our soldiers. I'm sure these drugs have improved since I left. Those drugs make our men feel invincible. German soldiers will soon be able to fight for days without sleep and survive wounds that would kill your men."

Meeker cut in. "So, you think you will win the war

because your research facilities and the men behind them are far more advanced than ours?"

"That, and our men have far more passion and strength than those they fight. We are a race of supermen who are just finding out our own potential. We are carefully breeding new generations of men and women who will be smarter, stronger, and purer than any people to ever walk this earth. With our Fuhrer's leadership, we will soon seem like gods to you."

"So, it is Hitler who comes up with ideas that will make you superior?" Bryant asked.

"He inspires and leads us," Hess agreed, "but it's our scientists who propel us."

"And who is the greatest of those?" Meeker asked. "Who is the man who directs all this brain power?"

"The shepherd is Van Halpton. He's the brightest of the bright, and the one who identifies and guides the minds who will shape our future."

Nodding, Meeker pushed her chair away from the table and slowly walked to the door. She knocked once, and the British officer reentered.

"We are finished," she announced.

"Did he give you what you needed?"

Meeker smiled and nodded.

She turned back to Hess, "Sir, I hope you live long enough to see the fallacy of your views. I hope someday you will have the opportunity to dip your fingers into Hitler's blood and discover it's the same color as Teresa's. I hope you die knowing how many people—most far superior to you—you helped murder. I hope that for as long as you live, their voices haunt your dreams."

Meeker glared at the former Deputy Fuhrer a final

time before turning and walking out the door. As Bryant caught up, Meeker whispered, "I need a shower."

Bryant added, "Vermin come in all shapes and sizes. It's a shame that Wallace couldn't share a cell with Hess."

CHAPTER 5

Monday, October 5, 1942
2:15 a.m.
Over southern Germany

As the British Air Force Douglas C-47 Dakota roared toward the rendezvous with the underground team, Helen Meeker considered the mission ahead. Though she didn't yet know all the men he'd assembled for this team, she was happy to be working with Holsclaw. The Dutchman employed military-type precision in each of his operations. His plans and execution rivaled that of the best United States elite military units. Therefore, she and Bryant would be in excellent company for the next few days. On top of that, having her old partner, Henry Reese, along shored up her faith as few other things could.

Thanks to what had once seemed an unnecessary stop to visit the former German Deputy Fuhrer, Meeker also had a much better idea as to what to look for in the mountain research facility. Based on what she'd gleaned from Hess's boasting, she needed to concentrate on getting one man's files back to the Allies. Thankfully, once she'd learned the scientist's name, MI6 had been able to provide her with some background on Wolfgang Van Halpton.

After stellar academic work in Hamburg and gaining a master's degree at St. Andrew's College in Scotland, Van Halpton had earned a doctorate in physics in 1928 from the University of Munich. He was immediately hired by Bayerische Flugzeuwerke, a firm specializing in automotive and airplane development. He had quickly risen through the ranks until his talent was noted by none other than Rudolf Hess. Over lunch in early 1934, Hess and Van Halpton spent hours talking about the dramatic changes in weaponry and how technological development would ultimately determine which nations could rule the world. Hess invited the scientist to a dinner party that included Hitler and Himmler. The Nazi's three powerful "H's" felt it was vital to bring Van Halpton on board. In 1935, a research facility was set up for the physicist, and he began developing concepts for strengthening the German military. Working with the nation's top industrial leaders, Van Halpton used his deep knowledge of the automobile industry and aircraft production to create a plan to revamp the entire military structure. In his mind, the key was not more men or more weapons, but rather weapons that were deadlier and more precise. Tours of England and the United States allowed Van Halpton to deepen that focus by observing the evolution of these industries in the free world. In Detroit, he realized the importance of putting together a team of experts and creative minds and getting them to buy into his vision.

Back in Germany, Van Halpton gathered the most inventive minds in every field of mathematics and science and gave them free rein. He encouraged them to dream of things that weren't and to find ways to get there. When Hitler invaded Poland and noted the signs of an upcoming war stretching to all corners of the globe, Van Halpton encouraged his men to set their sights on space. Not that he dreamed of going to the moon, but he realized to get there, new types of propulsion systems and fuels would have to be developed to drive them.

In private meetings with Hitler, Van Halpton proved to be the voice that steered the Fuhrer beyond the concept of tanks and massive armies of men carrying the latest weapons and into a world where bombs weren't delivered by planes but by rockets. He painted verbal pictures of weapons being launched from Germany that could wreak havoc on New York or Los Angeles. There would be no way to stop these destructive killers, he had argued, and no German lives would be lost as the weapons delivered their explosive packages. The image of skies filled with bombs, traveling over a thousand miles an hour, provided the scientists with unmatched funding and Hitler's full support.

Thanks to a drunk SS officer bragging on German military strength, an MI6 undercover agent had recently discovered Van Halpton was centering his focus on atomic energy. He had come to believe splitting the atom was the key to putting his vision into action. He'd thus gathered a new team and put them to work in a secret facility in Bavaria. Meeker guessed that was the facility hidden inside the mountain. Thus, destroying that mountain and those working there would set the program back months, if not years. But thanks to the underground, MI6 also discovered not all the vital work needed to create the arsenal of super weapons was located inside that mountain.

While Himmler and Hitler sensed an atom bomb would make them gods, Van Halpton knew a bomb control with a guidance system was far more valuable. Thus, he was personally involved in developing wireless navigation technology that could not only guide an unmanned rocket but also allow that weapon to be monitored along each mile of its trek. The key to Meeker's mission would include finding and destroying the radio facility and if possible, securing that research and bringing it back to the States. Sadly, the intelligence MI6 had gained did not point to a location for Van Halpton's pet project.

Meeker had a theory she hoped to test. She figured the radio lab had to be close enough to the mountain facility for the different research units to coordinate their research. If the underground team was successful in destroying the mountain plant and if the radio research was not very far, they might be able to hit both. Thus, two missions would be completed on the same trip.

Even on paper, accomplishing both assignments with a small team seemed impossible, but there had been one more thing placed on the team's plate that made this outing even more difficult. The Allies wanted Van Halpton kidnapped or killed. Now that they knew how much power the man had, MI6 and OSS had decided he could not be left in Hitler's hands. It would likely be far easier to pick all three winners at the Kentucky Derby than making good on the MI6 wish list, but they had to at least try.

Meeker reopened the file she'd been given on Van Halpton, pulled out her flashlight, and studied it for the fifth time. He spent about a third of his days in Berlin and the rest in unknown locations. Meeker guessed that meant he was splitting his time between the radio research facility and the mountain. The key was not only to be lucky enough to hit one of those places when he was there but to also recognize him among the scores of other researchers. She glanced again at Van Halpton's official Nazi photo. The black and white image showed a handsome man with a chiseled, clean-shaven jaw and large light eyes. His hair was either blonde or light brown. From the numbers scratched on the back of the photo, she guessed him to be about six feet tall and one hundred and seventy pounds. He was forty-five, athletic, and neither smoked nor drank. As he'd obtained his master's degree in Scotland and traveled extensively in England and the US, he was fluent in English. He had never married and had no known living relatives.

"Miss Meeker."

The flight's navigator's voice took the woman's attention from the files. After switching off her light, she answered, "Yes."

"We haven't been spotted, and we'll be landing in about five minutes. You'll need to secure yourself before setting down."

"What about the munitions?" she asked.

"The Goony Bird that left two hours before us sent us a coded message confirming they'd been delivered and unloaded. They are in the hands of the underground team." The young Brit looked back to where Bryant was leaning against a stack of parachutes. "I'll tell Miss Bryant we're almost there," he offered.

"No," Meeker cut in, "I'll tell her. You return to your post."

She pulled herself to her feet, waited twenty seconds to get her flight legs, then strolled back to her partner. She didn't have to verbalize the obvious, but she did anyway. "It's time."

"The waiting is over," Bryant noted with a smile. "I hate waiting. In that way, I'm much more like your people than my own."

"You stay undercover on this one," Meeker reminded her. "If anyone sees your skin color, you'll likely be hauled off to a concentration camp."

Bryant nodded. "Don't worry. Those who see me won't live to tell about it. And, after visiting with Hess, I'll admit there is a part of me that relishes the idea the last person a Nazi will see looks nothing like the master race."

CHAPTER 6

Monday, October 5, 1942
5:15 a.m.
Thirty-four miles northeast of Berchtesgaden, Bavaria, Germany

The plane set down in a pasture about two miles from the rendezvous point. After unloading, the Dakota's crew quickly got back into the air and headed for home. Suddenly the women, now dressed like locals, were very alone.

Even though there were no sounds of war, Bryant and Meeker shared the sobering reality there were thousands of men around whose job it was to capture or kill them. On top of that, there were eyes in every village, home, and even in hills and fields that would likely report strangers seen roaming the roads.

"Nothing like being a tourist without a guide," Bryant opined.

"For the moment, no one has apparently been unnerved by our arrival," Meeker replied, as she carefully eyed the surroundings. "I will say it's beautiful here."

"I've found the most beautiful snakes can also be the most deadly."

"Thanks for making me feel so much more secure," Meeker snapped. She pulled a compass from her pocket and studied the needle. "It's south of here. We're supposed to look for a white stone farmhouse with a green roof. Behind the house is a large log barn."

"I'd guess we're headed to an underground safe house?"

"It was when we left London," Meeker assured her, "but no safe house is safe forever."

Tossing their packs over their shoulders, the women hiked across the pasture to a dirt road. Darkness was transforming to twilight as they began their southern trek. By the time they spotted their destination, there was enough light to reveal something they hadn't expected.

"SS," Bryant whispered as she dragged Meeker off the road and behind a tree. "Six of them. Doesn't look like the safe house is safe any longer."

The Germans had parked where those in the house could not have seen them arrive. Meeker noted two staff cars and a truck sitting on the road just around the bend from the house. The SS had their guns ready and were moving cautiously. This was obviously a raid.

Meeker grimly whispered, "They must know Holsclaw and his men are inside."

"Helen, what's your plan?"

"Teresa, why don't you share yours first."

Bryant glanced from the house to the barn and back. "The SS party is concentrating on the house, but I doubt the entire team is inside."

"There's smoke coming from the chimney," Meeker pointed out.

"Yeah, and that likely means someone is up preparing breakfast. They're expecting us? Right?"

"Right about now, in fact."

"Then Holsclaw will be up and likely prepared for our arrival. Let's wait here until the SS knocks on the door. Perhaps this is just a random check, and they will move on."

"Two Mercedes and truck, each of those men is carrying a rifle, and they are making absolutely no noise. I don't think it's a random check."

"Do you think we should move in?" Bryant asked.

"No, I'm sticking with your plan. Let's wait and see what happens. Then, if the shooting starts, we can be the cavalry."

"Quit using that term," Bryant quietly demanded. "It doesn't offer me much security."

As the SS men fanned out, two to the edges of the front wall and two to the back, the other pair walked to the door. Bryant had been right; they were ignoring the barn. While the one picked to announce the team's arrival pointed his rifle at the front door, the other knocked. A few seconds later, the wooden entry opened, and a woman dressed in peasant clothing stepped into view.

"It's Gail Worel," a shocked Meeker whispered.

The SS leader spoke for a few moments. As he finished, Worel shook her head. The answer didn't seem to satisfy him as he pushed her out of the way and barged into the home. A second later, two shots rang out, and in the blink of an eye, the farmhouse became a war zone.

An instant after the shots, the officer who entered the home staggered out backward, grabbed his gut, and fell to the ground. As he did, the other SS troopers dropped to their knees and began firing through windows. Their fire was immediately returned.

"We've walked into a hornet's nest," Bryant calmly noted. She then dropped to the ground and pulled a rifle out of her backpack. After loading and securing the M1 Garand, she rose, braced herself against a tree, and got ready for action.

"Helen, how far would you say we are from the house?"

Meeker, digging out her Colt, answered, "A hundred yards."

"And no wind," Bryant noted, as she squeezed the trigger. The woman had the eyes of an eagle and nerves of steel. A split second later, the German positioned just outside the front door fell forward.

"One down," Bryant coolly whispered.

As Bryant fixed her sights on a trooper positioned on the right of the house, Meeker noted the barn door open. Stepping out into the open, guns blazing, were three of Holsclaw's men. In the face of their surprise onslaught, one of the Germans positioned at the back of the house dropped forward into the grass.

"Well," Meeker quipped, "it seems they weren't ready for the livestock."

"Not funny ..." Bryant replied. She squeezed the trigger for the second time and took down another SS man, "... but clever."

Sensing a need to retreat, the officer to the left of the front of the home retrieved a grenade from his belt, pulled the pin and lobbed it through a window. Four seconds later, the house rocked on its foundation, and a part of the roof fell in. As the man turned to run toward his car, Bryant fired again, dropping him in his tracks. She didn't have to shoot a fourth time as Holsclaw's men took care of the remaining stormtrooper stationed at the back of the house.

"That's everyone," Meeker noted. "Let's go down and see if any of the good guys got hurt and find out what in the world Gail's doing here."

Leaving their backpacks behind, Meeker and Bryant rushed up to the now half-demolished house. They were just arriving at the front walk when Holsclaw and Worel pushed out through a door that had been knocked off its hinges. A step behind was Henry Reese. When he saw Meeker, he shook his head in disbelief.

"You're the experts we've been waiting for?"

Meeker nodded, "As you're here, I'd guess Hans must have given his best men a few weeks off." She paused and smiled before adding, "It's good to see you."

As the trio approached from the barn, the leader, frowning and obviously upset, explained, "The grenade killed two of my best men. Now we're really undermanned. With this mess, there's no time to wait for replacements."

Mess was right. The house was in shambles, and the yard littered with German bodies. Those who lived in the general area surely didn't think fireworks created the noise that had echoed up and down the valley.

"What do we do with the SS officers?" one man asked.

Holsclaw grimaced. "We take them, along with George and Herman and put them in the barn. Then we'll torch it." Holsclaw walked far enough into the yard to spot the pair of Mercedes and the truck. "At least we have a means of getting to the next safe house. Since we were going to have to steal a couple of cars and a truck as part of our charade, this saves us one step. Come on, let's take care of the bodies and get our gear packed into the cars. Then get the truck back to the barn and load it with the munitions. There'll be a time for mourning later."

As Holsclaw's men began to drag the Germans toward the barn, Meeker approached her old partner. "So, you're back in the underground, and you brought Gail with you."

"We needed a woman for this job," he explained. "She speaks perfect German."

Meeker eyed the Brit. "She seems to have all kinds of talents."

"It's good to see you, Helen," Worel announced. Like always, her voice was sweet and honest. Why couldn't it be raw and haughty instead?

"Nice seeing you too," Meeker answered. "It's a shame we had to meet again on a day when two good men died."

"Death seems to follow both of us," Worel replied.

"Yeah," Meeker muttered, "that's not something I'm proud of." She glanced at the bodies of Holsclaw's men, then added, "I'm beginning to think I'm the grim reaper."

For a few seconds, as the sound of birds singing once more filled the air and the noise of war evaporated like dew under a desert sun, no one spoke. Strange—eight men were dead, their blood staining the soil, and yet, nature moved on as if nothing had happened.

Reese broke the silence "So you and Teresa are our carrier pigeons?"

"I seem to always be a pigeon," Meeker replied.

"We'll need to know what you found out," Reese continued. "It's good to have solid folks who will take the information back to the Allies."

"We need to walk back down the road," Bryant said,

changing the subject. "We left our gear back there when we joined the fight."

Reese agreed. "While you do that, we'll get this mess cleaned up and the explosives loaded,"

Meeker remained in place, seemingly glued to the ground, looking at Reese and Worel. Bryant gently grabbed her by the arm and pulled her away from the house. After they were well out of hearing range, she whispered, "I thought you were over your jealousy. That's what you told me in Chicago—you had put your feelings aside and knew Henry and Gail were meant for each other."

"It's not easy," Meeker shot back. "I wasn't expecting to see them here ... together."

"Get over it," Bryant said firmly. "We have a mission to accomplish, and the odds aren't in our favor." Pausing, she added, "This is old news and old memories. We don't need these supposedly buried feelings coming into play. Besides, did you notice their hands?"

"What?"

Bryant stopped, grabbed Meeker by the shoulders, and turned her until they were face to face. "Helen, they're wearing wedding rings. Gail has a new last name, and if I might add an observation, this is not the way I'd want to spend my honeymoon."

Meeker turned back toward the house. Here she was, halfway around the world, far behind enemy lines, and the only things on her mind were a love lost and a door finally closing. Just like her high school prom all over again.

CHAPTER 7

Monday, October 5, 1942
3:15 p.m.
Forty miles northeast of Berchtesgaden, Bavaria, Germany

The trip from the original safe house to the deserted mountain chalet that would serve as the setup point for their operation took about an hour. The women dressed in business suits in case the two Mercedes staff cars and truck were stopped. The five men donned SS officers' uniforms. Their cover story, fortunately unnecessary, was the women were secretaries being transported to a new secret aircraft factory.

Though she attempted to turn her thoughts to locating files concerning the Nazi's atomic development and Dr. Wolfgang Van Halpton, for most of the drive Meeker's eyes never left Worel and Reese, sitting close together in the front seat. Though she tried to mask her jealousy, a glance into the car's rearview mirror showed she wasn't successful. Her expression matched that of a spoiled child who'd just been told to go bed. While she wasn't proud of her emotions, she wasn't ready to let go of them either.

She found a strange comfort in her jealousy, making for a delicious if destructive, pity party.

The new safe house, perched on the side of a hill, had breathtaking views of the Bavarian Mountains. The scene was made for color photography, but even as she climbed the stairs to the porch and walked through the front door into a room with towering ceilings and intricate woodwork, Meeker failed to notice. Her thoughts remained on Reese and his new bride.

"Grow up," Bryant whispered to her partner as she tossed their gear into one of the four bedrooms.

"How dare you!" Meeker quietly shot back.

After closing the door, Bryant, her dark eyes alive, delivered a lecture usually reserved for a petulant child. "Your attitude will endanger the entire mission. Reese made his choice; they are now married, and it's too late for you to change your mind and open your arms and heart to him. Now's the time to focus on why we're here! In five minutes, Holsclaw will outline the plans for this caper. Based on what I know, some of us won't be coming back. In fact, for the mission to be a success, only one of us is needed to deliver the files to the Allies. Now if you can't focus on what you're going to do, maybe you need to stay on the hill and let me go into that mountain."

Meeker shook her head, "Yeah, that'll work! Hess knew you weren't white the moment he saw you. Those people in that facility will spot it too. They'll likely think you're a Gypsy, and Hitler sends those folks to the concentration camps. I've got to go in, and you've got to stay outside as a spotter."

"Then focus," Bryant suggested.

"But ..."

"No, don't offer any excuses. You gave him up, and you have no right to complain or be jealous. You have to realize and accept this situation doesn't fall on Gail's shoulders or even Henry's. It falls on yours. I just hope you have the strength to carry that load."

"What gives you the right to lecture me?" Meeker demanded.

"Friendship."

Meeker hated when Bryant was on target, but in this case, she was. The situation was her fault. No one had made her lie to Henry. She'd lied because of fear and uncertainty. When asked, she couldn't tell him she loved him, though she really did. So, naturally, he moved on. And like it or not, the woman he married was probably just what he needed—smart, charming, and tough.

"What about it, Helen?"

Meeker glanced back. "Yeah, you're right. But, I don't like your being right."

"In this case," Bryant quietly noted, "I don't like being right either. For your sake, I wish I could have rewritten history. And if I had known you back then, maybe I could have talked some sense into your head. A life fully lived is about taking leaps of faith. Gail was willing to do that."

"I know," Meeker acknowledged, "and I wasn't."

Meeker looked around the room. The log walls and arching roofline offered the perfect setting for a romantic Hollywood film. The views from the window would have inspired artists and tempted skiers. And now they were about to use this magical setting to lay out plans leading to countless deaths.

"You ready?" Bryant asked. "I hear them gathering in the main room."

"Yeah, as ready as I can be to once more be the grim reaper."

By the time the two exited the bedroom, Holsclaw had gathered his team around the large dining room table. Nodding at Meeker and Bryant, he spoke.

"The two men we lost back there," he began, "the two good people we left in that barn, demand that we finish the job they couldn't. If we don't bring down that mountain, their deaths will forever be meaningless. I don't want to go back to their wives and children and explain they died for nothing."

The strong Dutchman wiped a tear from his cheek. As everyone in the room watched, he took a deep breath and cleared his throat. Yet emotion prevented him from finding his voice. To give him time to focus, Meeker spoke up.

"I've studied MI6's files on the facility. From those reports, I had the chance to get to know a great deal about the man behind the research. Hans is right; we must succeed. What Dr. Wolfgang Van Halpton is working on with his team of scientists has the potential to not just change the course of the war, but blow the earth apart. We have to stop them."

Meeker was ready to deliver some of the things she'd learned from the files and her conversation with Rudolf Hess, but Holsclaw, regaining his composure, began to lay out his vision.

"Because I speak German like a native, I'll be the SS officer in charge. Max will join me as the other member of the military assigned to bring you to the facility." The Dutchman looked to Bryant. "Teresa, you'll dress in black and wait on top of the ridge. I had heard you're very good with that rifle, and you proved that today. Still, I hope you don't have to use those skills.

"Henry and Olaf will act as inspectors from Berlin. The two of you will set and wire the explosives." He glanced first at Meeker and then at Gail. "Helen, you're an accountant with top-secret clearance. Your papers will clear the way for you to check the files and make sure they have been filed properly and the materials being used are covered in the plant's budget. Essentially, they will think you are looking into efficiency and the possible misuse of funding. The Germans worship efficiency, so they won't see anything out of the ordinary with your assignment. Gail will be your assistant and will do the speaking for both of you, as her German is excellent. Hopefully, we won't have to explain Helen's accent."

"When do we go in?" Reese asked.

"At midnight. Our observations show there are fewer guards on duty at that time. Most of the scientists will be at the hotel in town. This gives us much more freedom than working during the day. Also, most German plant inspections happen at night, so this will seem normal to those working there this evening."

"How much time will we have?" Meeker asked.

"The charges need to go off in the morning when the plant is at peak performance. That way we take out the most people. And as these scientists are the best minds in Germany, we must take them out."

"There will be slave laborers in there as well," Bryant pointed out. "How do we get them to safety?"

Holsclaw frowned. "I had this discussion earlier with Gail. We can't get them out. Those who have been exposed to the radiation are going to die anyway. The rest are being worked to death. In other words, they are all doomed. In truth, the death we're giving them will be much more humane than what the Nazis are offering."

"How many will be in there?" Reese asked.

"Hundreds."

The room became silent as the team considered the ramifications of their actions. This was far more than just war; this was cold, calculated murder.

"About the explosion," Meeker asked, "will it be on a timer?"

"No," Holsclaw answered, "it can't be. A timer could be discovered and defused. The charges will be wired into what the Nazis will think is a radiation warning device. There are enough lights and buzzers, as well as a series of switches will make the device appear legitimate. To engage all the explosives, the four switches will need to be flipped in order, from left to right. Then, if we've done our job, the whole mountain comes down.

"Now, before those switches are engaged," he warned, "you'll need to be well clear of the entrance."

"Who flips the switches?" Bryant asked.

"That will be my job," the Dutchman calmly replied.

"Will you be able to get out?" Meeker demanded.

"There is a fifty-fifty chance. But, if this is indeed my last job, I can't think of a better way to go."

"Hans," Olaf cut in, "let me do it. You're too valuable."

"No, my friend, I'm the one in charge. This is my plan, and I have studied the box the Brit's built for us. If something goes wrong, I can fix it. You can't. Now, there's food in the kitchen. Make yourself some sandwiches and then try to get some sleep. And each of you study your personnel files and memorize your names and history."

As the meeting broke up, Meeker walked to the window. The view indeed was postcard perfect. Despite what they'd just planned, for the moment, the war seemed far away.

"Hitler's retreat is not very far from here," Worel pointed out as she joined Meeker. "It's a shame he's not in his mountaintop lair right now. We could plant a few of those bombs there too."

Meeker nodded but remained silent. This was not the person she wanted to talk to right now. Maybe this was not the person she ever wanted to talk to again.

"Helen, I need to thank you."

"For what?" Meeker asked. She turned to study the Brit's far-too-perfect face.

"Henry explained he wouldn't have ever felt free to fall in love with me if you hadn't been so honest with him. He loved you for a long time, dating back to a case you worked on with the FBI."

"That *was* a long time ago," Meeker quietly noted.

Worel continued. "When he found out you didn't feel the same way, he told me it broke his heart."

"I didn't mean to do that."

"He understands," Worel assured her. "But by breaking his heart, you gave me the chance to put it back together. I can't begin to tell you what he means to me."

"You don't have to," Meeker replied. "I see it in the way you look at him. And don't wonder about Henry and me. It wasn't meant to be. I'm not certain I'm wired for love. I'm singular minded. I focus on what I need to do to prove myself at that moment. As someone close to me recently pointed out, I want the world to see me as being as good as any man."

"Everyone does. Everyone who's met you is in awe of

you. Even Churchill talks of you in quiet tones. You're a trailblazer who is going to open doors for women everywhere. On top of that, you have more courage than anyone I've ever met ..." Worel paused and licked her lips before adding, "... and you're so noble."

"Me, noble?"

"Absolutely. You could have treated me badly because I took your old partner. No matter what you told him, it's easy to see that you loved him and still do. In fact, he's the only one who can't see it. But despite that, you've never appeared jealous, and you always take the high road. I don't understand how you can do it."

Meeker didn't answer, partially because she couldn't find any words, but also because she was ashamed. She hadn't taken the high road. She wasn't noble. She was still that spoiled high school girl wanting someone else's prom date. Rather than reply, she looked back toward the mountains.

"You need to grab something to eat," Worel said.

"Yeah," Meeker agreed before turning back to the Brit. "I'm glad Henry has you. You deserve him. In this crazy war, there are no guarantees for tomorrow and the future is as fragile as a rose petal, so make each second count. Live a lifetime between life's moments so that if anything happens, you'll have no regrets."

"I promise I will."

"Good. Now, you go get something to eat. I'll be along in a second."

After Worel had joined the men in the kitchen, Bryant approached Meeker.

"Where have you been hiding?" Meeker demanded. "Have you been spying on me?"

"No, I was just sitting in a chair thinking about the mission. But 1 wouldn't be human if I weren't curious about what that was about."

Meeker shrugged. "It wasn't a conversation I wanted or asked for, but it was one I needed. I could never love Henry like she does. I'm not sure I could love anyone like she loves him. I sure hope that if someone dies tomorrow, it's not one of them."

Bryant nodded.

"And thanks, Teresa. My conscience needed a good kicking, and you sure delivered it at just the right time. My ego will be showing bruises for weeks."

"Maybe wisdom does come with age," Bryant quipped. She then hurried to the kitchen before Meeker could ask an obvious follow-up question.

CHAPTER 8

Tuesday, October 6, 1942
12:01 a.m.
Bavarian Mountains, Germany

As Meeker and the rest of the team looked on from the "borrowed" Mercedes staff cars and truck, Hans Holsclaw, outfitted as an SS officer, stepped from the backseat of the first vehicle, paused to straighten the small Nazi flag displayed beside the headlight, and strolled over to the two uniformed sentries.

Helen Meeker hated moments like this. She had absolutely no control over what was about to happen. If the sentries smelled something fishy, she and the rest of team were likely experiencing their last minutes of life. It was strange to consider mortality measured in seconds rather than years. The mere thought put her nerves on edge and caused her to reach into her bag to wrap her fingers around the only security she knew at this moment—her Colt. How sad to put all of one's faith and hope for the future in a man-made hunk of metal whose purpose was to kill.

She tried to peer through the darkness to read the sentries' expressions in the dim light cast by a security light. Still longing for control, Meeker swallowed hard and leaned closer to the open window, attempting to hear the exchange between Holsclaw and the German guards.

"Good evening, Oberfuhrer," a sentry announced. Both men snapped to attention at Holsclaw's approach.

The Dutchman, playing the role of a heavily decorated officer, returned the salute and studied the pair. From Meeker's vantage point, she guessed them to be in their early twenties and likely thrilled to draw this post rather than to be fighting in the snow and bitter cold on the Eastern front.

"I'm Oberfuhrer Schmidt," Holsclaw announced. "I've driven in from Berlin with specific orders to escort these people inside. Here are my papers. I believe you'll find everything in order."

Taking the documents, they strolled over to the guardhouse. After taking a few moments to study the typed and signed pages under a lamp, he returned them to Holsclaw and carefully eyed the visitor.

"I trust you found them in order."

"Yes, sir, but you'll also have to show them to the group leader whose office will be to your right at the end of the tunnel. His name is Hoggmeyer."

Holsclaw nodded. "I'll have my people unload here. The men have a cart on the truck. They will remove the devices to ensure none of our men are exposed to radiation, and then they'll bring them in." The Dutchman held his stoic expression and level tone as a soldier exited the tunnel pulling a wagon. Inside the wagon were two corpses in soiled striped uniforms, their bodies little more than badly scarred and bloody flesh and bone.

"The Jewish pigs don't last long in the pits," one of the sentries casually noted.

"The pits?" Holsclaw asked, managing to hold onto his composure.

"The area where the radioactive materials from the experiments are dumped. Once they're no longer able to work, they're closed into the pits, and our scientists record how long they're able to live. They call it a medical experiment."

Meeker couldn't believe the casual manner in which the men spoke of murdering innocent people. But, as her eyes studied the bodies that were little more than thin flesh stretched over brittle bones, she recalled the meeting with Hess. The sentries, like the former Deputy Fuhrer, had grown to accept the people they were working to death as subhumans.

"What happens to the bodies?" Holsclaw asked. Meeker turned her attention back to the man who currently held the team's life in his hands.

"They're loaded onto a truck," the sentry offhandedly explained, "and taken to the other side of this mountain. We toss them into a hole dug just for that purpose. A little lime, a little dirt, and it is like they were never here."

"How many have been deposited there so far?"

"Thousands."

The Dutchman grimly nodded before looking back to the vehicles and waving for Helen and the others to step out. Before following Holsclaw into the tunnel, she glanced up to the top of the ridge. Bryant was there somewhere, surely ready for action. Comforted by that thought, Meeker smoothed her skirt, straightened her jacket, and entered the tunnel. There, she and the others waited for the mission leader to get them past the next checkpoint, located fifty feet down into the fifteen-foot-high tunnel cut into the mountain.

"I see," Hoggmeyer, short, balding, and heavyset, said after looking through the papers. Meeker figured he couldn't jog twenty yards without suffering heart failure. If this man were ever put on the Eastern front, he'd roll rather than march.

Hoggmeyer glanced up from the papers. "You're here to install some safety equipment and audit our files and books. Is that correct?"

"That is correct," Holsclaw assured him. "And we would like to get this done tonight. I have a meeting tomorrow evening in Berlin."

Hoggmeyer shook his head. "I wonder why I was not notified of this?"

Meeker tensed. For the first time since they'd arrived, there seemed to be a hint of trouble. How would the Dutchman handle the challenge? His next words proved he'd anticipated just such a question.

"A train was bombed a few days ago. Perhaps the notification was lost when the mail car was destroyed." Holsclaw's voice showed no hint of apprehension.

"Perhaps," the SS officer agreed, "but I'll need to check with headquarters. Please wait."

Glancing back to his team, Holsclaw nodded grimly. While Hoggmeyer made his call, Meeker and all the others prepared for expected action. One minute became two, and two became three as the SS officer talked on the phone. As she fingered her hidden Colt and counted the armed men between the team and the exit, the German officer returned from his desk.

"It seems that Reichsfuhrer Himmler is having a party tonight and his staff is with him. The person I spoke with told me your assignments seemed to be in order. He pointed out we did have a man who died from radiation disease last week. He figured that triggered Himmler's decision to put in the detectors. I'm guessing you're not going to place them in the areas where the slaves are constructing new rooms?"

"Yes," Holsclaw explained, "we will. There will be times when both the German military and our top scientists will go into those new areas, and we'll want to make sure they are clean when they exit. As you probably know, almost any exposure can be fatal."

Hoggmeyer nodded. "That's why I stay well away from that stuff."

"My men will be moving through the entire plant, but where can the women accountants find the file room?"

"The files are in the labs with our scientists. Except for one or two who are working late, none of them will be back until eight tomorrow."

"Are the cabinets unlocked?" Holsclaw asked.

"Of course. We're inside a mountain. Everyone who comes in here is checked in and out, so there's no need for locks."

"Very good." The Dutchman looked back at his team and smiled. Clicking his heels together, he then barked orders. "Let's get going. I want those detectors set up and wired before the main work crews come back in the morning. We don't want to be in their way."

Hoggmeyer started to return to his desk when he

noticed Meeker and Worel. Making a U-turn, he hurriedly approached. "Perhaps, I need to escort the women to the files."

Holsclaw smiled, "I'm sure they would appreciate it. Miss Duitsman is in charge. She will ask you if she needs anything. Miss Schluter is mute. She lost her voice a few years ago in an accident, but she is one of our best accountants. If she needs something, she will write out her wishes to Gertrude, I mean Miss Duitsman, and you will be alerted. Now, come on men. It seems the women have an escort. Herman, help Willie with that cart. And don't drop anything. Those detectors are expensive and rare."

After Holsclaw and the men had passed, Hoggmeyer grinned and signaled for the women to follow him. Once they walked into the main lab, he asked, "Is there anything I can get you?"

"No," Worel announced in German.

As the officer watched, the women set their large briefcases onto an empty desk and approached a wall lined with file cabinets. They were looking for anything marked "Atomar." A lone scientist, dressed in a white lab coat, looked up from a table for a second before turning his attention back to his work. Meanwhile, Hoggmeyer positioned himself to Worel's right and went into hover mode. After five minutes, she turned to him, frowning.

"If I don't finish this work," she announced, "I will have to explain you were the reason it was turned in late. I doubt if Himmler would be amused by your feeble attempts at flirting." She cocked an eyebrow and added, "Besides, he thinks of me as his toy."

The last remark caused the officer to rush out of the room and back to his post. Once he was gone, Worel went back to work. There was a lot to do, and they couldn't miss anything dealing with atomic research or containing the name Van Halpton.

CHAPTER 9

After Meeker finished searching the files, she had taken those she felt were significant and placed them into hers and Worel's now bulging briefcases. Stepping out of the lab, she looked down the hall into a large room filled with what appeared to be life-sized props from a Buck Rogers film. Worel joined her, and they casually strolled to what they quickly ascertained was the facility's manufacturing center.

"My Lord, Helen, this looks like something out of a Jules Verne novel."

Staying in character, Meeker remained mute as she studied rockets ranging in size from four feet long to some large enough to carry several men. Van Halpton's work appeared much further along than MI6 had imagined. As frightening as the number and variety of missiles, in the next room behind thick glass walls were what appeared to be bombs. They looked nothing like conventional bombs dropped by the tons daily. These were larger and far more imposing. On the side of one closest to her was written "Uranprojekt."

"They say it will blow up the whole planet."

Shocked by the unsolicited comment, Meeker turned and found herself face to face with Hoggmeyer. Turning his eyes from the weapon to the woman, he added, "Just hearing about its potential makes me think of the way my childhood priest used to describe the book of Revelation. It's kind of biblical if you think about it. The Fuhrer once said in a radio speech he was here to finish Christ's work. Maybe this is how."

The theological reference caused a chill to run down Meeker's spine as she turned once again to look through the glass. Several men, wearing what appeared to be heavy-duty diving gear, were working on a bomb in the far corner of the room. Around those in protective gear, emaciated slaves, many covered with bleeding sores and wearing little more than rags, were doing the heavy lifting.

"They'll be in the pit soon," Hoggmeyer casually noted, "but we get the most out of them while they're here. They build our projects and dig out the mountain for expansion. When they break down, they are used in medical tests that will show us how the enemy will respond to radiation after the bombs are dropped. And when they die, we pull out their gold teeth and fillings and melt them down so the radio laboratory down the road can use them in connecting wires to relays and such. Nothing is wasted, and they free up German men for service or jobs in factories."

Just like with the sentries, the men who worked here were completely callous about the deaths of those whose labor was necessary to construct their destructive machines. For the moment, it was all she could do to maintain her composure and her role as a mute. What she really wanted was to tear Hoggmeyer apart.

She glanced over to Worel, who was now facing Hoggmeyer. Just as Meeker had hoped, the Brit began a slow dig for more information on the radio facility.

"I understand Dr. Van Halpton is working on radio guidance systems at the lab."

"You know more than I do," the officer replied. "I've only been there once to drop off a load of gold fillings. I saw the radio components but had no idea what they were doing."

"It's just down the road, isn't it?" Worel cooed.

"Well, it's on the road, but fifteen miles south. I still don't understand why they are working out of an old barn. The building doesn't look like much on the outside, but you should see it on the inside. It has to be the cleanest, most advanced facility in the country or maybe the world."

Meeker smiled. Finding Van Halpton might be easier than she had anticipated. She was even more pleased when Worel seemed to read her mind with the next question.

"Do you think the doctor is there now?"

"He was a couple of days ago. In fact, he came up here to inspect the work on the bombs. I think I heard him say he's going back to Berlin next week. Your men have been working hard." He pointed to one of the boxes that did appear to be a radiation detector. "The guy, Willie, explained they had to be wired in a series. If they weren't, then the master console wouldn't be able to identify which area was being contaminated. He said that if they didn't get everything wired perfectly, it could cost us a lot of lives."

"He's right on that," Worel agreed. "Where are they setting up the control console?"

"Right in my office," Hoggmeyer proudly announced. "The Oberfuhrer is going to teach me how to run it. He told me if I do my job properly, my career could explode."

"It seems that all of the detectors here are in place, so why don't we head back to your office and wait for our team to finish," Worel suggested.

Hoggmeyer rubbed his hands together and grinned. "I'll lead the way."

The facility was starting to fill up. There were now more than a dozen men in the lab. The rocket assembly room was also starting to hum with activity.

"More than two hundred of Germany's finest work here," Hoggmeyer explained as they walked out of the rocket room into the hall. "And everyone here lives to serve the Fuhrer."

Meeker shook her head. If all went well, in a couple of hours, they would die serving Hitler as well.

CHAPTER 10

Tuesday, October 6, 1942
7:15 a.m.
Bavarian Mountains, Germany

On top of a ridge, hidden behind brush and trees, Teresa Bryant waited, observing the entrance to the research center. Her weapon was loaded and ready. The night had been long and slow, a few men going out and a few coming in, but now, as dawn gave way to a full morning sun, activity had picked up markedly. Scores of people, civilians and military, were arriving, parking their vehicles, showing their passes, and entering the mountain facility. Her instincts yelled that if trouble were to happen, now would be the time.

After checking her watch, she took a long, deep sigh. Just one hour remained before the final facets of the plan fell into place. By now, Holsclaw, Reese, Max, and Olaf should have the explosives planted, and hopefully, Meeker and Worel had the files they needed. The explosion had to be timed to ensure all the top scientists were in the facility when it went up—or, in this case, came crashing down.

The next sixty minutes really mattered and would likely seem much longer than the seven previous hours.

Looking from the entrance back to the parking area, Bryant noted what might be the first sign of trouble. A troop truck, following an SS command car, pulled up beside the vehicles the team had "borrowed." One of the men was inspecting the staff cars. Odds were good the burning barn with six dead stormtroopers and two members of the underground had been discovered, and this unit was assigned to apprehend those responsible.

Bryant frowned as she observed the two SS officers discussing, then pointing to the cars and the facility. What would they do next? The most likely option would be to track down the intruders and haul them off to SS headquarters. If that was indeed what the SS officers were planning, Bryant knew her team wouldn't give up—they'd fight to a sure death.

Retrieving a handgun to go with her rifle, Bryant carefully worked her way down the hillside to the edge of the road. She waited in the shadows until she was sure no one was looking her way, then jogged to the other side of the highway, where she stole into the trees and moved toward the back of the parking lot. She was now only fifty feet from the Mercedes sedan which was still running. Better yet, she was close enough to hear the officers talking. Her German was just good enough to grasp the most important aspects of the discussion.

"Where do you think they are?" the taller man asked.

"They have to be in the mountain."

"So, do we go in or do we alert command?"

"We don't even know who they are. The tip said they

were from the underground, but they might be some of Himmler's own, trying another purge."

"What do you mean, Joseph?"

"Don't pretend you don't know. Those officers who died weren't clean. They were dealing in the black market. If Himmler found that out, he might have set them up to die."

"Then who were the other two?"

"I don't know, but we just can't charge into that facility and ask everyone to line up so we can see if there is anyone there we don't know."

"There's a phone in the sentry's post. Why don't we call the higher ups for instructions?"

"That at least gives us someone to blame if things go wrong."

"Wait here for me," the taller man advised, "I'll make the call."

Things were about to blow up. If they got their superiors on the phone, more stormtroopers would be brought in, and Holsclaw's team would be wiped out before the mission could be completed.

From behind a tree, she observed the waiting SS officer step away from his vehicle and move over to the truck. After sharing something she couldn't distinguish with the men in the back of the vehicle, he pulled a cigarette from inside his coat. He'd just lit up when his friend returned.

"They want us to go inside and search the facility. Our guards stationed in the building will be able to tell us who are the new faces. Once we find those men, we are to haul them in. They are likely underground people posing as SS."

After taking a drag on his smoke, the other man

nodded. "Do you think they're here to try to blow up the facility?"

"That's too big an operation. My guess is they are trying to kill key researchers and delay the development of our new weapons. Think about it, how would you distribute explosives in a place this large without being detected?"

"There's no way. Our men are everywhere."

"Did you tell the sentries what's going on?"

"No, those guys aren't bright enough to grasp what needs to be done. They'd get excited and gum things up. For right now, we're the only two who are aware of this."

"So, what's the plan?"

"We'll find Hoggmeyer, explain what's going on, have him get a few of his men, and then grab the ones who are new."

"Sounds like a piece of cake."

"It should be."

Bryant glanced at her watch. It was twenty till eight, far too early for cake. Shooting the officers would be easy, but would create chaos and cause the mission to go south. Her next move required something much bolder.

Crouching, she emerged from the woods, made her way between two parked cars, and crept to the side of the SS staff car. The two officers were still smoking and watching the entrance. Quietly turning the handle on the front passenger side door, she opened it just enough to crawl in. Keeping her head low, she eased behind the wheel, setting both her automatic and rifle on the seat beside her.

After releasing the parking brake, Bryant, her head still below the top of the seat, took the wheel in hand, slipped the clutch, and slid the huge car into first. She adjusted the rearview mirror to observe the officers. They still hadn't noticed her. Easing the clutch out and applying just a touch of gas, the car almost silently moved forward. She'd covered twenty feet when the storm troopers finally realized their car was leaving without them.

There was no reason for Bryant to be coy now. Sitting up, she hit the gas and made the first hard left. The stunned officers were reaching for their sidearms when she made the second left. By the time she roared out of the parking lot and hit the road, their Lugers were out, but they were unable to get a clean shot. Now, the question became what they would do? She hoped they would take the troop truck and follow. As she slipped the Mercedes into second, she glanced back toward the parking lot and noted the truck backing up. They had swallowed the bait.

Bryant slowed the car enough to allow her pursuers to close a bit of the distance. Once she found the right speed to maintain her advantage, she inventoried her surroundings. The road was paved, but because of the terrain, was curvy. The landscape was mainly tree-covered, with power and telephone lines running along the road. So far, she'd met hardly any traffic, and she was already at least three miles from the facility with the truck still on her tail. She drove two more miles, then hit the gas. Within thirty seconds, the truck was out of sight and at least two curves behind. After another minute of hard driving, Bryant noticed a side road. Slowing, she turned right and drove the Mercedes about twenty yards. She then stopped, turned around, and headed back to the main road. She pulled the car behind some brush and left it running. Grabbing her rifle, she moved back toward the highway and hid behind a tree, waiting for the truck to come into view.

One of the SS officers perched on the running board, holding onto the window as he looked down the road. The other stood in the bed between the benches where the soldiers sat. The truck was going about thirty as it approached. Bryant wished she could just allow the vehicle to pass, but she was afraid the officers would give up, turn around, and still have time to alert the facility. Thus, even though it pained her, she was forced to embrace a far deadlier plan. From her hidden position, she leaned into the tree and set her sights. With a single squeeze of her finger, a projectile quickly found the side of the first officer's head. Perhaps reflex, but he hung onto the door for a few seconds before rolling onto the road. As of yet, no one seemed to have noticed.

Slightly shifting her position, Bryant waited for the truck to pass before taking aim at the only other man who knew her team was inside the mountain. When her bullet found him, he pitched forward and landed in the lap of one of the soldiers. Now, the driver became aware the unit was under attack, but surprisingly, he didn't stop the truck. That likely meant he was looking for cover. Aiming at the passenger side wheels, she squeezed off four more rounds. Two of the tires blew, one on the front and one on the back, causing the vehicle to pull hard to the right, running off the road. The truck then bounced through a ditch and into a pine tree before rolling over onto its side. The collision's force tossed men and equipment in every direction.

After grimly assessing the damage, Bryant lowered her weapon and hurried back to the Mercedes. She pulled the large vehicle out of its hiding place and hit the highway. As she turned back toward the mountain facility, she glanced over to the truck. Those not injured were helping their comrades out of the vehicle. None were grabbing their rifles and readying for action. After weaving around the body of the first SS officer she'd taken out, Bryant hit the gas, shifted from first to second, then to high. A mile later, she slowed the Mercedes and stopped on the shoulder. She got out and studied the lines that ran along the poles beside the road. Spotting the one dedicated to phone service, she pulled out the rifle and, with one shot, split the line in two. Now, no one could make a call to report the havoc she'd just created.

Satisfied her fly-by-the-seat-of-her-pants plan had bought some time for the team, she returned to the Mercedes and headed back to her post. If all went well, she'd soon sneak into one of the "borrowed" staff cars and head back to the safe house with Meeker and the rest of the band.

CHAPTER 11

Tuesday, October 6, 1942
8:21 a.m.
Bavarian Mountains, Germany

By the time the work was finished, and Holsclaw's team met in Hoggmeyer's office, the research facility was brimming with life. Meeker, feeling calm but impatient, watched the Dutchman hook up the last of the wires to the console and plug the unit into the wall. Standing over his shoulder was the ever curious Hoggmeyer.

"So those lights indicate what?" the German asked.

Holsclaw pointed to the eight multicolored small bulbs on the top of the large metal box. "As long as they are not lit up, you're fine. Each of the detectors in the plant has a number. I've written those numbers on the box beside the lights associated with a particular part of the facility. If the third light were to go on, that means the box with the same number has detected a problem. Therefore, you should immediately order an evacuation of that area until the problem is found." He pointed to a switch on the side of the unit, "Let me turn it on, and we'll see if any of the bulbs light up."

Hoggmeyer observed with great anticipation as the box came to life. "There is one on!" the German excited exclaimed. He leaned closer and pointed. "It's number eight."

"It's in the room where the weapons are being constructed, and the uranium is being used," Holsclaw explained. "It should always be on."

Meeker smiled. The Brits had thought of everything. Here was a box that was nothing other than an ignition switch for a series of bombs, and yet it actually seemed to be a necessary piece of technology for the facility.

"I think we are finished," Holsclaw said. He put his hand on Hoggmeyer's shoulder and added, "We won't be needing the cart we used to bring the materials into the mountain, so we'll just leave it for you." He glanced toward his team and added, "Now why don't you people get out of the way. I'll meet you at the car."

"We can wait," Reese offered.

"No, I won't be long. I just have to show Hoggmeyer how to test the machine so he can teach his men what to look out for." The others made their way out of the office, Meeker waited by the door as Holsclaw directed the German's attention to the unit. "There are four switches at the bottom. Look closely as you need to remember this. Every eight hours, those switches need to reverse positions. Let's look at the clock. We are coming up on eight-thirty, so at that time, we will need to flip them upward. And we don't do it slowly. We will need to switch all of them as quickly as possible. I can stay here and do it the first time, or you can. That is up to you."

Hoggmeyer nodded, "So in six minutes, I go over and flip them toward the top. Do I do it one at a time, or should I just use both hands and do it all at once?"

"You quickly flip them from left to right," the Dutchman advised. "Do you understand?"

"From left to right."

"Perfect. Hoggmeyer, you're a bright man! You might be able to handle it on your own the very first time. Himmler will be impressed when I tell him the caliber of officer I've left in charge."

"So, we just leave them in the up position for the rest of the day?" Hoggmeyer inquired.

"Yes," Holsclaw agreed, "after you flip it at eight-thirty. Then have your afternoon manager switch them back down. He should only switch them from right to left. Now, do you want me to do it the first time or would rather tackle it on your own?"

The German glanced over at his clock. "So, I make the switch in five minutes?"

"Exactly." Holsclaw smiled. "I feel confident with you in charge, so I'll be leaving now."

The Dutchman gently pushed Meeker out the door and toward the entrance. As they hurried toward the exit, they met about a dozen men walking in. None of them had any idea what was about to happen. Mixed in with that group was one person who did—Gail Worel.

Meeker stepped to the side and grabbed the Brit by the arm. "What are you doing?"

"I forgot my briefcase. There's vital information in there."

"It's too late now," Meeker whispered. "This whole place goes up in about four minutes."

"I'll make it," Worel assured her. "My watch is set at the time of the clock in the guard's office."

Holsclaw leaned close, "Fine. Go get it, but make sure that Hoggmeyer doesn't throw those switches until you have left. You got that?"

"Yeah," she assured him as she pushed away and raced down the corridor.

Concerned, Meeker suggested, "I need to go with her."

The Dutchman grabbed her arm and held her in place. "No, you don't. She made the mistake; she has to be the one to take the risk." He looked toward the exit. "Besides, she has time. Let's get moving."

Grudgingly, Meeker headed to the exit, but every five steps she glanced over her shoulder, waiting to see if Worel was heading back. Even as they exited the tunnel, the Brit was still not in sight.

"We have to go back," Meeker argued.

"No," Holsclaw ordered as he squeezed harder. "Get to the cars."

As they moved by the sentry, Reese ran up.

"Where's Gail?"

"She forgot her briefcase," the Dutchman explained. "She had to go back to get it."

Before anyone could say a word, Reese gritted his teeth and took off toward the entry. This time Holsclaw didn't attempt to stop him.

"Get into the car, Helen," the Dutchman snapped.

"But …"

"Get into the car. You can't do anything now."

Meeker opened the back door of the Mercedes where she found Bryant crouched down and waiting. In the front, sitting behind the wheel, was Olaf. She glanced to her left and saw that the other team member, Max, had already started the second staff car.

Meeker looked at her watch and frowned. It was time. Hearing footsteps, her head popped up. Holsclaw, briefcase in hand, raced toward the first Mercedes, tossing the bag with the files through the window before giving an order.

"Olaf, get going. I'll stay with Max, and we'll meet you back at the safe house."

"How did you get the briefcase?" Meeker demanded.

"Gail passed it to me."

"Where are she and Henry?"

"They somehow missed each other as he went in and she came out. She rushed back in to find him." He shook his head and spoke softly, "I tried, but I couldn't stop her."

Meeker thrust her head out the window and shouted, "We can't leave them here."

"I'll stay for them," he assured her. "You have the files; get them to safety. Go, Olaf! Go!"

Olaf hit the gas and hurriedly exited the parking lot. The car was less than a half a mile down the road when the explosion hit. It felt an earthquake. Looking back over her shoulder, Meeker saw smoke but no flames.

CHAPTER 12

Tuesday, October 6, 1942
1:17 p.m.
Forty miles northeast of Berchtesgaden, Bavaria, Germany

The first car arrived safely at the chalet just after twelve-thirty. Along the route, Olaf filled in Teresa Bryant on how the work had gone. Bryant then explained what she'd done to make sure the team wasn't interrupted. Uncharacteristically, Meeker remained mute during the entire trip along the winding mountain roads. When they arrived at the cabin, Meeker walked silently into the house. After retrieving the two briefcases containing the files, Bryant followed.

"Helen, Olaf's hiding the car behind the house. He'll stay outside and watch the road until our other car arrives. Can I get you something to eat or drink?"

Meeker shook her head. After dropping into a chair, she began to sob.

"You don't know that they didn't get out," Bryant argued. "Gail and Reese might be coming through that door any minute now."

There was no response.

After setting the briefcases on the table, Bryant walked into the kitchen and drew a glass of water. In terms of the mission, no matter how many were lost, they'd had a good day. The team had stolen the files and blown up the most important research and development facility in Germany. In doing so, they had also taken out some of the Nazi's top scientific minds. Yet in times of war, victories often rang hollow. And their assignment was not over. There was more to be done. She wondered if, during their work inside the mountain, the team had uncovered the location of the radio research facility. She sensed now was not the time to ask.

Wandering back into the living room, she positioned herself in a chair by the front window and waited. As the minutes slowly ticked by, she began a mental battle that had once been foreign to her. In the past, Bryant had always been patient. Waiting and watching were a part of the nature of her people. But the more she'd worked and lived in mainstream American society, the more she'd lost the ability to embrace the long, quiet moments. She no longer wanted to wait for the action to come to her; she wanted to force the action. Yet, history and her own experience had shown that was the surest way to earn an early greeting from the Great Spirit.

Pushing into the chair's cushioned back, Bryant glanced from the road to Meeker. Her partner was no longer the strong woman she had come to know over the past few months. At this moment, she was a hurt and suffering child. As emotions of loss consumed her, her eyes were not seeing, and her mind was no longer working. Meeker was trapped in a world somewhere between hope and hopelessness. The winner of that tug of war depended on how many team members returned to the chalet.

"Damn war."

The words shocked Bryant. In her time with Meeker, she'd never known the woman to curse.

"Cussing doesn't become you, Helen." The observation was not meant to scold her friend, but rather open a line of conversation. Meeker needed to talk. After several seconds, she finally did.

"Neither does war." The words hung in the air like a heavy dark cloud, hinting at a woman whose spirit had been broken.

"War doesn't become anyone," Bryant agreed. She resisted the urge to walk over and hug Meeker. "The only glory in war is to be one of those who stops it. Today, we did something that might have helped do just that."

"When this war's over," Meeker whispered, "won't we just start another one? Will wars ever end? Do we have to destroy every person on earth to actually have peace?"

"I can't answer that," Bryant admitted, "but I hope not."

The sound of a car's engine caused her to turn her eyes back to the window. Soon, she spotted the other SS staff car.

"Is that them?" Meeker asked, likely afraid to rise and see for herself.

"Yes."

"How many are in the car?" Meeker demanded.

Bryant watched the vehicle pull into the drive and stop by the chalet. After the engine shut off two doors opened.

"How many?" Meeker again asked.

"Hans and Max. They're talking to Olaf."

Suddenly angry, Meeker exploded off the couch, raced

to grab one of the briefcases, and flung it into the wall. Somehow it bounced off without opening. Bryant was stunned by the power she'd witnessed in the act.

"That stupid briefcase is what cost us two people!" Meeker shouted. She turned back, glaring at Bryant, and screamed, "Was it worth it?"

"Personally, no! I would not wish anyone I knew and loved to die for a few thousand sheets of paper." Her eyes once more met Meeker's. "But like it or not, that briefcase might well contain information that's worth hundreds or thousands or millions of lives."

"Never in my mind will it be worth anything," Meeker vowed.

"Maybe not," Bryant admitted, "but the odds were always against us getting out clean. We knew that going in. In truth, I figured we'd all die. The mission beat the odds."

"I don't care about odds or missions. I care about people."

Bryant closed the distance between them. Standing directly in front of Meeker, she lowered her voice and asked, "Which person are you talking about? Is this about losing Henry all over again?"

Meeker looked down at the floor and sadly shook her head. "No, I now know that Gail was perfect for him." She looked in Bryant's dark eyes. "I really wanted them to build on the love they had. I really did. And if Gail hadn't forgotten that briefcase, they would be here now."

"That's right," Bryant agreed, "and if he'd waited rather than rushed in to get her, they'd have been here too. They both screwed up. Maybe that just means they were meant to leave this world together, doing something they both believed was important. Maybe they had the chance to die when their love was most alive."

Meeker shook her head and sniped, "If you're trying to make me feel better, you're not."

"I don't have the words to do that," Bryant admitted. "I've never known anyone who did. Helen, I've seen more people die in my life than you could imagine. Watching loved ones die left scars on my soul that will never heal. The scenes of those deaths still bring nightmares and streams of deep, dark depression. But some way and somehow, the reasons I loved them still inspire me."

"I'd rather just forget," Meeker whispered. "I don't want to remember!"

"Death is God's way of showing how much someone really meant to us. If we mourn only a little, then those people didn't make an impact, but if our heart is torn into pieces, that person blessed us in ways that will sustain us forever."

Meeker, her blue eyes clouded with tears, shook her head. That Bryant's words weren't making an impact was painfully obvious. The strongest woman she'd ever known had lost her strength.

Meeker, now almost choking in an attempt to not break down, announced, "Teresa, I've lost everybody. My folks and now, the one man I loved. And just when I got to understand what he saw in Gail, I lost her too."

"You still have Alison," Bryant gently reminded her. "That's much more than I have."

Meeker stepped back and wiped her eyes. After regaining a bit of composure, she whispered, "Your folks are gone? You don't have any brothers or sisters?"

"Helen, my people are gone along with the way of life

they knew for centuries. Like smoke from a campfire, my history has dissolved into thin air. I have no home to go back to, and no one waiting for me even if I did."

For ten minutes, the ticking of an antique German wall clock was the only sound breaking the silence. Only after the clock had chimed twice, did either woman move. Hearing footsteps on the porch steps, Bryant turned to face the door. Holsclaw, his face grim, led Max and Olaf into the room.

"They didn't make it out," the Dutchman sadly explained.

"We guessed," Bryant answered.

"Well," Holsclaw almost regretfully continued, "we've created quite a stir. Once the dust settles, they'll be on our trail. They'll be knocking down every door in these mountains until they find someone to blame this on. We need to radio London and get back to a meeting point so a plane can get you two back to England. I'm going to suggest they pick you up where they dropped you off ..." He paused and took a deep breath before continuing. "Once we get you loaded up, the boys and I will move north."

"Not yet," Meeker announced.

Bryant was stunned that her partner had found not just her voice, but also her resolve. One look in those eyes showed Meeker was once again ready for action.

"Our mission's not over. We've lost four friends, and the best way to honor them is to fulfill our goals. I know where the radio facility is. We need to take the building and Van Halpton out. Once we get that last element behind us, I'll get on that plane. But I'm not leaving before we do."

"Do you have a death wish?" Holsclaw demanded.

"No, Hans, I have a life wish. I want the four we left behind, the four we didn't have a chance to bury or say prayers for, the four who may never have a grave or a marker to have one more reason to have lived."

"Can we complete the mission with just five?" the Dutchman asked.

"I will do it by myself," Meeker shot back. "That is if I have to. None of you have to go with me, but I'm going to do this."

"Where is it?" Bryant asked.

"In a barn about fifteen miles on the other side of the mountain we just blew up. It's the biggest building in the region, so it won't be hard to spot."

Holsclaw looked at his two men before warning, "After what happened today, that place is going to be well-guarded."

"We took down a mountain," Bryant chimed in. "Surely, we can knock down a barn. Besides, the magnitude of taking down that mountain means they won't be expecting another attack. Normal plans of operations would dictate lying low until things cool off. Of course, that's a man's way of thinking, so I tend not to put much stock in it. I figure the best time to hit a second time is while things are still hot."

"I hate to admit it, but there's some logic in that," Holsclaw noted. "But we'll need clean uniforms and new covers."

"There are some uniforms in the back room of the house," Max noted. "Lots of weapons and ammo too."

"Who will we be this time?" Meeker asked. "That is if we're stopped."

"Are you sure you want to do this?" the Dutchman asked.

"As sure as I can be."

Holsclaw nodded and folded his arms over his chest. He seemed lost in thought for a few moments; then as if by magic his energy was renewed by a vision.

"There is a women's branch of the SS. We have one of the uniforms in our batch. Helen, you're about to enter the Reichsshule-SS."

"What about me?" Bryant asked.

"You don't fit the requirements," he explained. "If we're stopped, about all we can do is claim you're a Gypsy prisoner suspected of helping those involved in the explosion."

"Wonderful," Bryant announced, "I'm the low man on the totem pole again. I hope you don't mind my attempt at Indian humor."

"Actually, having you gives us a reason to be on the road in a staff car and for having a female member of the SS with us. And, as they will assume you are not armed, you might be the ticket to our survival if anyone gets suspicious."

Bryant looked back to Meeker. "Are you sure you're up for this?"

"Yeah, this means more to me than anything right now. I need some revenge."

"No, you don't," Bryant warned. "You have to go into this with an objective point of view. You have to be cool. Being bloodthirsty clouds the mind. I want the Helen who was with me on that yacht in Chicago, the Helen who was by my side at the power plant. Do I have your word you can put everything that's happened here behind you and be that woman again?"

Meeker nodded.

"I need to hear you say it, Helen."

"I'll be that woman."

Bryant turned back to the others. "Let's get the gear and go. There will be plenty of time to sleep when we get back to London."

CHAPTER 13

Tuesday, October 6, 1942
8:17 p.m.
Werfen, Bavaria, Germany

From the back seat of the Mercedes, Helen Meeker, now dressed as a female member of the SS, sat next to the door. Teresa Bryant sat in the middle, with Olaf on the far side. Max drove, and Holsclaw sat on the passenger side. The only illumination on this cool, cloudy evening came from the yellow glow of the Mercedes' instrumentation.

Though they had not been stopped, patrols seemed to be everywhere. The episode at the mountain had literally and mentally shaken the area, perhaps all of Germany, to the core, yet the Nazi propaganda machine had not even mentioned it on newscasts. They couldn't. The facility was so secret most of those in the government hierarchy knew nothing about it. The conspirators felt a certain and undeniable satisfaction in taking down something that few realized existed, and even those who did know had to pretend they didn't.

As they wound through the mountains, Meeker

attempted to put the loss of Reese and Worel behind her. Getting the files back to the Allies had to be the main focus. That meant she or Bryant had to live to return to London, but before they could fly out, they needed to knock out the facility developing new radio technology.

The concept of guided bombs shook Meeker to her core. To drop explosives from a plane and hope they hit their target was one thing, but the ability to control a weapon from hundreds or thousands of miles away was almost beyond her grasp. The tactical advantage this technology could produce would shift the whole dynamic of war. Even if those radio signals only controlled conventional bombs, the kind currently dropped by the thousands by both sides, they would be precision-driven and oblivious to attacks from the air or ground, making them deadlier than anything ever developed. This plant might even be more important than the one now buried under the mountain.

"What's on your mind?" Bryant asked.

"Radio-controlled bombs," Meeker admitted.

"That's not the answer I was expecting."

"Teresa, the thought horrifies me. Imagine having the ability to wipe out entire cities without sending a single person into harm's way."

"Pushbutton murder," Bryant quipped.

Meeker shook her head, "Are we headed in a direction where machines fight wars?"

"The results would be the same, Helen. The bottom line is still killing more of the enemy than he does you. War is about human blood, and always will be. Even if machines are tools that don't bleed and do all fighting, the targets will always be flesh and blood."

"But, you and I know the toll killing takes on a person. Even if they are enemies of the state or criminals, we see their faces and understand in part their humanity. Killing by remote control will erase that element. Those who do the killing will never hear the cries, see the blood or smell the gunpowder. They will never witness the last breath escaping from someone's lungs. Death will cease to be real."

"That's nothing new," Bryant responded. "Wars have almost always been framed by people buying into the concept that they are superior to those they are fighting. Propaganda convinces folks they are God's chosen people and the enemy is a lower-life form. In their minds, they're not really killing humans—they are killing animals that don't deserve to live. What was the name the American whites once called my people?"

"You mean savages?"

"Yes. And by simply putting us in those terms, you took away our humanity and made murdering us much easier. So, our final breaths, our blood and our cries became the prelude to a victory song for those standing over us."

Meeker quietly asked, "Are you bitter?"

"We must never forget the history because it's history that puts our inhumanity into perspective. Thus, we owe future generations to write history honestly. We need to point out where we have failed, and the price moral failure has taken on our souls. Still, there is no time for bitterness. There's only time to move past what happened, learn the lessons and look to the future."

"Teresa, or should I say Morning Star, when you talk about history, it's like you were there and witnessed it."

"I've seen much more death than I wanted to see, and

today I not only witnessed it, but I served as an aide to the grim reaper." She frowned and studied Meeker before adding, "And I blame you for the way I feel right now."

"What?"

"I'd gotten to the point where I had become a machine. I had a mission, and I did what was necessary to complete it. Morals didn't matter, and I quit feeling death's sting. Teresa Bryant did things that Morning Star had been taught not to do. In a very real sense, I gave up my humanity and my soul. And then, I made the mistake of meeting you."

"What did I have to do with it?"

Bryant stared deep into Meeker's eyes. "Killing bothered you. Even if the person you took out was garbage, you still thought of their families. In a sense, each time you had to take a life, the act stole a piece of your heart. You didn't want to become what I had become ... a cold machine. Today, when I killed those SS officers, I did so not because they were evil but to save my teammates' lives. But those deaths brought me no sense of satisfaction. They offered no glory. Someone will mourn those men, and I was the instrument that delivered that overwhelming sadness. I'd forgotten that element of this job until I began working with you."

"I'm sorry."

Bryant shook her head. "Never be sorry for holding up a mirror and forcing others to see themselves as they really are. After all, looking at the darkness that a mirror reflects is the first step in bringing some light back into our lives. You have helped me reconnect with the sanctity of life that my tribe embraced for hundreds of years.

My grandmother would have probably told me that my ancestors sent you to open my eyes and my heart."

"Don't praise me too much," Meeker suggested. "I didn't feel anything when I killed Spoons. Maybe I'm headed to the dark side as you rediscover the light."

"Ladies," Holsclaw announced, "we have a roadblock ahead. Only speak if spoken to. I will do the talking."

"We are about to arrive at a point where we might be instruments of death again," Meeker noted.

"Not sure I'm ready for that," Bryant replied.

As the car rolled to a stop, a German soldier glanced into the driver's window. "Good evening, Oberfuhrer. May I ask what your orders are and where you are going?"

Holsclaw, his voice gruff, spit out the reply with a machinegun-like burst. "We are headed to Hamlin. We are taking a Gypsy woman there for interrogation. She was seen not far from the explosion."

The soldier glanced into the back seat. "Do you think she knows anything?"

"I doubt it, but my orders are to let those who specialize in that sort of thing get a crack at her."

The sentry directed the flashlight to Bryant. "She's a pretty thing," he cracked.

"Take a good look," Holsclaw said. "She won't be pretty for very long. I'm betting by this time tomorrow night, she'll be dead. Now may we pass? I want to get this distasteful exercise behind me and return to my real duties."

"All seems in order," the soldier announced as he shut off his flashlight.

"By the way," the Dutchman added, "I'm supposed to drop one of my men off to guard some big barn. I know that sounds stupid, but that's what I was told before we left the site of the explosion. For the life of me, I can't understand why they would want Max to guard a barn."

The soldier nodded. "You're not the first to ask about it. A truck carrying about a dozen men came through here an hour ago, looking for a barn. The only thing that matches their description is about three kilometers ahead on the left. There must be something important there, but I have no idea what."

"Thank you."

As Max slipped the car into gear and eased by the checkpoint, Holsclaw looked back to the women. "I was afraid that security for the facility would be beefed up."

"That's all right," Meeker assured him. "We'll just have to spend a bit more time scouting." She glanced toward Bryant and quietly added, "I doubt your ancestors sent me to guide you. I think it might be the other way around."

Bryant, her eyes fixed on the road, nodded. "My people teach the road goes in both directions. Perhaps this is an example."

Meeker wasn't sure what the other woman meant, but now, she would have something else to consider other than the deaths of people she loved and the odds against completing the next mission. For the moment, having that to ponder was a gift.

CHAPTER 14

Wednesday, October 7, 1942
11:36 a.m.
Three miles outside of Werfen, Bavaria, Germany

"It's a small fortress," Meeker reported from her position on the mountainside, about two hundred yards—as the crow flies—from the barn. "They seem to have guards to guard the guards."

Holsclaw nodded. Picking up his field glasses, he studied the scene. "Objectives sometimes change. This is a mission we need to pass on. We can just put it off until another time. I'll organize a group and come back in a month or so."

Meeker immediately disagreed. "No, we can't wait. There's a man in there we have to get. If we can just take him out, the German scientific research arm of this war will be set back by a year or more. That could well be a crippling blow."

"Van Halpton?"

"Hess assured me he was the most important scientific mind in the country. He has both Himmler and Hitler's ear. In fact, he may have them in the palm of his hand. They give him free rein and unlimited resources."

"That's certainly interesting," Holsclaw admitted. "Yet, look at that place. Even if we had more manpower, I doubt we could get to him."

Meeker carefully studied the facility and the guards. She then glanced up the road in both directions. "The way this site is nestled in on the mountainside, I don't think bombing from the air would be effective either."

The Dutchman shook his head. "We're down to just five people, and there are never fewer than eighteen guards stationed around the facility. There is no way to come in from the backside. It's too steep, and the three other approaches leave us wide open."

Meeker wasn't ready to give up that easily. She knew, if they just thought hard enough, they could find a way to take the place out. But—and this was a large qualifier— she, like the Dutchman, was not prepared to lose any more lives. Was there a way to accomplish this mission without doing that?

While stalling for time to think of a plan Meeker noted, "Imagine, Hans … a radio-controlled bomb. We know that the Germans are now working on a rocket program. You put that with a radio-controlled bomb, and that turns the tide of the war!"

"But, the rocket program's likely years away."

"We don't know that, and really, does it matter if it is? There are several ways to distribute bombs. Consider this, we blew up the facility with a series of small bombs. We didn't have to drop them. We just put them in place."

"Helen, I don't see what that has to do with this."

"Just listen a second, Hans. What if you could have

simply set those explosives out without having to wire them up? You then bid Hoggmeyer ado and drive away. When you're a few miles down the road, you turn on your wireless remote console and push a button. Your setup time would be nothing, and you'd be miles away when the explosion ripped the mountain apart."

Holsclaw stood, walked over to a tree and leaned against the trunk. Meeker got up and followed him.

"Hans, I'd love to steal those files, but if we can't, and if we can't grab Van Halpton, then at the very least we have to destroy the facility and take out the men developing this technology."

"How?" he demanded. "I have been doing this type of thing for years, and I see no way to accomplish what you want."

"We're the SS," she explained. "Or at least we appear to be. We have the uniforms and the paperwork. We just invite ourselves in through the front door."

"Oh, we could do that," he assured her, "but getting out is impossible. We can't grab the files, kill the scientists and then just leave. Every one of those guards would be ready to blow us apart. Our efforts would be suicide, and we'd accomplish nothing."

Meeker smiled, "I know that, but would setting off explosions a hundred yards up the road be difficult?"

"Helen, that would be easy, but what good would it do?"

"We employ human nature to destroy that plant. Human nature is more powerful than any weapon ever developed or used."

"Human nature? I don't understand what you're saying."

"Okay," Meeker explained, excitement now clearly evident in her tone. "After a natural disaster or an unexpected attack, people's fears are magnified. When the Japanese hit Pearl Harbor, the West Coast literally went dark. For weeks, folks figured San Francisco or Los Angeles would be hit next. That there was no way a Japanese force could escape detection and actually pull something like that off didn't matter. Logic flew out the window, and panic took over."

She set her jaw and looked down at the barn. "Hans, right now those people in there are wondering if they will be next. It doesn't matter that they have been assured time and time again that their facility is unknown. In their minds, they are in danger. They think they're sitting ducks. Every branch that falls in the woods causes them to jump. Every visitor looks like the grim reaper. They're one small event from going into a full panic."

"And how do you create this panic?" he asked. "And even if you can, how do we get access to those files?"

Meeker turned back to the road. There were no houses within at least a mile in either direction, and her two hours of observation had noted there was almost no traffic.

"I'm waiting for your idea." Holsclaw was growing impatient.

"Do we have enough explosives to blow up a vehicle?"

"We brought a couple of boxes of grenades with us. We can rig something with some of those."

"Good! Now can you, Max, and Olaf find a way to borrow two trucks? One would need to be a military rig and the other civilian."

"We've done much more difficult things. It might take a day or so."

"We'll need a place to hide and prepare. Besides, I want to look my best when we're invited to enter that barn."

"Invited."

"Yep, Hans, they'll want us there."

Holsclaw shrugged. "What is the phrase that Americans say when someone has suddenly gone crazy?"

"You think I've flipped my lid?"

"Yes."

"I assure you I haven't. Now, what about a place we can work, eat and sleep."

"I saw a house when I went to buy food. It's about a half mile out of town, set off in the woods with a couple of buildings behind it. A sign indicated the place was available for rent."

"Then see if you can take out a lease," Meeker suggested. "Tell them the house will be used by the SS as a temporary headquarters."

"You're sure your plan will work?"

"I'll tell you what I'll do. You get the trucks and the house, and after that, I'll lay things out. If you think the operation has no chance, you have the veto. How does that sit with you?"

Holsclaw finally smiled. "I'll give you the benefit of the doubt, but you must give me a couple of hours to get the house. We'll work on getting the trucks later tonight. If we're lucky, we won't have to steal them. I'll just convince the Nazis to loan us the military vehicle and then find a civilian truck to buy. I always pack a lot of money."

"Where did you get the cash?"

"We knocked over a payroll train a few months ago. I've been saving the money for a rainy day."

She grinned. "I love a man who invests wisely. Let's get back to the camp and get this operation started."

CHAPTER 15

Thursday, October 8, 1942
3:32 p.m.
One mile east of Werfen, Bavaria, Germany

Meeker and Bryant stood in one of the two barns behind the small, wood-frame, country house they were using as their headquarters. The Americans studied what they had been told was a 1936 Opal Blitz farm truck. The old utility rig looked as if it had been pulled out of the mountain they'd brought down earlier in the week. It would have been harder to find a place where it wasn't dented than where it was.

"If that were an animal," Bryant commented, "they'd put it out of its misery."

"They wouldn't have to," Meeker noted. "I think it's already gone to that great wrecking yard in the sky." As Olaf and Holsclaw worked on wiring a small bomb under the bed, Meeker asked, "How much did they pay you to haul it off?"

The Dutchman looked up and frowned. "I'll have you know it runs like a top."

Meeker smiled. "As long as we can drive two miles, we're fine. I just don't want to have to push it."

"I wouldn't hesitate to drive this rig all the way home."

Meeker turned to Max, who was resting against the fender of the Nazi military vehicle they'd be using. It was a large truck, sporting six wheels and a canvas top over the bed.

"Now that will do," Meeker noted. "It actually looks good."

"That bed is big enough for a small square dance," Bryant added.

Max shrugged. "It was the easiest one to borrow and had a full tank of fuel."

Holsclaw cut in, "Helen, when are you going to share your plan? After all, if I decide it's too risky, we're doing all this for nothing."

"What about the phone lines?" Meeker asked, ignoring the Dutchman.

"I took care of that," Olaf assured her. "We have a tap about half a kilometer from the barn. We can listen to all the calls, and as per instructions, if they call out, we can intercept the call and answer."

"That's critical," Meeker noted. "They will make a call, and that will give us our invitation to visit them."

Holsclaw stepped out from behind the Opal truck. He rubbed his hands together in an attempt to get rid of some grease as he approached the two women. After packing and lighting his pipe, he posed the question each of the men needed to have answered.

"The bomb's ready. So is everything else. We have the papers and identification, but you haven't shared the plan. We have to know that."

Glancing out the door, Meeker looked up to the sky. The clouds were gathering. Within a few minutes, the rain would begin. That worked in their favor as well. The darker the skies, the better off they'd be.

"Helen," the Dutchman pleaded.

Without turning, Meeker asked, "What about the three small bombs with timers. Are they ready to go?"

Holsclaw's patience was all but gone. "They're in three footlockers," he assured her. "They are ready."

"Okay," Meeker announced, "you all have done a good job. If this goes as planned, there won't be a shot fired. We'll get what we need, and the facility will be leveled."

"But ..." the Dutchman cut in.

"I know what you need to know, Hans," Meeker assured him. "Teresa and I have worked out the details. I'll let her fill the three of you in. Then, you decide if it's worth the risk."

"Okay," Holsclaw replied. "I'm ready to listen."

"I've spent part of the day ..." Bryant began, then paused and waited. Only when she saw six male eyes locked on her did she continue. "During the time I've been watching the facility, I've noticed that everyone's on edge. You can see the apprehension even from the top of the ridge. Now, enough time has passed since we brought down the mountain that they've cut back a bit on the guards. They are rotating them in two shifts of eight—twelve hours on and twelve off. If we set off the truck bomb in thirty minutes, the men on duty will be nearing the end of their shift. They'll be tired, and that will probably cause them to overreact. I'm sure the first thing someone will do is call the SS and ask them to rush a team to the barn ..."

Meeker cut in. "That's why we're taking over the phone

service. When the call is made, Max will answer." She turned to the tallest member of the team. "Max, you have to convince them you are at headquarters. If they ask to speak to your superior, explain he is either out or busy on another line. If they ask who you are, tell them you were sent from Berlin after the bombing. They likely will be so nervous they won't press you anymore and will then beg for help. You will assure them an SS team will be there within thirty minutes to take care of the situation. You will also ask them to be calm but vigilant, then hang up. To make sure no other calls go through, cut the line. In fact, cut it in several places, so it will take time to repair. At that point, come back here and meet us."

"Got it."

Meeker looked back to Bryant who picked up explaining the mission details. "The team needs to arrive about half an hour later."

"Why not sooner?" Holsclaw asked.

"Because we want them to be on edge," Bryant explained. "The longer they're kept waiting, the more nervous they'll become and the fewer questions they'll ask."

"Okay," the Dutchman agreed. "I'm now beginning to understand what Helen meant when she was talking about manufacturing panic."

"When folks are really rattled," Bryant added, "they don't think logically. Things that they know can't possibly happen suddenly become accepted. You have to look no further than when Orson Wells panicked millions on October 30, 1938. He presented a radio drama that indicated Martians were invading the United States. People died in the effort to race from places where they thought the Martians had landed. The broadcast created such chaos, the program's timeline, which was completely skewed to fit the hour-long program slot, was ignored. So was the fact that only one network was carrying the news. There were traffic jams and city leaders called governors demanding the National Guard be sent immediately to provide protection. A few folks even committed suicide."

"You're serious?" Olaf was incredulous.

"Dead serious," Bryant assured him. "The men in that facility are scientists. They don't know war like we do. On top of that, they've likely all been to the mountain that we brought tumbling down. None of them ever expected their colleagues to die. The truck bomb will create a new sense of mortality that will sweep over these people who never expected to be in danger." She turned to Holsclaw. "In fact, you're going to explain to them the truck was meant to drive right up to their door and blow up. The only reason it didn't was because of a malfunction of the bomb. That will really drive the point home."

"There are still eight soldiers there," Max noted. "They're trained fighters."

"They're trained," Meeker agreed, "but there's a reason they're not on the front lines. They are either very raw, or they know someone who has the pull to keep them out of harm's way. Most of those men have likely never had a bullet fired at them."

"Hans," Bryant continued, "you must act as if you are speaking for Hitler himself. That's the kind of authoritative figure we need to make this work perfectly. You're not going to ask anything, but you are going to give clear, concise orders. And if anyone dares challenge them, you're going to run them over like a Sherman tank."

"And what am I going to tell them that will cause them to follow every order I give?" Holsclaw asked.

Bryant smiled, "Tell them the area is filled with special teams of Americans and Brits who were dropped behind German lines with two missions. The first was to blow up the mountain. The second was to find and destroy the radio facility and murder everyone in it. Because of that threat, the facility must be moved immediately to a safer location. You order them to take the most important files and equipment and load it onto the truck."

Meeker then picked up the instructions. "While that is going on, Max and Olaf will bring in the footlocker bombs and, when we are finishing loading, set the timers for ten minutes."

"Hans," Bryant continued, "you will inform the scientists and soldiers that a bus will be coming within half an hour to transport them to the new location. Tell them they would be safest waiting inside the building. At that point, I'll work my way down the hill and sneak into our car, which shouldn't be that hard as you will have everyone else occupied."

"Then," Meeker added, "we get as far away from here as possible. We need to take everything with us and leave nothing at this house. We won't be coming back." She turned to Holsclaw. "What do you think?"

Holsclaw looked to his men before nodding. "We're in." He paused and smiled before posing a final question. "Every mission is supposed to have a code name. What do you call this one?"

"Panic Attack," Meeker coolly replied. "It's time to get that truck in place. And Max, you get to your position to intercept the call for help."

As the men went to work, Bryant pulled Meeker to the side and said quietly, "You realize we're about to kill a lot of people?"

Meeker grimly nodded. "But, as you recently pointed out, how many more are we saving?"

CHAPTER 16

Thursday, October 8, 1942
4:45 p.m.
Three miles outside of Werfen, Bavaria, Germany

The truck explosion set off the initial round of panic Meeker expected. Within seconds, a frantic call went out begging the SS to come to the besieged facility's aid. That call was intercepted, and Max assured them help was on the way. Exactly twenty-eight minutes later, Holsclaw, dressed as an Oberfuhrer, led his team down the road. When they came upon the still-burning farm truck, he and Max got out, and with three soldiers looking on, walked around the destroyed vehicle. Meeker sat in the back seat almost amused by the way the Dutchman played his role, going so far as to point to imaginary pieces of evidence. Seemingly satisfied, he glanced back to one of the soldiers and demanded to know who was in charge of the facility.

"Dr. Wolfgang Van Halpton."

Holsclaw threw his hands in the air and barked, "It's come to this! Now we have scientists ordering around

German troops! No wonder things like this happen!" Before slipping back into the car, he snarled, "Take me to this Van Halpton, whoever the devil he is!"

When they arrived at the barn, Germany's top scientific mind was waiting just outside the facility's only door. Recognizing him from the files she'd studied, Meeker leaned forward and whispered to Holsclaw, "That's the brain. He's running this place, and he was also in charge of the mountain facility."

"And soon he will just be running," the Dutchman countered.

As Max, Holsclaw, and Meeker exited the vehicle and made their way to the barn, Olaf pulled the truck up beside the Mercedes.

"Where are the rest of your men?" Van Halpton demanded, obviously unnerved by the limited amount of protection the SS was providing.

Angrily shaking his fist, Holsclaw snapped, "I don't need more men." He glared at his host. "You must be Van …" He paused and snapped his fingers before turning to Meeker. "What's the name I'm looking for?"

"Van Halpton."

"Yes, of course." He sneered at the scientist as he grumbled, "Van Halpton, what kind of name is that? And why put a civilian in charge of a research facility?"

"Hitler puts a lot of stock in my work," the man explained.

"Hitler also consults with palm readers," Holsclaw retorted, "so that puts you in really good company."

"I beg your pardon," Van Halpton snapped, indignant.

"You should!" Holsclaw leaned forward and shouted, "You got me out of bed!" He then glanced back at his car, stuffed his hands in his pockets, and added, "Nevertheless, the Fuhrer does feel this work is worth saving, and that's why we are here."

Van Halpton was obviously agitated. "We need more troops for protection. We need tanks too."

"And you'll have them at your new facility" the Dutchman lied.

The offhanded remark caught the scientist by surprise. "What do you mean new facility?"

"Let's go inside and talk," Holsclaw suggested. "Looks like it's about to rain again, and I don't want to get wet." He turned back to Max and said, "You keep Olaf company, and I'll signal when I need you."

Van Halpton opened the door and led the visitors into a large building filled with more than a dozen different workstations and tables covered with tubes, wires, and speakers. But what surprised Meeker most were four different screens showing live images from the front, back, and sides of the building. She could even see Max and Olaf waiting by the truck.

"We have cameras on the outside," Van Halpton explained. "They feed video images to those screens. It's kind of a security system."

Impressed, Meeker replied, "Interesting." She didn't dare to employ any more of her German than necessary.

"Boys and their toys," Holsclaw added.

"Those toys will help us win the war," the scientist confidently boasted. "That's why this building and what we do here is so important."

Holsclaw nodded as he pounded his right fist into his left palm. "So I've been told. How many men do you have here right now … that is, not counting the eight guards?"

"Ten of the top scientists in Germany and six assistants."

"Okay, that tells me what size bus to send."

"Oberfuhrer …"

"Schmidt," Holsclaw filled in the blank. "I was not given a royal moniker at birth as you were."

"Schmidt, you don't seem too concerned about whoever blew up the truck."

The Dutchman nodded but didn't answer. Instead, pointing to a table, he ordered, "Your men need to pack up all your files and whatever you consider the most important projects you're working on now, then place them in the truck I've brought with me."

"What?" Van Halpton was not grasping the concept of moving.

Holsclaw turned to face the scientist. "Only the most vital files, the ones you couldn't afford to have fall into enemy hands."

"I can't do that," Van Halpton argued. "Everything here is important."

Holsclaw cut in. "But some things are always more important than others." He said, staring directly into the scientist's eyes. "If this building were on fire, what would you save?"

Van Halpton glanced around the room. "Those file cabinets on the left wall and the experiments and equipment on the two tables right in front of me."

"Then direct your men, as well as the guards outside, to get all of it onto the truck right now."

"But we need more time!" Van Halpton snapped.

"You asked about the blown-up truck," Holsclaw replied. "It is a portrait of failure. I had inspected it before I came to meet you. The truck was meant to be driven right into this building, to blow this whole place sky high. If it hadn't gone off early, you'd be dead now, and everything here would be in ruins."

"The underground?" the scientist asked in a whisper.

"After you get your men and those guards working," the Dutchman continued, "I'll fill you in on why it's so important to move the most valuable material now."

Van Halpton nodded and called his carefully chosen team together to explain what needed to be done. The frightened scientists didn't argue but got right to work. He then exited the building and returned with the guards.

When Van Halpton finally had everyone moving and had returned to his guests, Holsclaw smiled for the first time. "Thank you. Now I will have my men look over this building and see if they can spot anything else that needs to be loaded up during our initial move." With that, the Dutchman exited.

"Have you worked for him long?" Van Halpton asked.

"No," Meeker admitted, keeping her limited German under wraps. She then moved to the side of the building and watched.

When Holsclaw returned, he approached the scientist. "We have a couple of footlockers taking up space in our truck that should be reserved for your materials. I'll have my men store them here, and we'll pick them up later."

Observing a facility alive with activity, Holsclaw leaned close to Van Halpton and whispered, "Do any of your men speak English?"

"Schultz does."

"Then have him stay in the truck as a loader."

"Why?" Van Halpton demanded.

"Because I know you speak English as does my aid. I

would rather give you more details about this operation in a way that your men would not understand. Is that all right with you?"

Van Halpton nodded and walked over to Schultz. After they had spoken, the younger man moved outside. When the lead scientist returned, Meeker once more joined the men.

"What's this all about?" Van Halpton asked.

"She'll fill you in," the Dutchman replied. "She's actually with intelligence."

Van Halpton turned to Meeker and spoke in English. "What's going on? Who was behind that truck bomb?"

"There is a mole," Meeker explained, "who somehow found out what you were doing and shared that information with the Allies. The reason we are being forced to use English right now is that the mole might well be in this facility."

"And, they instructed the underground to hit us."

"No." She chuckled as if surprised by the man's ignorance. "The peasants couldn't pull off something like this."

"Who then?" he demanded.

"I'm not at liberty to tell you," she shot back, "but I can assure you it was the same group that destroyed the mountain facility."

"I lost so much work in the mountain," he complained. "Years of research went up in that explosion. I have a right to know who was responsible."

"Perhaps you do," she whispered, "but if I tell you, you have to keep it quiet. If the people in this area learn what is going on, it will create mass panic. Do you understand?"

"It's that bad?" he asked. His face was now framed by obvious apprehension.

Meeker led him to a far corner and quietly explained, "Here's the deal. The Allies dropped in specially trained units the day before the mountain was hit. We don't know how many, but we'd guess perhaps two hundred. They have two objectives. Obviously, the first they have already accomplished. The second is to destroy this research. That's why it's so essential we get the most important elements out tonight."

Meeker glanced across the room and observed the scientists and guards quickly moving the essential equipment out to the truck. They were so caught up in their efforts they hardly noticed Olaf and Max bringing the footlockers into the building. So far ... perfect. By now Bryant had likely come down from the ridge and snuck into one of the staff cars.

"Where are we going?" he asked.

"An unused ski resort about fifty miles from here. No one would ever think of us placing important research there. To add to the charade, your men will need to actually hit the slopes from time to time in the winter."

"That sounds wise," he agreed. "When will we move the rest of the stuff?"

"Other trucks will come back later tonight," she assured him. "It will take a number of trips. Your men will need to stay here and load items in order of importance."

"I understand."

As the last of the file cabinets were moved and the essential lab tables were cleared, Holsclaw strolled over to join Meeker and Van Halpton. "I'm leaving the guards you already have here. They will stay outside." He paused and looked at Meeker. "Did you tell him who was behind this?"

"Yes."

"Well," the Dutchman noted, "that changes things. Van Halpton, tell your men to stay inside. They don't need to go anywhere unless the SS is guarding them. Why don't you go over and explain the situation but try not to scare them. I don't want them to know about the Allied units in the area."

"Yes, sir," the scientist quickly replied, then hurried over to the confused scientists who were still waiting. Meeker observed the color draining from the faces as they heard the news.

"Helen, Max and Olaf just got in the truck and left. We have ten minutes to get as far away from here as possible."

"We have one more package we need to pick up," she added.

As the scientists grabbed cups of coffee and huddled around worktables to wait for the next load, Van Halpton returned and assured Holsclaw everything was in order and his men would wait as told.

"Good," Meeker replied, "but because you've been told about the situation, we can't leave you here. One slip of the tongue could cause complete panic and chaos. Besides, it would be best if you were at the new facility when the materials and files are unloaded."

"That's no problem," Van Halpton assured them. "I would feel safer with you."

"Then let's move," the Dutchman urged as he checked his watch. "I'd like to be far away from here in eight minutes."

"Why eight minutes?" the scientist asked.

"I have a date," Holsclaw cracked.

The trio hurried outside. As they passed the loaded truck, Max and Olaf nodded and smiled. It looked as though the mission was going to come off without a hitch and this time, with no loss of life.

Arriving at the staff car, the Dutchman opened the door and slid behind the wheel. As Meeker took her place in the front passenger seat, she pointed to Van Halpton and said, "You can ride in the back."

He opened the door and slid in before noticing another passenger just to his left. His jaw dropped as he studied the woman crouched in the floorboard.

"What's this?" he asked.

Bryant, gun in hand, smiled. "It's a gun. If you want to live, you won't even squeak. Do you understand?"

As Holsclaw pulled the Mercedes away, Van Halpton, still in shock, whispered, "What's going on?"

"You'll be taking a trip," Meeker explained, "and it won't be a short one."

"I don't understand."

"You don't need to understand," Bryant added, "just sit back and relax." She then looked toward Meeker, "Our Uncle Sam will be very happy. Maybe he'll even give us a bonus!"

"And," Meeker added, "Dr. Van Halpton may have a new lease on life."

CHAPTER 17

Friday, October 9, 1942
2:15 p.m.
Mountain Top Estate twenty miles north of Berchtesgaden,
Bavaria, Germany

The Mercedes sedan veered off the road and down a trail, then pulled into the deep woods. Teresa Bryant wearily stepped from the car and stretched. After three long days with hardly any sleep, she was beat.

As Meeker emerged from the Mercedes, she announced, "In twelve hours, we'll be on our way back to England."

Bryant nodded. A part of her couldn't wait to escape Germany and start the trip to American shores. But another part of her yearned to stay behind the lines, stymieing everything Hitler did. After what she'd witnessed on this trip, she would relish being a thorn in his side.

"Helen, if my skin were the same color as yours, I'd skip the plane ride and work with Hans. There's a purpose here I haven't found anywhere else."

"You hit the point," Meeker replied. "Your skin color

would make that impossible. We're better off to go home and fight to create a world where race doesn't matter than stay in a place where only one race survives. You can do more good back in the States."

Holsclaw joined the two women as they reflected on the state of the world. "Our scientist is bound and gagged in the truck. He won't be any problem."

"Is that necessary?" Meeker asked. "I mean, we are in the middle of nowhere."

"Actually, we stayed in this same place on the way to the mountain. There's a Lebensborn home about a hundred meters over that hill, so we'll need to remain quiet until we leave for the new rendezvous point," the Dutchman explained.

"What time will that be?" Meeker asked.

"About midnight. You'll have time to get some rest."

"What's a Lebensborn home?" Bryant inquired.

"Gail asked that same question," the Dutchman answered. "It's a breeding program the Nazis use to mate perfect specimens of Aryan women with SS officers to produce the next generation of the master race. Other children who already possess those unique traits live there too. The older ones were either removed or kidnapped from their families. Everything the Nazis do in the place, from education to recreation, centers on giving these children a sense of entitlement simply because of the way they look."

Bryant shook her head, trying to displace the image of breeding humans like prize cattle. "How many are in the home?" she asked.

"This one's not large—most are much bigger. Based on my observations, I'd say no more than twenty. Most of these kids are very young. The oldest are likely between ten and twelve. This estate is where some of the breeding takes place. They bring in the strongest SS men and give them a woman with the right traits."

"Do the women have any choice?" Meeker asked.

"A few might, but most are forced into this situation. When the child is born, they're immediately moved elsewhere, so the mothers don't have any contact with their offspring. The state supervises everything."

"So, there is no love?" Bryant noted.

"Not in a family sense," the Dutchman explained. "I'm sure some of the staff members grow fond of their charges, but there is no real devotion as we would know parenting. This is really about business. If you want to see the place, we can walk up to the top of the ridge. In fact, this might well be something you'd want to tell your President about."

"Just when I thought things couldn't get any darker or more perverse," Bryant said. She shook her head and glanced up the steep rise to the top of the ridge. Did she really want to see any more examples of how the Nazi machine had turned life upside down? Wasn't viewing the dead slaves through her field glasses enough shock for one trip? But curiosity now had her by the throat and wouldn't let go. Saying nothing, she began the trek through the woods and up the hill. The Dutchman and Meeker followed close behind.

As she topped the rise, Bryant was immediately impressed with the astonishingly beautiful old estate. The lawns were perfectly manicured, the huge house and barns shone like beacons in the sun, and the children, who almost all looked alike, were clean and well-dressed. And they seemed happy as some played near the house and a few older kids participated in an archery competition that would have made Robin Hood proud.

As if reading her thoughts, Holsclaw said, "Sometimes, hell looks a great deal like we picture heaven."

"It's nothing like the orphanages I've known," Bryant observed. "In the daytime, the children dreamed of escape, and at night, their nightmares were of monsters. Those homes were dark, dingy, dirty places where play was replaced with survival."

"It sounds as though you speak from experience," the Dutchman noted.

"I've been inside a few of them," she admitted. "I can still smell the odor and hear the sounds in the halls. I will never forget the longing in the kids' eyes as they looked to visitors, hoping they were there to take them somewhere … no, anywhere else."

Bryant's horrific memories put a damper on the conversation as the trio hidden in the trees observed Hitler's next generation of perfect Aryans playing in a world created to reward them for their appearance. Then, with no warning, the idyllic scene was transformed into something far different. Two large women dragged a screaming blonde-headed girl—about ten or eleven— from the house. The child was hitting and kicking as she was pulled across the yard. When she begged them to let her go, they took turns slapping the girl's face.

"I won't do it again," the child promised, her words choked by tears.

"No, you won't," one woman yelled.

The wrestling match between two adults and a child continued until they arrived at a small, windowless, stone building. While one woman held onto the girl, fighting off flying fists and kicking feet, the other unlocked the door. When the door was opened, the child was roughly shoved inside, and the door was slammed and relocked.

"Wonder what that was all about?" Meeker mused.

"I have no idea," Holsclaw admitted.

As she watched the women casually stroll back to the house, Bryant pulled her arms together to fight off a sudden chill. This was more than just discipline; something else was at work here.

"Helen, Hans, did you notice the other kids?"

"No, my eyes were on the girl and the women."

"They didn't quit playing," Bryant noted. "It was as if they were blind to what was happening. Even now, none of them are looking at the building or responding to the girl's screams. That makes no sense. All they have is each other, so there should be a bond, like siblings, and yet they aren't concerned."

"Perhaps the compassion has been bred out of them," Holsclaw suggested,

"No, those kids care about each other. You can tell by the way they play together. This child has been set aside for some reason. I wish I knew why."

"That, Miss Bryant," the Dutchman noted, "would be pretty much impossible to discover."

"You're an SS officer," Bryant retorted. "Why don't you go find out. No one will challenge you. Drive up there and ask for directions to somewhere. Then, as you hear the little girl's cries, find out what's going on."

"It's not worth it," he argued. "She's probably just being disciplined."

"I think it's more. I feel it in my gut. And I really don't believe it's a very big risk. No one knows we're up here."

Looking to Meeker for support, Holsclaw repeated, "It's not worth the risk."

Meeker spoke up. "Hans, we'd be dead, and the mission would have failed without Teresa taking a few risks. I think we owe her. And if you don't want to, I have an SS uniform. I can drive up and knock on that door too."

"Fine," Holsclaw answered. "I should have learned in twenty years of marriage there's no arguing with a woman or in this, case two women. I'll be back in fifteen minutes."

Meeker and Bryant watched the Dutchman work his way down the hillside to the car. After signaling for Olaf to drive him, the two climbed into the Mercedes and left. Three minutes later, they arrived at the estate. From their vantage point, the women watched Holsclaw as he spoke with the woman who answered the door. Just before ending the short conversation, he pointed toward the building.

"What do you suppose she told him?" Meeker mused.

Bryant saw no reason to guess. She continued to study a strange world where a child was screaming for help while a dozen other children acted as if they heard nothing. She'd only seen something like this on one other occasion. She remembered a time when a Negro boy was disciplined, and the other kids seemed not to notice. It was as if he had been invisible. Ten minutes later, she was still trying to marry that memory to the current situation when she heard Holsclaw climbing back up to their position.

"What did you find out?"

"It would be better not to know."

Bryant turned and shook her head. Her body language spoke loudly, and she didn't need to use words to get an answer.

"You were right. It isn't discipline," the Dutchman quietly admitted. "The child has begun to have seizures, making her inferior stock. Later tonight, the SS will send two men to execute her. The woman explained that was much easier than taking her to a concentration camp where she would suffer the same fate."

"Inferior," Bryant whispered.

"That was the word the woman used," Holsclaw said. "Evidently, the girl has always been high-spirited and hard to handle. The seizures are the final nails in her coffin."

Bryant turned and studied the Lebensborn estate once more. Even through the children's excitement and laughter, she could still hear the cries for help. They were weaker now, but the child was still begging for another chance.

"We're going to save her," Bryant vowed. "She's going back with us."

"We can't risk that," Holsclaw objected. "The information you're taking back to London is too valuable. There will be no more changes in our plans. The mission is over!"

Bryant, her dark eyes burning, turned to Meeker. "We're taking back a piece of scum who was figuring ways to kill millions. We set up explosions that took the lives of who knows how many men and women whose families are now mourning them. We lost Gail and Henry, and Hans is also going home without two of his men. We did all that in the name of war. In time—I'm not sure how many years that will be—I'll learn to live with it. But in God's name, I will never be able to live with a small girl being executed just because a society views her as inferior. You can leave me behind. You don't need me to deliver that stuff and Van Halpton back to the Allies. I'm going to save that child."

Meeker, her expression stoic, looked from Bryant back to Holsclaw. "Hans, you say the SS squad is coming tonight?"

"The woman said around ten. She didn't want them to come until the other children were asleep."

"Okay, then we wait until the activity settles down and make our last raid of this trip."

"I don't think …"

Meeker didn't allow him to finish. "I'm with Teresa. I can justify a lot of things in the name of war, but I can't allow a child to be executed just because she's not perfect in the Nazi world." She glanced back to Bryant. "Why don't we go back down the hill and work out the details?"

"Thanks," Bryant whispered.

"No thanks needed," Meeker assured her. "I wasn't going to leave her behind either."

CHAPTER 18

Friday, October 9, 1942
9:30 p.m.
Mountain Top Estate twenty miles north of Berchtesgaden,
Bavarian, Germany

The easiest plan, the one Meeker thought of first, would have quickly blown up in their faces. They would simply send two men up to the home, pretending to be the SS hit squad. But, as Holsclaw explained, the woman he'd spoken with had mentioned the storm troopers' names. If those two didn't show up, the staff would realize immediately something was wrong. They also couldn't take the child before the SS men arrived because a dragnet would be thrown out, shutting down the entire area. This would place the current mission in jeopardy and make a covert plane landing impossible. Running out of options, Holsclaw suggested they simply take out the assassins after they'd pulled the girl from the barn.

"And how will you do that without setting off alarms?" Bryant asked. "A scuffle will be heard from the house, and we obviously can't shoot anyone. If there's any unusual noise, I have to believe the dozen or so stormtroopers on holiday at the estate will come out, guns blazing."

"Fine," the weary Dutchman agreed. Taking a sip of coffee, he gazed up at the star-filled sky before continuing. "We've been knocking this thing back and forth for hours, and we're no better off than we were when you stubbornly suggested we risk everything to rescue the girl. This is your baby, so why don't you rock it?"

"Do you want me to come up with my own plan?" Bryant asked.

"Yah, since none of the rest of us can find a workable one." Holsclaw scowled as he tossed the rest of the coffee on the ground.

They'd had little sleep and had lost too many close friends. Mentally and physically exhausted, they were dangerously close to going for each other's throats. Ironically, this should be the easiest mission of the trip, but no one could agree on a workable way to accomplish it. Someone needed to step up and offer a plan that was silent and required little risk.

Bryant knew responsibility was falling into her lap. After considering the various options, she made a suggestion, "Why don't we go back to the top of the ridge?"

As the team had now been up and down the hill a dozen times, this trek was not as difficult as the first. They had all but carved out a trail, and they knew which trees to grab.

Bryant studied the estate's layout for the tenth time. As she inventoried once again every nook and cranny, Meeker asked, "When and where do you think they'll execute the child?"

Holsclaw scratched his head and frowned. "Based on what the woman told me, I think they'll do kill her there.

That's why she wanted the deed done late, so the children would be sleeping. If they weren't going to kill her on site, I don't think the time would matter."

Meeker continued to probe. "And what method will they use?"

"My guess is they'll shoot her. It's clean and quick. I also figure they will do it as soon as they unlock the shed."

"So," Bryant summarized, "we have to allow the SS to announce their arrival, pick up the key to the lock and make their way to the back yard. Then, do we grab them before they get to the shed?"

"As we've mentioned a few hundred times," Holsclaw argued, "there are no walls or trees to hide behind, so there is no way to surprise them."

Bryant grimly nodded as she turned to Max. "You watched the house all afternoon. Did you see what they did with the equipment and toys the children were using after they quit playing?"

"The staff picked them up and put them in the barn."

"The one on the near side or the far side?" Bryant asked.

"The one closest to us."

"That would make it about halfway between us and the shed." She glanced up to the sky. The fact there were no clouds made it easy to see even in the darkness, but it also would be easier to be seen. She grimly smiled and looked back to the team as a plan formed in her mind. "There would be no reason for the SS officers to return the key. Since they would be carrying the girl's remains away, they'd likely just leave that key in the lock. All we need to do is wait for the SS officers to return from the back with the girl in their arms, then get into the staff car and drive away."

Holsclaw was now exasperated. "Teresa, we recognized those facts this afternoon. What you've just said is nothing new."

"But," Bryant replied, "there is one thing that's new. Everyone agrees we have to take out the SS killers without making any noise. We can't use a gun, so what other methods can we employ?"

The silence lasted for a few seconds. Finally, Meeker spoke up. "Stabbing or strangulation seem to be all that's available, yet, there's simply no way we could sneak up behind them. The grounds are too exposed. We'd be shot as soon as we made our move. I don't know of anything."

"Where you see no way for a silent kill, I see the opportunity to revive something my ancestors used against man and beast."

"What's that?" the Dutchman asked.

Bryant pointed toward the barn. "The archery sets the children were using are high quality. I noticed the arrows had hard tips that dug deep into the wooden targets. I could tell the draw on the line produced plenty of power. Best of all, you don't have to get close to deliver a fatal blow, and I'm very good with a bow and arrow. So, my weapon is waiting for me inside that barn. I can stand just inside the door, cloaked by the shadows, and pick off the SS officers when they approach the shed."

"But," Holsclaw noted, "While you might be able to nail one of them, you couldn't reload fast enough to get the second. He would fire in your direction, waking up the whole household. Not only would we not be able to save the girl, we'd lose everything we worked for and probably die."

Meeker smiled and cleared her throat. "I don't mean

to brag, but I was a championship archer as a child, and I even used my skills when I worked with Henry during my stint with the FBI. The distance we'll be shooting is only twenty-five yards, and I can steady myself against the doorframe. If Teresa and I shoot at the same time ..." Meeker paused and smiled at her partner, "those two will be dead before they hit the ground."

"You think you're that good?" Bryant prodded.

"There are three buttons across the breast of an SS uniform jacket," Meeker said. "The one on the left is directly over a man's heart. I can put my arrow within an inch of that button."

"Well, I can get within a half inch."

"Winner buys a steak once we get back," Meeker offered.

"You're on."

"Cowboys and Indians in the middle of Bavaria." The Dutchman shook his head. "Now I've heard everything. But, just in case your skills are a few levels beneath Robin Hood, we'll have our guns ready, and at least one of them has a silencer."

"You won't need them," Bryant assured him. She looked to the last two members of the underground's crack squad. "Hans, you and Max come with us and hide in the barn. Once we have taken out the SS men, I'll get the key to the shed and you drag their bodies back into the woods. Helen and I will free the girl and explain what we're doing. We'll have to convince her she has to play dead. When you join us, we'll need to fire a shot in that shed. Take a minute so it appears you're cleaning up, then take the kid back to the staff car and drive off."

"By the way," Meeker suggested, "search the SS officers'

pockets just in case they took the keys to the car. We can't afford to waste time hotwiring the Mercedes."

"We'll take everything in all the pockets," Olaf assured Meeker.

Bryant looked down and checked her watch. "We only have about fifteen minutes to get ready." She glanced back to the house. "All the lights on this side are off. Olaf, you wait here while the rest of us will sprint to the barn."

Meeker solemnly added, "Olaf, if anything goes wrong, you get the papers and the scientist to the rendezvous point."

He nodded.

Meeker looked back to Bryant. "This is your war party. We're waiting for your orders."

"Okay. When Hans and Max take the girl to the staff car, Helen and I will hurry back down the hill. Olaf will drive the truck, and we'll take the other staff car." She looked at the Dutchman. "We'll wait to pull away until you arrive. At that time, Max can join us and take over as driver in case we hit any sentry posts along the road. Now, let's get into position."

Bryant set her jaw. She was finally in her element and immersed in an operation that she deeply believed in.

CHAPTER 19

From her position leaning against the frame of the barn door, Bryant was bathed in shadows. No one could now see her or Meeker unless they approached to about ten feet. What was even better than being in position was having extra time to prepare and become confident with their unique and somewhat antiquated weaponry. After entering the barn, the women spent five minutes picking out the best bows and testing them by shooting into bales of hay. Once they were familiar with the spring in the bows and tension in the string, they took the positions needed to make the shots. Now they had to wait, though neither was in a patient mood.

"There's no wind," Bryant whispered.

"How close do you think we should allow them to approach before shooting?" Meeker asked.

"I suggest we take them out about twenty feet in front

of the shed. They'll be walking almost straight toward us until that time, but right after that the path turns a bit to the left. As it's night, I believe they'll stay on the stone walk where the footing is better than in the grass. As soon as you fire, grab another arrow and get ready for a second round."

"I will," Meeker assured her partner, "but I won't need a second shot."

"Neither will I," Bryant cracked.

After watching Meeker test her skills, Bryant was confident that both of them were fully ready for action. The key was not just hitting their targets, but also stopping them in one shot. If the targets cried out or managed to fire off shots, getting away from the house would be a challenge. Reaching the rendezvous point would be all but impossible.

Five feet behind the women, dressed in SS uniforms and with guns ready, Holsclaw and Max waited. From their grim expressions, Bryant could tell they didn't have much confidence in the women's archery skills.

"A car's driving up," Meeker warned.

Bryant turned her gaze from the barn to the road. A dark Mercedes phaeton pulled up in front of the house. Seconds later, two black-clad men stepped out and strode resolutely up the walk. In the stillness of the night, she could hear one of them knock three times, followed by a door creaking open. She knew just enough German to understand what was being said.

"Willie, Jon, it's good to see you."

"And you, Emma," one of the men replied. "Do you want this done just like the last time?"

"Yes, shoot her in the shed, then wrap her body in this blanket and take her away."

"What's wrong with this kid?" one man asked.

"She's having fits."

"Is she one of ours?"

"No," Emma assured them, "she doesn't have any SS blood in her. She was kidnapped years ago. Even if she wasn't having seizures, she wasn't going to be selected. She's bright enough but a real handful. She's stubborn and always questioning. Here's the key to the padlock."

"We'll take care of it just the way you asked, then we'll dump the body in the lake. We'll weight her down so no one will ever see it again."

"Thanks. Good evening."

"And sweet dreams to you, Emma."

As the door closed, Bryant glanced at Meeker. "Did you hear that?"

"Yeah, they're really cold. That makes what we're doing a bit easier."

"Hans," Bryant whispered, "did you hear the part about rolling up the child in the blanket?"

"Yes."

"Aren't there some bags of feed behind you?"

"Yeah."

"After we take out the SS hit squad, grab the blanket and wrap one of the feedbags around it. That way you don't have to worry about Emma looking out a window and seeing something that makes the child appear alive. Helen and I will bring her with us."

"Got it," Holsclaw assured her, "but this still depends upon your skills. Without them, we'll have a firefight and every life that's been lost on this mission and the files we have gathered will be worth a bit less."

"Don't worry about that," Bryant replied. "These men admitted to executing other innocent children. We won't miss."

Her attention now on the SS hit squad, Bryant noted their pace and calculated the amount of time before they got into position. As they slowly moved forward, keeping to the stone walk, she smiled. Luck seemed to be with them. They looked about the same size and build as Hans and Max. In the darkness, no one in the house should be able to see a difference between the two men who arrived and the two who would be leaving. Also working in their favor, the lights were off and curtains drawn on this side of the house.

"Mine's the one on the left," Meeker whispered, "the one holding the blanket."

"I'll take the other guy," Bryant agreed.

When they were only fifty feet away, the men stopped unexpectedly. Had they sensed something?

"Do we need to shoot now?" Meeker quietly asked.

"Not yet. They have to come closer to get the girl. Let's just see what they're up to."

The men looked toward the shed as if sizing up a dangerous mission. Then came the first hint they were not enamored with their orders.

"Want a cigarette, Jon?"

"Yeah, that'd be good."

Willie pulled out two cigarettes. He handed one to Jon, then stuck the other between his lips. After lighting up with a shared match, they stood quietly smoking for a few minutes.

Jon broke the silence. "Who pulls the trigger this time?"

"Want to flip for it?"

"Not really. You took out the boy at the Hamburg house, so I guess it's my turn."

"Does it bother you?" Willie asked. "If it does, I can do it."

"It doesn't bother me," Jon insisted. "If you think about it, these kids are just pieces of machinery."

"But a couple of them are yours," Willie pointed out, irony in his voice.

"Are they really mine? I've always believed kids are not yours if you don't raise them."

"Yeah, I get that. Besides, what makes these kids any different than the ones we load on the boxcars and ship to the camps?"

The men stood in the dark, the glow from their cigarettes dimly illuminating their faces. After killing another minute, Jon announced, "Okay, I'll shoot her and you wrap her up and carry her back to the car."

After tossing his spent cigarette, Willie grimly smiled and moved ahead. A step behind, Jon followed. Fifteen steps later, Bryant whispered, "Ready?"

"On your mark."

Behind Bryant, Holsclaw pulled his gun and took a step closer to the door. As he did, his boot hit a can, sending it rolling across the ground until it hit a wall. The two SS men stopped and pulled their weapons, then turned toward the barn door.

"What was that?" Jon asked.

"Let's go find out."

Suddenly the mission was turning in a new direction, but it was not time to panic. The women steadied themselves against the doorframe and pulled the bowstrings back, their arrows held in place between their fingers. Bryant took a deep breath, allowing the men to come closer. Pausing, Jon cocked his gun and announced, "There's someone in there."

"Now," Bryant whispered.

Willie must have heard the slight rattling sound made by the bending wood and snapping string because he turned slightly to his right. But even though his gun was drawn and ready, he didn't have time to respond before the first arrow penetrated his black uniform, digging through his skin and into his heart. An instant later, Jon dropped his weapon and the blanket as his hands wildly sought the spot where Meeker's arrow found its mark. As the women readied for a second round, the SS officers staggered forward two more feet before falling to the ground.

Tossing her bow to the side, Bryant was the first one out of the barn. Rolling Willie over, she began to go through his pockets. Among some change and an address book, she found a key.

"This must be it," she whispered as the others joined her, "but let's check the other guy's pockets too." That search resulted in a couple of letters, some cash and a set of car keys." She tossed the car keys to Holsclaw and pointed to the woods. The men picked up the officers and carried them to the ridge where they dumped the bodies behind some trees.

"Let's get the kid," Bryant led the way to the shed. Seconds later, the two women stepped in, closing the door behind them. Finding a light switch, Bryant pushed a button, and the tiny room was bathed in a soft yellow glow. Huddled in the corner, tears running down her cheeks, was a blond-haired girl with the bluest eyes Bryant had ever seen.

"My name's Teresa." Bryant spoke softly in German. "My friend and I are here to take you away from this place."

"Are you going to kill me?" the child asked. "Emma told me I was going to be killed."

"No," Bryant assured her, "we're here to keep you safe. What's your name?"

"They call me Heidi," the child stated, reaching for Bryant, "but my real name is Elga."

As she picked Elga up, Bryant whispered to Meeker, "Let's get moving."

"What about the shot?" Meeker asked.

Before Bryant could reply, Holsclaw opened the door and stepped into the shed. Behind him stood Max, holding what appeared to be a body wrapped in a blanket. As Meeker turned off the light, Bryant stepped around the men and out the door. Only when she was clear of Elga's prison did she speak.

"Wait until Helen, the child, and I get back to the woods, then fire off a round. Don't hurry back to the car. We don't want to draw attention to ourselves. Make sure you close the door and leave the key in the padlock. We need to be on that plane before anyone figures out what happened here."

Meeker, Elga, and Bryant were across the yard and halfway down the far hill before they heard a shot. They could be thankful now that the shot had no real impact. The child was alive and for the moment, they were safe.

"It worked just as you planned," Meeker declared.

"Too soon to tell," Bryant cautioned. "A lot of things have to go just right between here and the plane."

CHAPTER 20

Saturday, October 10, 1942
12:15 a.m.
Ten miles from Berchtesgaden, Bavarian, Germany

Two hours passed, and the rescue of the young girl appeared to have come off without a hitch. Apparently, no one had noticed the two SS who came to the estate were not the same two who left. After being traumatized, Elga babbled for the first sixty minutes. Now she was sleeping in Bryant's arms.

Bryant spoke quietly to Helen. "She's eleven; she'll be twelve later this year. Her memories of her life before she was kidnapped are pretty strong. She was an only child, living on a farm in Norway. She remembers her mother telling her how beautiful her eyes were, and they reflected the hope found on clear, spring days. She also remembers a man in a leather coat shooting her mother."

Watching the sleeping child, Meeker agreed. "It's a horribly tragic story, and I hesitate to even consider how many children like her were stolen."

"Or how many have died in pursuit of perfection," Bryant added.

After gently brushing a few strands of blond hair away from the girl's face, Bryant stared out the window. The car's headlights revealed the thick woods and rugged terrain surrounding them, but those same lights couldn't illuminate the unseen horrors hidden just outside of public view. As the Nazis' power grew, the earth itself had opened and hell had exploded like a volcano, hot lava threatening every corner of the planet. She wondered if all that pain and suffering could ever be buried or would the devil forever have his mail forwarded to an address on the surface. Consumed by those thoughts, Bryant made an overdue observation.

"You're right, Helen."

"About what?"

"Back at the chalet, when you were angry and hurt, you spoke about the toll of constantly taking lives. Even in times of war, when the lines are clearly drawn and it is either them or us, it just doesn't seem like the blood can be washed from our hands. In the last few miles. I think I've seen the face of every life I've taken on this trip."

"You want to go back to the States and just solve mysteries?" Meeker asked. "Maybe we should devote our lives to finding hidden wills or exposing men who are cheating on their wives?"

"I don't know about that," Bryant admitted, "but it seems the deaths I've caused weigh on me even more with the passing of time."

"Are you about to tell me your age?" Meeker teased.

"No, I think I'll pass on that. A bit a mystery is always good for any friendship."

"Then why don't you tell me how you got the name Teresa Bryant? We all know that's not even close to your real name."

Bryant smiled as she ran her hands through the sleeping child's hair. "You never actually lose a name. The Nazis changed Elga's name to Heidi, but before she fell asleep, she told me she still considered herself Elga. Thus, over time, as I move from one name to another, deep in my soul I still think of that little girl whose parents named her Morning Star. It was an honor to have that name. The stars were very important to my tribe, and the dawn was our symbol of new life and new chances."

"How did you choose Teresa?" Meeker prodded.

"It was at the suggestion of the President."

"Which President?"

Bryant smiled. "I'll pass on giving that bit of information. Let's just say he wanted something that was easier to pronounce."

"You didn't mind?"

"I was told it originally was from a word that means 'She knows.' That seemed to fit me pretty well." Bryant turned her gaze from Meeker to the windshield. Her body tensed as she became aware of a new prospect of taking even more lives. After taking a deep breath, she said, "Enough about names and history. We might just have some problems in the present."

A hundred feet up the road was a barricade with a dozen German soldiers stationed on either side. The unit was a mix of regular enlisted men and SS officers. Holsclaw, driving the lead car, slowed down. Both Max, piloting their staff vehicle, and Olaf, driving the truck, eased onto the brakes as well. As they slowed to a stop, the drivers and passengers could easily hear every word spoken by the lead officer and the Dutchman.

"Identify yourself!"

Holsclaw calmly declared, "Hans Schmidt, Oberfuhrer, stationed at SS headquarters in Berlin. If you need, I will show you my papers."

"How many different names and sets of papers does he have?" Meeker whispered.

"One for every day of the week," Max quietly replied.

"Schmidt, what are you doing so far from Berlin?"

"I was sent here to investigate the explosion and search for those responsible. When I discovered the investigation was in good hands, I commandeered a truck and secured vital files from our radio development facility to transport back to Berlin for safekeeping. I understand I picked up the files none too soon as the facility was recently blown up as well."

"That's true," the SS replied. "Who is in the other staff car?"

"One of my right-hand men and my female interrogator. Another of my officers is driving the truck at the back. I had two other men with me, but I left them to guard the radio facility. They likely died with all the others. Oh, and I also have a possible hostile witness to the bombing of the mountain facility. I'm taking her to Munster for interrogation. She's a Gypsy who says she saw several Allied soldiers in the area that night. The little girl in the second car also claims she saw Englanders outside her home. I'm now thinking the entire operation might have been a sneak attack by a small group of American and British paratroopers who are now working their way back to Switzerland. I've shared my theory with Berlin."

"Interesting," the SS officer replied. He looked back toward the other two vehicles before adding, "I guess that would make some sense. Stay here while I radio this information to my superiors."

"That will be fine," Holsclaw calmly replied. "I'll go back and inform my men about the delay. Is that all right with you?"

"Go ahead."

The Dutchman exited his car and casually stretched before slowly strolling back to the vehicle Bryant and the others were using. He glanced toward the barricade before speaking in a low tone. "Did you hear?"

"Yes," Max replied.

"When they make that radio call, they'll find out we're not who we say we are. I have about a half-dozen grenades in my car. After I alert Olaf, I'm going to get back in my vehicle and get ready. When the lead officer steps back to my side, I'll shoot him, hit the gas, knock down the barricade and toss a grenade at the place where most of the men are standing. Have your guns ready and follow me through." He looked at his watch. "We have less than two hours to make the rendezvous, so this is our only choice. Anyone have any arguments?"

"We're with you," Meeker assured Holsclaw as she readied her weapon.

The Dutchman nodded and moved to the truck to update Olaf. A few moments later, he casually returned to his vehicle while the trio of adults in the second car prepared for trouble.

"Elga," Bryant whispered to the child. "I'm going to put you on the floorboard. No matter how much noise you hear and no matter how scared you are, you stay there. Do you understand?"

The sleepy child nodded as Bryant gently lowered her to the floor and covered her with a coat. Within seconds Elga was once again asleep.

"Oh, to be a child," Bryant observed.

"You got your gun ready?" Meeker asked.

"Yeah," Bryant assured her, "but I hope I don't have to use it. Imagine getting this close and running into a routine checkpoint. Our fortunes may be changing."

"Do Indians believe in luck?" Meeker asked.

"We believe there is a road we travel and getting from one place to another requires making good decisions. I believe luck is more about good decisions than having things happen in your favor."

Meeker nodded.

All eyes were now on the SS officer who was stepping away from the car likely containing the radio. Even as he said something to his men and pulled out his gun, Holsclaw didn't move.

Meeker grimly noted, "It appears our fate has changed. If someone gave me a fortune cookie right now, it would read, 'Dark clouds threaten your future.'"

In front of them, the Dutchman appeared completely unconcerned. Only when the SS officer was standing beside his door did Holsclaw pose the obvious question.

"Is there some problem?"

The German nodded. "There seem to be a great many things wrong. Get out of the car and give me your weapon."

The Dutchman answered with a single blast from his automatic and then hit the gas. A soldier standing just in front of the Mercedes was knocked at least six feet in the air as Holsclaw splintered the makeshift wooden barricade. As the rest of the checkpoint guards reached for their weapons, a grenade flew from the Dutchman's car and landed in their midst. At least four of them would never be surprised again.

Seizing upon the chaos, Max and Olaf gunned their vehicles and raced through the opening the Dutchman had created. Only two of the Germans were in position to fire. Neither of their rounds hit the team, but they did dig into the Mercedes driven by Max.

A hundred yards past the barricade, Holsclaw pulled to one side and waved the other vehicles by. With Max now leading the way, the trio of vehicles were about a mile away from the scene by the time the Germans could regroup and pursue.

Max punched the gas, but the car slowed down. "We've got trouble," he noted, shaking his head. "One of the rounds must have hit the petrol tank."

As the big phaeton drifted to a stop, Olaf and Holsclaw followed suit. While Meeker, gun drawn, exited the car and glanced back down the road, Bryant jumped out and looked forward. About one hundred feet ahead, the road cut through a pass. The hills on each side were steep, climbing up several hundred feet.

"Everyone pile into the truck," Holsclaw ordered. "I'll stay here and hold them off as long as I can."

"The truck can't outrun them," Bryant protested, "and one man won't stop them from catching up with us." She eyed Meeker. "You grab Elga and get her into that truck, then take her, the Nazi scientist, and the materials we've obtained back to England. Olaf, you drive them."

"I'm not leaving you," Meeker announced. "Besides, you said the truck couldn't outrun them. I'll die or be captured if I run."

"No, you'll make it," Bryant assured her. "I have an old Indian plan I'm sure the Germans don't know about. If everything goes well, I'll catch up with you and join you on the plane. Now, get going before the Germans get here. If you're not a mile down the road in the next two minutes, even my plan's not going to save us."

"But!"

"Go," Bryant snapped.

Meeker frowned, gathered up Elga, now frightened but silent, and climbed into the truck with Olaf. As they slowly pulled back onto the road, Bryant turned to the other men.

"How many grenades do we have?" she asked.

"Five," Holsclaw replied.

"Okay, we pile into your car and head into the pass. Once we're a hundred feet in, Hans and I will climb up the sides of the mountain. I'll take left and you take right. There's no shoulder in the pass and the road is barely two cars wide. We're going to lob grenades onto the Nazis from above, and when those cars explode, the road should be completely blocked. We'll meet Max at the car and then try to catch up with our truck. Any questions?"

No one replied.

"Then give me three of those grenades, and let's go."

In two minutes, they were deep enough into the pass to put the plan into action. In five more minutes, Bryant had climbed through brush and around trees until she was about two hundred feet above the road. On the other side of the road, Holsclaw found a spot about fifty feet below the woman's elevation. Now it was time to wait.

The radio call had surely confirmed they were not who they claimed to be, so there was no doubt the Nazis would come. Holsclaw's killing the commanding officer and several other men put an exclamation point on how dangerous the Dutchman and his party were, so this chase was likely being followed even in Berlin.

As she waited, Bryant was comforted by one thought. Elga was going to escape and get a second chance in life. Maybe there would be a family in the States who would step forward with the love she needed, and perhaps a doctor could diagnose and heal her medical issues. There were so many things worth living for and few worth dying for, but this was one of those few.

Looking down the road, she thought back on her own life. Perhaps it was time to greet the ancestors she'd lost so many years before. After all, she'd lived enough adventures for a dozen people. She had lost her soul and had recently rediscovered it. Her life had been like no other, and she was now getting tired of the strain it created.

Looking up to the clear sky, she whispered with pride, "My name is Morning Star."

The sound of several different engines echoing through the hillsides caused the hair on the back of her neck to stand on end. Thirty seconds later, she made out five vehicles coming down the road. The first three were cars, followed by a troop truck, with another car tailing behind, each about a hundred feet behind the other. The key was making sure they got the first two. That should be enough to block the road. Anything they torched after that would be gravy.

Squeezing the triggering lever, Bryant pulled out the first pin and waited. From her position, she figured the speed of the lead car and decided to aim about thirty feet in front of the Mercedes. That should allow the explosive to hit right on top of the target. Holsclaw knew to wait on her—she'd made that clear. If she got the lead vehicle, then he was to go after the next one. If she missed the car, his job was to take out that first one, and she would go after the next one as it pulled around the wreckage.

As the car entered the pass, Bryant silently counted to three and tossed her grenade. She heard it hit the car's hood then bounce backward before exploding. Pieces of metal flew in all directions. A steering wheel landed against a tree about fifty feet below her position. A second explosion, even larger than the first, hit as the gas tank detonated. The right half of the road was now blocked.

As Bryant reached down to grab another grenade, the second car slowed to a stop about fifty feet behind the burning wreckage. The driver froze in place for at least ten seconds before pulling the staff car to the left, easing by the burning debris. His caution spelled his doom. It was easy for Holsclaw to literally drop his grenade right on top of the vehicle. The fireball that followed rocked the entire pass.

For the moment, the road was blocked, but Bryant reasoned the Germans might still be able to clear a path when the fire stopped. Thus, she felt a need to stick around and inflict a touch more damage. The other three vehicles had pulled to a stop just inside the pass. Bryant grabbed her two grenades and, still hidden by the darkness and trees, jogged along the side of the hill until she was above the troop truck. Aiming at the vehicle's canvas top, she pulled the pin and lobbed the handheld bomb. Once again, her aim was true. The explosion caused the truck to jolt to its left, and then roll over onto its side, ejecting its human cargo. Now the road was blocked in two places. Seeing no reason to race back to the car with the other grenade, she tossed it at the next staff car. She missed by about five feet, but a second later Holsclaw's hit dead center.

With no need to check out the damage, Bryant raced along the wooded hill toward their parked car. She tripped in the brush twice before emerging from the woods. Bleeding from scratches on both arms and scrapes to her right knee, she still managed to sprint to the Mercedes. Max was already behind the wheel with the engine running. Bryant then looked toward the other hill. Thirty seconds later, the Dutchman, a rifle slung over his shoulder and panting like a steam locomotive, rushed from behind some trees and leaped in through the open front door.

As the car sped off, Holsclaw glanced at Bryant. "So, your people used that tactic?"

"Well, we didn't have grenades. We only had rocks and arrows, but it was still like shooting fish in a barrel."

The Dutchman grinned. "Get this crate moving, Max. Miss Bryant's got a plane to catch."

CHAPTER 21

Saturday, October 10, 1942
12:55 a.m.
Thirty miles from Berchtesgaden, Bavaria, Germany

Max pushed the Mercedes staff car to its limits as they roared along the mountain road toward the rendezvous point. Along the straightaways, the black car was nearing eighty. On the curves, Max rode the brakes, tossing Bryant from one side of the back seat to the other. No doubt, the driver was determined to get the woman to her appointment on time or die trying. She prayed for the former rather than the latter.

In truth, Bryant wouldn't have been concerned about catching the flight back to London if it weren't for the child. She was confident Meeker could handle everything needed to close this mission, and she had no fear of being trapped behind enemy lines for a bit longer. She knew that within a week or two, Holsclaw could find another way for her to get back to England. But she and Elga had bonded, and she had promised the child she would protect and stay with her. The child was fragile and sick. This was promise she must not break.

"I think we'll make it," the Dutchman assured his passenger. "Besides, knowing Helen, she'll force the pilot to hold the plane for you."

The C-47 would be sneaking back to England with no fighter escorts, so the window for take-off was small. Meeker would likely demand the crew to wait as long as they could, but even as overbearing and intimidating as she could sometimes be, there was a limit to how long they could hold the flight.

A few minutes before, Bryant had been ready to die; now she was anxious to live. She silently willed the driver to give the staff car everything it had.

Just as he had twenty or more times in the previous ten minutes, Max eased off the gas, turned the wheel, and hit the brakes as the Mercedes started another slide around a sharp curve. At that moment, everything that seemed so right turned upside down. A single light, seemingly in the middle of the road, was heading right for them, and there was nothing Max could do to avoid it.

"Motorcycle," Max yelled as he desperately yanked the steering wheel to the right.

In the glow of the headlights, Bryant saw the bike's driver throw his hands up in the air just before the staff car's bumper and right fender struck. A clanking of metal followed and then, as the Mercedes eased to a stop, the only sound was the car's idling motor.

Bryant was first out. As soon has her feet hit the ground, she raced toward the motorcycle, now resting along the side of the road. There was no possible way it would ever roll again. The front wheel was gone, the frame was twisted, and the ruptured gas tank leaked fuel. The driver, dressed in black leather and knee-high boots, was about twenty feet further up the road. He wasn't moving.

Holsclaw, flashlight in his hand, jogged up behind Bryant and shined his light at the victim. The beam quickly identified the man.

"He's an SS courier," the Dutchman explained. "I'm sure there's a satchel tied to the bike. He was likely delivering communications or reports."

Bryant nodded as she slowly closed the distance between herself and the unmoving victim. Thanks to the flashlight, she could see he was not dead, but seeing the way the body was twisted, he was not in good shape either. She knelt and leaned close. After gently placing a hand on the man's shoulder. she used her limited German to gain some information.

"How are you feeling?"

The courier opened his eyes. He immediately looked behind Bryant to Holsclaw and whispered, "I'm sorry, Oberfuhrer. I shouldn't have been in the middle of the road."

Bryant considered the irony of the man's apology. It was so like the German military. Even though the accident was as much their fault as the courier's, the junior officer still deferred to the man who outranked him. Or in this case, appeared to outrank him.

Holsclaw, playing his role as an Oberfuhrer, leaned forward and posed a question. "Where were you going and what materials were you carrying."

"I don't know what I was carrying," he explained, his voice labored. "The package was given to me, and I put it into the bag and locked it. I'm not allowed to know what I'm transporting."

"Where's the key?" Holsclaw asked.

"As you know," he whispered, "I don't have one. It can't be opened until I get to headquarters." He managed a breath before adding, "It must be important. An Englander gave it to me, and then I gave him a package filled with American dollars." He moaned and spit out a bit of blood before asking, "Will you see that it gets to Himmler?"

Bryant looked from the dying man to Holsclaw. As it was intended for Himmler, whatever was in the satchel had to be important. As she watched, the Dutchman hurried to the wrecked motorcycle and retrieved that bag tied over the rear fender. He was slinging it over his shoulder as the courier grabbed Bryant's hand, squeezed once, and then went limp.

"He's dead," she announced, placing the man's hand over his chest.

There was no time for prayers. They had to hide what had just happened and get back on the road.

Quickly moving toward the body, Holsclaw called to Max, "Drag the bike into the woods. I'll get the man."

While Holsclaw and Max moved the courier's body and the bike out of sight, Bryant jogged about twenty feet up the road, picked up the front wheel, and tossed it into the woods. A few moments later, the three returned to the car.

After the Mercedes was back on the road, the Dutchman handed Bryant the brown satchel, saying "Now, we really have to get you on the plane. If what's in this bag was important enough for Himmler to pay American dollars to a Brit, the Allies will want to see it."

"I wonder where the Brit came from?" Bryant asked.

"Who knows?" the Dutchman answered with a shrug.

Bryant nodded. Now there was reason beyond Elga that demanded she get to that C-47 before it left the ground. She patted the locked satchel. No matter what it took, she had to make that flight.

CHAPTER 22

Saturday, October 10, 1942
1:32 a.m.
Thirty-four miles from Berchtesgaden, Bavaria, Germany

Helen Meeker stared out the open door of the C-47 toward the road leading to the pasture used as a landing strip. She and Elga were on the plane, along with Van Holfman and the materials, but Teresa Bryant was nowhere in sight. Had the Nazis found them? Were they all dead? Her watch told her it was half an hour past time to leave. She had stalled the British pilot as long as she could. He'd promised her fifteen minutes, and she'd been given twice that amount.

The sound of small arms fire suddenly broke the silence. Where was it coming from? Her eyes scanned the horizon before fixing on a grove of trees. There, emerging from the woods, were a half-dozen German soldiers, likely a patrol that had accidentally stumbled upon their position. There could no longer be any doubts; the gig was up.

"Miss," the copilot called out, "do you see that?"

"Yes."

"We need to move before they get close enough to do any damage. I'm sorry about your other team member, but we can't wait any longer."

"Understood," she sadly agreed. "Can I leave the door open until we get into the air? I might be able to give us cover if they get close."

"I'll close it after we get wheels up," he yelled, "but don't get shot!"

As she looked around the door, more fire broke out, but this time it was coming from a different direction. Had another patrol spotted them? What she saw created more anxiety than facing another squadron. Olaf, driving the empty German truck that had been hidden in the woods, was spraying the Nazis with bursts from his pistol. Meeker understood Olaf was trying to buy time, but it was suicide for him to take on the unit alone. He should have stayed safely hidden in the woods.

As the goony bird's pilot fired up the left motor, the one-sided battle continued. No longer were the Germans directing their fire at the plane. Instead, they were now ducking back into the woods, no doubt wondering why in the world one of their own was shooting at them. And that must have been what prompted Olaf to act. Dressed as a German and driving a Nazi truck, his move was brilliant. Swinging the truck around, he headed for the road. He had bought them some time and was smart enough to know when to make an exit.

As the plane's second engine caught, Meeker followed Olaf's race for freedom. When he made it to the road, she hoped against hope that Bryant and the rest of the team would appear. Sadly, they didn't.

The Germans, still confused but no longer focused on

the truck, emerged once more from the woods and raced toward the C-47. Within a few seconds, the plane was being sprayed by gunfire. A couple of rounds flew through the door and bounced off an inside wall. After squeezing off four shots from her Colt, Meeker rushed back to where Elga sat on a bench. The noise had awakened her, and she cried out in fear. Sitting beside her, Meeker wrapped the child in her arms and whispered, "It's going to be all right. We're leaving this horrible world behind."

"Teresa," Elga whimpered. "I want Teresa."

"We all do," Meeker admitted as the plane started to move. She grabbed a belt and secured the child, then warned her in German, "Now you stay right here. I need to see what's going on."

The plane was now moving forward, its tires bouncing over the pasture's rough surface, forcing Meeker to grab onto slats screwed into the cabin's frame and slowly, hand over hand, work her way to the back. Even over the motor's roar, she could hear gunfire. Sneaking a glance around the edge of the entry, she spotted a familiar Mercedes emerge from the road and race onto the field. The team had survived! Boldly stepping into the open, she waved toward the car, then made her way to the cockpit.

"Our other rider's here," she yelled.

"Too much gunfire," he screamed back. "We have to take off."

Meeker glanced around the plane and noted a coiled rope tied to the wall. Rushing across the plane, she grabbed the end, tested the knot, then worked her way back to the door.

The C-47 was now picking up speed. Tossing the rope out, Meeker signaled for Max to drive toward the plane.

He must have understood because he gassed the sedan and pulled forward. Meeker grabbed the rope and showed it to Max. A few seconds later, as the "borrowed" staff car grew closer, Teresa Bryant opened a back door and, holding onto the window frame, crouched on the running board. With the wind fiercely blowing her dark hair, she remained in a kneeling position, hands locked on the front doorframe, as Max drew closer to the plane.

"What's he doing?" the pilot demanded.

"They're with the underground," Meeker yelled. "They're trying to complete this mission."

No longer fearing the gunfire that occasionally whistled over her head, Meeker made her way back to the rear of the plane, held the door with one hand and leaned out to wave her comrades closer. The car was now about fifty feet away, and the C-47 had just gained enough speed to begin to lift off the ground.

"Come on!" Meeker screamed.

Max, sensing it was now or never, willed another burst of speed from the sedan. With the plane now ten feet off the ground and rising fast, Bryant made a mad leap from the car and managed to grab the thick rope with one hand. Her added weight caused the plane to lose a bit of altitude, and as it dipped, her knees dragged along the pasture. Somehow, she managed to hold on and pull her other hand to the rope just as the plane regained its upward thrust.

"Hang on," Meeker screamed out an order she didn't need to give.

Secured by ropes against a wall at the back of the plane and surrounded by his research, Van Halpton shook his head. "You're one crazy woman."

As the plane climbed, Bryant, dangling fifteen feet below the door, was now being blown toward the tail and plane's fuselage by the rising air speed. Meeker attempted to pull the rope upward, but due to the bumpy ride combined with the plane's rising speed, she couldn't get enough traction to lift the rope more than a foot. As she struggled, Meeker, unable to grab onto anything but the rope, rolled across the cabin and through the door. Her fall was only stopped when Bryant grabbed the collar of her SS uniform. In panic, Meeker seized the rope just above Bryant's head.

Buffeted by the wind, their bodies now pushed up against each other. Bryant hollered, "Is this your idea of a rescue?"

"I just wanted to check how you were doing," Meeker yelled back.

"It's lovely out here. The only way to travel." Bryant, taking a deep breath, looked up at the plane's door and called, "Climb over my body and use my shoulders for knee rests. Then go hand over hand while hugging the rope with your knees. Your legs will give you a way to rest your arms. Go slow, but only release one hand at a time and try to block out the pain that you're going to feel in your shoulders."

Meeker nodded, then, hugging Bryant with her legs, she placed her right hand over her left, managing to move up a foot. The wind tore at her hair, causing her eyes to water, but she kept moving a few inches at a time. When her feet were on Bryant's shoulders, she took a deep breath and paused for a few seconds before pulling up four more inches.

Glancing down, she realized in the time it had taken her

to move eight feet, the plane had now climbed a couple of thousand feet. Looking up, she realized she still had another eight feet to go. She was about to push up another few inches when the copilot's face appeared in the door. Moments later, the navigator joined him. After assessing the situation, they stepped out of sight and began pulling on the rope. Now all the women had to do was hold on. In less than a minute, Meeker reached the bottom of the door. As the copilot held the rope, the navigator lifted her inside. Then, returning to the rope, they lifted eight more feet until Bryant grabbed the inside of the opening. She didn't wait for any help, but rather just rolled in.

The copilot shut and latched the door, then looked down at the two exhausted women lying on the plane's floor. "Welcome aboard, ladies. I hope you enjoy your flight."

Bryant somehow found the energy to roll over and drop a satchel from her shoulders. She then pushed up onto her knees and crawled over to Elga. When the child opened her arms, Bryant pulled herself up and accepted the hug.

From the other side of the plane, Van Halpton again shook his head and muttered, "Crazy women."

CHAPTER 23

Saturday, October 10, 1942
3:30 a.m.
Somewhere over Europe

Once the excitement of Bryant's unorthodox entry onto the C-47 was over and the women changed into flight suits, the droning of the plane's powerful motors quickly lulled Elga to sleep. On a bench often used by paratroopers as they waited to launch themselves into the air, the child slept with her head on Bryant's lap. Meeker smiled as she watched her friend gently rub the girl's back.

About ten feet from Meeker, Dr. Van Halpton sat, secured to the opposite bench. He was wide awake, and his face wore a bemused expression. His deep voice noted the irony of what he'd witnessed.

"So much for the superiority of German men."

"What do you mean?" Meeker asked.

"Your actions pretty much prove we have been clinging to a myth. I would guess you were a part of what happened at the mountain too."

"We were on that team," Meeker acknowledged. She

considered the mission that now seemed long ago and far away before solemnly adding, "In fact, I lost some friends there."

"As did I," Van Halpton added, speaking just loud enough to be heard.

She was sure he had lost some friends too but that was the price they paid for working slaves to death. At least at this moment, she felt little sympathy for him.

Van Halpton looked toward Bryant and studied her for a moment. "Where's she from?"

"If you're asking what country," Meeker replied, "she's a lot more American than I am. Her people roamed the United States long before Europeans got there."

"So, she's an Indian?"

"Yes."

"Another example of the fallacy of a master race."

Meeker grimly smiled. "From your tone, you sound like you don't believe in the master race."

He shrugged. "I'm a scientist, so I have to test everything before I believe it. In this case, the tests didn't match the propaganda."

"And you worked for Hitler anyway."

"You seem to think I sold my soul to the devil," he replied, "and it does look that way. But I've traveled all over the world. I have friends in the countries Germany is fighting. I'm no different than you. I see the Nazis for what they are."

Meeker couldn't believe what the man was suggesting. He was nothing like her. Maybe he didn't believe in the superiority of one race over another, but he still worked for forces that did. In a sense, if he didn't buy into what they were selling, he was even worse than those who bought the propaganda.

"Let's say what you just said is true." Meeker's contempt could be heard in every word. "If that's the case, the fact you knowingly sold out to evil makes you even worse than the men who are marching lockstep out of loyalty to their country."

"How long until we land in England?" he asked, deftly changing the subject.

Seeing no reason to push further, Meeker answered, "The pilot tells me we're taking a roundabout route where we're least likely to be detected by your air force, so we probably have another two hours."

"There are no direct flights in times of war," he agreed.

He was right. There were no direct routes anywhere now. War made travel a dangerous nightmare. But how could a man who was that guilty be so casual? How could he even look at himself in the mirror, much less face anyone else? Shouldn't the weight of the innocent dead be crushing him?

Oblivious to what Meeker was thinking, Van Halpton glanced toward Bryant and asked, "Who's the little girl?"

Bryant, who'd remained mute since take off, jumped in to explain. "She was a child your government kidnapped because she appeared to be the perfect ideal of the Aryan race."

He nodded, "Lebensborn, another Nazi myth that will in time be unmasked as a fraud." He studied the sleeping child for a few moments before asking, "But why did you take her? She was a liability to the mission. She was going to hold you back. She could have stopped everything you worked to accomplish."

Her voice cold, Bryant explained, "Because the SS was going to execute her. She seems to have not been so perfect after all."

Van Halpton's eyes narrowed into slits as he carefully studied the child. "What was her problem? Did she not measure up to their intelligence standards? Does she walk with a limp? Or is she blind or deaf? What was their excuse this time?"

"She has seizures."

He shook his head. "By the time the SS sends all those who are imperfect to the death house, there will be no one left."

Meeker wryly commented, "And you knew all this and worked for them."

The scientist shrugged before asking, "How did you find out about me? Most Germans don't even know who I am or what I do. My work has been kept under wraps to the point few outside Hitler's inner circle know my story."

"Hess," Meeker calmly replied. "He couldn't stop bragging about you."

"Crazy Rudolf," he chuckled. "I guess he still buys into everything Hitler says."

"He thinks he's a genius, the greatest man the world has ever known. God's gift to the universe."

"He would," Van Halpton answered.

"You might just be rooming with that guy," Bryant suggested.

He looked from Bryant and back to Meeker. "You want to know why I jumped at the chance to go with you when you left the radio facility?"

"That's easy to answer," Meeker replied. "You wanted to help us unload the files and equipment. You wanted to be with your work." As she spoke, her eyes went to materials about ten feet to her right.

"That's not really why," Van Halpton explained. "Yes, I wanted to go with you but not to set anything up. I ran out when I got to thinking about the footlockers you brought in."

"You guessed they were bombs?" Bryant asked, suddenly very interested.

"Yeah," he admitted, "and then everything made sense to me."

"Why didn't you just warn everyone?" Meeker demanded.

He paused a moment and studied the satchel Bryant had brought on board that was still where she dropped it.

"That must be important," Van Halpton suggested, "for you to not drop it as you clung to that rope."

Meeker, now curious, rose from her spot on the bench, retrieved the bag and retook her seat. Noting the latch was locked, she looked to her partner for an explanation.

"We ran into a SS courier," Bryant explained. "That's why I was late. He was taking the satchel to Himmler, so we felt the need to bring it along."

"What's in it?" Meeker asked.

"I have no idea, but the lock shouldn't be that hard to force."

"Why not cut through the leather?" Van Halpton proposed, "and just pull out whatever's in there?"

Meeker raised her eyebrows and smiled. "That doesn't sound very German."

"It's the easiest way," he noted. "You're not going to keep the bag anyway."

Nodding, Meeker set the satchel down and walked back

to where the crew and the women had tossed their duffle bags. She sorted through them until she found her own. Pulling out a knife, she jammed it into the leather and started sawing. After a bit of elbow grease, she managed to create a slit around a foot long. Reaching in, she pulled out a small cloth bag.

"That's all?" Bryant asked.

Meeker nodded as she untied a knot in the drawstring and looked in. She only knew *The Cat's Eye* from the file photos Roger Richards had shared aboard M.E. Wallace's yacht, but nevertheless, she was sure she was now looking at the real McCoy. Why did Himmler want a necklace worth only a few thousand dollars?

Meeker walked back to Bryant and tossed her the bag. She watched as her partner took out the jewelry and examined it.

From across the plane, Van Halpton exclaimed, "*The Cat's Eye*! Himmler told me last week at a party he had secured the necklace. Supposedly cost him more than a million American dollars."

Meeker glanced from the scientist to Bryant. None of this made any sense.

CHAPTER 24

Saturday, October 10, 1942
4:02 a.m.
Somewhere over Europe

Bryant took a second look at *The Cat's Eye*. There was no apparent reason for the jewel to be worth any more than what they'd been told on the yacht. Sure, Himmler loved to steal art, but why this piece? She held it up and looked at Van Halpton.

"Why, in the middle of a war, would Himmler want this junk?"

"It once belonged to Mata Hari," he explained. "Supposedly, the gem was given to her by a German general during the first war."

"That might be its history," Bryant observed, "but it's not an answer."

Van Halpton nodded, "I was told that an American had the necklace and Himmler wanted it back. As I told you a minute ago, he told me *The Cat's Eye* cost him a million dollars in gold plus transportation costs."

"So," Meeker noted, "Wallace wasn't lying. But why does it have such great value?"

"I don't know," their prisoner admitted, "but I will tell you this. Hitler sees price as no object when he buys something, but Himmler is different. He measures what something is worth and pays no more than that amount. If he said it was worth a million, it's worth that much or more."

Bryant again studied the necklace. This time she focused on details, but found nothing, not even engraving on the back. Her finger then traced around the large sapphire in the middle of the setting, the one that gave the piece its name. At the top, she felt a slight rise in the edge. As she worked her way around to the bottom, she discovered another rise. Using her thumb and forefinger, she pushed both ridges at the same time. The blue jade stone moved slightly upward. When she turned the pendant onto its side, two pieces of microfilm dropped into her palm.

She held up the microfilm. "Wallace had something he didn't tell us about."

"And we won't know what it is," Meeker added, "until we can look at those under a microscope. But obviously that film's worth a fortune."

As Bryant considered her chance meeting with the SS courier, her blood suddenly ran cold. After placing the microfilm back into the necklace and snapping it shut, she slipped it into the cloth pouch and passed it to Meeker. Then, with no explanation, she quickly moved to the back of the plane. With a confused Meeker looking on, Bryant began to go through the duffle bags.

The first one, with the name O'Hara stenciled on the outside, contained nothing out of the ordinary. The second belong to someone named Blair. As soon as she unzipped it, she smiled and returned to sit by Meeker. In an almost inaudible voice, she asked, "Who's Blair?"

"The navigator," Meeker replied.

"How long was the plane on the ground before you arrived?"

"I was told about two hours."

"When we get back to the base, have Blair arrested. He's the one who passed *The Cat's Eye* to the SS courier. I don't know how he managed, but there's enough American cash in his bag to buy a large home in Yorkshire."

"You sure?"

"Oh, yeah. But I think it'd be best not to let on until we're on the ground."

Bryant moved over to Elga. After gently placing the child's head onto her lap, she looked back to Van Halpton.

"Did you find something interesting?" he asked.

"Nothing that would concern you," Bryant replied.

"Can I ask the two of you another question?"

"Shoot," Meeker answered, "we've got nothing else to do for a while."

"How many people did you lose on your mission?"

"Four that we know of," Meeker replied. "I have no idea if the three who were fighting the patrol when we took off made it out alive or not. It could be seven, meaning only the two of us are left."

"Such a waste," he noted.

"We destroyed your facilities," Bryant pointed out, "and many of your top scientists were killed in the process."

He nodded. "But the work we were doing was a sham. You'll discover that when your scientists look at the files. I had full control over which ideas and plans were used. I always chose the ones that just *seemed* to be on the right track while rejecting those I knew had potential. Hitler was convinced the scientists I had chosen were brilliant, but they really were only men who believed I had all the answers. So, because they basically worshiped me, when they actually had a great idea I could convince them it wasn't."

"What are you saying?" Meeker demanded.

"I'm telling you we were no closer to splitting the atom than we were two years ago. I'm letting you know my radio guidance technology was as much Jules Verne fiction as German fact. Oh, yes, Hitler was very impressed by the way the bombs and rockets looked. He also saw the effects of radiation on the workers and dreamed of what it could do in American cities. On top of that, during his visits, he was fascinated by my television security system, so he kept funding my work. But all I was doing was diverting research money from areas where it could be far better spent. In truth, I was pulling the biggest con game of all time. You don't have to believe me, but I was on your side. I was working against the Nazis even while they thought I was working for them."

Bryant let the man's words sink in. If he was telling the truth, everything they'd done had been for nothing. Henry and Gail had died for a myth. Meeker would be crushed when that sank in.

"I see you're having problems believing what I've told you. The files will prove I'm telling the truth."

"Why did you turn on Hitler?" Bryant demanded.

"I was never really in his camp, but I also realized I was never going to get away from him either. So, I did what I could. At first, I slowed things down, and then, as my pitches caused Hitler to believe I was his top mind, I actually vetoed almost everything that might help the war effort."

"If that's true," Meeker suggested, "then why work so many Jews to their deaths. Why expose those men to radiation?"

"You can believe me or not—and if I were in your place I wouldn't believe me—but my control only went as far as the science and research. I had nothing to do with who built the facilities or how they were treated. In fact, I argued for using only military men. The SS overruled me in that matter." He frowned before adding, "And, at the time you showed up, I believed my string of luck was about to run out. I think a few in the SS close to Himmler were beginning to figure out I was hindering the war effort and not helping it."

"But even if all you say is true, so long as Hitler believed in you, then it would seem the SS couldn't touch you," Bryant argued.

Van Halpton smiled. "Himmler would have me shot and then blamed my death on the underground. That's how they handle those they suspect are not in their camp. So, without meaning to, you essentially saved my life."

Had this mission been for nothing? If what Bryant was hearing was correct, it sure seemed so. She walked over and stood directly in front of their prisoner.

"If they had killed you, what would have happened to the research? Who would have taken it over?"

"There are three or four they could have chosen," he explained.

"Would they have been able to clean up your roadblocks?" Meeker joined in. "Once they figured out your deceptions, could they have pushed forward in developing atomic weapons? Would they have been able to design and put into operation a radio guidance system for those weapons?"

He nodded, "In time, yes. They could go back through my research, see where I'd blocked good ideas and build on those. It might have taken a couple of years, but with the facility in the mountain and the equipment they had, many destructive weapons could have been developed." He paused and smiled. "But on the radio guidance system? I don't think the war will last long enough for that research to pay off. That technology will likely be used in the next world war."

"So, our mission wasn't for nothing," Bryant said. "What we destroyed might not have been doing much for the Nazi war effort now, but it could have been a game changer when the SS executed you and put the right people in charge."

"I guess you're right," Van Halpton agreed. He paused as if reconsidering his admission, then added, "Yes, in thinking about it, I have no doubt you are right."

The deaths of the team members were no easier to deal with, but the knowledge those they'd lost had given their lives for a purpose that would save thousands, perhaps even millions of lives helped put things into perspective. And the man they were bringing back might also prove a key to helping the Allies develop technology that could end the war a bit sooner. Perhaps, this would allow Meeker to sleep a bit better. At least, Bryant hoped so. And when they found out what was hidden in *The Cat's Eye,* maybe everything would come into even sharper focus.

PART THREE

CHAPTER 1

Thursday, October 15, 1942
10:15 a.m.
Meeker's Suite, 12th Floor, Lincoln Hotel, Chicago, Illinois

Helen Meeker, still exhausted, sat in her suite at the Lincoln Hotel and reviewed the latest news in *The Chicago Tribune*. The war reports were largely filtered so as to not demoralize those on the home front. Rather than spell out the details that Guam was under attack, the media shielded the sizable losses from the nation. But Meeker knew the whole unvarnished truth, and even if the best-case scenarios played out, likely another year would pass before the war could be turned in the Allies' favor. Right now, the United States was still playing defense, yet it could have been far worse. One of the pieces of microfilm Bryant had discovered hidden in *The Cat's Eye* listed the names of more than four hundred OSS operatives working behind lines in Europe. All those men and women, along with their underground teams, would likely have died if Max hadn't literally run into the SS motorcycle courier.

While Meeker could feel good about that, the mystery

of what was on the other part of the film confused her. The film recorded more than one hundred names, but none were affiliated with anyone in the US or British governments or any of the intelligence teams. So, who were those people and why did the Germans believe they were important enough to pay a million dollars in gold to M.E. Wallace?

Tossing the newspaper onto an end table, Meeker switched on the radio. After the console's tubes warmed, a disk jockey announced the new number one song in the nation: Kay Kaiser's "He Wears a Pair of Silver Wings." The piece opened with a soft piano accompanied by woodwinds before giving way to a tenor's lead vocal. Meeker listened closely to the lyrics, telling the story of a girl who was in love with a pilot. The song honestly focused on the sacrifice both were making for their country. As it was a romantic number, the music should have inspired a positive vibe, but Meeker noted a melancholy edge that others might miss. She knew the odds were against that pilot ever getting home to marry the young woman who was so proud of him. In her mind, the last, yet unwritten, verse would end with a visit to a grave.

Her mournful thoughts of a love destroyed by war were interrupted by a knock at her door. After switching off the radio, she smoothed her floral print dress and walked across the room. At the door was her friend and associate Dizzy Vance, wearing a snazzy brown fedora and matching suit. His hand-painted blue tie was perfectly knotted and his wingtips freshly shined. Gone was the sloppy drunk in the rumpled clothes who'd joined them a few months before. What a transformation!

"Sorry to bother you," he greeted. "You must still be catching up on your sleep."

Meeker stepped aside and pointed to a chair. "Sleep seems to reveal faces I don't want to see and voices I will never again hear, so any interruption is welcome. I know you know what I mean."

"Yeah," Vance replied with a slow, understanding nod, "I have those dreams more than I care to admit."

After Meeker sat on the couch and he grabbed a chair, Vance volunteered a bit of information. "Based on what I've been able to learn after interviewing Elga and doing some homework, she's the daughter of Sven and Anna Olson. Before the Nazis kidnapped her, she lived on a farm a few miles outside of Oslo. While the father was away on business, two men killed her mother and took the child. Our contacts in Oslo informed us Sven almost lost his mind. He couldn't deal with the double loss. A year later, he sold his farm and moved into town to work at a shoe factory. A few months after that, he moved again."

"So Elga has no mother. Where did her father go after he left Oslo?"

Vance looked at his notes. "Sven had a brother in Glasglow, so he spent some time there. In 1939, he moved to London. He appears to have started to get his life together at that point. He obtained a regular job at a dairy farm and within a year was managing it. He also met Lois Pennington, a widow with two children. They married on June 4, 1941. Lois was originally from Canada, so they moved to Ontario where Sven managed another dairy farm, owned by a man serving in the Canadian Army. When the owner, Private Noah Moon, was injured and sent back home, Sven was out of a job, so, in March 1942, he and his new family moved again. That's where I hit a dead end. I can't find anyone who can tell me where they moved."

"What about her family?"

"Her parents died in a car wreck about three months ago, and she was an only kid."

"We have to find the father," Meeker whispered, as much to herself as Vance.

"I'm working on that," he assured her. "If it's all right with you, I can leave for Ontario tonight and try to track down someone who went to school with Lois. They might have heard from her."

"Do whatever it takes," Meeker agreed. "He needs to know his daughter is alive and we have her. For his sake and hers, they must be reunited."

"I'll be on the first flight, and I'll call you the moment I find out anything." Vance paused before quietly adding, "She's a beautiful girl."

"Yeah," Meeker agreed, "and she bright, but she's also damaged. The garbage the Nazis taught her will not be easily erased. Knowing that she was deemed unfit to live has created scars as well. She has nightmares, and there are moments when she clams up and goes completely mute. Then there are the seizures. She had two in London and two more on the trip home. They seem to be coming more often. Teresa is afraid to leave her alone for a second."

"Can the doctors do anything about that?" Vance asked.

Meeker shook her head, "We don't know. We have an appointment to have her examined tomorrow. We'll learn more then."

"Were you able to find out when they started?" he quizzed.

"If Elga is correct, they began after one of the women who runs the home beat her. That was about five weeks ago."

The man sadly shook his head. Meeker knew what he was likely thinking. The same thought was renting space in her mind. But neither of them could punish a woman who was a half a world away.

"Have you told Teresa what you've found out?" Meeker asked.

"Not yet."

"I'll take care of that," she assured him. "You hit the road and track down her father."

Vance moved toward the door, then stopped and looked back at Meeker. "Have you considered he might not want a child who is damaged and has been brainwashed?"

"Yes," she quietly admitted, "and I'm praying that's not the case. She's already been rejected once because of her seizures. I couldn't stand for that to happen to her again."

Vance nodded and left. After the door shut, Meeker moved to the radio. When it warmed up, the sounds of Glen Miller's latest hit bounced from the ten-inch speaker. Even the upbeat tempo and lyrics of "I've Got a Gal in Kalamazoo" did nothing to lift her spirits.

CHAPTER 2

Friday, October 16, 1942
1:15 p.m.
Cook County Hospital, Chicago, Illinois

Bryant and Meeker had been stuck in the children's wing waiting room since nine a.m. Both had read every available magazine and newspaper and memorized the street scenes outside the third-floor windows. Parenting a sick child, even as a foster parent, was exhausting.

For the hundredth time on the cold and overcast autumn day, Meeker looked out the waiting room window, studying the Chicago streets. People were going about their routines, likely trying to forget the war raging in Europe and the Pacific. That wouldn't be hard, if you didn't read the newspapers or listen to the radio since, after all, America was a long way from the fighting.

"That black Oldsmobile has been parked in front of the pharmacy for three hours," Meeker observed. "That must be a big drug order to fill."

Bryant glanced at the spot and shook her head. "Is

waiting this long a good thing?" Her voice revealed her deep concern.

"For us or the people who own the Oldsmobile?" Meeker asked.

"You know what I mean."

Meeker continued to stare out the window. "We're dealing with the human brain. That's complicated stuff. We might just be here a lot longer." She took a breath before adding, "It could be a lot worse."

"How?" Bryant asked as she looked up at the clock.

"We could be dealing with your brain. You've built so many walls inside your head, they'd never get to the real problem."

Bryant didn't have time for a comeback.

"Miss Meeker, Miss Bryant," a young woman's voice called out.

"That's us," Helen volunteered as they turned to face the nurse. "I'm Meeker and that's Bryant."

"If you'll follow me, the doctor will see you now."

The nurse led the pair down a long hall to a flight of stairs leading to the second floor. Another extended trek along another hall was followed by a left turn that took them to a door reading "Chief of Neurology." The nurse knocked, and a baritone voice answered. Within seconds, the women were seated across the desk of a thin, gray-haired man with green eyes and sharply chiseled features.

"I'm Dr. Halaby," he announced. "I have been evaluating Elga."

Meeker glanced at Bryant. Apparently, her normally bold associate was too apprehensive to pose the question they both wanted answered, so it was up to Meeker to lead.

"I'm Helen Meeker; this is Teresa Bryant. We brought Elga in for tests, and we're both looking forward to hearing your report. At least, I hope we are."

Halaby grimly nodded. "As Elga speaks no English, I'm betting neither of you is actually related to her. Before I answer any of your questions, I need to know where the child comes from and why she is with you?"

"I'm afraid we can't tell you how Elga came to be with us," Meeker calmly explained.

The doctor frowned. "I have been faced with cases where children have been kidnapped. If you don't level with me, I'll have to call the FBI and ask them to investigate."

"Dr. Halaby," Meeker quietly replied, "I would love to tell you the truth, but doing so might place a lot of people in danger. Even contacting the FBI would create issues that go far beyond what you can imagine."

"You're not helping your case, Miss Meeker."

"Okay," she conceded, "I will tell you that my associate and I did kidnap Elga."

"What?" The stunned doctor gasped.

"We didn't kidnap her from her parents. Her mother is dead. We snatched her from the ones who did kidnap Elga seven years ago. We were forced to act because, if we hadn't, those who held the child were going to kill her simply because she was suffering seizures. She doesn't speak English because she has never been in an English-speaking country until a few days ago."

"I have to call the authorities!" he explained, reaching for the phone.

"Before you do ..." Meeker opened her purse and pulled out her Colt. She held it in her hands for a few seconds before setting the gun on the desk. "I have another suggestion."

Suddenly shocked, Halaby eyed the gun nervously. "Are you threatening me?"

"Not like you think," Meeker replied. She glanced at Bryant and added, "In truth, Teresa is far better at threatening than I am." Returning her gaze to the doctor, she continued, "I anticipated we might run into issues, so I have written a suggestion for you." She pulled a piece of paper from her purse and handed it to him, then returned her Colt to her purse.

"This is a long-distance telephone number," he noted.

"Also written there are the names you will need to ask for to get to the proper person. Now, if you will simply make the call, I believe you'll decide to give us the information about Elga."

Halaby glanced from Meeker to Bryant and back at the page. After taking a deep breath, he dialed the long-distance operator and gave her the number. He seemed stunned when a few moments later, someone answered his call. He looked back at the women and putting his hand over the phone's mouthpiece, whispered, "A woman just told me this was the White House."

"Just follow the directions," Meeker encouraged.

As was typical when dealing with the White House during wartime, four minutes passed as the doctor moved through three more people. Thoroughly confused, Dr. Halaby drummed his fingers on the desk as he waited for the final connection.

"Mr. President?" Halaby was stunned when the voice came on the line. "I'm Dr. Ralph Halaby at Cook County Hospital in Chicago. I apologize for bothering you, but a

Miss Meeker gave me this number. She and a Miss Bryant brought me a child and admitted they had kidnapped her. I have run some tests and examined her, but protocol prevents me from sharing any information with them. I was going to call the FBI, but ..."

Halaby's face suddenly went pale as he listened to the Commander in Chief. He nodded three times, then said, "I see. And yes, it was good to talk to you as well."

As he slowly placed the receiver back into its cradle, Halaby whispered, "That was the President."

"I'll take that paper," Meeker announced. After he handed the note to her, she restated her question. "What can you tell us, Doctor?"

Halaby, still in shock, opened a file and studied it for a moment before speaking.

"Elga's seizures are caused by blood that is slowly seeping from her brain and gathering in the back part of her skull." He then looked hard at the women and demanded, "How were you able have me speak to the President?"

"I've known him since I was a child," Meeker explained. "I still do some work for him. In fact, that's the reason we have Elga. Now, you were saying?"

He glanced back at the file and picked up where he'd left off. "A portion of the blood is being absorbed, but when the remainder fills the cavity to a certain point, pressure builds up and causes a seizure. She is suffering severe headaches in the hour or so before the seizures hit. When she's not active and in a resting mode, her body absorbs enough of the seeping blood to give her some peace."

Bryant finally spoke up. "What can be done?"

"Brain surgery," he replied bluntly.

It was Meeker's turn to be stunned. "What? You want to operate on the child's brain?"

"Many people are shocked, but brain surgery is the oldest of the surgical arts. The Romans even practiced it, but only in this century have we started to perfect the art. There's a good chance surgery will allow us to stop the child's bleeding and end her seizures."

"What are the odds?" Bryant demanded.

"About fifty-fifty," he admitted.

"Is that fifty-fifty you can fix it," Meeker asked, "or fifty-fifty she survives the surgery?"

"The latter," he admitted. He paused and rubbed his brow. "But if a seizure causes her to fall and strike her head, the bleeding will likely get worse. I'm sure that will happen at some point, so there is a one hundred percent chance she'll die without the surgery. In short, there's really no choice."

Meeker glanced at Bryant and then back at the doctor. "And the surgery will end the seizures?"

"That's the best-case scenario," Halaby admitted, "but there could be other damage I won't see until I operate. I can't make that promise any more than I can assure you she will live through the procedure. But, none of this is your choice or my choice right now."

"What do you mean?" Bryant was confused. "If the only way she has a chance at living is to have the operation, you have to do the surgery."

"Are you her legal guardian?" Halaby asked.

"No," Bryant admitted.

"That is the issue," the doctor explained. "Even the President can't give the okay for this operation. Before I can do the surgery, one of you has to become the legal guardian or the state will have to be made the legal guardian or you will have to produce the father. I believe you said the mother was dead."

"How long do we have?" Bryant asked.

"If we keep Elga here, we can likely control her seizures and prevent any more damage. We can keep her sedated enough that she will sleep more than usual. But in time, without the surgery, the bleeding will increase, leading to a myriad of problems that could kill her. So, the sooner the better."

Meeker nodded. "One of my men is currently tracking down her father. We believe he's in Canada. While we work on finding him, we'll also set in motion the legal machinery to allow the state to have guardianship until he is found. With my connections, we should take care of this issue by the middle of next week."

"I now have no doubt about your connections," Halaby admitted. "We'll keep Elga stable here at County until you get the right documentation." He smiled for the first time. "I'll bend some rules and let you see her now if you wish."

"Yes, we do," Bryant rose and eagerly headed for the door.

As Halaby stood, he offered another suggestion. "My wife's family is from Norway. I detected the child was trying to communicate in both German and Norwegian. Would it be all right if Rachel stayed with the child a few hours each day and perhaps a bit at night? That way Elga could voice any wishes she has and perhaps feel more secure."

"That would be wonderful!" Meeker replied. "And we'll be here whenever we're not working on closing out another case."

"You're investigators?" Halaby asked.

"Among other things," Meeker cryptically replied.

CHAPTER 3

Saturday, October 17, 1942
10:30 p.m.
The Wallace Estate, Wilmette, Illinois

"How did you enjoy your stay in jail?" Meeker asked M.E. Wallace as a police officer escorted the anxious man into his large home.

"Do you need anything from me?" the uniformed cop asked.

"No," Meeker assured him. "You can leave."

Wallace, dressed in a wrinkled white shirt and suit pants, looked frantically back to the door as his police escort walked out. He was obviously agitated, frowning and running his fingers through his gray hair.

"You look like you're ready to cry," Meeker observed.

"I was safe in jail. I'm a target now."

Meeker shrugged and walked out of the foyer and into the mansion's huge, ornate living room. Moving across the oriental rug, she dropped easily onto a thickly padded velvet loveseat before turning to watch Wallace follow. Apparently, he wasn't interested in resting, but he must have been very thirsty. He moved quickly to the bar and poured whiskey into a glass. He gulped it down, then followed with another.

"I'd go light on that stuff," Meeker suggested. "Whiskey will dull your wits, and you will need all your faculties. Who knows who'll be gunning for you? You might have to move really quickly, but you won't react well if your mind is clouded by the booze."

"You're setting me up to be murdered," he complained as he poured a third drink.

"Well, if you keep drinking, they won't have to embalm you when it happens," she quipped. Crossing her legs, she smoothed her olive-green skirt before adding, "You didn't play ball with us. You went to jail and clammed up. You now have a final chance to give us your contact in the organization. You level with me, and I'll see you're returned to a safe place."

"I don't know who it is," he whined. "I never met my contact in person. Elliot and the guy you people called Bauer are the only two I ever actually came face to face with. I wouldn't recognize anyone else if they walked into the house right now."

"And they might," Meeker said. "You failed to lock the front door when the cop left."

She smiled as Wallace put down his drink and hurried to the main entry. After turning the lock, he rushed to every window and door on the main floor to make sure they were secure as well. When he finally returned to the living room, he found Meeker grinning like a cat who had just swallowed a canary.

"What's so funny?"

"You are. You're scared to death."

"And I can't help you," he pleaded. "I really can't. I'd tell you all about the contact if I knew, but I really don't know."

"Oh, you're wrong." Meeker stood and walked over to the radio. After flipping the Zenith console on, she turned back to her nervous host. "You will help. Someone will show up to silence you, and that someone will be a link in the chain, leading me back to the person calling the shots."

"What good am I to you dead?" he demanded.

"Well, perhaps the bullet we dig out of you can be traced to the person I need to find. If that's the case, you'll be a lot of help to me."

The radio's tubes warmed up just in time for a local news reports. After a blurb on the battle at Guam and a commercial for Wrigley's Doublemint Gum, the announcer launched into a story of far more local significance.

> *M.E. Wallace, the Chicago industrialist who has been locked up in prison since October 1st, was released on bond today from the city jail. The police recently dropped Wallace off at his Wilmette estate. A local police official, who asked not to be named, told this reporter Wallace had shared information with the FBI needed in a case of high significance, which led to his release from confinement.*

Wallace hurried across the room and switched off the radio. He rubbed his hands together as if suddenly experiencing a chill, then, shaking his head, he ranted, "You mean this is all over the radio?"

Meeker casually strolled over to the coffee table and opened the evening newspaper. "It's all over the papers. In fact, I made sure the story was released about three hours before you got out, so everyone would know. It wouldn't surprise me if some of the friends you tried to blow up on your yacht might drop in. Mr. Wallace, you've made a lot of enemies."

After tossing the newspaper on the sofa, Meeker crossed the room to a table by a far wall. She reached into her purse, then looked back at her host. "I picked up something you might want back." She tossed a necklace his way. He didn't respond fast enough, and the piece fell at his feet.

"*The Cat's Eye*," he whispered.

"By the way, the fact you once again have that valuable piece of jewelry in your possession is in the newspaper story as well. We used your own story as to its value—a cool million. Who knows who might come visiting tonight?"

"You want me dead, don't you?"

"I need information in order to save lives and perhaps make sure this war ends a bit sooner. The only way I can get that information is to pin a target to your back."

He pointed toward a window, "But you're not stupid. You have this place surrounded by cops."

"I'm not stupid," she agreed, "but there are no cops out there. None of my people are out there either."

"What?" he announced. "How dumb can you be?"

"If this place were surrounded, the people I need to meet would stay away. This is a private party, and we are waiting on the guests to arrive."

"I would tell you if I knew," Wallace shot back. "I really would. And you need to call the cops. We can't be alone like this!"

"Because you can't tell me your contact, we have to play things this way."

"It's not fair," he whispered.

"You should have thought of that before you sold out."

"I had to have money," he argued.

"A lot of folks have chosen failure over treason. You knew the risk of a dark heart when you made the opposite choice. Now why don't you sit down and get comfortable? After all, waiting is pretty much all we have left to do."

"You're cold," he spat.

"I'm anything but," she replied. "I'll take risks all day long to save good people. Each person I'm forced to kill—even if they are in league with the devil—haunts me. I've been responsible for the deaths of scores of Nazis in the last few weeks, and I pity the pain their families are feeling. The Germans I've killed might have been serving evil, but I can rationalize their loyalty to their country. You sold out your country and even your Japanese wife who came to love America. If someone walks in trying to kill you, I'll do whatever I can to save your life, but if I fail, I won't mourn. In fact, if someone does stop your heart, I don't think I'll lose any sleep. Now why don't you grab a book and sit down. And while you do that, I'm going to unlock a few doors. We need to make this as easy possible."

Meeker left Wallace alone as she made her rounds. Not wanting to advertise too much carelessness, she only unlocked the outside kitchen door and a window in a first-floor bedroom. As she made her way back to the living room, she was shocked to hear voices. Reaching into her jacket pocket, she retrieved her gun and moved closer.

"I swear," Wallace protested, "I didn't tell them anything."

Peering through a crack between the hinges of the double doors leading into the living room, she saw a dark figure pointing a gun at Wallace. With the person's back turned, she had no idea of the person's identity, gender, or how he or she had gotten inside. She was certain no one had yet come through the two entrances she'd unlocked. She glanced toward the front door and saw it was slightly ajar, so either Wallace had opened the door or the intruder had a key. Either way, it didn't really matter. Now was the time to hear what the uninvited guest had to say and to try to use the stranger to get closer to the person in charge. She pulled out her Colt and turned her attention to the scene playing out in the living room.

"I can prove to you I'm still on your side," Wallace assured the visitor. Meeker leaned close to the door. "Give me a gun, and I'll take out Meeker. But if I do, you have to get me away from here, to someplace where no one will ever find me."

Meeker watched the industrialist reach into his pocket. Holding up *The Cat's Eye,* he promised. "We take care of Meeker, and I'll give you this. It's a win-win deal for you."

Meeker's goal was to get the person assigned for the hit without having to kill them, but the problem was complicated. If she barged into the living room, the person would turn and take aim, and she'd have to take them down. Perhaps a better way to orchestrate her little game was to play cat and mouse. By making some noise in another room, she'd force them come to her. Then perhaps, she'd only have to wound the shooter and not kill them.

As she turned to make her way to the study, she glimpsed something from the corner of her eye. An instant later, something came down hard on her head. Meeker's knees turned to rubber, then everything went black.

CHAPTER 4

Saturday, October 17, 1942
11:41 p.m.
The Wallace Estate, Wilmette, Illinois

The voices sounded as if they were filtered through a pool of water. The words reverberated and bounced around but didn't make sense. The pain pushed through Meeker's head like waves, from the top of her skull to her spine and down her back. As the droning in the background continued, she tried to make sense of the black void she'd somehow fallen into, but she could remember nothing.

As one minute became two and two limped into three, a story began to build and a bit of the darkness began to fade. She was back in the living room. Someone had placed her on a couch. Forcing her eyes open just enough to glimpse the foggy scene in front of her, she noted three men. She knew Wallace, but the pair he was arguing with were foreign to her. She'd never seen them, but as her hearing sharpened, their words served as a wake-up call to reality. They were talking about her.

"She'd didn't see us," the first stranger argued. "Let's just do our job and evaporate."

"Fine with me," the second agreed. "Let's take care of this joker and get out of here."

"Wait!" Wallace broke into the discussion. "You may have been sent here to kill me, but Meeker's the one they really want. If you let me kill her, I'll bet your boss will not only reward you, but he'll let me live and provide me a safe place to hide."

"Meeker was mentioned," the first man said. "Is that who this is?"

"Yeah," Wallace eagerly confirmed.

"Joe, we were told if we had a shot at her, we were to take it, but no one said anything about her death giving Wallace a pass. Why don't you make a call and see what we should do? We've got time. She's sleeping like a baby."

Closing her eyes, Meeker listened to Joe make a local call. When he was connected to his party, she paid careful attention to his words.

"No problem; we found a hidden key. Amazing that folks still hide those things under rocks by the front door. How stupid can they be? Anyway, Wallace is breathing because he wants to make a deal. The Meeker woman is here and out cold. Yeah, that's right, we have her, and she's on ice. Wallace wants to take her out in exchange for your people giving him a ticket out of town and to a hiding place." Joe listened for a few seconds before picking up the conversation. "Yeah, I got it." He then hung up.

"Okay, Wallace, she's going to pass the word on. We're supposed to wait for her to call us back. So just get comfortable."

Meeker heard footsteps coming her way and felt hands

on her shoulders. As she remained limp, she was shaken and then pulled up into a sitting position.

"You must have hit her hard," Joe noted.

"Is she still breathing? If not, our bonus is already on the table."

"No, she's breathing. Want to throw some water in her face?" He paused before adding, "And what a face it is. I've never been out with a doll like this before. She's Grade A from top to bottom."

"Yeah, but as dangerous as a box full of rattlesnakes. Quit dreaming about the merchandise because you're never going to get to sample it."

Joe didn't back off, but instead drew closer.

"Wonder what kind of perfume this is? I could get drunk just breathing this stuff."

He was close enough now she could smell his cheap, minty aftershave and the odor of cigar smoke. He reached forward and ran a rough hand over her cheek before tracing her lips. That same hand was drifting toward her chest when the phone rang. Stepping back, he made his way to the desk and answered.

"Joe." He waited for a few minutes before closing the short conversation. "I got it."

Meeker heard heavy footsteps come back in her direction, but this time they stopped about five feet short of the couch. She could also detect Wallace's nervous breathing to her right.

"Wallace," Joe began, "our contact went through the system and checked with the person who pulls the strings. You'll walk, and they'll hide you if you murder the dame with her own gun. Is it a deal?"

"How do I get away from here?" Wallace asked.

"We'll take you with us. But Hank and I get the necklace, and no one will ever know about that but us."

"What choice do I have?" Wallace answered, obviously anxious. He reached into his pocket and retrieved *The Cat's Eye*. "Give me the gun," he demanded.

Meeker opened her eyes just enough to size up the situation. There was one light on in the room and it was beside the couch where they'd propped her up. Joe had pulled her gun out of his pocket and was now emptying the bullets.

"What are you doing?" Wallace demanded.

"You'll only need one," he explained. As he finished, he handed the Colt to Wallace and smiled. "Hank, splash some water on her face. I want her to be looking at Wallace when he pulls the trigger. That'll be a good test of just how heartless he really is."

Hank set his thirty-eight on a table and left the room. As he waited, Wallace fidgeted with the weapon. He held it in his right hand but was having problems making it look natural.

Joe, his forty-five casually gripped in his left hand, grinned. "I don't think you're going to have the stomach for this. And if you don't take her out, we get to drop you right here in your house and walk away."

"I can do it," Wallace assured him.

"Okay, let's just get her awake." Joe glanced at Meeker and added, "I think maybe her clothes look a little tight. It might be better to loosen a few buttons. After all, it's no fun to get a present and leave it fully wrapped."

Slipping his gun back into his suit jacket, Joe moved closer to Meeker. As he reached for the top button of her dress, she flung her arm out, sent the lamp flying, then raised her knee hard, catching the stunned man in the place that was now doing his thinking. With the room bathed in darkness, Meeker scrambled over the arm of the couch and dashed to the entry. Finding the switch, she turned the light off in the foyer and raced back toward the study, but she didn't stop there. She kept running until she got to the back staircase. Slipping off her shoes, she used one to shatter the glass of a French door, then dropped her other pump and quietly made her way upstairs.

While the men on the first floor gathered their wits, she ran down the upstairs hall, turning out all the lights before arriving at the front stairs. She stopped and ran her hand over the large bump on her head while considering her options. The yard and grounds were well lit by security lamps, so she'd be a sitting duck if she went outside, but she didn't have much of a chance inside the house either. Once one of the hit men caught up with her and flipped on a light, she would be like a deer caught in a car's headlights. So, both inside the house and out, the lights were working against her.

She heard Joe yell, "She could have gone up the back stairs. Wallace, what's up there?"

"Six bedrooms and four baths. There's also a door leading to the attic steps."

"We know she's not armed. Hank, get up there and go room to room. I'll take Wallace, and we'll look in the back yard just in case she smashed this window to get out."

Meeker counted to ten before silently easing down the winding front staircase. After rushing across the foyer, she worked her way to the kitchen and began opening drawers. After securing the largest butcher knife she could find, she moved out the back to a small utility room.

One door led to a well-lit patio area, so she tried the other, which turned out to access the basement. Closing the door behind her, she climbed down the steep, wooden steps and took an inventory of the musty room that appeared to be used for storing unwanted furniture. The cellar also served as home to the coal furnace and a small woodworking area. On a far wall was the most beautiful thing she'd ever seen—a fuse box.

Quickly moving to the home's electrical command center, Meeker opened the metal cabinet. A dozen round fuses were waiting. Wasting no time, she began unscrewing them one by one. After she completed her mission, she took them, as well as the unopened boxes of new fuses she spotted on the shelf, and hid them under the cushion of a discarded chair. When she had unscrewed and hidden the last fuse, she felt confident that every light in the house was out. While the odds were still long, they'd swung a bit in her direction.

Feeling her way back up the stairs, she quietly waited just inside the door. She listened, and hearing no voices, she cracked the door open. The house was dark inside, but the outside lights were still on, most likely controlled by a fuse box in the garage.

Still clutching the butcher knife, she stole back into the kitchen. The outside landscape lights bathed the rooms in a strange mixture of shadows and dim light. She had explored the house while waiting for the police to bring Wallace. Now, she mentally retraced her earlier tour to ascertain the best and safest place to wage battle.

"What's going on?" Meeker recognized Hank's voice.

"She must have been to the fuse box," Wallace said.

"Fine," Joe said. "Wallace, lead me to wherever that

is. Hank, we know she's not upstairs, so you start going through the other rooms one by one until we get the lights back on."

Meeker quickly slipped into the foyer, then, as she heard footsteps growing closer, silently hurried to the study. She was sure Hank would soon be in the room, so she had to come up with a plan. There were no closets, but there was that large desk. Rolling the chair back, she slipped under the desk and pulled the chair into what would look like its normal resting spot. Kneeling, with the knife ready, she waited.

She heard Hank open the door and walk in. He'd found a flashlight, and he flashed the light in all directions as he slowly moved around the study. Peeking out, she observed him looking behind the curtains. His gun was in his right hand and the flashlight in his left. Next, he turned, concentrating his light on the desk. He set down the light on the desktop before pulling the chair back. As he reached for the light, Meeker made her move.

Thrusting upward, she plunged the knife between his legs, lifting until all ten inches of the blade were buried in the man. The shock and pain caused him to fall forward onto the desktop, knocking the flashlight to the floor. Rolling out, Meeker picked up the phone and brought the heavy receiver down onto Frank's right hand, causing him to lose his grip on his thirty-eight. Meeker immediately dropped the phone, picked up the gun and pushed the man to the floor. As he lay there groaning in pain, she retrieved the flashlight and switched it off.

"Help me," Hank screamed.

Knowing the man's cries would bring Joe, Meeker quickly moved out of the study. Her goal was to make it back to the room she knew best before Joe and Wallace came up from the basement. She heard them trudging up the stairs as she raced through the foyer and into the living room. As the house was still dark, and she had a gun, the odds were now about even.

Joe and Wallace emerged from the kitchen. The hit man was carrying the pair's only flashlight. By the time they got reached the study, Hank was no longer crying out for help; either he'd passed out or was dead from blood loss.

"Where is that she-devil?" Joe screamed.

"She's still in the house," Wallace answered, perceptibly frightened. "Maybe we just need to get away."

"Yeah," Joe agreed. "I was sent here to shoot you. I'll just do that and leave. No reason to take any more chances now."

Just as something heavy hit the floor in the study, Meeker heard footsteps racing down the hall. There was just enough light coming from outside to highlight Wallace, moving toward the front door. He'd managed to unlock the entry when Joe appeared, flashlight in hand.

"Both of you stop where you are," Meeker yelled.

Joe slid to a halt on the marble floor and turned toward the living room. Meeker was too deep in the shadows to be seen, and his sweep of the flashlight didn't catch her hiding behind the door. Yet, the beam made Joe an easy target. She aimed and pulled the trigger. The man gasped and tumbled forward.

"Joe," Meeker called out, "I got your knee that time; the next one won't be as forgiving or so low."

In the mix of shadow and light, she watched him let go of the flashlight. Not missing a beat, Wallace rushed over and picked it up.

"Drop the light," Meeker ordered. She then quickly added while noting the obvious, "You're making yourself a target."

Wallace didn't listen. A second later, Joe fired, dropping Wallace to the floor. Joe had been good to his word and fulfilled the obligations of his contract.

"We can stop this right now," Meeker suggested.

"I die now or I die a few months from now in the chair," Joe muttered as he struggled to his feet.

"Maybe not. You have information that might lead us to a person the government needs to stop."

"I've got nothing," he moaned as he tried to rise, using his one good leg.

He was determined; she had to give him that. He could barely stand, but he was still attempting to lift his gun. Meeker watched with almost detached interest as Joe wobbled over to a wall, trying to find the strength to pull up his gun from his side.

As Joe struggled, a car pulled up the drive and stopped in front of the door. For a moment, Joe's eyes moved to the entry. As the door swung open, he slid to his left to redirect his aim. Meeker locked her arm and fired again. This time the bullet pierced his hand, sending the gun flying.

Stepping into the room, the visitor picked up the flashlight, shining it first on the wounded Joe, then at Wallace, and finally toward the living room before asking. "Is that your Colt Wallace is holding?"

"Yeah," Meeker answered. "What time is it?"

"Almost one," Teresa Bryant replied.

"You're early."

"Actually, this room makes it look like I'm late. What happened to the lights?"

Meeker smiled grimly. "It's a long story." She switched on the flashlight she'd taken from Hank and moved into the foyer. "Get Joe's gun and then call the police and have them send an ambulance. There's another guy in the study. He might still be alive. I'll head back down to the basement and put the fuses back in."

"Where's the phone?"

"In the room I just left."

"Where are your shoes?"

"I'll explain that later."

Meeker stopped and retrieved her Colt, then calmly walked to the back of the house and down the stairs. After retrieving the fuses from under the cushion, she screwed them back into place. By the time she'd finished, there was no need for the flashlight. She made her way back to the living room.

"Did you get a hold of the cops?" Meeker asked.

"Yeah. They're on the way. You think that guy on the floor knows anything?"

"I'm sure he doesn't know the person behind this mess, but he can get us closer. He made a local call, so that should help us. I'm pretty sure I know the number. I counted how long each spin of the phone's dial took to return to the beginning position."

"I'm not impressed. I mastered that skill years ago."

"Then call Jupiter 5-4871 and see what you get."

Meeker watched as Bryant made the call and asked, "Is Mable there?" A second later she added, "Sorry I must have the wrong number." She glanced back at Meeker and explained, "It's Hefflin's Bar. The guy who answered is the janitor."

"We'll get Joe to tell us who he talked to there; then, we'll visit with the owner and staff."

A siren wailing in the distance assured Meeker that help was on the way. She smiled as she looked back at Bryant. "It might have been safer behind the lines in Germany."

CHAPTER 5

Sunday, October 18, 1942
5:05 a.m.
The Wallace Estate, Wilmette, Illinois

Still in her stocking feet, Meeker relaxed on the same couch where she was almost molested, watching Roger Richards and his crew conduct their investigation. After going through the house from top to bottom, Richards spent some time on the phone, speaking to police departments up and down the East Coast. He also sent a crew to grill the owner of the bar Joe had called. Finally, after they'd spent hours waiting, he approached the women with a spiral tablet filled with notes.

"So," Meeker asked, "what can you tell us about the two hoods who came to take out Wallace?"

"They're both East Coast thugs," he replied. "The guy you know as Joe is Joseph Denelli. No one has ever been able to pin much on him other than stealing a couple of cars when he was younger. For that, he spent two years in prison. Even though we can't prove it, we know he's a hired gun. Hank's last name is Smith. He and Joe have been a team for years. From their hotel reservations, we know they arrived in the city two days after we nabbed Wallace. Joe told us the down payment came from Washington DC. The cash was mailed to him in an envelope from the Hotel Royale, but as there's stationery in every room and in the lobby, that doesn't narrow it down much."

"It gives us a hotel," Meeker noted. "How is Joe?"

"You shattered his kneecap and pretty much destroyed his hand, but he'll live. So will Hank. He lost a lot of blood and will never be able to produce any offspring, but he's going to make it as well. Sadly, neither of them knows the top dog."

Bryant, who'd been quietly listening to the conversation, chimed in, "They wouldn't. Most modern hit men are hired by what I call the ladder method. One person goes through another and then another until they get to the bottom of the ladder. That would be Joe. The key is the money. If you're paying big bucks for a kill, you don't trust the ladder to get the money to the triggermen. You send that yourself. We will need to begin our work at the hotel."

"Still a long shot," the cop noted.

"It's likely the only one we have," Bryant explained. "After all, if the ladder method was used to employ Elliot and Wallace, then neither one of them will know much beyond a rung or two."

"I really can't give you much more," Richards said as he thumbed through his notes. He paused for a moment before adding, "Oh, I can tell you this. The contact at the bar was a waitress who started the day after we arrested Wallace. We checked her home address, and it was phony. The manager told us she quit last night, telling him she wouldn't be coming back."

"Just another rung on the ladder," Bryant quipped.

The cop closed his notes and strolled back into the foyer where Wallace's corpse was about to be put on a stretcher and taken to the morgue. Meeker walked to the living room door to observed the process.

Bryant joined Meeker at the entry. "Did you get more or less than you expected?"

"More. And yes, before you ask, it was worth the risk. Still I'm glad you came in when you did."

"Richards said you were crazy to try this alone. Even now, after you brought down Wallace's assassins, he still believes that."

Meeker rubbed the large knot on top of her head and nodded. "It was crazy but was the only way to find out if Wallace had any real information … and he didn't. But I got something out of Joe. Our target for the ring appears to be in DC, and they have no idea we know that. I'll send Dizzy and Napoleon to the Royale Hotel as soon as Dizzy finds Elga's father."

"Then he'll be packing his bags for Washington very soon," Bryant said.

Meeker turned her attention from the scene in the foyer to her partner. "You mean he's found Sven Olson?"

"He knows where he is. He's working in Detroit, building bombers for Ford. Dizzy will be meeting with him tomorrow."

"Did he tell Olson what it was all about?"

Bryant shook her head. "He didn't speak to Olson; he spoke to his wife. Olson was at work on the assembly line when Diz called. They set up a time to meet. Diz caught a train and will be there when Olson gets off work."

Meeker rubbed her head and winced before asking, "How do you think he'll take it?"

"I wonder if he'll even believe it," Bryant answered.

"We'll know much sooner than I figured. At the very least, even if he decides it's too painful to reconnect with Elga, he'll surely sign off on the surgery and allow us to find a guardian."

The ringing of the phone pulled both women's eyes to the desk. The cops were now outside, so answering fell to them.

"You or me?" Bryant asked.

"Why don't you grab it. My head's still pounding. It's probably for Richards anyway."

As Meeker looked on, Bryant answered the phone on the fourth ring. "Wallace residence."

Meeker watched as a perplexed look crossed Bryant's face. "No, there's no Joe here. Mr. Wallace isn't here either. May I take a message?"

Pulling the phone away from her ear. Bryant explained, "She hung up."

"Who was it?"

"I don't know, Helen. She didn't say, but I swear I've heard that voice before."

"Give me the phone." Meeker dialed the operator. When she heard a voice, she demanded, "I need to know where the call that just came to this number originated."

"We can't give out that information," the operator replied.

"Let me speak to your supervisor."

"Yes, ma'am."

Meeker waited for about a minute before a second woman's voice came on the line.

"I need to know the number of the person who just called this number."

"I'm sorry, we can't give out that information."

Meeker wasted no time. "Do you have your war code book with you?"

"Yes, ma'am."

"Look up A47D22X19."

Meeker waited. When the woman came back on the line, she was much more accommodating. "If it was a local call, I can't help you, but if the call was long-distance, I can at least give you the point of origin."

"Please check."

"You have an idea?" Bryant asked, as Meeker waited on a response.

"Just a hunch," Meeker replied.

Two minutes later, the supervisor obtained the needed information and hopped back on the line. "The call came from Washington DC."

"Do you have a location?" Meeker asked.

"The call came from a pay phone," the operator explained.

"Was the phone located in a business or in an outside booth?"

"The phone was located at the Royale Hotel."

Meeker smiled, raising her left eyebrow. This was even better than she had hoped for. "Operator, can you connect me with the hotel's front desk?"

"Just a second."

As the phone company employee went to work, Meeker brought Bryant up to speed. "The call originated from a payphone at Royale Hotel, the same location as the envelope containing Joe's down payment for taking out Wallace."

"Do we need to get there as fast as we can?" Bryant asked.

"No, I don't think so. If we lead the parade, we could spook the person we're trying to track down. We'll use Dizzy and Napoleon as the advance team since no one in DC knows them. Then we'll wait to see what they dig up."

Suddenly a man's voice filled the phone's receiver. "Royale Hotel."

"This is an information operator at the FBI," Meeker lied. "I need to ask you about your pay phones."

"We have a bank of eight of them," he replied.

"Can you see them from where you are?"

"Yes."

"Did you notice a woman using any of them over the past ten minutes?"

"Yes."

Meeker smiled. "Can you describe her?"

"Ma'am, at least a dozen women have used those phones as well as a dozen or more men. They line up from five in the morning until well past midnight. I can't remember what any of them look like. Ever since the war started, no one seems to sleep in this town."

"I understand," Meeker replied. "Thanks for your time."

"Nothing?" Bryant asked.

"No way for specific identification, but I just wonder how far up the ladder the person is."

"If she sent the money, she's at or near the top."

"Why would she call here?" Meeker mused.

"Maybe to check if Joe and Hank did their work. This

could have been a confirmation call because they hadn't called to let anyone know the job had been completed."

Meeker snapped her fingers as she recalled the phone conversation she'd overheard when Frank and Joe thought she was unconscious. "Yeah, she had to approve the change in plans where they agreed to let Wallace knock me off in exchange for spiriting him to a safe place."

The front door opened and Richards strolled in. The lanky cop called from the entry, "Hey, we're through here. Do you need anything else?"

Meeker strolled out to the foyer. "Have you told the press about this?"

"No," he admitted, "but they'll find out. After all, we fed them the story of Wallace getting out of jail and returning home."

"Can you just release the news Wallace was killed but give no details on Joe and Hank? I want whoever paid for this job to think they got away."

"Why?"

"Because she'll need to pay them for completing their work."

"Did you say she?" the cop asked.

"Yeah. And I don't need to be mentioned in this matter either. I'm too high profile and the ruse wouldn't work for long if I'm connected. You can take the credit for this job."

"What job?" Richards complained. "The way you described the situation, Wallace was nailed, and we didn't protect him. The DA will be all over me."

"Work a big deal for Joe," Meeker added, ignoring the spot she was placing the cop in, "Tell him he can serve only a few years at a work farm if he gives us all the information on how, where, and when he was going to get the back end of his payment."

"He's a hired gun," Richards argued. "He needs to pay for what's he's done."

"This is bigger than that," Meeker explained. "Joe might well lead us to the people who are in charge of an espionage ring as well as what a second piece of microfilm we found means. We need to know who they're working for—the Nazis or organized crime. If we can bring those folks down, we will save hundreds if not thousands of lives. The course and length of the war might even be changed."

The cop agreed. "Okay, if that much is at stake, I'll play the game. But I'm not sure the DA will want to go along."

"I'll let him talk to FDR. That should convince him."

"I'll put the squeeze on my buddies to keep their lips sealed," he said as he headed to the door."

"I've got another plum for you," Meeker announced. The grumbling cop stopped in his tracks. "The DA will owe you big time for this, as well as the FBI and the OSS. And you can have all the credit."

"What?"

"Follow me." She walked down the hall to the study, then through the French doors to the patio. When Richards and Bryant joined her, she pointed to a small painted wall at the end of the patio. "I can't tell you why—that's highly restricted information—but *The Cat's Eye* really was worth a cool million. I also can't tell you who paid off Wallace, but on many of those bricks in that wall, if you scratch off the paint, you'll find gold."

"What?" Richards asked.

"Take your knife and scrape off some paint," Meeker

suggested. She watched as the cop hurried over, pulled out his pocketknife and went to work. After he was convinced, he turned back to Meeker.

"How did you know?"

"Teresa and I were on another case where I discovered Wallace had been paid in gold for *The Cat's Eye*. I thought of your crime scene photos and remembered a new brick wall that didn't make any sense. Why create a short little wall when the patio and backyard had fallen into disrepair? Wallace put up the wall himself to disguise the payoff."

"You're amazing," Richards noted with genuine admiration.

"A woman often notices things that a man doesn't. Now, is Joe well enough to make some calls?"

"Yes," Richards said.

"Good. Have him stay in touch with those who are paying him off and find out the specifics of when that's going down."

"I'll do it." the cop promised.

"Let's get going, Teresa."

"You've forgotten something," Bryant pointed out.

"What?"

"Your shoes."

CHAPTER 6

Tuesday, October 20, 1942
10:39 a.m.
Cook County Hospital, Chicago, Illinois

Wearing a simple black dress, Helen Meeker leaned against the wall of the hospital's conference room, concern etched on her face. Dizzy Vance had called as soon as his train arrived in Chicago. The detective had convinced Sven Olson to make the trip from Detroit to the Windy City but under false pretenses. Olson thought he was coming to the city for a shot at a better job. He had no idea his daughter was alive. Vance was leaving the task to Meeker to deliver the shocking news.

With only half an hour to prepare to share information that was both miraculous and horrific, Meeker felt like a painter with a blank canvas. Where was the best place to start?

"Dizzy shouldn't have lied to Elga's father," Teresa Bryant complained. She sat in a chair next to the window on the far wall. Like Meeker, Bryant had chosen a simple dress for the occasion. Hers was red. She watched her friend take two more trips pacing back and forth across the room, before adding, "Diz should have told him and not dumped that on you."

Meeker shrugged. "I think he wanted to. He just couldn't find a way to share the good news, then follow with news that sounds very bleak. He couldn't simply tell Olson that Elga is alive. The problem is adding, 'And by the way, she was raised by Nazis and has a medical problem with a fifty percent chance of killing her.' And don't forget, Dizzy watched his daughter shot and killed when she was about the same age Elga was when she was kidnapped. So all of this has likely reopened some old wounds."

Meeker walked to the far end of the conference room, pulled the dark green curtain back and peered into a small observation room. On the other side of the wall. a nurse was playing with blonde-haired, blue-eyed Elga. The child had no idea she was being watched through a one-way glass. For all the world, she looked healthy, but there was a time bomb in her tiny head that could explode at any time.

Meeker wondered about Olson's personality. He was from a place she'd never been, and he had experienced traumas she couldn't imagine—traumas so horrific that he'd wandered from place to place, looking for peace. How had the events of seven years before and his experiences since then affected him? Had his wounds healed or were they still festering? And what of his new family? Had this created a roadblock that would prevent Olson from reclaiming his past and bringing her into his present?

When the conference room door swung open, Meeker took a deep breath and turned. This was the moment! But the man was not Sven Olson. He was Dr. Ralph Halaby. As she looked in Halaby's kind, green eyes, a sense of relief poured over her.

"Good morning, ladies," Halaby greeted. His reserved tone indicated he was as apprehensive about the upcoming meeting as Meeker.

"Good morning," Meeker answered for both. "I'm very, very glad you could be here. I don't think I could explain this by myself. Sven Olson is going to need all the knowledge he can get for this to soak in. Remember, he believes his child is dead. He hasn't seen her since she was five. He has no idea she's alive, and when he finds out, we have to drop the next bombshell."

"I appreciate the report you sent me," Halaby replied. "I still don't understand how you got out of Germany and why you were there, but the report helps me get a handle on the situation. This Lebensborn concept is unbelievable. I can't fathom it."

"We can't either," Bryant assured him. "Even after seeing the kids in person, I can't fully grasp the belief that maintaining and strengthening certain aspects of physical appearance has become the building block for an entire society."

Halaby nodded. "If you work with children like I do, you realize there is no look or no race that has the corner on creativity, love, athleticism, strength, or character. All the children I treat have the potential to impact the world and reshape tomorrow. This sounds trite, but I truly am grateful you saved this child from a fate I can't begin to imagine."

Meeker attempted to deflect the man's praise. "Why we were there had nothing to do with the little girl, so don't give us too much credit. When the war is over, I'll be happy to tell you the rest. For reasons of security, I just can't right now."

"But even if you were there to do something else, you stepped away from the mission when you discovered a need," he argued. "Most folks wouldn't have done that."

Meeker shook her head and looked from the doctor to Bryant. "Give Teresa the credit. She's the one who wouldn't leave Germany without Elga. Some members of our team thought the risk was too great, but she wouldn't let her go."

A knock pulled three anxious pairs of eyes back to the door. Dizzy Vance walked in with a tall, thin, blond-haired man. His handsome face was marked by the saddest eyes Meeker had ever seen. Vance pointed to the table, and Sven Olson sat down. The others quickly took places on each side and across from the guest. Once the introductions were completed, Meeker began to explain the situation.

"Mr. Olson, the reason Dizzy brought you here from Detroit has nothing to do with a job."

"What?" Olson asked. Stunned, he glared at Vance before declaring, "I was told this was an opportunity to give my family a better life. How could you lie to me? If this isn't about a job, then what's this all about?"

Olson had a thick accent, but his words still packed a punch. The emotions created by the false promise made Meeker's task much more complex.

"Please don't be upset," Meeker continued, trying to reassure Olson. "Mr. Vance had to get you here, but he was unsure how to tell you why."

"Am I in trouble?" Olson asked. "I have my papers. I came into the country legally. I can assure you of that."

"No," Meeker promised the man who was growing

more confused by the second, "you are not in trouble." She paused while trying to find a way to explain why Olson was sitting in a hospital conference room with four strangers. After a few awkward moments, she realized there were no magic words.

"Mr. Olson, let me apologize for bringing you here under false pretenses. But what I'm going to share is far more important than any job you can imagine. I can't go into details as to how or why, due to matters of national security ..." She looked into his green eyes and continued. "Miss Bryant and I have news about your daughter Elga."

"Elga is dead," he announced with no emotion. "She died a long time ago. Whatever news you have is unimportant."

"We know what happened at your farm on November 18, 1935," Meeker continued. "I can even tell you a bit more about the day Elga disappeared."

"I don't want to hear," Olson bluntly announced. "I don't want to know any more. I have spent my life not just trying to forget that day, but to forget Elga as well. It's too painful!"

Olson looked away from Meeker and turned his eyes to a painting of a nurse on the far wall. He wasn't seeing the picture because his expression showed him to be a long way from the room. Meeker allowed Olson to stay in whatever place his mind had taken him for several moments before again sharing the story he had to hear.

"On that November day, your daughter was kidnapped by members of the Nazi SS. They were taking children possessing what they considered the ideal Aryan features to Germany to create the next generation of the master race. They killed your wife when they grabbed your little girl. The Nazis struck not just one, but two horrible blows on that day."

"The SS?" he whispered, his eyes returning to Meeker.

"Yes. They had likely been watching your family for a long time. They waited until you were not there and moved in. They took Elga to Germany where she lived in a special home in Bavaria, a place where the Nazis kept and trained children with certain physical traits. Last week, Teresa and I found Elga just as the Germans were about to execute her."

"Execute a child?" he whispered in disbelief.

"Yes. Your daughter was beaten, causing bleeding in her brain that led to seizures. The Nazis only want perfect children in this program, so when Elga developed medical issues, she was scheduled for death. Miss Bryant and I, along with a team from the underground, prevented that from happening. We brought her back to the United States, and she is currently in this hospital."

Olson shook his head, too stunned to speak. As he attempted to make sense of what had to be the most unexpected news he'd ever heard, Meeker looked to Halaby.

"Mr. Olson," the doctor began, "your daughter needs surgery. We have a donor who will pay for the operation, so money is not a concern. The operation, if all goes well, should stop the seizures and restore her to perfect health. But it is brain surgery, and there are risks."

"Risks?" Olson asked.

"Yes," Halaby solemnly admitted, "but she will die otherwise. The surgery is her only option. And we need your permission, as her father, to perform the operation."

Olson shook his head. "Are you sure she's my daughter?"

Bryant leaned across the table toward the guest and softly explained, "Mr. Olson, she remembers you. She described your house to me. She talked about the love you showed her. She told me about a yellow cat, named Toby, that slept with her. She spoke of a brown cow, Molly, that she loved like a pet. The church you attended was small, made from logs, and there was a wooden cross on the back wall that she watched you shape in your workshop. She's not only your daughter, but despite all the years with the Nazis, she's never forgotten you."

"I can't believe it," he whispered.

Bryant got up and took the man's hand. "Come over here."

Olson followed Bryant as she led him to the window. She pulled back the curtains and pointed to the glass. "She can't see or hear us, but that is your daughter."

As if made of stone, he remained frozen in place, his eyes locked on a child reading a story with the nurse. As tears ran down his cheeks, he whispered "Elga," again and again.

A knock on the door pulled Meeker's now misty eyes away from Olson. Walking across the room, she opened the door and found Roger Richards standing on the other side.

"I need to speak with you for a moment," the cop said quietly. "I called your hotel, and Lancelot told me where to find you."

"Let's step out into the hall," Meeker suggested.

After the two found a quiet corner, Richards explained, "I got Joe Denelli on board. He figured the plea deal was too good to turn down. He made the call and here's the tale on how he's to get paid for knocking off Wallace. He's supposed to fly back to the East Coast. The money will be delivered by messenger to a safe house outside of DC on Sunday night. He gave me directions." The cop handed the information to Meeker. "Joe was supposed to go alone, but I'd already told him that was out. So, he explained that he'd been dinged up and was having a driver accompany him. He was supposed get his next assignment that night along with the payment. That should have told you who was orchestrating this game and who they wanted to knock over next. But sadly, it's all a moot point now."

"Why?" Meeker asked. "You can assign a driver and he can keep an eye on Joe."

"Denelli died an hour ago," Richards explained. "The doc is guessing he threw a blood clot that led to a stroke. There's no one to go to the meeting."

"Just when things were going right," Meeker muttered.

She was trying to come up with another plan when Vance emerged from the conference room. "Helen, if you don't need me for anything, I'd like to catch some sleep. The last few days have been long."

Meeker nodded.

"My goodness!" Richards exclaimed. "Does this guy work for you?"

"Yeah, he's one of my best."

"Look at him," the cop said. "He could be Joe's twin."

Meeker turned to study Vance. Richards was right. Dizzy was about the same height and build of the hit man. But the facial features were just enough off to close the door on the possibilities.

"Close but no cigar. They'd spot him."

Richards disagreed. "I don't think so. Joe told me he'd never met the contact. The guy had only seen a copy of his picture." The cop pulled a photo out and showed Meeker and Vance. "Helen, if your man wore his hat low and turned his coat collar up, he could pull off the act and get you a step closer to whoever is pulling the strings."

"I still think it's too big a risk."

"Up to you," Richards said, "but I'll keep Denelli's death quiet for a few days in case you change your mind." The cop turned and walked off.

"What's this all about?" Vance asked.

"It's the Wallace case I told you about on the phone. You know, the one that began on that yacht ride."

"The guy that got knocked off?" Vance asked. "The case where you were working alone again and almost got yourself killed?"

Meeker nodded. "The lead hit man is—or I should now say was—the guy you look like."

Vance smiled, "I could put on my acting chops and go get the money and possibly some information too."

"But the deal could go south." Meeker argued.

"Hey, I'll take Napoleon with me as the driver. If this is our best route to finding out who's behind this and whether they're connected to the Nazis, then it's worth the risk. And, looking at this photo, I can easily pull it off."

"I won't order you to do this," Meeker said firmly.

"But I can volunteer. And I am."

"I still don't like the odds."

"Helen, if they needed someone who looked like you to get some needed information, would you go?"

"That's not fair."

"I'm going."

"Only on one condition."

"What's that?"

"That Lancelot feels as strongly about this as you do. If Napoleon's not on board, it's no deal. You got that?"

"Yeah. But what if he says yes?"

Meeker handed Vance the address with the date and time before explaining, "If he says yes, then you'll have to get back east in the next couple of days. The pick up is only three days away. And you're supposed to get your next assignment from the messenger. That's far more important than the cash. In fact, the assignment's the only reason to go."

"So, we have your blessing?" Vance asked.

"You'll need to wear gloves. We need to see if we can get fingerprints off the package, the paper, and the money."

"Got it," Vance assured her. "And I'm sure Napoleon will be on board."

"We have to visit before you leave," Meeker warned as she pointed a finger into the man's face. "I want this planned in detail."

"We'll do that after I get some sleep and see if Nap is looking for a bit of adventure."

"Give this some real thought," Meeker warned.

"I will. Now why don't you get back to that meeting? Those folks need you a lot more than I do right now."

Meeker watched Vance stride happily down the hall before turning back to the door. He was right. At this point, Elga was the most important concern.

CHAPTER 7

Tuesday, October 20, 1942
11:17 a.m.
Cook County Hospital, Chicago, Illinois

As Helen Meeker reentered the conference room, Teresa Bryant looked and shrugged. Even after giving Sven Olson more details on what his daughter had endured and what she remembered about her life before the kidnapping, the man had surprisingly not asked to be taken to the room where Elga played. Bryant was stunned. She figured by this time Olson would have demanded to be allowed to hold his child in his arms and to smother her with kisses.

Leaning closer to the man who was staring at his child through the glass, she quietly prodded, "Sven, Elga has been gone a long time, but she's still your child. That much hasn't changed."

He nodded, attempting to put words to his thoughts. "I know, but so much else has happened."

"Don't worry," Bryant said. "Professionals can help her work through the issues brought on by being kidnapped.

Kids are resilient. They can overcome trauma much more easily than adults."

He turned to face her. "How do you know that?"

Solemnly, Bryant told him something she had never shared. "I saw my parents murdered."

Olson studied her expression for more than a minute before whispering, "Really?"

"Yes."

"Did you get over it?" he asked. "Have you put it behind you?"

"I've put it behind me," she assured him, "but I haven't forgotten."

"Can she forget what she's been through? Can Elga forget seeing her mother murdered? Can she forget, or put behind her, being in that place run by the Nazis?"

Olson's questions were pushing Bryant down a path she didn't want to take. She glanced from Olson back to Elga. The girl's future was far more important than the pain Bryant would experience by revealing her past.

"She will forget many things, but not all. You see, I was taken from my parents too. After they killed my mother and father, they dragged me away. I was crying and screaming. I was taken somewhere and held against my will, then educated in ways and about things that had nothing to do with my heritage. People tried to make me forget who I was and to mold me into something I was never intended to be. But despite all that, I survived, and I never lost my love for my parents or my memories of the life they gave me."

He considered her words before asking a question Bryant hadn't expected. "And if one of your parents had lived and you'd been returned to him, how would he have responded to the things you'd been taught?"

"I don't know," Bryant admitted. "I never got the chance to find out."

"Miss Bryant," Olson quietly replied, "this is more than what has happened to Elga. This is also what has happened to me. I no longer live on that farm, and I never want to go back there. When I returned that day and found Anna lying in her own blood, the scene created an image I cannot shake. Even though I ran away from where it happened, to this day what I saw visits my dreams. Elga's intelligence and beauty was what brought the Nazis to my door, and those things also caused my wife to be murdered. How can I erase that thought? How can I not blame the child for Anna's death?"

Bryant had no answer. Earlier, she'd believed only the child's mind carried deep scars, but now she knew the father's wounds might even be deeper and far more profound. And she wasn't sure how to address them.

"I heard what you both said," Meeker shared, as she approached. "I, too, can understand. Few of us escape tragedy. I know I haven't. My mother essentially died because my sister was kidnapped. In time, that killed my father too. I will admit the situation even shaped my life. But those events, as well as what happened to Teresa as a child, motivated us to risk our lives and the outcome of a very important mission to save your daughter."

"There is more," Olson replied. "I have a new wife now and she has two children I consider my own. Lois is pregnant, and we are looking forward to having our baby. Can I ask Lois to bring another child into our home, especially one who has been damaged?"

Damaged! Just hearing the word cut like a knife. Bryant had all she could do to keep from shaking the man and screaming in his face. Yet, rather than react as her heart demanded, she chose to quietly shock him.

"Elga's odds of surviving the operation are only fifty-fifty. It's even money you'll never have to hold that little girl or listen to her sing her favorite songs. All we ask is that you sign the papers allowing the surgery and sign a few more giving her to the state. Then you can just walk away."

"But …" he interrupted.

Bryant held up her hand, "No, let me finish. Down the road, you can choose to tell the two children you consider your own, as well as the child who is on the way, that you gave up another little girl because she was damaged."

"But …" Olson interrupted again.

"No," Bryant continued. "Elga has a medical issue, that's true, but you thinking that she's damaged makes you no better than those who kidnapped her and murdered your wife. If she's not perfect, then you don't want her. That's what it sounds like you're saying. Well, let me tell you something. Yes, Elga has a medical issue, but she's not damaged. You are. And unless you break down that wall around your heart, you'll never be the kind of father any child should have."

"Miss Bryant," he protested, "you don't know what you're saying."

"Yes," she quietly shot back, "I do. Now, I'm going to challenge you. Are you ready?"

Olson didn't reply.

"Dr. Halaby told us he could do this surgery in two days. That would be Thursday. For those forty-eight hours, I want you to be Elga's father again. She has stories about you that she's shared with us. She has memories that are as fresh now as they were when they were made. She's about to go through a surgery that might kill her, so she deserves to have the man she considers a hero to at least pretend he loves her. Can you just do that for two days?" Bryant's dark eyes sparkled and her nostrils flared. "Is that asking too much? If she does live and you want to walk away, then do it. We'll come up with some kind of lie that, I hope, will not break Elga's heart into so many pieces it can't be put back together again. In other words, we'll let you off the hook."

"But, I will see Anna's blood when I look at her."

Bryant replied, "If you're the man Elga believes you to be, the one she remembers from that farm in Norway, you'll look at your daughter and see all the love your wife had for her. You're only promised two days to treasure a life you thought you lost seven years ago. If I were you, I wouldn't pass up that gift."

She watched Olson as he turned back to look at the child on the other side of the glass. For several long minutes, he stoically observed Elga. Finally, he whispered, "I'd like to see her."

Dr. Halaby placed his hand on Olson's shoulder. "Follow me," he said.

As the men left the room, Meeker whispered, "I didn't know that about your parents."

"That was the day Morning Star quit shining," Bryant replied.

As the women looked on, the door to the other room opened and Olson, still hesitant, walked in. Amazingly, without a word being said, Elga knew who he was. The child ran toward her father, Instinctively, he opened his arms. As they hugged, Olson cried, but his eyes no longer looked sad.

"I now understand why you had to save that child," Meeker noted.

"And I now understand why you let me."

CHAPTER 8

Wednesday, October 21, 1942
9:41 a.m.
13th Floor, Lincoln Hotel, Chicago, Illinois

Meeker sat at the head of the conference table in the team's headquarters, looking at her three associates. Though Vance and Lancelot were eager and ready for the mission, she still had reservations. If this were a normal case, she would have passed, but this case involved the war and preventing vital information from falling into the wrong hands. They had to find, identify, and capture whoever was giving the orders, and this might be their only chance.

"I liked things better when we were dealing with Bauer," Meeker said. "I had a feel for what he wanted and how he'd respond. I'm completely in the dark now."

"He was crazy." Bryant got up from her seat and leaned on the conference table. "The person we're dealing with now is crafty. Crazy stands out; crafty does not."

"The voice on the phone …" Meeker inquired, "have you figured out where you heard her?"

"Not really," Bryant admitted, "but the other time I heard her wasn't over the phone. And fairly recently too. If I could just hear her once more."

"Odds are against that," Meeker said.

Vance was growing impatient. "We need to get moving. I have reservations on American Airlines. Nowadays, those aren't easy to come by."

Vance hadn't been tossed into real action for a while, and he was anxious to get moving. Dressed in a gabardine suit, white shirt and tie, and topped with a new fedora that could be pulled low over his brow, he was both anxious and ready. But was Meeker ready to send him?

"Diz, did you study Richards's notes on Joe?"

Like a school boy eager to prove his smarts, Vance rattled off facts. "Denelli was born in the Bronx in 1902. His father and mother were fresh off the boat from Italy. He gravitated to petty theft as a teen and by his twenties completed his first contract hit. He likes blondes, Irish whiskey, and jazz. He dresses nice and is detail-oriented. Anyone who calls him Joseph gets a smack in the kisser. He had a perfect record in taking folks out and leaving no clues … until he ran into you."

Meeker shrugged as she looked at Lancelot, dressed in a black suit, white shirt, black tie, and a cap that fit his cover as a hired driver. Though he'd been a part of their misadventure on the yacht, he appeared just as ready for action as Vance.

"You want me to give you my backstory?" Lancelot asked.

"I take it you've created one?"

"My name for this job is Jacob "Wheels" Gordon. Joe discovered me in Chicago. I was a driver for Big Jim

O'Toole until the big guy was taken down. When Joe found out I was as good with a gun as a car, he brought me onboard. My main draw is I'm a mute."

"That last part will take some real discipline." Bryant laughed.

"It fits what Denelli would want in a driver," Lancelot suggested.

"Okay." Meeker cut into the good-natured verbal sparring. "The safe house is on Route 301, about two miles north of Marlboro. The meeting is set for eleven at night. The meeting spot is a place where hoods hang out to cool off. There's not supposed to be anyone there except you two and the messenger."

"How do we recognize the house?" Vance asked.

"There will be a Lux Soap billboard on your left as you drive toward Marlboro. Just past that sign is a dirt road. You make a right there and go about a mile. On your right, you'll see a white, two-story house with a porch wrapping around the front and north sides. The name on the mailbox is Jones. You just park the car, walk up and knock. The messenger will be waiting. He'll hand you two envelopes. One will contain your money. There should be ten grand in the first. Joe always counted the dough on the spot, so you should too."

"Count the money," Vance muttered. "Got it!"

Meeker continued, "The second envelope will contain the name of your next target and a five-grand down payment. You will not pay any attention to the name, but you will count the money." She paused to emphasize what she considered the most vital part of this mission. "You both must wear dress gloves. I want to see if we can pull fingerprints off the envelopes, the instructions for your next hit and the money. Make sure you don't forget that."

"I've already purchased the gloves for both of us," Vance assured her. "Anything else?"

"Be careful. And when you finish, get to your hotel and call us. No matter how late, I'll be waiting by the phone. Once you've checked in, get back here as quickly as you can so we can use what you gathered to lead us to the person calling the shots."

"Literally calling the shots," Bryant added.

"Got it," Vance announced. "If you have nothing else, we need to get going."

"Be careful," Meeker warned again.

"Always am," Vance assured her, "and on this run, I've got a great guy watching my back."

On paper, this was simple; the risk was much lower than anything that had been attempted in Germany. Yet, for some reason, Meeker was worried.

CHAPTER 9

Thursday, October 22, 1942
11:17 a.m.
Cook County Hospital, Chicago, Illinois

Elga had been in surgery for two hours. During that time, Bryant and Meeker, along with Sven Olson and his wife, Lois, who had taken a train from Detroit, waited for news in a small room near the fifth-floor surgical unit.

As she stared at the wall clock on the far side of the sterile, fifteen-by-fifteen-foot room, Helen Meeker assessed how she'd arrived at this place and time.

"One life for at least four," she thought, not realizing she'd spoken the words out loud.

"What do you mean?" Teresa Bryant asked.

"Isn't there a pop machine down the hallway?" Meeker asked, ignoring the question.

"Yes."

"Why don't we get a Coke?"

With Meeker leading the way, the women bought two nickel soft drinks, then found a deserted spot in a different waiting area. Once they were seated, Meeker began to explain the cryptic meaning of her verbalized thought.

"We lost at least four people—Henry, Gail, and two of Hans's men. For all we know, we might have lost the rest of the team as well. At the very least, four folks died, possibly seven, and we came back with one child. If she dies, what was it really worth?"

"Van Halpton is talking." Bryant began a list. "We set back Nazi research for a long time too. And the Nazis still don't have the names of our agents. Who knows how many lives that saved."

"Yeah, but if we hadn't stepped in and saved Elga ..." Meeker paused and thought of the chaotic scene when the C-47 took off. "I wish I knew if Hans, Max, and Olaf are alive. No one has heard from them since that day." She took another sip of Coke before turning to her partner and friend. "Shouldn't we have put the war effort ahead of everything else? In that sense, didn't we fail? Hans and his men are likely dead. They probably died saving us, and they wouldn't have had to if we hadn't saved Elga. How many more lives would Holsclaw and his team have saved over the next few years?"

"No one can answer that, Helen, so let me ask you this. How do you judge the value of one life as opposed to another? Is the Army private fighting on some remote island in the Pacific of more value than you, me, or even the President? It often seems that war is all about using those who have nothing as fodder to protect those who have everything. But I think the fodder is still the most important part of a society, both in times of war or peace. A nation is defined not by how much we respect the wealthy, but how much we respect the poor."

Meeker shook her head, "That's the way it's supposed to be, but …"

"In Germany, it's not that way at all," Bryant continued. "In the United States, at least in principle, I think it really is that way. I believe most of us don't look at the lives of the rich and powerful as being any more essential than those who have nothing. You once told me that FDR's first question about any legislation is, 'Will this help the guy who drives the truck or picks the crops?'"

Bryant paused to finish her Coke and set it aside. "I've given a lot of thought to what I've witnessed in my life, and I've come to this conclusion. I've told you this before, but it's worth repeating. War is not as much about being on the side that is morally perfect as it is about making sure you aren't fighting for the side that is the most immoral. What we saw in the mountain, the way the Nazis used and murdered those people they called subhuman—we don't see that here in our country. In the minds of those in charge in that mountain, the Jews, Gypsies, and other ethnic groups have no value at all. Those same people are also murdering innocent children because they aren't perfect. That's why we saved Elga. That says all I need to know about why it's important for us to keep doing what we are doing. So yes, even if she dies on the operating table, we made the right decision."

"We didn't save the slaves in the mountain," Meeker pointed out.

"We would have if we could have," Bryant argued. "You can't save everyone, but you have to save the ones you can. When my parents were murdered, those who killed them were going to kill me too. A soldier stepped in and stopped the men pointing their guns at me. In doing so, he disobeyed orders to wipe out all the savages. Besides me, he saved a dozen other children. He gave us to a missionary. I later found out that man was court-marshaled for leaving any witnesses behind, and he was hung. Was saving me and few other Indian kids worth it? He thought so. His actions gave me a bit of hope that not all white people were servants of the devil."

Once again, Meeker was stunned by the scope and depth of Bryant's experiences. "How many layers are there to your life?"

"More than you'll ever guess. But, here is the point I want you to know. In the mountain and at the Lebensborn house, we confronted the devil and saved those we could. No, we didn't do all we wanted to do, but at least we did something. Life is about doing something when we are given the opportunity."

Meeker nodded. Setting her empty bottle to one side, she suggested, "We need to get back."

As she rose, Bryant added, "You started this by asking whether four lives lost equal one life saved. In life, things don't add up like they do in math. Trying to make them balance is a formula for frustration."

"I think I liked you better when you talked less. The more you talk, the dumber and more selfish I feel."

Before Bryant could respond, Dr. Halaby, still wearing his surgical gown, his mask hanging around his neck, stepped into the hall. He waited for Meeker and Bryant to join the Olsons before speaking.

"The surgery went as we expected, and I'm very optimistic. We were able to stop the bleeding, and it shouldn't recur. I'd like to keep her here a week to make sure there is no infection and that we have eliminated the seizures. She's not going to be conscious for a while but Mr. Olson, if you'd like, you can sit by her bed and wait."

"Can my wife come as well?" Olson asked.

"Absolutely. I'll send a nurse down to fetch you when we get Elga into her room."

Showing fatigue mixed with relief, Halaby headed to his office. As he left, Lois Olson turned to Bryant.

"Thank you for saving *our* daughter. I think in doing so you might have saved Sven too. In the past few days, I've begun to know him in ways I don't think I ever would have without Elga coming back into his life. He talked about his past for the first time. He cried some, but he found memories that made him smile and laugh too."

"We did the right thing," Bryant replied, "yet doing the right thing doesn't erase all the wrongs that were done to Sven and Elga."

"But," Lois said, "doing the right thing does make the wrongs easier to handle. Hitler's war machine killed my first husband just like it killed Sven's first wife, but now we have been given back something unexpected." She smiled before softly adding, "If our baby is a girl, she will be named after you."

A nurse appeared and motioned for Sven and Lois to follow. Only after they were out of earshot did Meeker tease, "I wonder which of your names they will use?"

Bryant grinned but didn't reply.

CHAPTER 10

Saturday, October 24, 1942
11:03 p.m.
A farmhouse outside of Marlboro, Maryland

As Lancelot pulled up the drive, Vance eyed the farmhouse from the back seat of the three-year-old Buick. The modest home was as Meeker described with the most impressive feature being the porch on two sides of the house.

"What do you think?" Lancelot asked. "This type of thing is kind of new to me."

Vance took in the whole picture. The house was large enough to hold a big family and likely had been constructed for just that purpose. There were three outbuildings; a barn, a structure that looked like a hen house, and a single car garage. A 1935 Ford sedan was parked in the garage. A swing and two rocking chairs were the only furniture on the porch, just three steps up from the yard. To his right, a child's swing hung from an oak tree. Shades were drawn tight, allowing not a single opportunity to peek inside. For a house so far off the main road and away from any neighbors, that seemed unusual.

"What do you say, Diz?" Lancelot asked again, growing impatient.

"I think the clouds work to our advantage." Vance pulled up the collar of his trench coat and adjusted the fedora so the front brim all but covered his eyes. As he pulled his gloves from his pocket and slipped them on, he went over his mental checklist. The most important thing, a well-known element of Joe's personality, was to count the money. Failure to do that could make or break the deal.

Lancelot looked back toward his partner and asked again, "Are you ready to do this?"

"Put your gloves on," Vance ordered, "then come back and open the door for me. This guy has to buy that you're my driver. And don't forget, you're a mute."

Lancelot just nodded. After putting on his gloves, he strolled deliberately around the front of the car and opened the huge car's back passenger door. Vance stepped out, shrugged his shoulders and straightened his coat. Keeping his head down, he led the way to the house, climbed the three steps to the porch and knocked on the front door. A thin, balding man, wearing bib overalls and a flannel shirt, pulled back a shade and studied his two guests. Seemingly satisfied, he unlocked and opened the door.

"Denelli?" The messenger's voice was deep and gravelly, like someone who had smoked for decades.

Vance studied his host before asking, "Have we met? You look familiar."

"No," the man assured him. "I know who you are. I've

seen your picture, but we've never met." His eyes trailed from Vance's face to his hands. "Why the gloves?"

"I spent a bit of time in jail when I was younger, so there is a record of my prints. I don't plan on the FBI ever getting another chance to view them."

"I heard you were smart," the man replied. He studied Lancelot, then said, "The newspapers didn't say how Wallace died."

"Does it matter?" Vance asked.

"No, but I'm curious."

"He was shot. Took only one bullet."

"And the weapon?"

"Do you think a man who doesn't leave fingerprints would use the same gun over and over again? You gotta give me more credit than that. If you want the gun, you'll need to get a diving suit and jump into Lake Michigan. Now where's the money? I was raised in the city and being out here in the woods gives me the spooks."

The messenger reached into his back pocket and fished out two envelopes. One he immediately handed to Vance. The other he held onto.

Vance retrieved a knife from his pocket and carefully opened the blade, slitting the envelope's flap. When he finished, he gave the knife to Lancelot, saying, "Hang onto it. I've got another one coming."

Vance peeked into the opened envelope before looking back to their host. "Not much wattage in that porch bulb," he observed.

"It should be enough."

Vance nodded and pulled out the cash. After carefully slipping the envelope into his pocket, he counted the thousand-dollar bills. When he finished, he glared at the messenger and growled, "It's a grand short!"

"I should get a cut," the messenger replied.

Vance stepped forward and grabbed the man by his shirt collar. As he pulled him closer, he threatened, "Give me the grand, or I might be forced to give you something you don't want—a funeral!"

"But …"

"No buts. You get paid to do what you do, but I'm not the one who pays you. Fish into your pocket and give the grand to my driver. That's his cut you're trying to steal."

The man briefly considered his options before reaching into a front pocket and retrieving the bill. Never taking his eyes off Vance, he handed the grand note to Lancelot.

"Now, I think you have something else for me. And if it's not all there, I'll be leaving here with one of your fingers. This knife is sharp enough to slice right through your pinkie."

"It's all here," the man assured Vance, pushing the second envelope forward, then quickly hiding his hands in his pants pockets.

Lancelot handed Vance the knife, and he cut the flap. After pulling out and counting the five bills, he retrieved the folded paper and stuck it and the empty envelope into his pocket.

"Aren't you going to read who your next target is?" the surprised messenger asked.

"Is it you?" Vance asked.

"No."

"Then I'll worry about it later. Now I think it's time we get back to the city. Nice doing business with you, but if you ever try to skim anything off the top again, I'll kill you."

Vance didn't have time to see if his warning made much of an impact. In the distance, he heard the sound of a car coming down the road. The detective instinctively pulled his gun from his coat and turned. For the first time, Vance was on edge.

"There's nothing to worry about," the messenger assured him. "It's just a torpedo coming in from New York to cool off for a few days."

Vance and Napoleon watched from the porch as a dark-colored Cadillac pulled into the drive, easing past the Buick. A big man in a dark suit stepped out.

"Hey, Benny," the messenger called out.

"Who's the company?" the stranger demanded.

"Denelli and his driver. They're here for a payoff."

The visitor shook his head as he pulled out his gun. "That ain't Joe." Without warning he fired two rounds. The first flew by Lancelot's ear, while the second caught Vance in the chest. Surprisingly, Vance didn't fall, but rather raised his gun and squeezed three times. All three shots drove into Benny's torso, driving him back against his car before he slid to the ground.

"Let's go," Vance growled.

With Lancelot leading the way, the pair climbed into the Buick. Within twenty seconds, the car was out of the drive and speeding down the country road. It had almost gone as planned.

CHAPTER 11

Sunday, October 25, 1942
2:11 a.m.
Helen Meeker's Room, 12th Floor, Lincoln Hotel, Chicago, Illinois

As Dinah Shore's version of "Blues in the Night" played on the radio, Helen Meeker checked her watch for the ninth time in ten minutes. She grew more concerned with each tick. At this point, she regretted not learning to drink coffee because she sensed the need for a shot of caffeine. Rubbing the sleep from her eyes, she got up and walked over to the radio. Just as she turned it off, her phone rang.

"Meeker," she answered, praying this was the call she needed and hoping it would bring only good news.

"Helen, it's Napoleon." The man paused for a moment before spilling the story. "It went south. I should have done something, but I just didn't anticipate …"

"You didn't anticipate what?" Meeker interrupted.

"It all went just like it was supposed to," he continued. "Dizzy played it perfectly. The messenger bought everything he said and gave us both envelopes. We were about to leave when another car drove up. The guy who got out evidently knew Denelli. Before we could react, the guy, his name was Benny, shot twice. One went past my head; the other caught Dizzy. I was digging for my gun when Diz squeezed off three rounds and took care of the shooter. We then made it to the car and drove off."

"How bad is Dizzy hurt?" Meeker asked. "Did he just get winged or is it more serious?"

"He died about five minutes after we left," Lancelot explained, his voice filled with regret. "He got it in the chest."

"No," Meeker whispered.

"He told me to assure you we got all we needed. The last thing he did was have me turn on the dome light so he could read the name of the person Joe was supposed to hit next. Helen, it's you!"

The news didn't faze Meeker. She'd been a target for months. But losing another member of her team drove a stake through her heart. Once again, she'd become the grim reaper. It seemed that knowing her was the same as meeting death. As she mentally flogged herself, she leaned her mouth against the phone's receiver.

"Where's Dizzy?"

"I didn't know what to do with him," Lancelot explained. "He's still in the car. I covered him with a blanket."

"Okay, Napoleon." With tears streaming down her face, she switched to professional mode." My sister's number in DC is Jupiter 3-4444. Have you got that?"

"Jupiter 3-4444."

"Call her right now. Tell Alison what's going on and that we need to make sure this stays quiet. The people she sends will keep you out of this and take care of the body. Do you understand?"

"Jupiter 3-4444."

"Yes, and when the Secret Service takes over, explain where the safe house is and that Dizzy was brought down by a thug he killed. Don't tell them about the money or that I'm next on the list. I want them to find the man they call "The Messenger" and put him in the deep freeze. You got that?"

"Yeah."

"Don't touch those envelopes, the note, or the cash. We need to test those for fingerprints. We don't need anyone but us involved in that part of this operation."

"Okay," he replied.

"Pull yourself together and make the call. Try to get back here as soon as you can."

"Helen, I watched him die. I watched Dizzy die."

"I know," she quietly replied, "but that's not on you. It's on me. Now take care of business. Okay?"

"I will."

Meeker gently set the receiver back into the cradle and tried to ignore her pain long enough to put the facts together. This couldn't be a coincidence. Had there been a leak? Had Richards shared the information with someone at the local police department and, if so, was that person a mole? She'd start digging into that in the morning. Now she needed to confront her grief.

She was about to collapse onto the couch, drowning in confusion and pain, when she heard footsteps in the hall. A large manila envelope was slipped under her entry. After retrieving her gun from her purse, she hurried to pull the door open. The hallway was empty. Sliding her Colt back into her pocket, she closed and locked the door, then tore open the envelope. Inside, she found a stack of eight-by-ten photos. On the top was a headshot of Dizzy Vance with a large red X painted over the image.

She considered the implication of the not so subtle message before setting the image to the side. The next photo was of Dr. Spencer Ryan. Another red X was painted over his face.

"My Lord," Meeker whispered as she dropped that photo only to see a similar image of Alistar Fister. Next, were shots of Henry Reese and Gail Worel, also covered with the same blood-red X. The final shot was of Teresa Bryant with an X covering her as well. At the bottom of the stack was a typed note that read, "Your time is running out."

Suddenly, all thoughts of Vance evaporated. Tossing the message and photos to the floor, Meeker retrieved her Colt and raced out the door toward Teresa's room. She lifted her hand to knock, but stopped when she noticed the door was cracked about an inch. With her weapon ready, Meeker eased the door open with the toe of her pump. What greeted her almost took her breath away. Lying face down on the floor was a man in a bellhop's uniform. He wasn't moving.

Stepping over the body, she silently stole through the living area and into the bedroom. It was empty. So was the bath. Bryant was nowhere to be seen. Had they already killed her and taken her body away?

Her heart racing, Meeker backed out of the room. In the living area, she studied the man on the floor. She noted a gun, complete with a silencer, that had partially slid under the couch next to the body. That had to mean he was part of an assassin's team. But why leave his body and take Bryant's?

The sound of footsteps in the hall pulled her eyes from the floor to the half-open door. Ready for action, Meeker set her feet and aimed. The footsteps paused for a moment before the door slowly opened and an unexpected figure stepped in.

"Teresa?"

"Yeah," Bryant quietly replied.

"I thought you were dead." Meeker was weak with relief.

"Someone was pretty serious about making it happen," Bryant admitted.

"Did you kill that guy?" Meeker asked, pointing at the man on the floor.

"No, his gun misfired. I knocked him out with the Coke bottle I had in my hand. It will likely take the maid a good while to get the stain out of the carpet. There was another guy with him, so I chased him down the fire escape before losing him in the alley." She glanced down at the unconscious man and asked. "How did you know about this?"

"It's a long story," Meeker sadly replied. "One that includes counting chickens before they hatch."

"You seem to be talking in riddles?"

"I'll explain later," Meeker assured her.

Bryant studied Helen's face. "You've been crying."

"Dizzy's dead. Some hood knocked him off. The deal went south."

"Napoleon?"

"He's shook up, but fine. He has the money and the envelopes, as well as the name of the person Joe was supposed to take out next."

"Anybody we know?"

"Me. I'm guessing that Joe drew the assignment because

he got so close to getting me the first time. We have to find the identity of the voice you heard before she kills us."

"Then, Helen, let's start by waking this guy up. Maybe he can give us some answers."

Meeker wasn't sure she was ready to get involved in another case. Could she think clearly enough to make sense of anything?

"Helen, are you okay?"

Meeker shook her head. "Teresa, I killed Dizzy just as surely as if I'd pulled the trigger myself."

Bryant frowned. "No, you tried to talk him out of going. He demanded this assignment."

"But ..." She whimpered as she bit her lip.

"No buts, Helen. There will be time for mourning when we solve this mystery."

Meeker nodded. "I need vengeance."

"No," Bryant countered. "No one needs that. What we need is justice."

Meeker heard a noise. Turning toward the door, she watched a large tabby cat, its head badly scarred, enter the room. It stopped, looked up and stared intently at her with one eye. The cat's other eye had apparently been lost in a fight years before.

ABOUT THE AUTHOR

Ace Collins is the prolific author of more than 80 books including *The Stories Behind the Best-Loved Songs of Christmas, Lassie A Dog's Life, The Color of Justice* and *Service Tails*, and the thirteen-book (so far) series, *In the President's Service* for Elk Lake Publishing Inc. Ace and his wife, Kathy, live in Arkadelphia, AR, where he happily writes, fixes up old cars, and plays his vintage Fender guitar.